THIS
ANIMAL BODY

THIS
ANIMAL BODY

a novel

MEREDITH WALTERS

Published by SparkPress, a BookSparks imprint,
A division of SparkPoint Studio, LLC
Phoenix, Arizona, USA, 85007
www.gosparkpress.com

Published 2024
Printed in the United States of America
Print ISBN: 978-1-68463-242-8
E-ISBN: 978-1-68463-243-5
Library of Congress Control Number: 2023915564

Interior Design by Tabitha Lahr

"How Eternity Could Be Endured" and "But What Can Die" from the Penguin publication *A Year With Hafiz: Daily Contemplations* by Daniel Ladinsky, copyright 2011, and used with permission.

"So Many Gifts" and "Now is the Time" from the Penguin publication *The Gift: Poems by Hafiz* by Daniel Ladinsky, copyright 1999, and used with permission.

To my mother, whose spirit and writing contain beauty beyond measure. Without your love, support, and example, this story would remain untold.

Now is the time to know
That all that you do is sacred.

—Hafiz, "Now Is the Time,"
translated by Daniel Ladinsky

PROLOGUE

I run.

Shadows pass over me, then golden sunlight, then more shadows, large and dark. They are tree trunks. Rocks. Nameless things. The earth is cool and moist beneath my feet. It propels me forward with every step. Between steps, I am flying.

I feel other animals around me: birds singing, squirrels leaping, spiders spinning. I cannot see them, but know they are there, just as I know without seeing there are hills up ahead, a river after that, and then, eventually, mountains. I feel all of them and none of them at once.

The white wolf runs beside me. She breathes softly, and I feel her power next to me, pulsing like a heartbeat. She has always been there, and will be forever; we are two, but we are also one.

Her fur is thick and brilliant like fresh snow, her eyes dark and deep and full of shadows. When she looks at me, she takes in everything, strips me naked. I can hide nothing. Her eyes reflect only light and goodness, deep love for all that I am and can ever be. The wolf's affection is a corporeal thing, something enormous and solid that holds me, and this forest, and everything else within its embrace. Silently, I return it.

Muscles ripple beneath my skin. The cool air breathes life into my lungs. My two legs become four. My tongue gets long and flaps inside a panting mouth. Earthy, familiar smells come alive within my nose. My four legs turn into wings.

As I feel the wolf's heart beating within my own chest, a fullness expands within me. It is as if the golden sunlight has passed through my skin to flow through my veins. I feel filled to the brim with a warm, glowing light that leaves space for nothing else.

Nothing in the world can possibly harm me. There is darkness around me, in the shadows and the trees and the depths of the wolf's eyes, but there is nothing to be afraid of. I am too big, too bright, too like sunlight for anything bad to reach me. What could damage sunlight, after all?

I am the strength of the wolf. I am the knowing of the trees. I am the free movement of the wind. I am all of this and more.

I run with the white wolf, play in the trees with her, share a perfect, wordless understanding with her. There is no time as we run, only trees and air and sunlight and joy.

There is no room for anything else. Freedom and love are all that there is, all that have ever been.

And then I would wake up.

Alone in the dark. Small, confused, and achingly separate.

Just a dream, I would tell myself, trying to make it a smaller thing to lose. But no matter how many times I said it, the wolf felt more real than the mattress beneath me.

Dream or not, the running stopped when I turned five. For months, I would lie on my princess sheets, trying to call the beast into the darkness. But no matter how hard I tried, the white wolf never returned.

I looked for her in the woods behind our house, slipping past my mother's vigilant eye to race into the trees at the edge

of the creek, even though they were shorter and more sprawl-
ing than the ones in my dream. My mother would drag me
into the house as I cried that it wasn't fair.

The matter came to a head one muggy night just before
school started.

I sat on the couch, twisting the corner of a red corduroy
pillow I hugged to my belly while my parents looked at each
other with tight faces. Something was wrong.

Finally my father cleared his throat. "So, Frances," he
said in the deep, throaty voice that I loved. "You remember
how we talked about how babies are made?"

"Yes." I released the pillow and watched it slowly uncurl
to reclaim its previous shape. "The man inserts his penis into—"

"When a man and a woman love each other very much,"
my mother corrected.

"Yes." I kept staring at the pillow in my lap. "That's when
the man inserts his penis into—"

"That's right, Frances." Something in my father's voice
made me look up; his face had turned bright red. "You've got
the gist of it. The man's, ah, sperm fertilizes the woman's egg,
and a baby begins to grow in her belly. Your mother tells me
you were asking some questions recently, and that you might
be, ah . . . a little confused. The thing is, sweetheart, you didn't
actually grow in your mother's belly. You grew in the belly
of another woman."

I looked down at the pink stars on my shoes.

"Frances, we love you very much." My mother's voice
sounded hollow and distant, as if she'd been swallowed by a cave.

"How did I get here then?"

"Well, your mother—er, the woman whose belly you
grew in—didn't want—um, couldn't keep you," said my father.

"Goodness gracious, Mitch." My mother used the same
tone she did when I tracked mud into the house. "Frances, it's
just this: we wanted you to be part of our family, so we adopted

you just as soon as we were able to. And we are so glad we did because we love you very, very much."

"So . . . you're not really my mother?" I twisted the pillow again.

"Of course I am!" Her eyes glistened. "It's just that somebody else brought you into this world."

I twisted the corner of the pillow until it wouldn't twist anymore. Something occurred to me. "And James, did he grow in this other woman's belly too?"

My mother flinched. "No, sweetie. He grew in mine."

I couldn't breathe. I leaped off the couch, letting the pillow fall, and darted to the back door. Wrenching it open, I rushed out into the humid embrace of a warm summer night.

I ran as fast as my legs would carry me toward the trees by the creek, but when I heard our back door slam, I changed course, silently slipping through the shadows of our neighbor's house, then racing up their driveway and to the park at the end of our street. My brother belonged to our mother, but I belonged . . .

The pounding of my feet kept the burning sadness from flooding down my throat.

When I reached the trail that stuck out like a tongue between the trees to lap up the dark pavement of the road, my eyes scanned the shadowy woods for flashes of light and my ears sought sounds of panting.

But there was no sign of the white wolf.

I weaved through the trees, hissing my pleas, and searching every crevice where a wolf could hide, and even those a tiny voice whispered were too small.

Nothing.

Just as a sucking emptiness filled my chest, I heard a noise. My heart leaped, but the sound was wrong. The wolf had been silent except for the soft noise of her breath, and besides, this sound had come from somewhere up above me, too high for a wolf to climb.

It was hard to make anything out in the darkness, but then two eyes glimmered above a bough that was nearly as thick as me. They were large and wide, almost human. A ghost? But after a few more moments of staring, the shape of an owl emerged from the shadows.

Something stirred in my chest. "Where's the white wolf?" I called up to the owl. "Are you here to help me find her?"

The owl didn't say anything, just looked at me.

"I lost my friend. And I really need her." My father's words echoed in my head. *You grew in the belly of another woman.*

I stared at the owl with hungry eyes. "Can you please help me? Just tell me how I can find the wolf. Or show me. You can fly, I'll run behind you. I can run fast, I swear."

The owl was silent and still.

Water filled my eyes, and my breath grew ragged. *No, sweetie. He grew in mine.*

I remembered a story I'd read about an owl who carried messages to a human village from the world of the spirits. The humans couldn't interpret the messages at first, until a little girl appeared who knew how to understand the owl.

My breathing steadied. I wiped my eyes so I saw the bird more clearly. "Do you have a message for me?"

The owl said nothing, but his eyes disappeared for a split second and then reappeared again.

I stood up straighter. "Okay. That's good. Is it about the wolf?" The owl stood motionless. "Is it about the woman whose belly I grew in?"

He only stared at me. I met his eyes. They were large, close together, and surrounded by a circle of white feathers that accentuated their depth. They looked like portals to the night sky.

Somebody else brought you into this world.

The longer I peered at the owl's black eyes, the more alien they looked. And then I understood.

"You're not from here!" I screamed in triumph. "You come from another world, and you came here tonight to tell me that *I do too!*"

The black pools disappeared, then reappeared again.

I jumped up and down. The emptiness in my chest broke apart and was carried away by a warm tide that filled me.

"Where do we come from? Where is home?"

A branch cracked behind me, and I spun. My parents were eating the trail with large, rapid bites. No time to hide. They saw me at the same time and started talking at once. I looked back just in time to see the owl take flight. He was huge but moved so silently in the darkness that my parents never saw him.

The warm tide receded back into the dark earth, leaving me empty. I forced my heavy feet to follow my parents back to the house.

I didn't dare talk to them about it because I didn't want to upset them, but the question of where I was from burned in my mind night and day like the incandescent light on the porch outside our front door that nobody bothered to turn off.

As time went on, however, and as the rhythm of school took over my waking hours, facts and science crowded out the possibility of a giant white wolf running wild in Atlanta. Eventually, knowing the right answers for my homework and tests became more important than knowing where I came from.

As the memory of my run with the white wolf receded, I had to accept that she was gone and—far worse—had never been real in the first place. The realization left a hole in my chest that never quite went away.

I believed I'd finally grown up, accepted reality, and come to terms with the fact that I had an overly vivid imagination, and that magic wasn't real.

Until one day when I was twenty-five a strange thing happened, and I no longer knew what to believe.

PART 1

CHAPTER I

Twenty Years Later

approached the first day of my neuroscience PhD program at UC Berkeley like a determined turtle crossing the road: focused, stubborn, and trying my best to ignore the rumbling engines of doubt threatening to run me over.

My classmates' resumes were already crammed full of publications and awards for scientific breakthroughs. My work history, on the other hand, told the story of someone who had taken Winston Churchill's assertion that "Success is going from failure to failure without loss of enthusiasm" a little too literally.

But this time would be different.

I walked past the Crescent Lawn on the way to my first lab, excitement heating the inside of my chest, sunshine warming my back. I'd lived in Northern California long enough to be grateful that the sun was giving off heat for once.

I arrived at the lab at the same time as a woman with thick, black hair and even thicker glasses. Her hair fell in waves over her shoulders, which had the rich, brown glow of acorns. I recognized her from orientation the week before but couldn't for the life of me remember her name.

"Frankie!" Her voice was strong, unwavering, like she'd never forgotten a name in her life. "You're in this lab? I've always been fascinated by sharp wave ripples. Is that why you chose it too?"

I hadn't even heard of sharp wave ripples before reading the description of the lab. Choosing a lab had been harder than getting into the exclusive program in the first place. "I heard the faculty won a Gruber Foundation Neuroscience Prize." I tried to sound like I hadn't had to look that up too.

"Oh, I know. The professor is supposed to be brilliant. Though I've heard he can be a little—"

The door swung open, revealing a middle-aged man in a rumpled sweater and khaki pants, his skin so pale it was nearly translucent. The man's blue eyes shook slightly, like he'd had too much caffeine, and landed first on my anonymous classmate and then on me. "Why don't you come on in so we can get started on time?"

I checked my phone. It was nine fifty-seven, three minutes before the lab was supposed to begin. But the man stared at me with those quivering eyes.

"Sure." I ignored the sinking feeling in my gut and prayed he wasn't our professor.

He nodded once, without conviction, as if he had expected more opposition, then turned and shuffled back into the room.

"Intense." My classmate finished her sentence under her breath.

We walked into the lab.

Cold light spilled from rows of fluorescent lightbulbs, forcing itself like an unwanted houseguest into every nook and cranny. Several computer screens lined the walls, but no windows. An X-Acto knife sat on a table in the center of the room, abandoned.

At the front of the room was another student, tall and near my own age. He reminded me of a lion at rest—tawny, lean, indifferent, with a mane of perfectly unkempt, sandy-blond hair piled thick on his head. He looked like he'd woken up after a night on the savanna ready for a *National Geographic* shoot. Something about him felt untouchable, like he was in a museum, the example of a perfect specimen.

Just then his eyes caught mine. I went rigid, unable to breathe or look away.

His mouth stretched into a crooked half-smile, one corner higher than the other. He had a dimple. Just the one. It disarmed him, breaking his untouchability, and adding to the lopsidedness of his smile. Warmth emanated from him like dancing flames.

I put my backpack on a table and focused all my attention on unzipping it.

"I'm glad to see we're all here," said the older man from the front of the room. His tone cast doubt on his words.

There were only four of us in the room—the middle-aged man, the guy with the lopsided smile, the woman whose name I'd forgotten, and me.

"I'm Dr. Stephen Porter." My hope vanished as the man in the rumpled sweater rubbed his wild gray goatee. "I'll be running this lab with the help of Brian here, my research associate." He jabbed his thumb at the man I'd thought was a student. "As you can see, this is not a big lab. For once I find great wisdom in a hackneyed cliché. Quality is always more valuable than quantity. I'm very selective about who I let into this lab, and the pickings were slim this year." He glanced between me and the other woman. "Which one of you is Lillian?"

The other woman raised her hand.

Lillian, Lillian, Lillian, I repeated to myself. *She's small like the Lilliputians. And pretty like the flower.*

The professor turned to me. "Then you must be Frances."

"Yes, though I prefer Frankie." Was it my imagination, or did he roll his eyes before writing something in his notebook?

"As you should know, we'll be studying sharp wave ripple complexes to determine their exact nature and function in the learning process." Dr. Porter peered over his reading glasses at the two of us as if trying to gauge our comprehension. Seeming satisfied but not pleased, he walked around a table to open a door into a room not much larger than a closet. Shelves covered with metal cages lined the walls. Inside each cage were several rats.

"One of your jobs"—Dr. Porter looked back at Lillian and me—"the most pressing one at the moment—is to feed the rats. Which one of you would like to start?"

I raised my hand.

"Frankie it is. Lillian, come with me. I'll show you how to record the daily logs. Brian, please show Frankie the proper method for feeding the rats."

Brian did a mock bow, extending his arm toward the small room.

I walked inside. As soon as Brian followed, I smelled his scent, somehow both musky and fresh, like earth and plants just after rain mixed with sweat. I also smelled the pungent odor of urine but decided to give him the benefit of the doubt and assume that was the rats.

"Nice to meet you, Frankie." He held out his hand, but all I saw was that dimple.

"Nice to meet you, Brian." I shook his hand. It was warm and smooth and soft. I didn't want to let go.

Joe, I reminded myself quickly, yanking my hand back to my side. *I have a boyfriend, Joe. Joe who just moved across the country to be with me. Quiet, handsome, dependable Joe.*

Brian's smile didn't falter or become any less magnetic. "First thing to know about Dr. P is it's his way or . . . his way.

He claims to encourage independent thinking, but he's particular about how things are done. Case in point—the feeding. Very, very precise instructions are posted on the wall in case you forget." He pointed to two solid pages of tiny text with numbered steps and footnotes.

I skimmed the instructions then peeked in the cages. There were no wheels, no tunnels, no toys—nothing except the animals and a sad plastic bottle of water shackled to the bars of the cage.

"Don't the rats get bored without anything to do?" I tried to pet one of the rats, but my finger wouldn't fit through the bars. "Why don't you give them something to play with?"

"Bored? No, rats aren't like us. Their brains are much less complex. They're not capable of getting bored, and besides, toys could interfere with the experiment results."

Unformed words rose in my throat, but I couldn't get them out.

I picked up a bowl from the table in the corner and went to the food bin. After metering out the prescribed amount, I double-checked the measuring cup. "This can't be enough food." I checked the cup again. "I had a gerbil growing up. He was smaller than these rats and ate at least twice as much."

"Have you never worked in a lab before? It's common practice to restrict calories for the rats. We give them enough to maintain a healthy weight, but this way, they're more motivated to run the mazes."

My pulse lurched in my temple like it was trying to escape. "Sure. Maybe we should starve grad students too, to encourage us to do our best work." I looked into his golden lion eyes. "And no, I've never worked in a lab before. My undergraduate degree was in wildlife biology, so all my work was in the field. Not as exciting as rats and mazes, but at least we didn't have to starve the animals to study them."

Brian's eyes were steady on mine. "So why did you switch?"

I tried on different ways to explain in my head. *Because I finally figured out what I'm meant to do. Because I realized if I study brains, I can find out what went wrong with mine. Because if I can fix my own defect, I can fix it for millions of others too.*

I couldn't think of a way to say it that didn't sound either grandiose or pathetic. "It's complicated."

For a moment, the only sound was the light scratching of paws on plastic. Then Brian dismissed my response with a single chuckle. "No need to be so sensitive, Frankie. You'll need to have thick skin around here or the barbs of Dr. P will make you bleed."

"Thanks for the advice."

Brian shrugged, then turned and left. When the door creaked shut, the room got cold.

My whole life people had been telling me I was too sensitive, but I wasn't sure what part of not wanting to be cruel to the rats made me so frail. The cup of food in my hand weighed almost nothing. I wanted to go back to the bin and fill it higher, but it was my first day, and Dr. Porter didn't seem the type to appreciate student initiative. So I made a vow and bent over the first cage.

"Sorry, y'all. This sucks. But as soon as the experiment is over, I'll bring in some strawberries and sunflower seeds and cardboard for you to shred, and we'll have an awesome rodent party."

When I slid my hand in the cage, a small, white rat with brown shoulders raced over and ran headlong into my hand.

"Miscalculate your landing there, buddy?" But the rat kept his head against my hand, so I stroked the soft fur between his ears. When I pulled my hand away, the rat tried to follow. Curious, I moved my hand to the other side of the cage. The rat ran over.

This time when I stroked his fur, he rolled over onto his back and exposed his belly. I tickled it the way my gerbil had loved when I was a kid. The rat rolled his head back and forth and splayed out his adorable little toes.

I laughed, the sound boomeranging off the walls of the small room.

"You're not ticklish, are you?" I touched the rat's front paws, but he stayed still. When I moved to his hind feet, he rolled his head again and stretched out his toes.

"You are ticklish. Is that a giggle?"

A current of warm air wrapped itself around me. When I turned, Brian's lean form blocked the doorway. "I forgot to tell you about cleaning the cages." He squeezed past me into the room. "But first, don't let Dr. P hear you talking like that. That's what I was just trying to tell you. He's big on not making unsubstantiated claims about the cognitive abilities of the research subjects."

"The cognitive abilities of the research subjects? I'm not suggesting the rat solved an algebra problem. I'm saying he's ticklish. I swear he was laughing, but only when I tickled his belly and hind feet. When I tried his front paws—nothing. Just like us."

A sharp exhalation cut the air behind me.

"Those are complex processes." Dr. Porter's thicker frame now darkened the doorway. "Your evidence this rat is ticklish is . . . what exactly?"

"Well, the way he was moving, rolling his head, and splaying his toes. It looked just like the kids I used to babysit when I tickled them."

Dr. Porter rolled his eyes. "Oh, well, by all means then. That does sound like irrefutable proof."

Someone coughed. Lillian stood a few feet behind the professor, watching us with fierce eyes.

"Frances—er—Frankie." Dr. Porter's words dropped low and loud. "I don't know what type of lab you've been in before, but in this one, we try to hold ourselves to stricter standards of scientific proof. Have you heard of Morgan's Canon?"

I hoped he couldn't see the heat rolling off my cheeks. "No, sir."

"Ah, yes, well, you'll want to make a note of it then." He cleared his throat. "*In no case may we interpret an action as the outcome of the exercise of a higher psychical faculty if it can be interpreted as the outcome of the exercise of one which stands lower in the psychological scale.* In other words, the simplest explanation is the better one."

Since when was being simple better than being right? My hands rose from my sides like angry birds. I pushed them back against my thighs and pressed my lips shut.

"Above all else, we don't want to make the grave scientific error of anthropomorphizing animals or assuming they're more intelligent than they are." The note of absolute certainty in Dr. Porter's voice fanned the fire in my cheeks. "It's likely some previous graduate student trained that rat to exhibit the behavior you saw by rewarding it with extra treats when it did. Graduate students are regrettably prone to such blunders."

Heat consumed my entire body now. On what planet was someone accidentally training rats to act ticklish more likely than rats actually being ticklish? I knew I shouldn't say anything, but my mouth was a dog that had slipped its collar—I no longer had control of it. "With all due respect, Dr. Porter, I really don't think—"

"*With all due respect,* I don't give a rat's ass what you think. I care what you can prove. And unless you can prove that rats are ticklish, we are required as responsible scientists to assume they are not."

"Okay." I bought some time to take a deep breath, try to tamp down the fire, find a solution. "If I design an experiment, could I use two or three of the rats to see if I can prove it?"

Dr. Porter's pale eyes burned like liquid nitrogen. "Don't be ridiculous. We have many more important things to focus on. To start with, you need to have a banner made with Morgan's words for us to hang on the wall. That way, perhaps you'll think twice before wasting our time with any more idiotic ideas."

The fire inside me exploded. My vision filled with sparks, my ears with a sizzling hiss.

I couldn't breathe, couldn't speak, couldn't meet anyone's eyes. But it didn't matter. I was a rat fighting an eagle—there was no way for me to win.

So I did the only thing a rat can do. I squeezed past Dr. Porter, avoided Lillian, and scrambled away as fast as I could, hoping no one would follow.

CHAPTER 2

ater that afternoon, after my first Advanced Cellular Neurobiology class, I took a mushroom wrap from the Mediterranean place on Kittredge Street to a small grove of eucalyptus trees I'd seen earlier in the middle of campus. As soon as I sat down on a little concrete bench, my backpack vibrated.

I dug my phone out, hesitated—but only for a moment—and swiped my finger across the screen.

"Frankie." My mother's voice was warm and excited. I could almost see the flush on her pale cheeks beneath her freckles. "How are you? How was your first day?" Before I could answer, she yelled in a tone with much less warmth, "Mitch, Frankie's on the phone!"

Maybe my decision to answer the call hadn't been such a good one.

"It was fine," I said. But even I could hear the frustration in my voice.

There was a click.

"Hi, sweetie." The voice was deep, rich, and commanding.

"Hi, Dad."

"Are you okay?" Anxiety oozed from between my mother's words. "Is something wrong?"

"No, it's just . . . I'm not sure about the lab I chose. The professor was kind of a jerk." I told them what had happened with the rats.

As soon as I got to the part where Dr. Porter made the comment about not having any more idiotic ideas, my mother interrupted me. "That's horrible. What a nasty, cruel man. I can't believe he said that to you."

Frankly, I agreed. But with the help of some time and distance, I tried to give him the benefit of the doubt. "I don't know. I think he wants to see what I can prove. I just don't understand why he won't let me try."

My father grunted.

I hesitated, even longer than I had to answer the call. But clearly he had something he needed to say. "What do you think, Dad?"

"You really want to know?"

Something told me I didn't, but it was too late now. "Yes, of course."

"I think you're taking this too personally, Frankie. You have to see it as a learning opportunity. You do tend to project your own experiences onto others."

There was a sudden pressure in my chest, as if I'd tried to swallow the words but they went down the wrong pipe.

"Do you remember when you were a girl and you slept with all your stuffed animals in your bed?" Dad went on. "There was hardly any room left for you, but you insisted. Sometimes in the middle of the night, I heard you picking up the ones you'd kicked off in your sleep. You said they got cold and lonely on the floor. I believe you fed them Cheerios sometimes as well." He paused. "You have to admit, you have a vivid imagination and a tendency to anthropomorphize."

More words lodged in my windpipe, blocking my air. "I guess I do have a strong imagination."

My mother started to say something, but my father overrode her. "Don't worry, Frankie. It'll get better. You're different from most people in these programs." I knew what he meant even before he said it. "What with your . . . mood issues." *You mean depression*, I corrected him in my head. "You're more than smart enough, but you're so sensitive." *Overly emotional*, I thought. *Weak.* "You can do it, but if you want to achieve the kind of breakthrough you're hoping for, you're going to need to be disciplined and strong."

Heat flared, but it wasn't angry heat. It was queasy, contaminated, can't-stand-to-be-in-my-own-skin heat.

"Frankie." My mother spoke before I could put any words together. "Why don't you come home for a visit? You haven't visited in so long."

My shoulders tightened. I didn't need a reminder right now of my mother's constant disappointment in me. "I would, but I don't have the money."

"We'll pay for it." She said it almost before I finished speaking. "We'd be happy to buy the tickets."

"Thank you, Mom, but I really don't have the time, either. I mean, classes are just starting. What would it look like if I missed labs so early in the program?"

"You could come for the weekend."

"The weekend? It takes an entire day just to get there from here. We're on opposite ends of the country. By the time I got there, I'd have to turn around and come home."

My mother's disappointment slithered through the phone and wrapped itself around my neck. "Okay. I just thought with all that happened today you might want to come home. But it's okay. I understand. You have more important things to do out there."

I groaned. "They're not more important, Mom, but coming home just isn't practical right now. Listen, I'll look at tickets for Thanksgiving, okay?"

"Only if you want to. I don't want to force you to do anything you don't want to do."

"Of course I want to." But my words sounded rote. I was already thinking about a bigger problem than my mother's never-ending guilt trips.

I barely heard my feeble excuse to get off the phone, barely registered my parents' goodbyes, barely tasted the mushroom wrap that I began eating from habit more than anything else.

All my attention was on two words that kept cycling through my mind.

Mentally ill is one of those phrases you don't think about much until someone applies it to you. I never felt mentally ill, but I'd scored a thirty-eight on the psychiatrist's test, enough to qualify my disorder—my depression—as not just severe but borderline extreme. I couldn't deny it. The medication the doctors gave me worked so well it was hard to remember why I took it, but when I didn't—when I went out of town and forgot to bring the little pink pills—the pain reminded me. I was unbalanced. Defective. Sick.

How had I already lost my determination to find a fix?

Far from disciplined and strong, my behavior in the lab had been reactive and irrational. I'd let my emotions get the best of me, embarrassed myself in front of my peers, been defensive and rude to a professor. Dr. Porter was right to call me out.

I promised myself I'd do better. I had to—I couldn't do any worse.

CHAPTER 3

It took me a few minutes to figure out what was missing from my apartment when I got home after my first day as a neuroscience PhD student.

I walked up the stairs, exhausted. But when I reached the door and turned my key, it was already unlocked. Suddenly I was wide awake.

Joe should have been at work. Nobody else had a key to our place. *Should I call the police?*

My neighbors were home—the drone of their television rose through the floorboards—so I decided it was safe to investigate. Maybe Joe had forgotten to lock up when he left.

I opened the door.

Everything looked normal. The television, the stereo, the tablet my father had given me when I was accepted into my program, were still there. Nothing looked out of place or disturbed.

"Joe?" Maybe he'd gotten off work early. "Joe, are you here?"

Nothing.

I walked through the living room into the bedroom. Everything was in order. The bed was made, the few pieces of jewelry I had were untouched in the stand on my dresser, and the painting of the wolf my mother had bought me, my most valued possession, was still on the wall.

Only when I turned to check the bathroom did I notice the first disappearance.

Joe had put his favorite beanbag chair, the only furniture he owned, in the alcove between the closet and the bathroom door.

Only now it was missing.

In the bathroom, Joe's ancient toothbrush with the permanently splayed bristles was gone as well. I walked back into the living room on legs that no longer promised to hold my weight. The framed poster for the 1939 World's Fair in San Francisco I'd given Joe for his birthday the month before had vanished.

My heart thrummed in my throat. Somehow, I made it to the kitchen. On the counter was a note, a single key on top of it.

I didn't want to read it. I already knew what it said. But maybe it would offer an explanation to stall the growing emptiness inside me.

I picked it up.

Frankie—
I know I haven't done a good job telling you what
a great girlfriend you are, and now isn't the time to
start. I'm going back to Chicago. This doesn't feel
right anymore.
Joe

My breath was shallow. The yawning, frozen abyss swallowed my stomach and most of my intestines. The edges of it threatened my lungs. My knees gave out and I sank to the floor.

Good riddance, I told myself. I'd repeated it to friends when they found themselves dumped. But the words were hollow. I didn't want to be rid of Joe. I liked Joe. I thought he liked me.

Clearly I was wrong.

Something *tap-tap-tapped* on the counter behind my head. When I turned, I was face-to-face with the largest cockroach I'd ever seen.

"No!" I shot back up to my feet. "Not okay!"

A helpless panic rose within me.

"You know I can't kill you." The last time I'd tried to kill a roach, I nearly threw up. I couldn't stop seeing the wide-eyed fear on its face, stop hearing the sickening crunch.

The roach stared at me, unmoved.

I couldn't kill it, but I also couldn't let it creep around my apartment. I went to grab a plastic cup and envelope from the recycling bin. Overly emotional or not, I had to do something.

But when I got back to the note, the creature had disappeared.

I kept the cup and envelope close for the rest of the evening. Lying in the steaming water of my bath, I tried to figure out what I'd done to make Joe want to leave. So many ideas rolled into my brain they backed up in a traffic jam.

My chest heaved with heavy sobs. Tears streamed down my face as if competing with the faucet to see who could fill the tub faster.

An urgent and unfamiliar sound broke into my sobs. I jumped out of the tub, grabbed my towel, and followed the noise. It led me to the living room closet where what I'd assumed was a defunct phone I inherited with the apartment yowled.

"Hello," I said, out of breath. Silence. "*Hellooo.*" More silence. "Hello!" Not even breathing answered. I hung up the phone.

When I walked back into the bathroom, the larger-than-life roach was perched next to a watery footprint. Its head bobbed up and down. Like a dog's. *Drinking the water I'd spilled on the floor.*

I clutched the towel to my chest, fumbled for the cup on the vanity. The roach just watched me. Shivering, I bent down, tried to catch the insect under the cup. But at the last minute it darted under the baseboard, leaving only one large, hairy leg exposed.

Vomiting became a real possibility.

I got back into the bath, washed as quickly as I could. My head swiveled nonstop, looking in four directions at once.

By the time I lay down in bed, I was exhausted. I wanted to lose consciousness, only wake up once this day was so far gone I'd need binoculars to see it.

But sleep didn't come. Instead, I thought about Joe. I should have seen it coming. He didn't talk much. He assured me he wasn't angry, but I knew he was unhappy. If only I'd paid more attention. If only I'd done something different—

Something moved near the ceiling on the other side of the room. I looked up to see the roach launch itself off the wall, fly straight toward my face. My limbs turned to ice. All I could do was scream.

At the last second the roach veered to my right. It landed on the wall behind me, on Joe's side of the bed, then calmly continued its climb.

"No." I leaped out of bed and ran past the cup, the envelope. "No!" I went as fast as I could to the kitchen and scooped up a catalog. "NO!" Weapon in hand, I ran back to the bedroom, resolved.

But when I raised the magazine, the roach lifted its head and gazed at me.

I froze.

Such dark, liquid eyes. I recognized something in them, something familiar. Fear, but also something else—something deep and aware and alive. Trying to place what it was, I realized something. The roach's antennae were waving softly, but it was otherwise perfectly still.

It wasn't moving to avoid my blow.

I couldn't do it. I couldn't kill the roach. "Fine." I threw the catalog to the floor. "Who am I kidding? You win."

And in that moment I knew I'd made a huge mistake. There was no way I was going to figure out the cause of my depression, let alone find a cure. I couldn't even get rid of a defenseless roach.

I pulled the pillows and blanket off my bed and stumbled to the living room. Lying on the couch, hugging my knees to my chest, I tried not to think about angry professors, missing boyfriends, or flying cockroaches.

CHAPTER 4

At first, everything was dark and silent.

Then a small voice asked, "Is she here yet, Mama?"

A moment of stillness. Then a deeper, throatier female voice: "Yes, I believe she is."

Another silence. Then the small voice again, impatient. "Then why can't I see her?"

This time the answer came right away. "Because she can't see you yet. Give her a minute, Sweetpea. This is all new to her."

Who were they talking about?

I waited to hear more, or for the lights to be turned on, but the darkness remained and the only sound I could make out was a slight scuffling, like feet scratching the bare earth.

"She does realize we're all waiting for her, right?" This was a new voice, male and sharp.

The deep female voice came again, kind and gentle. "I don't think she does. I think she's confused." The tone of the voice changed then, became higher and stronger, meant to carry. "Frankie," it called. "Frankie, can you see us?"

I started. I wasn't sure what to do. I couldn't see anything and didn't know what was happening. Suddenly, the darkness was thick and malevolent like in the nightmares I sometimes had where everything dimmed and blurred, and I couldn't make anything out clearly.

My heart pounded.

"Now we've scared her," said the female voice. "Frankie," she called again more loudly. "There's no need to worry. I think you can't see us. Is that correct?"

My pulse throbbed in my neck. "Um, yes," I said, wondering if it wouldn't be a better idea to hide or run.

"Don't worry," the female voice said again. "You're perfectly safe. Something's not working right, but it's okay. We'll fix that shortly. Is it possible your eyes are still closed?"

I started to say no, then realized I should check. When I did, I found my eyes were squeezed shut, the muscles actively contracted like when I used to pretend I was asleep as a little girl. "Oh. I guess they are."

Embarrassed, I forced my eyelids open. It was harder than usual, as if they weighed ten pounds each. Shadowy figures stood before me. It was dark, clearly nighttime, but a pale, silvery light fell in patches, illuminating a few shapes.

I first made out the trees. Thick trunks clustered around a small clearing, some dark and rugged, others smooth and ghostly in the moonlight. As leaves above me rustled, stray stars flickered momentarily through the canopy.

Inside the clearing was a large stump that came up to my waist. Studying it, I discerned two forms sitting in the shadows on top—one small and round, resting directly on the stump, the other larger, more oblong, and upright, floating a few inches above it. I squinted my eyes, trying to understand what I was looking at.

The throaty female voice sounded from behind me. "Sweetpea, Roo, move into the light so she can see you." The round shape and the oblong one shifted, coming forward into a patch of light falling on the front of the stump.

I first looked into the excited eyes of a young squirrel, then met the incisive stare of a large rooster.

"She saw me!" squealed the squirrel in delight. "Mama, she saw me!"

A short laugh rumbled behind me. "Well, go ahead like we practiced," said the deep voice. "Introduce yourself."

"I'm Sweetpea!" shouted the squirrel, showing her teeth in a wide, lopsided smile. "Nice to meet you!"

I laughed. "Nice to meet you too, Sweetpea." I turned to the rooster. He was not smiling but glaring hard at me with one black eye.

"I hope you don't expect the same level of enthusiasm from me," he said. "I would hate to disappoint you."

"Um, not at all," I said, uncertain.

Something grumbled, sounding half like a growl, half like a throat clearing. Roo's eyes darted past me to the source of the noise, then came back to meet my own. "Oh, fine. I'm Roo." His tone was chill but not frozen. "Pleasure to meet you."

He didn't sound pleased, but I appreciated the gesture. "The pleasure's all mine, Roo," I said, relieved to at least know what to say.

I turned to the voice coming from behind me. Nothing. Until a dark form moved out of the shadow of a tree and into the light of the clearing.

My breath caught in my throat. But the color was wrong, and the eyes weren't quite right. She was huge though. Her paws were wider than my hands, and her shoulders almost reached my waist. Her movements were soft and quiet but filled with a clearly contained power.

"I'm Mama," said the sooty-gray wolf, her yellow eyes flecked with bits of dark gold. "There're five of us, but one is running late."

"He's always late!" complained Sweetpea.

"I know," said Mama. "He has important work to do."

"What could possibly be more important than this?" whined the squirrel.

"You're right. Not much. He'll be here soon."

I had a doubt, then confirmed it with a quick count. "There're only three of you, four with whoever's late."

Mama's eyes searched my own. "You didn't see Nameless One? Behind Sweetpea and Roo?"

I turned. "I don't see anybody else there."

The rooster snorted. "You're still young in human years, but not nearly as nimble as you used to be, eh?"

I gave him a questioning look.

"When you were a kid, you never had a problem seeing Nameless One."

I thought about it but came up blank. I shrugged.

"Even at night . . ."

I furrowed my brows.

"Especially when you were upset . . ."

I frowned.

"Oh, for goodness' sake," he said. "Or just found out you were adopted . . ."

Understanding dawned. I moved my gaze off the stump and into the treetops. There—two white circles of feathers surrounding wide, unblinking eyes. *Of course*, I thought, *the owl*.

"Nice to meet you, Nameless One," I said. He made no response, not even bothering to blink.

Roo chuckled. "That one doesn't talk much. And when he does, you kind of wish he hadn't."

"Oh." I moved my gaze back to the rooster and the squirrel. "Okay."

Silence once again.

It was broken by the rooster. "Still not sure what you're here for, are you?" His voice was dry.

"No," I said, confused and embarrassed. "I guess not."

"Roo, be nice," growled Mama. "She's had a rough day. You of all creatures should understand that."

Roo grunted. "What's a rough day for a human compared to a chicken? Was her waterproof, temperature-controlled nest not big enough to hold all her shiny, plastic toys? Or was she bored because she didn't have to spend all day fleeing hawks or stray dogs? Wait, no—I know, it took too long to cook the decaying carcass of some poor animal caged and tortured for their entire brief existence all so she could consume their flesh, and she got hungry—so very hungry!" By the time he finished, the feathers on the back of his neck stuck straight out.

I stared at him. Sweetpea looked like she was going to cry.

"Roo," Mama said softly. "Frankie's vegan."

The rooster's eyes widened, and his head jerked back. "Really?" The sarcasm was gone from his voice.

"Really," Mama said. I nodded. "So maybe you can give her a chance to tell us why she's so upset."

Upset? I wasn't sure what Mama was talking about. Then the memories came surging back—the lab, my failure, the way I'd snapped at my parents, losing Joe, my defeat by the cockroach—and my heart plunged into my stomach.

I started to tell them, from the beginning, everything that had happened. When I got the part where Dr. Porter turned down my request to test for the rats' ticklishness, Sweetpea squeaked, and Roo hopped from one foot to another.

"What a mite-brained bonehead!" He clucked. "That man wouldn't recognize responsible science if it hit him in his bunghole!"

Mama's head whipped around to face the bird. "Roo." Her voice was a knife. "We've talked about this."

Roo stopped hopping. "Sorry, Mama. I know. I shouldn't insult boneheads like that. They don't deserve it."

Mama's canine teeth shone suddenly white in the darkness.

The rooster's head dropped level with his shoulders. "Okay, fine. I know what you mean. It's just hard to, you know, practice compassion in the face of such asininity. Everyone knows rats communicate ultrasonically. Just because his fat ears are too primitive to hear—" He broke off at a hard look from Mama.

"Try," she growled at him. When he opened his beak to respond, she cut him off. "Try harder."

"Yes, ma'am." Roo shifted uncomfortably in his stance. "What I meant to say was, that man is—um—disappointingly misguided. Frankie, please continue."

I told them about the conversation with my parents, then coming home to find the door unlocked. Movement caught my eye—Sweetpea trembling on the stump.

"Don't worry." I made my tone as reassuring as I could. "Nobody was inside. It's just that Joe had left the door open."

Sweetpea looked up at me with wide, dark eyes. "Who's Joe?"

I told them. I tried not to sound as sad as I felt. I explained how we'd met and bonded over our different work studying wildlife, how he'd moved in with me after six months, how I'd driven him out just four weeks later. When I recalled the note, and the cockroach next to it, I shuddered.

"What's wrong?" Sweetpea asked.

"I just remembered someone had broken into my apartment, though it wasn't a thief or a murderer. It wasn't even human. It was a terrifying—" The leaves next to me rustled. I looked down but couldn't see anything. "A disgusting—" Something crawled over my bare foot. Shrieking, I picked up my foot and kicked wildly. A shadow shot forward, then opened its wings, slowed, and landed on the stump in the shadows beside Sweetpea and Roo.

"A disgusting what?" said a bass voice so resonant it reverberated off the tree trunks around us. "Please do tell us: Who was this vile intruder?"

With the echoing, I couldn't tell where the voice was coming from. Maybe Nameless One was speaking? But when I looked up, the owl was motionless. I peered through the darkness trying to locate the creature to which the voice belonged but found no source.

"It was—it was—" Cold tendrils of fear wrapped around my heart. *It's not what you think*, I told myself. I pulled my hands inside my sleeves. Opening my mouth, I was about to try again when something moved in the shadows of the stump.

Even before it entered the moonlight, I knew what it was. The soft clicking of multiple feet on wood confirmed it. My stomach turned. "No! It was you!"

"I'm afraid it was." The cockroach's deep, reverberant voice was far too large for his size. He raised one of his front legs and extended it to me. "I believe this is how you humans prefer to greet one another. I'm Cockroach."

I wanted to run, but my training to be polite overrode my fear. "Just Cockroach? You don't have a real name?"

"You can call me Mr. Cockroach if you like." He pulled his thorax back and straightened up, appearing to grow bigger. "Or *Señor Cucaracha*. Which reminds me, did you know they wrote an ode to me in Mexico? And now every schoolchild in the country sings in homage when we cross paths." The roach chuckled, his laughter sounding like thunder rolling in the distance. "Not many insects can say that." He tilted his head toward his front leg, which was still extended. "But I don't get too big for my britches, see? I still observe the niceties of society. Which appears to be more than I can say for you."

Embarrassed and nauseated, I stepped forward. "Nice to meet you then, Mr. Cockroach." I used all my willpower to reach my index finger forward and touch the roach on what I assumed to be his foot—or, in this case, his hand. I shuddered and pulled my finger away.

"Cockroach." Mama padded forward from where she had been sitting at my side. Her eyes were fiercely intent on the insect, but he made no effort to retreat. "You made contact with Frankie before our meeting?"

"I did." The insect's voice was sonorous. "We planned for the school thing but didn't anticipate the boyfriend. Fortunately, one of my cousins alerted me at the last minute. I didn't have time to let y'all know, but I thought it best that one of us be there."

I stared, unbelieving, at the cockroach. "Why? To terrorize me on top of everything else?"

"Ha!" hooted Roo from his spot on the tree stump. His voice sounded almost shrill in comparison to the roach's. "Once again your peepers fail you. I'm beginning to think human eyes aren't the paragons of perception they're cracked up to be."

I looked at him, confused.

"I think what Mr. Roo is trying to say is that I wasn't terrorizing you," said Cockroach. "That you did well enough on your own. Truth be told, I believe I was more frightened than you were. I've never heard of a human, after all, who's been whacked, zapped, flushed, or squashed beneath the shoe of a giant insect."

He had a point, but still. "You sure didn't act very frightened." I recalled the roach's unflappable calm.

"Yes, well, as Mr. Roo just pointed out, looks can be deceiving. I've picked up a thing or two from human beings over the years, having had so much"—he cleared his throat—"intimate contact with them. Y'all are good at hiding what you're feeling. It's part of the reason we're here." He paused, looking up at me. I bit my lip, but he didn't explain. "Well, I suppose I've learned how to do it too. It's quite easy to fool a human. You tend to see what you already believe."

"We don't hide what we feel."

Roo exploded with laughter. "And how in the world could you be so sure using those hopeless eyeballs?"

"Frankie," came Mama's throaty voice from the other side of me. "I believe what they're trying to say is you're not so different from us. All animals get scared when they sense danger, whether from predation, competition, or even rejection. It's a good thing. It helps us pay attention more closely to the situation at hand. And it's true for all of us, regardless of whether we look frightened or not."

"I believe you call it 'fight or flight,'" said Roo. "Though of course freezing is an option too."

My belly vibrated, then the deep, baritone voice rumbled again. "Yes, and while some animals tend to fight when scared"— the roach's voice had a cutting edge—"others much prefer to flee."

Heat rushed into my cheeks. I remembered running out of the lab earlier that day and abandoning my bedroom to the roach.

"I didn't mean to run away. I just didn't know what else—"

"I didn't mean you." Cockroach's voice was softer. "I was talking about somebody else."

Despite my unease, I moved in close to the insect to get a better look. I was missing something. "What do you mean? Who are you talking about?"

"You'll realize soon enough. Fear makes us do some absurd things. The trick is to see through our own fear to theirs. That's the trick." The roach nodded like a bobblehead doll going over a speedbump.

I was still missing something. "I don't understand."

"I know," said the insect. "But you will. And I'll be here to receive your thanks whenever you do."

The degree of certainty in his tone rubbed me the wrong way. Anger and confusion fought in my brain. I looked at the other animals for guidance, but Roo avoided eye contact, Sweetpea appeared to have fallen asleep, and Mama just met my gaze with kind eyes.

The confusion won out. I must have been slower than molasses for failing to puzzle out the roach's meaning. All my breath escaped through my nose, leaving me deflated. "I feel like I've failed yet again."

Mama padded silently to my side. "When have you ever failed, Frankie?"

I snorted. "Didn't you hear what I said earlier? In one day, I managed to convince my professor I was an irrational, oversensitive tree-hugger, disappoint my parents, drive away my boyfriend, and let a teeny tiny insect—no offense, Mr. Cockroach—get the best of me in my own home."

"None taken," said the roach.

Mama looked at me with her gold-flecked eyes. "Yes, I heard all that. But I still don't hear any evidence of failure." I opened my mouth, but before I could say anything, the wolf continued. "Yes, you're very sensitive. Yes, it sets you apart. And yes, it can cause some discomfort in this world as it is, for you and for others. But never, ever think it's a weakness, Frankie. It's one of your greatest strengths. Your sensitivity is the source of your compassion. It's why you were chosen to come here, and it's the reason you're going to be able to accomplish what you're here to do."

My mind swam with thoughts, but none of them made any sense. "What do you mean 'chosen to come here'? Do you mean here to this clearing on this night, or here to this earth in this lifetime? And what exactly am I here to do?"

"What do you mean 'what do you mean'?" asked Sweet-pea in a tremulous voice. Her eyes had opened and were wide and liquid in the night. "Don't you know who you are and where you're from?"

"I'm Frankie. And I'm from Atlanta, Georgia." The squirrel's face fell. "I'm sorry if you wanted a different answer, but that's the truth."

"I thought you said she already knew!" Sweetpea wailed, close to tears.

Mama looked at the squirrel and smiled. "She knows, little one, but she doesn't remember yet."

Suddenly I heard a familiar voice in my head. *Somebody else brought you into this world.* I shuddered and took a step back. "Does this have to do with seeing the owl that night?" My throat was dry. "About him telling me I was from another world? I made that up. It wasn't real. I'm sure I made that up."

Sweetpea was sitting upright now, leaning forward, squirming next to the rooster. "Can we tell her, Mama? Can we, please?"

Mama's voice was as soft and rhythmic as a lullaby. "No, Sweetpea. We talked about this, remember? We can't tell her what she needs to know. She has to remember herself."

I swallowed to keep the fluttering in my belly down. "But I never did know. I tried to find out. For years after that night, I tried to figure out where I was really from. I searched, checked my birth records, and tried to find my biological parents so I could ask them questions. But I couldn't, no matter how hard I tried."

Silence. The wind lifted my hair. I swept it out of my face.

"Maybe you were looking in the wrong place," said the rooster softly.

"But that's the thing." I knew my voice sounded agitated, but I couldn't slow down enough to control it. "I didn't just look for my birth parents. I also read everything I could find about UFOs and aliens. I even tried using my radio to communicate with extraterrestrials. But I never found one clue or piece of evidence to tell me I was from anywhere other than the local hospital. I made it all up. You have no idea how hard it was, to know something in your gut so clearly, and then find out it's not even remotely true." My hands were shaking. "There's nothing to remember. Nothing I didn't invent."

Mama took a step closer and touched her muzzle against my arm. "Oh, Frankie. Be patient. You will remember soon."

My throat narrowed and I fought to keep control of my voice. I was about to respond when a deep noise reverberated through the darkness. It took a moment for me to recognize the words within the rumble.

Please forgive me
If I break into a sweet laughter
When your heart complains of being thirsty
When ages ago
Every cell in your soul capsized forever
Into this infinite golden sea.

I looked at the cockroach for the first time with more curiosity than discomfort. "What is that? What does that mean?"

"It means exactly what Mama said. You'll remember soon enough."

I wanted a better explanation and was about to ask again when the air suddenly felt cold against my skin. A sharp and insistent noise cut the night. I tried to ignore it, but after a moment I could no longer feel Mama's muzzle on my arm or make out the shapes of Sweetpea and Roo in front of me. Nameless One was the last thing I saw, gracefully taking flight from the branch where he had been resting.

My eyes filled with light. The sharp noise continued, persistent. After a moment I made out the form of my legs in front of me covered by polka-dotted pajama bottoms and a bright window somewhere past my feet. A blanket lay crumpled on the floor next to me. I felt frozen in place.

Helpless, immobile, grief flooded me. The familiar despair rose like a tsunami, breaking inside my chest.

Wiping away my inexplicable tears, I reached for my phone to turn off the alarm. As I did, a movement caught my eye. A cockroach ran along the baseboard of my living room. It paused just before the front door and turned back to look at me. The surge within me subsided. But before I could move, the roach turned back around and disappeared beneath the door.

Sorrow crashed over me, wave after relentless wave.

CHAPTER 5

Endless clusters of diagrams and dots stared up at me from the paper, screaming.

I sat, entering the incoherent results of Dr. Porter's maze experiment into statistical software for analysis. It was mind-numbing—or had been, until I had the strange sense the data were trying to tell me something. Something important. Something that might as well have been in Russian for all I understood.

Everyone knows rats communicate ultrasonically.

Instead of helping me decode the cryptic message, my brain was usefully providing a soundtrack of randomly-remembered quotes from my encounter with the animals the week before.

I clicked again on the browser window I had minimized moments ago and reread the definition for the two hundredth time:

Ul-tra-son-ic
/əltrəsänik/
Of or involving sound waves with a frequency above the upper limit of human hearing.

I'd had to refresh my memory of what the word even meant. When I read the definition, I remembered that some animals like bats and dolphins used ultrasound waves to locate objects they couldn't see, but I'd never heard of anything communicating that way. I'd spent the entire weekend scouring three libraries on campus trying to find out if rats really did communicate ultrasonically. I'd even skipped lunch—an unprecedented accomplishment for me—but my search had ended in failure.

Groaning, I minimized the window again.

I was avoiding Dr. Porter—and Brian and Lillian too for that matter. Dr. Porter hadn't raised his voice at me again, or brought up the incident, not even when I shuffled to his lab early one morning with the banner I'd made and the hardware to hang it on the wall. He was on his phone when I reached the door, his face as tart as a lemon through the glass. He waved me inside but ignored me as I walked to the far wall, didn't look at me once while I hung the banner, and barely acknowledged me when I said goodbye.

Brian fired me from feeding the rats. He let me know in a note taped to the wall in the rat closet that reminded me of Joe's terse breakup letter. This time I got an explanation, though it was a dubious one—he claimed Dr. Porter wanted him to do the feeding since he had more experience. My new job was to take notes as the rats ran the mazes and enter the recordings of their brain activity into statistical software.

Nobody asked me to draw conclusions from the data. Still, that didn't stop me from having the unshakable sense that I should understand something important about the results. But like with everything else, my mind refused to help me figure out exactly what that was.

Every cell in your soul capsized forever into this infinite golden sea. The deep rumble of the cockroach's voice rolled through my brain.

I clicked another tab—also open for the past week and scanned hundreds of times—to conjure a poem by a fourteenth-century Sufi master named Hafiz called "So Many Gifts." It read:

There are so many gifts
Still unopened from your birthday,
There are so many handcrafted presents
That have been sent to you by God.

The Beloved does not mind repeating,
"Everything I have is also yours."

Please forgive Hafiz and the Friend
If we break into sweet laughter
When your heart complains of being thirsty
When ages ago
Every cell in your soul
Capsized forever
Into this infinite golden sea.

Indeed,
A lover's pain is like holding one's breath
Too long
In the middle of a vital performance,
In the middle of one of Creation's favorite
Songs.

Indeed, a lover's pain is this sleeping,
This sleeping,
When God just rolled over and gave you
Such a big good-morning kiss!

There are so many gifts, my dear,
Still unopened from your birthday.

O, there are so many handcrafted presents
That have been sent to your life
From God

I'd never heard of Hafiz before, certainly never read this
poem that left me more bewildered than enlightened. How did
my brain reference it in a dream with such specificity? Some
hidden understanding lay buried here, too, calling my attention
like an idea raising its hand to be heard, but I refused to call on
it and turned back to the diagrams and their inscrutable secrets.

The previous studies into sharp wave ripples I'd read
were bloated and tedious, puffed up with extra words and
fancy jargon. Only after removing their most overdressed
phrases did I get to the heart of their findings—that the brains
of many animals create replays during the learning process,
firing cells in sequences that mirror their previous actions,
like the ones in front of me that recreated the paths the rats
ran through the maze.

The images of the rats' brain activity resembled artists'
sketches of the maze routes they'd run with gray, wayward
lines curving off the main paths like unruly hairs. Vibrant blue
and purple dots clustered around the most efficient path to
the reward, blues indicating the first brain cells to fire, purple
pointing out the laggards. I admired the hues and the fact that
anyone would think to turn firing neurons the color of spring
violets and forget-me-nots.

The colorful diagrams told a story. After exiting the maze,
the rats ran it again in their minds, reviewing the routes that
led to the reward. I leaned forward in my chair as if trying to
get a better view through this strange and fascinating window
into the inner workings of a rat's mind.

But I couldn't let myself get carried away. My eyes flicked to the banner I'd hung the week before, a perfectly proportioned testament to my failure.

I knew what the others would say if they heard me talking about the inner workings of rats' minds. Just because the rats were processing information didn't mean they were having thoughts. Don't be delusional.

I was about to turn the colorful diagrams over so they would stop distracting me when the purple and blue dots muttered something in a language I understood. Many of the diagrams mapped the same route through the maze but bore opposite color schemes. Some had blue dots on top and purple on the bottom. Others were identical except the colors were reversed.

I jumped out of my chair and threw papers around like they were confetti on New Year's Eve, casting about for my notes from yesterday's experiment.

"Hey."

My stomach leaped into my throat. I spun around.

Lillian walked through the door, clutching books to her chest with both hands and wearing a black mini backpack over a black-and-white striped tank top. "I'm so glad you're here." She eyed the papers on the floor. "Everything all right?"

Her voice was so effusive and affectionate I resisted the urge to look around and see if she was talking to somebody else. I was the only other person in the room. "Yeah." I put the papers back on the table. "I'm just looking for my notes. How's it going?"

"Not bad." Lillian pulled out a chair and lowered herself into it. "Except for the fact that my back is killing me. I know it's irrational to wear this tiny backpack instead of one that would actually fit all my shit and, you know, serve some kind of purpose." She rolled her eyes. "It's just I saw this one in the thrift store and it's Prada, and for five bucks I couldn't resist. So I may be permanently damaging my spinal column, but at least I'll impress the surgeons with my good taste when they go to sew my arms back on."

"It's very cute." I tapped my finger on the table. "Hey, I have a question for you about the experiment yesterday." The words spilled out all at once.

"Yeah, sure, whatever you want." Lillian's sienna brown eyes shone behind her glasses. "I had something I wanted to talk to you about too. You go first, though."

I forced myself to continue before she could change her mind—or I could. "I thought I remembered the rats only ran through the maze in one direction yesterday."

"That's right. We rewarded two different paths at different times, but they both started at the same point and went in the same direction."

I wasn't sure how much I wanted to share, but my discovery felt important. "The thing is, I've been looking at yesterday's results, and the sharp wave ripples"—I grabbed the top sheet of diagrams on the table—"go in opposite directions." I waited to give her time to see.

"Meaning what?" Lillian examined the paper with her head cocked to one side. "Ah, I see. They were replaying the path through the maze both forward and backward." Her eyes met mine. "So what?"

Doubt surged like a rogue wave. If Lillian didn't see it, I must be wrong. But it was too late to turn back now, and Lillian was staring at me, waiting.

"Well, it may be nothing. But I thought it could mean, or at least seems to suggest—"

The door creaked, and the words dried up in my mouth. Brian stepped through the door, his lion's mane even more tousled than last time, his lean frame humming with power. He broke into a wide grin.

"My two favorite lab partners." He strode toward us on long, athletic legs.

"Your *only* two lab partners," Lillian said. "But we'll try to forget that and pretend you're not full of shit."

Brian's flaxen eyes pinned me to the wall like a butterfly in someone's collection. "Hey, I'm glad you're here. I've been meaning to talk to you about the other day."

The only thing I wanted less than to talk about the other day was to talk about the other day with Brian. He seemed to think he knew better than everyone about everything and didn't mind saying so. "That's okay—no need."

"No, really. I want to. I felt bad." It took all my willpower not to look away from his intense gaze. "I should explain something to you now that Dr. P's not around."

"I know," I said. "You told me not to make unsubstantiated claims around Dr. Porter, but I did anyway. I get it. I jumped to conclusions. I won't do it again."

Something—regret or pity?—flickered across Brian's face. "No, that's not what I meant at all. It's true Dr. P doesn't like his students making unsubstantiated claims, but that's only part of what I was trying to warn you about."

I crossed my arms over my chest, hoping I didn't look as confused as I felt. What else had I missed?

"I ran into Dr. P at the registrar's office the morning before our first lab." Brian leaned against a table. "He didn't see me at first, he was so caught up talking to a woman who works there. He was pissed off, yelling that she wasn't doing her job. I think he had just found out there were only two students registered for his lab."

"Yeah, he's very picky," I said. "He told us that. Quality over quantity, slim pickings, and all that."

"No." He stretched the word out long. "That's just it. The lab isn't small because he wouldn't let people in. The lab is small because nobody wanted to study with him. I think his reputation for a quick temper and a sharp tongue finally caught up with him. And it's been a long time since his Gruber nomination." He took a deep breath. "Anyway, he argued with that lady for a long time. I could tell he was still pissed when we got to the lab. You just happened to give him as good an excuse as any to pick a fight."

Some animals tend to fight when scared. Cockroach's words rang like a gong between my ears.

Brian looked at me, waiting for a response, and I wanted to give him one, but I couldn't concentrate. *Fear makes us do some absurd things.* I tried to focus on what he'd said and think of an intelligent reply, but it was as if my brain were vibrating from the reverberations of the gong. *The trick is to see through your own fear to theirs.*

Something clicked in my mind. I knew what the animals had been trying to tell me. It seemed obvious now, given what Brian had just said. "It wasn't my fault," I muttered.

"What?" Brian and Lillian said together.

Dr. Porter was scared. That's what the animals had been trying to tell me. I wasn't too sensitive, or too irrational. I hadn't made some horrific, unforgivable mistake. My father may have been right about my imagination, but I still had a chance to be a good neuroscientist.

The irony made me want to laugh. Dr. Porter yelled at me because of his own fear. Fear that he wasn't liked, fear that students were avoiding him, fear that *he* was a failure.

Some animals tend to fight when scared. The trick is to see through your own fear to theirs.

I wished the animals were there so I could tell them I finally understood. Instead, Brian and Lillian continued staring at me. "Nothing," I said. "I just mean, that's good to know. Thanks for telling me." I made a mental note to be more forgiving of Brian in the future.

Lillian put her hand on my knee. "Dr. Porter was fucking miles out of line, Frankie. That's what I wanted to tell you earlier. My parents are professors, and they're hard-asses, but they would never treat a student that way, no matter what they did, and you didn't do anything wrong."

Brian looked at Lillian directly for the first time since entering the room. "Where do your parents teach?"

Lillian took her hand off my knee. "Here. But not in this department. Brian, Frankie was in the middle of telling me something she discovered about the experiment results when you got here."

I was talking about somebody else. Cockroach's deep rumble rang in my brain, once again leaving no space for other thoughts. I itched beneath their gaze, trying to focus on what Lillian had just said.

"Yeah, I . . . ." *Others much prefer to flee.* My brain had developed a mind of its own. I needed to get out of there. "I, uh, have to go to the bathroom. I'll be right back."

Luckily, nobody was in the restroom. I locked myself in one of the stalls and took a deep breath.

I was talking about somebody else. The words were insistent and strangely loud, like they were echoing off the bathroom walls despite being confined to my head.

I covered my ears—a futile attempt to address the noise in my brain—and saw something dart across the floor of the stall next to me.

Others much prefer to flee. Relinquishing all pretexts of sanity and hygiene, I got down on my hands and knees and peered under the divider. *Y'all are very good at hiding what you're feeling.* The useless soundtrack of remembered quotes continued as a small cockroach ran toward me as fast as he could.

I know I haven't been the best at telling you what a great girlfriend you are.

This time the voice in my head wasn't the deep bass of the cockroach. It was Joe's voice, imagined when I held his note in my shaking hands. The cockroach halted his sprint and my heart stopped dead in the same moment.

Joe was gone. Not angry. Not sunk into one of his frequent silences. Gone for good. He didn't want to fight for what we had. I wasn't worth it.

A water main burst behind my eyes.

I was talking about somebody else.

Again something clicked in my head. I scrubbed my palms across my face.

"Is that what Cockroach and Roo were trying to tell me? That Joe was scared too?" In my mind, Joe fled from me gazelle-like down a busy Berkeley street, pushing people out of his way in his terror. "I suppose if I'm being honest, we weren't a great fit anyway. He was never really here even when he was, you know?"

Was the roach nodding?

I leaned down to get a better look. "You know, this is the first time I've been close to an insect when I wasn't totally panicking." He stood frozen as if waiting for something. "Well, I'm not going to kiss you, if that's what you want. Maybe that would turn you back into a prince, but we'll sure as heck never find out."

The roach just stared at me. "Brian and Lillian are probably wondering where I am." I started to stand up, but paused midway, still held by the demand in the roach's gaze. "What is it you want?"

The roach's back legs twitched. And suddenly I knew.

"You want me to do the tickling experiment." I sank back to the floor to see the roach eye-to-eye. "You know that Dr. Porter explicitly forbade me to do it?"

The roach's eyes were implacable.

"He could fail me. Maybe even expel me. But . . ." I bit my lip. "He did also say he only cares about what I can prove. And if I could prove they're ticklish, maybe it would change his mind about the rats and me."

I could have sworn the roach's expression softened.

Remembering the blue and purple diagrams back in the lab, I decided. "Okay, I really do have to go. But I appreciate the input."

The roach didn't acknowledge my words, just turned and scurried up the wall.

When I got back to the lab, Brian sat at one of the computers and Lillian was checking her phone. For the first time in a long time, I knew exactly what to say.

"What I realized is about the rats." I walked up to them. "The results show sharp wave ripples going in opposite directions. That means the rats are replaying the correct path forward and backward. But that's bizarre, because the rats only ran the maze forward."

I waited, but neither of them said anything. "We've assumed the rats are replaying their recent experiences in the sharp wave ripples. But that can't be true if they didn't run the maze backward."

I paused. More silence. "The rats aren't just programming memories—they're creating a mental map of the maze." The words spilled out of me in a rapid, happy gush. "We have evidence that rats create mental models of their environments to help them solve problems!"

Lillian smiled, but the muscles in Brian's jaw clenched. "No, I know," I said before he could object. "Don't worry, I won't say anything to Dr. Porter. I'm not eager to repeat that mistake. But Dr. Porter was right about one thing. I shouldn't make unsubstantiated claims. So I'm going to do my own experiment on the rats."

"Are you sure that's a good idea?" Brian's words were enveloped in Bubble Wrap, like he was afraid they might break me.

But for once I didn't care. "No. Not at all. But I am sure of one thing. They are ticklish. And they are laughing. We just can't hear them."

Brian and Lillian's foreheads crinkled in confusion.

I allowed myself a grin. In truth, I couldn't stop it. "Everyone knows rats communicate ultrasonically."

CHAPTER 6

"How can you be so sure?" Doubt riddled my father's voice.

"I'm not." My confidence slipped away like rainwater through a sewage grate. "I told you, it's an idea I had to find out if rats really are ticklish. Lots of animals use ultrasonic sounds, so maybe rats do too."

"Why would you harp on this, sweetie?" His voice was strained; he was working hard to stay calm. "You already upset your professor once. He could make life very hard for you, maybe even get you kicked out of the program. Why would you take the risk?"

"He won't even know unless we tell him. We're only going to use a few rats that aren't being used in the other experiment, we can do it when nobody's around, and maybe I can get the scientific proof Dr. Porter says he wants."

"*If* it's even true."

"You may be right. But—" A door slammed in the background. "Is that Mom? Is she home now?"

"Yes, she picked James up from his hotel."

"James is there?" My brother had just visited them a couple weeks before.

"His new job has him working in Atlanta the next few months."

"That's great." I tried to make it sound like I meant it.

"Do you want to talk to him?" He didn't wait for an answer. "James. *James*! Come talk to your sister."

My brother's muffled protest was pointless. Neither of us had figured out how to defy our father. Sure enough, a moment later James's energetic voice was on the line. "Hi, Sis." He did a good job making it sound as if he'd really wanted to talk to me.

"Hi, James. How's it being home?"

"Great. How's it avoiding being home?"

"Not so great. Are you liking the new job?"

"It's awesome. They always are, though, 'til they're not."

James was a consultant. As if changing projects every few months wasn't enough, he changed jobs every couple of years as well. Despite the lack of loyalty on his résumé, he always managed to get whatever position he wanted. While I was racking up rejection after rejection, or worse, no rejection at all—just a giant black hole that sucked up all my applications— he was busy landing every job he applied for. Every. Single. One.

"That's great." I imagined his body buzzing with excitement like it always did in the beginning.

"Hey, you should come visit, Frankie. Mom and Dad miss you."

My shoulders caved into themselves. Mom's guilt was bad enough—I didn't need my brother reminding me that he was the golden child. Literally. His strawberry-blond ringlets were a perfect mix of Mom's red locks and Dad's dark blond curls, and his golden complexion combined Mom's fair skin with Dad's sun-darkened khaki cast. Everybody knew they were related right away. Unlike me, with my anomalous olive skin and dark brown hair.

I take a breath and force a response. "I'm working on it. I've got a few things going on."

"Yeah, Mom told me about Joe . . ."

He didn't say anything else. "It wasn't meant to be."

"Sorry, kid." I really hated when he called me that.

"It's okay. You know, it sucks, but I'll be okay. How's Jessica?"

Silence. I knew what it meant even before he explained. "It didn't work out. I'm seeing a woman named Elizabeth now." I didn't bother asking what happened with Jessica—it was usually the same thing anyway. You could almost see his enthusiasm for a woman fade after the first few weeks like a bright shirt washed too many times. His disappointment felt real when things ended, but he always had a new, beautiful girlfriend within a month. How in the world did we come from the same family?

"Frankie, don't let this get to you, okay? There'll be someone else, someone better. Don't worry about this guy. He didn't deserve you."

I knew he was trying to be helpful, but he was always saying things like "Don't let it get you down," or "Life's too short to be sad." He made being happy sound so easy, like it was something you ordered off a menu. "Thanks, James." My throat constricted, preventing me from saying more.

"Hey, did you hear Dad's drug baby passed Phase 3 trials? He's about to submit it for FDA approval."

"No, that's great." This time I didn't have to fake my excitement. My father's drug baby was the latest medicine he was in charge of developing. His last drug baby had died in Phase 2 trials, so this was good news.

"We're going out to dinner now to celebrate. I should probably get going. Hey, chin up, grasshopper. Life's too short to be—"

"No, wait, James, hold on. Is Mom there? I need to ask her something."

"Yeah, she's right here. But make it short, okay? We have reservations to make."

After a brief scuffling noise, my mother breathed into the phone. "Frankie, how are you? Is everything okay?"

"Yeah, everything's fine. I just had a few questions I wanted to ask about my birth parents." I waited for the hurt to flood back across the line.

It didn't. My mother's voice was even and firm. "What questions? I'm happy to answer any I can, though I've already told you everything I know."

"I know. But I was a kid then, and I'm not sure I remember everything you told me. I just want to make sure I'm not missing anything."

"Why? Has something happened?"

"No, Mom, nothing's happened. I just—" I didn't know what to tell her. "I've just had some weird dreams that got me thinking about it again. If you don't want to talk about it, we don't have to."

My mother took a long inhale and an even longer exhale. "It's no problem, sweetie. Ask me whatever you want."

Guilt nibbled the insides of my intestines. My conversation with the animals—their implication that I was wrong about who I thought I was and where I came from—had reignited my obsession to learn about my birth parents and the time before my adoption. Asking my mother what she remembered was the only way I could think of to get answers. I forced myself to read my first question. "How did you find me?"

"Through an adoption agency. Love's Promise, I think, or something like that. It's been so long. I could look through my papers and try to find the name if you like."

"That would be great. But I mean, how did we first meet? How did you find *me*?"

"We met at the adoption agency. One of the social workers had told us about this amazing four-year-old who was being fostered in California, and we were so excited—"

"Wait, I was *four* when you adopted me?"

"Yes, sweetie. I thought you knew that."

"No! I thought I was a baby. Why would you adopt a four-year-old?"

My mother hesitated. "Because we fell in love with you as soon as we saw you. We'd planned to get a baby. As soon as I had James, I wanted another one. But then I was in that car accident, and I couldn't get pregnant anymore. Your father was the one who suggested adoption. I loved the idea—I don't know how I didn't think of it—but there was a long queue for babies. Then a social worker mentioned they had a four-year-old we could adopt right away. She kept going on about how special you were, but she didn't have to convince us. As soon as we heard about you, we knew you were the one."

I didn't like the word *special*. Like *interesting* or *funny*, people used it when they didn't want to say what they really thought. I refocused. "California? What was I doing in California?"

"I don't know, Frankie. But I've always thought maybe that's why you ended up there. Because you were homesick." She laughed, a brief, obligatory bark. "The social workers never told us anything about your past. Your parents requested a closed adoption, so we never knew who they were. We never met your foster mother either or learned her name. It didn't seem important at the time."

"Does the adoption agency still exist? Maybe if we contacted them . . ."

My mother sighed. "Don't you remember? After that night you ran away, you insisted we find your birth mother." Her voice sank. "We went back to the adoption agency to try to get your records unsealed, but they'd had a fire. All the records burned."

Her words triggered a memory of my parents telling me about the fire, but at the time I'd thought they were lying because they didn't want me to find my birth parents. A fire was way too convenient. They never said anything, but their bodies always froze when I asked about my adoption. When I developed an interest in UFOs, they got explicit really fast and told me to stop wasting my time. But my mother wasn't lying to me now. I decided to ask the last question on my list.

"Do you have any other information about where I came from?"

"No, sweetie, I'm sorry. I really am. I know how important this is to you." She got quiet again, like she was deciding whether to say something. "Have you thought about using one of those reunion registries? Or going to an agency that could help you search?"

"No." The small electric shock of surprise gave way to a warm surge of gratitude. "But that's a really good idea, Mom. Thanks. How do you know about those?"

"You always wanted to know more about where you came from when you were young. I had a feeling it was only a matter of time before it came up again, and at some point, I did research to be prepared." My father called my mother's name from the other room. "Good luck, sweetie. I've got to go. Sorry I can't help more."

"You helped a lot. Have fun at dinner."

Her voice got lighter. "We will. It's so nice to have James here." Then plunged. "I only wish you could be here too."

And there it was. My stomach twisted in knots so intricate they would have made an Eagle Scout jealous. "Yeah, Mom, me too."

But a few minutes after I hung up the phone, my stomach had more butterflies than knots. All I could think about were registries and search agencies, and how much could happen in four years in a state larger than most countries.

CHAPTER 7

illian was running late. I hadn't asked Brian to come because I felt safer without him, and we really only needed two people for the experiment. But without either of them in the lab to distract me, I was a mere speck of space dust trying to escape the gravitational compulsion of the black hole in my backpack.

Sliding my phone out of the small pocket in front, I opened my email, ready to find only newsletters or spam, emails about class projects same as the last four hundred times I'd checked since the day before.

Instead, I found a reply from the Georgia Adoption Reunion Registry right on top. The air froze in my lungs, and my hands shook in mutiny, nearly dropping my phone on the floor when I tapped the message.

I scanned it, but the tiny words leaping off my phone's vacuous face couldn't be true. Even this close, my nose nearly touching the screen, they were too small, their implicit promise too big.

Martha Forrester, your foster mother, would like to contact you.

The door scraped open behind me. Lillian looked like I felt, her mouth open and chest heaving.

"Sorry I'm late," she said, breathless. I dropped my phone in my bag. She dropped an armload of books onto the table. "I did research on rats and tickling. Scientists have been stumped for a long time about ticklishness, why it evolved and what purpose it serves, so they've done a lot of studies. They claim only primates are ticklish. But from what I can tell, nobody's bothered to test rats."

Yet again I doubted the wisdom of doing this experiment. For the first few days, my decision had seemed so right, so solid, that I hadn't questioned it. But as worries had time to gather in my brain, they formed a mob, chasing me with burning criticisms and barbed what-ifs. What if there was a reason real scientists hadn't already done this experiment? What if Dr. Porter found out and took revenge? What if I was wrong? Even if I was right and rats were ticklish, our efforts would be too small to be conclusive, too illicit to be shared. What was the point in taking the risk?

But then I remembered the rats—underestimated, maligned, helpless—and I knew I had to keep going. For them, and for me. I was dying to know if what the animals had told me about ultrasonic communication was true.

So I filled my lungs with air and courage and got three rats out of the storage room.

"Which ones are those?" Lillian didn't look up from untangling the electrodes. "I can never tell them apart."

My cheeks got hot. "Calvin, Hobbes, and Wilbur." Lillian had overheard me call one of the rats by name the week before and made me tell her all their monikers. I wasn't sure what was worse—that I'd given names to all twenty-five lab rats and could remember each and every one—or that I'd named them all after my childhood heroes.

"I get Calvin and Hobbes. I used to love that cartoon. But who is Wilbur named after?"

"*Charlotte's Web*." My voice was barely audible.

"Of course, the pig." Her laugh was loud and long, and each iteration poked at another soft spot in my belly. "You know, the more I learn about you, the more I wonder what miracle it was that landed you in neuroscience."

I focused on setting up the ultrasound receiver Lillian had managed to borrow from another professor. "I figured Hobbes can be the control. Calvin can get the non-tickling light touch, and Wilbur can be the one we tickle for real. He's pretty responsive to touch and likes having humans around, from what I can tell."

A few minutes later, Hobbes looked like a mini-Medusa with a tangle of white wires snaking out from his head.

Lillian held her phone's camera up to the monitor. "The neural patterns of Research Subject Number 1, the control, have been recorded."

"Great." We pulled the electrodes off Hobbes and put them on Calvin. Something—an alien?—was doing somersaults in my stomach. Taking a deep breath, I stepped in front of the cage. "I am now going to touch Research Subject Number 2 lightly on the back." I stroked Calvin just below his neck, his white fur soft under my fingers.

"His Romandic operculum is activated." Lillian's eyes were fixed on the screen.

"Good. Let's get the electrodes hooked up to Wilbur." When I pulled out my hand, Calvin looked up at me. I ignored the request in his eyes.

A few minutes later, Wilbur was ready. "I'm now going to touch Research Subject Number 3 in the same way." I stroked Wilbur's gray-and-white back.

"Subject Number 3 is showing Romandic operculum activation as well," Lillian said.

"Okay, now I'm going to stroke his hind feet." I gently nudged Wilber over and he fell onto his back. I touched the bottom of his back feet as lightly as I could.

The room exploded into sound.

It took a minute to untangle the different strains of noise. First, I isolated Lillian's voice. I had to replay the words in my head before I understood them.

"His hypothalamus is lighting up! Romanic operculum and hypothalamus are both activated!"

Next, I identified a high-pitched squeaking like an insect chirping happily underwater. It came from the ultrasound receiver.

The last noise I managed to separate out was a door slamming and shelves rattling. I looked up, still tickling Wilbur's feet. Brian entered the room with a sour expression on his face.

I yanked my hand out of the cage. "What are you doing here?"

"Nice to see you too."

"Sorry, I mean, I wasn't expecting you."

Brian turned to Lillian. "You didn't tell her I was coming?"

Lillian planted her palm against her forehead. "Oh, shit! I totally forgot to mention that I invited you. Sorry, Frankie." Her face twisted in regret. Then she lowered her palm and narrowed her eyes at Brian. "But I told you we were starting forty-five minutes ago. Where have you been?"

Brian's eyes went from heated amber to burning ember. "Our soccer game went into overtime. Stanford handed us our asses in penalty shots."

Lillian nodded ruefully. "A true tragedy."

"It is," Brian said. "Stanford's undeserved arrogance is a stain on our otherwise bright state."

"You play for Cal?" I was still trying to figure out how Brian could be a superstar researcher and a star athlete.

"No. I did in undergrad. Now I just coach. Not that it did any good today."

"Brian, stop humble-bragging and come look at this." Lillian was staring at the EEG monitor again, waving her hand impatiently. "When Frankie touches the rats' backs, their Romandic operculum gets activated. But when she tickles their hind feet, the entire hypothalamus lights up. And they make sounds! Did you hear them when you came in?"

The sour look disappeared from Brian's face. "No, show me."

I nudged Wilbur again, rolling him onto his back, and began to tickle his belly this time. The underwater insect chirping began immediately. When I stopped, the chorus stopped. When I started again, it continued.

After a minute, I removed my hand from the cage. Wilbur jumped up and ran around the cage, leaping along its length.

"That's amazing." Brian's upper body quivered with quiet laughter. "And nothing from the control?"

"Not a thing," said Lillian.

"So the hypothalamus is activated when humans are tickled as well?" Brian had stopped laughing and was staring at the screen.

Ice invaded my veins. I looked at Lillian. "I don't know," she said. "The studies I found were older and didn't map the neural activity in that level of detail."

Brian looked back and forth between the two of us. "Well, I guess we'd better find out then, hadn't we?"

I took a step back. "But I'm not ticklish."

"Me neither." Lillian looked at Brian.

"Oh, for goodness' sake. Give me the electrodes." He distributed the tiny cups throughout his thick hair.

"I am now going to touch Research Subject Number 4 lightly on the arm." I stroked the back of Brian's forearm.

"Romandic operculum is activated," Lillian said.

"We will now lightly touch the belly of Subject Number 4."

Lillian and I tickled Brian, who wiggled and squirmed beneath us. It was oddly intimate, but I kept at it until Lillian turned to the monitor and yelled, "Hypothalamus activity!"

All the ice in me melted, replaced by a rising tide of joy.

Brian fished the electrodes out of his hair. "I have to admit, I didn't expect our little experiment to suggest that rats were ticklish *and* capable of ultrasonic communication. One or the other, maybe, but both? That's impressive."

For a second I was too hung up on the *our* and *little* to hear anything else. But then I realized he was complimenting me—or the rats, but either worked. "Thanks." I smiled.

But Brian's face stayed serious. "You know you can never tell Dr. Porter about this, right?"

"I know." But part of me didn't. Part of me was desperate to inform him how wrong he'd been.

I turned to Lillian to see what she thought, but she was staring at the ultrasound receiver, unhearing. "Frankie, how did you know about the ultrasonic thing?" she asked. "When I was doing research, I looked all over for studies supporting what you said, but I didn't find any. Not one. Nobody said anything about rats communicating ultrasonically."

My smile flatlined. I didn't want to admit the entire premise of the experiment was based on a dream I almost believed was real. "I, ah, just had a hunch."

Lillian's eyes dug into mine. "A hunch? How did you get the idea to begin with?"

I wished I was a better liar. "Um, well, it was a dream I guess."

"A dream?" Brian's eyes joined the excavation. "What kind of dream?"

"Just a regular dream. It was the night after our first lab. Someone in my dream might have mentioned rats communicate ultrasonically."

Brian and Lillian looked like they were watching a cheaply-made horror movie. "How did you get into neuroscience?" Brian asked.

I swallowed, praying my salivary glands would start working again. "My father."

"Your father's a neuroscientist?"

"No. He's a molecular biologist. He heads the R&D department at a pharmaceutical company." I looked down at my feet. "It was his idea. But I did it because of my . . ."

Lillian laid a soft hand on my arm. "Your what?"

My hands clasped together, as if seeking solace from one another. "Depression. I was depressed in high school. I got better just before college, studied biology, and worked in wildlife conservation for a while. But the funding dried up, and I couldn't find another job. The pay was terrible anyway, and my dad suggested I look into neuroscience." I forced my hands apart. "He pointed out the salaries are good, and there's a lot of demand. I wasn't sure, but then I remembered"—the pain, I almost said, that sprouted thick arms like the monsters in my dreams and wrapped them tight around my chest, slowly squeezing the life out of me—"but then I realized I could use neuroscience to do some good. You know, study the brain to find out how to help other people not go through what I did."

"That's so great," Brian said.

My brain struggled to come back to the lab. "What, depression?"

"Of course not. It's great you have such a noble reason for being here. I chose it because it's one of the few fields of science where you can make a lot of money."

Lillian took her hand off my arm. "Aren't there medications that work pretty well for depression?"

"For some people." I rubbed my hands together. "Not so much for others. And nobody knows why they work when they do."

Brian nodded. "My sister's always saying the same thing."

"Is she depressed?"

"She used to be suicidal, but now—" An old-school alarm clock beeped from Brian's pocket. He pulled out his phone. "Yikes, I've got to go." He stood up so fast the EEG machine skipped toward him. "Swim practice starts in a few minutes."

"You swim too?" My voice was a squeak I didn't recognize.

"Just for fun." Brian pulled the last of the electrodes off his scalp. "I mean, I am an assistant coach for the Cal team, but it's just for kicks."

And just like that my irritation returned—at the smug smile, the careful nonchalance, and the fact that there didn't seem to be anything Brian wasn't good at.

After Brian left, Lillian had a strange look on her face—perplexed but also piercing. She turned her fierce brown eyes to me. "So, do you always have dreams that lead to scientific breakthroughs?"

I didn't want to tell her about my dream, but with those eyes on me, I was scared not to. She was too smart for me to be able to hide anything. "Nope, that was the first. But it was a weird dream. Like, really weird."

Her eyes softened into ocher invitations. "Tell me about it."

I told her about the animals and what they had said. Without meaning to, I also told her about Joe and the battle with the cockroach. The only thing I left out was the part about the animals bringing up the question of where I was from and what I was here to do.

When I finished, Lillian didn't laugh. She didn't tell me I was nuts. She didn't find a polite excuse to get as far away from me as possible. Instead, she asked, "Why didn't you tell us earlier?"

"I don't know. I already feel like I don't belong here. I mean, everyone else is so brilliant and accomplished. I guess I didn't want to give anyone any more reasons to doubt me."

She pursed her lips and nodded. "Yeah, I know what that's like."

"You do?" Lillian was probably the most brilliant and accomplished person in the program.

"Are you kidding? My Dad's Black, and my Mom's Chinese. If someone isn't accusing me of getting in because my parents teach here, they're suggesting it must be because of affirmative action."

"Didn't California get rid of affirmative action in the '90s?"

"Yeah. Residents voted to make it illegal. And you know the funny thing—are you white?"

My nod was stiff as I waited for the funny part.

"Okay, so this isn't personal, but historically it's been mostly white women who challenge affirmative action in court, but they're also the ones who tend to benefit the most from it. Regardless, affirmative action at this school long gone, but that doesn't stop people from believing I don't deserve to be here."

I had a hard enough time when I was the only one questioning my worthiness. How much harder would it be if others were doing it too?

"That's messed up. I'm so sorry."

"Yeah, it's hella wack." Small vertical lines etched themselves into her forehead. "But it's still not as whack as your dream. Are you sure you'd never heard of that poem before?"

"I'm sure. I don't even remember the last time I read a poem. I mean, I suppose it's possible I read it years ago and forgot about it, but to remember it in such detail would be as strange as producing it out of the blue."

"And the thing about rats communicating ultrasonically. Like I said, I couldn't find any research about that anywhere. It's weird you would have known that."

"I know. I looked as well as soon as I had the dream. I couldn't find anything either."

Lillian shuddered, then hesitated, as if calculating her words. "Hey, I'm really sorry about Joe. What a spineless way to break up with someone."

"Thanks. It was pretty feeble."

"Do you want to go to the city this weekend? There's an international café that has great music we could go to. Maybe take your mind off Joe?"

The tiny words in the email from the Georgia Adoption Reunion Registry leaped into my mind. I had an idea. "Instead of going out, how would you feel about a road trip?"

"A road trip? Where to?"

"Eureka."

"Why there?"

I considered my answer. "I've been trying to find out more about where I come from."

"Are you from another country?"

"No. I'm adopted. I've never known much about my birth parents or where I was born, but I signed up with a reunion registry last week and heard back from them just before you got here." It felt like the butterflies in my stomach were trying to lift me off the ground with their flapping.

"What did they say?"

"There's no news from my mother. Or my father, for that matter. But I was with a foster mother until I was four, and she's been trying to find me." I rubbed my hands along the sides of my cargo pants. "Turns out she lives near Eureka. Says I'm welcome to visit her. I was just thinking . . . if you're willing to go . . . maybe we could . . ."

"Yes! Let's go! Maybe Brian will loan us his car."

"Actually, I'd rather he didn't know. I'll rent a car."

Lillian shrugged. "Whatever you want. But you know he's not entirely terrible, right? False bravado aside—he's actually a good guy."

Now I shrugged. "Okay. Whatever you say."

We said our goodbyes and I made my way out into the warmth of a hyperbolically sunny late afternoon. As I trudged home, a war raged in my belly. Part of me couldn't wait for the weekend to arrive, and part of me hoped it never would. Part of me insisted that telling Dr. Porter was the right thing to do, and part of me believed that part was suicidal.

If only I could talk to Roo, Mama, Cockroach, and the rest one more time. They could tell me what to do. But how many times had I tried to dream of a giant, white wolf?

The edges of sadness burned my throat and chest.

I should be used to losing the white wolf by now, but I wasn't. Would it ever hurt any less?

CHAPTER 8

Golden hills, clusters of gnarled trees, and a deep, endless blue rolled by the windows of the car. I itched to feel them on my skin.

"Do you mind if I roll down the window?" I asked Lillian as we passed a sign that said, *Eureka 230 miles*.

Her laugh from the passenger's seat was a little too amused. "You sound like my little brother. He hates riding in cars with the windows up. We always joke that he's part dog."

I bit my lip. "But no, I don't mind at all. I could use some fresh air." As if to convince me, she lowered her own window.

"Thanks." I fumbled to find the button for my side.

As soon as the wind touched my face and the smell of earth filled my nostrils, something inside me relaxed. I almost wanted to stick my whole head out the window, but I didn't tell Lillian that.

She reached over to turn down the music she'd put on earlier. "So what do you know about your foster mother?"

"Not much. Her name is Martha Forrester. She lives alone and works for herself, but I'm not sure doing what." I stared at the road, avoiding Lillian's eyes. Why was I so nervous? Was I afraid Martha would embarrass me? Herself?

I had no idea, but I was jealous of Lillian, the other drivers, and anyone who wasn't about to meet their foster mother for the first time.

Something moved into the road in front of the car's right wheel. I yelled and swerved into the left lane, barely missing it. When I looked in the rearview mirror, a small, box-shaped turtle inched across the highway, fully unconcerned about the massive cars whizzing within inches of his outstretched head.

"Shit," I said under my breath.

When I turned to check my blind spot, Lillian's mouth was forming a word—a question, I guessed—but I didn't hear it. I put on my turn signal and swerved again, this time to the right, then slammed my foot on the brake. We came to a stop several hundred feet later on the shoulder of the road.

"A turtle," I yelled as I opened my door and jumped out of the car. I raced back along the highway, propelled by the fear I wouldn't get there in time.

Somehow, miraculously, despite his small size and slow, determined steps, the turtle wasn't getting hit. People were either traveling in the fast lane or swerving at the last minute to avoid him like I had. But now, a large truck barreled toward him. I yelled, clapped my hands, flailed my arms like a drowning person, but I might as well have been invisible. As he approached the turtle, I put a hand over my eyes, my desperation turning to despair.

But when I looked up, the turtle was fine. He'd acknowledged the truck's passing enough to lower his head about a half-inch but was still making his way forward at the same dogged pace.

After what seemed like an eternity, I reached the little guy, scooped him up, and turned to run back to the safety of the shoulder.

When I looked down, he had retracted his head and feet inside his shell.

"Oh, *now* you're scared. Makes total sense." I studied his green-brown shell, wide eyes, and pointy little nose.

When something touched my shoulder, I jumped. Lillian was staring at me, panting. "How in the world did you see it?"

"I don't know. I almost didn't."

Lillian leaned forward to study the turtle up close. "It's kind of cute, isn't it?"

"He sure is." I held him up so we could both see him better. The turtle retreated further into his shell. "But I don't think he likes being this high off the ground. We should probably let him go." I walked away from the highway and put him on the ground. I made sure he was headed in a safe direction.

Without hesitating, he turned around and walked straight back toward the freeway. I picked him up, walked a few steps farther from the large, metal objects hurtling past at dangerous speeds, and placed him down again. He turned right around and headed toward the road.

"Sorry," I said to Lillian, picking him up one last time.

"Why?"

"Because we're going to have to take a slight detour."

I turned around at the next exit and pulled over just across the highway from where I'd found the turtle. I put him down facing the direction in which he'd been headed. As soon as he hit the ground, his head and legs popped out of his shell and he began to walk toward the hills.

I could feel Lillian's eyes on me when I got back in the car. "You think differently from most people, don't you?" she asked.

"Yeah, I guess so." I watched the grass waving on the edge of the highway. "That's what everyone tells me, anyway."

I could still feel Lillian's eyes on me, so I looked up to meet them. She didn't say anything for a moment, just sat there looking like she was trying to will something to happen. Finally, she shook her head.

"It's not a bad thing, Frankie." Her voice was unyielding. "It's not a bad thing at all."

———————

Martha's home resembled a cabin more than a house. Worse, it looked like it belonged in a fairy tale, as if Frodo—or, worse yet, the Wicked Witch of the West—might walk out at any moment.

The building was basically a hill with windows and a door stuck into it. Grass and a few orange wildflowers covered the roof, and small, crooked tree trunks stripped of their bark framed the windows and door. A curving path of river stones led up to the door, which had a rounded top and was about the right size to fit a hobbit.

Large, dark trees reaching impossible heights surrounded the cabin. Their trunks were so thick, they created an island of silence around them, stilling everything, including my heart. I'd seen redwoods before in Muir Woods, but the ones up here were different somehow. When we first drove into their shadows at Humboldt Redwoods State Park, I'd stopped breathing for a moment. Only when we entered a small clearing and I started gulping down air again did I realize I was holding my breath.

Now I put on the parking brake and turned off the engine. We sat in silence, both of us staring at the cabin. I had the urge to turn around and drive away.

"Okay," I said before I could act on my desire. "Let's do this."

When we reached the rough planks of the wooden door, I stooped and knocked three times.

Before my last knock was complete, the door flew open. A tall woman in a colorful sundress grinned in front of me. "Frankie!" she said, stretching her arms out for a hug. I took an automatic step back, then realized what I was doing. I forced myself forward, and she swallowed me in an awkward embrace. "I'm Martha, but please, call me Sundog," she said.

She let me go. "And you must be Lillian?" Lillian stepped forward with her hand outstretched, and Martha—Sundog—used it to pull her into a hug as well. "Please come inside."

We had to duck to make it under the doorframe. "It's a long-term lease," Sundog explained. "The owner is a good friend of mine. She's a lovely human being. A little obsessed with *Lord of the Rings*, but lovely nonetheless."

The interior of the house was much lighter and airier than I expected. The walls were painted white, and the floor was light wood, so the sunshine from the windows reflected throughout. Tree limbs made up the rafters and railings. A short stairway with a curved railing led up to what appeared to be a loft.

"Please, sit down." Sundog waved to a loveseat. Lillian and I sat in it, and she settled in a wooden chair across from us made of more gnarled branches the same creamy color as her skin.

"It's beautiful. Is this where I . . . where we . . ." My voice drifted off, and I couldn't find it.

"No." Sundog's graying curls swayed. "Child Protective Services never would have let me bring a child into a house like this. We lived a few miles down the road in some more traditional apartments. You probably passed them on the way in."

I squinted at her dress. It wasn't just colorful—it was tie-dyed.

"So what do you do for a living?" Lillian asked in a polite voice.

"I'm an energy healer." Sundog held her hands up, palms out. "I move blocked or distorted life energy to restore a harmonious flow. I also do psychic readings, but most people find those a bit too woo woo." She smiled and lowered her hands to her lap.

Unlike energy healing, I thought, *which is totally scientifically sound.* "How interesting." My voice was even more polite than Lillian's.

I glanced at Lillian to gauge how daft she thought Sundog was. But she was leaning forward, genuine interest in her eyes. "So when you say *life energy*," she asked, "do you mean *qi*?"

Sundog sat up straighter. "Yes. That's exactly right. Same as the Hindu concept of *prana*. It's the energy that moves through us and sustains us."

"My mom used to drag me to the acupuncturist all the time when I was growing up. I thought he was full of shit until my mother got fed up with my whining one day and explained that physicists are discovering all matter is pure energy, including humans. The rate of vibration of that energy determines the properties of each substance, so it's logical you can change human properties by shifting our energy. I would have argued with her, but she's a quantum physics professor at Cal."

Sundog clapped her hands together. "Fascinating. I love when science catches up with ancient wisdom." I had to stop myself from rolling my eyes. "So, what do you two do with your talents?"

"We're neuroscience PhD students at Cal," Lillian said. "We just started in August."

"Really?" Sundog sounded as polite as I had a moment before. "I wouldn't have thought . . ." She smoothed her dress over her legs. "Do you work with animals at all?"

"Mostly rats these days." I smoothed my own pants over my thighs. "Why?"

"I assumed you would work with animals, since you were always so good at speaking with them."

My stomach growled, expressing what I couldn't. "Um, speaking with animals?"

"Yes! A few years back I looked for you at the St. Francis School of Animal Communication because I thought you might have enrolled there. When you were young, if there was an injured animal within a two-mile radius of our apartment, you would bring it home and tell me what had happened to it. When I asked you how you could be so sure, you said, 'I asked him!' Like it was obvious. I assumed you were making it up, of course. Until Charlotte disappeared."

"Charlotte?" Lillian leaned forward so far she nearly tipped the loveseat over.

"Our cat." Sundog pointed to the picture of a gray tabby with large, green eyes on the table next to us. I didn't remember her—or anything Sundog was saying—but a wave of sadness rose in my throat. "I thought she must've gotten hit by a car. But when I said as much to Frankie, she insisted, 'No, she's *in* the car!' She wouldn't stop crying until we searched my old Camry top to bottom. But she wasn't there."

The loveseat lurched again—now I was the one tipping us forward. I pulled back.

Sundog stood up. "Would you like anything to drink, ladies?"

"No, thank you," Lillian and I said, releasing our breath together.

Sundog took her time walking to the refrigerator and picked up a bottle of what looked like dirty beer. When she sat back down, I made out the label: *Kombucha*.

"So where was she?" Lillian asked.

"Well, if it had been up to me, we never would have known. But Frankie insisted we could find her, so we canvassed the neighborhood and searched every car we could find." Her laugh was dry. "I'm pretty sure half our neighbors decided that day I was even crazier than they'd thought, which is saying a lot. But Frankie swore she saw an image of Charlotte looking up at a steering wheel. So we searched, I don't know, a dozen cars before we finally got to the farm at the end of our road.

"We searched their car too, but Charlotte wasn't in it. I was about to give up and call a therapist for Frankie when she asked if we could look in the car we saw behind the big building on the drive in. Turns out there was an old 1960s Ford pickup truck parked behind the barn—I just hadn't noticed it. Frankie walked over, opened the door, and sure enough, out leaps Charlotte, directly into the arms of her savior."

"How'd she get in there?" Lillian asked.

"They only used that truck once a week to go to market, so she must have gotten locked in there somehow after their last run. Poor thing probably would have died of thirst if we hadn't found her." Charlotte's stare haunted me from the photograph, stirring up ghosts of longing. "She never left Frankie's side for more than a few minutes after that, and I never doubted Frankie again. She would tell me all about her conversations with lizards and birds and bees, and I would listen just as carefully as if she were telling me about her class-mates at school. That's the way she talked about them, like they were her best friends."

I snapped out of my reverie. My best friends? Was she kidding?

I tried to think of a reason we needed to leave before my foster mother could share any more embarrassing stories, but Lillian spoke before I had a chance. "Sundog." Her face was deadly serious, as if the future of the world depended on the answer. "Did Frankie name Charlotte?"

"Yes, dear, she did."

"Was it for the spider in *Charlotte's Web*?"

"It was. That was her favorite book to read at bedtime."

Lillian hooted. "I knew it! She hasn't changed a bit. You know, she named one of our lab rats Wilbur."

I tried to disappear into the folds of the loveseat.

Sundog wiped her eyes. "I'm not surprised." She looked at me. "You really don't remember your conversations with the animals?"

"No."

Lillian stared at me, urging me with her long-lashed eyes, but I wasn't going to talk about my dreams. Not like this.

Not if it meant admitting I was as out of touch with reality as Sundog was.

"And you never speak with them anymore?"

"I do talk to them sometimes," I admitted. "But they never talk back."

"That makes me so sad." Sundog stared out the window. "It always seemed an amazing gift to me, such a sweet miracle."

I wanted to tell her she was wrong. It wasn't a miracle—it was a ridiculous lie made up by a ridiculous girl trying to impress her ridiculous foster mother. "And what about my birth parents? Do you know anything about them?"

Sundog stared out the window so long I wondered if she'd heard me. When she turned back, her blue eyes were glistening. "No, dear." Her tone was flat. "I'm so sorry. I don't."

Frustration sparked in my chest. I'd driven all the way up here, been laughed at and embarrassed, and still hadn't learned a single thing about where I came from.

I stood up. "We should go."

Sundog's face drooped. "Do you have to? I could make dinner. You could stay the night. It's been so long since I've seen you."

She sounded like my mother. I could feel a five-star, all-inclusive, no-expense-spared guilt trip coming on.

The spark of frustration fell into my stomach. Found kindling. Flared into flame.

"We have to get back. It's a long drive. We have so much work to do before Monday."

Sundog nodded as if her head weighed a hundred pounds. "I understand. I appreciate you driving all the way up here. There is one thing I can tell you, if you can spare a minute?"

I nodded.

"When you were a baby, I saw a woman lurking at your bedroom window. She scared the pee out of me, but it turns out she was a friend of your mother's. She didn't tell me the full story, but mentioned you were born under some type of duress."

"She was there? When I was born?"

"No. Apparently she was out of the country at the time. But she came to check on you as soon as she was back."

"She didn't say anything about who my mother was?"

"No. I've thought about it a lot since then, and I still can't figure out how she found us. CPS isn't supposed to release information like that to anyone who's not a relative, but Eureka is a such a small town, news travels widely. At any rate, she wouldn't let me wake you up to meet her. Said she just wanted to make sure you were all right. She rushed away before I could invite her in. But she did tell me her name. Stella Richardson. Maybe you can find her."

I closed my mouth. "Thank you, Sundog. Did she say where she lived? Do you have any idea where she is now?"

"No, dear, I'm so sorry. She didn't tell me any of that. She really didn't say much. But I am sure of her name—Stella Richardson—in case that helps."

Charlotte's picture caught my eye, triggering another wave of sadness.

Sundog's eyes followed mine. "Charlotte died five years ago, just before I moved in here. She never forgave me for your leaving. Oh, she would eat, and even sit on my lap on occasion, but mostly she just sulked around the house after you left. Not that I blame her. I did my own fair share of sulking after you left." Sundog wiped her eyes with the back of her hand. "My point is, I'd like you to have that photo. Charlotte would be happy to know you were reunited, even if it was after her death."

The sadness threatened to flood me, sink me, drown me. My lungs struggled to bring in air, which felt thick as water.

I picked up the photo. "Thank you." I wanted to tell Sundog I was sorry, that we didn't really have to leave, that we would stay for dinner and spend the night, but I needed to get away so I could breathe.

Clutching the photo to my chest, I waited for Lillian and Sundog to stand up. They did, as if stuck in slow motion, and hugged goodbye. I ducked outside. Sundog came through the door and stretched her hand out to me. "It was lovely to see you again, Frankie. I've missed you."

I shook her hand. "It was good to see you too." My body screamed for oxygen.

"You're welcome back anytime, okay?" Sundog's eyes were moist again. "This is your home. I know it may not feel that way, but it is. You're always welcome here, no matter what, for as long as you like."

"Thank you." I stepped back onto the river of stones without waiting for Lillian, gasping for air.

Why would Sundog say this was my home when every word out of her mouth confirmed there was nowhere in the world I would ever belong?

———

We drove down the long driveway. Lillian didn't say anything, but I could tell from her frown she was concerned.

She stayed silent when I hesitated at the intersection with the road, then turned in the opposite direction from which we'd come. She didn't utter a word as I drove two miles in the wrong direction, only coming to a stop when the road dead-ended at a farmhouse surrounded by red-roofed barns and dusty fields.

She still didn't say anything as I stared at the farmhouse, waiting for I wasn't sure what.

The limbs of the huge oak tree by the house swayed in the breeze. Shadows of the leaves shifted and danced in the dirt. A clanging sound came from the barn behind us, along with the faint scent of manure.

Only when something moved in the shadow of the house did I know why I had come. Out stepped a tall rooster with a familiar red comb, golden neck, and shiny, green tail feathers that curved like a triumphal arch. I gasped and leaned forward, but Lillian still didn't say anything; she just leaned forward as well, following my gaze.

We watched the rooster in silence as he pushed the dirt behind him with his feet, then pecked the ground, picking up things too small for us to see. After several long moments, he looked up, first to the tree and house, then to the road behind us, and finally at our car. One eye locked on mine. He pulled his head back and crowed. Then he turned around and disappeared back into the shadows at the base of the house.

I put the car in reverse and did a two-point turn. Neither Lillian nor I said anything until we were weaving through Redwood State Park on our way home.

"That was the farm where you found your cat?" she asked.

"Yes." It was all I could think to say.

"And did you see what you were hoping to?"

"Yes." I didn't want to explain about the rooster looking just like Roo.

She was silent for a long moment. "What happened back there? With Sundog, I mean? Why did we leave so quickly?"

Fleeting relief that she hadn't asked about the rooster gave way to my earlier shame and sadness. "I don't know. She wasn't as . . . rational as I expected. I mean, energy healing? Speaking with animals?" It wasn't the whole truth, but I couldn't put the rest into words.

"Did you see what was on the table next to the door?"

"No."

"An invitation to an alumni reunion at Harvard."

"Are you sure it was hers?"

"It had her name on it."

"Maybe she did too many drugs at Harvard and that's why she lost her mind."

"That's not fair and you know it." Her voice had an edge of anger. "You really don't believe you talked to animals?"

"Of course not. I mean, I'm sure I talked to them, but I don't believe they answered me. I probably told her they did, but it was just wishful thinking."

"You know the saying: *You have to see it to believe it?*"

"Sure."

"What about: *You'll see it when you believe it?*"

I shook my head.

"My mother taught me that one. She used to say it when I complained about going to the acupuncturist. She's always going on about how a lot of scientific discoveries would never have been made if someone hadn't believed in something that seemed impossible. I wouldn't have bought it, but . . ."

"She's a quantum physics professor at Cal."

"Yup. You believe in God?"

I slowed down to pass a group of people taking pictures next to the road. And to give myself a moment to think. "I'm not sure."

"Me either. I used to think the only reason to believe in something as illogical as a supreme being that's inherently unprovable was because you were weak or irrational. But when my grandmother died, I realized there was another reason." Lillian's glasses reflected dark tree trunks alternating with white light.

"Which is?"

"I'm so glad you asked. Sometimes admitting you're powerless and asking for help makes things better when nothing else does. And sometimes believing in something allows you to be a better person."

I didn't say anything for a while, just watched the giant trees pass by. "So you think I *could* talk to animals?"

"Oh, God, I don't know. But I have a feeling it's one of those things that has to be believed to be seen."

Soft rays of light filtered through the trees, falling in intricate patterns on the bright green ferns and thick, brown needles on the forest floor.

"Oh, God," I said, swerving onto the shoulder of the road.

"What, another turtle?" Lillian turned to look behind us. "I don't see anything."

"No." I couldn't breathe again. Something pressed against my heart. "No, it's not that."

I opened the door and got out of the car. Leaning against it for support, I sucked in small mouthfuls of air and searched the forest with wild eyes. Tree trunks. Rocks. Golden sunlight. Shadows. I pulled off one shoe and felt the cool, moist earth soft beneath my foot. A gentle breeze touched my cheek, and a stray patch of sunlight warmed my arm. It was all so achingly familiar.

I looked around in desperation, my heart pounding in my chest, but there was no giant, white wolf anywhere to be seen.

CHAPTER 9

All was black.

I waved a hand in front of my face but couldn't see it. I relaxed my eyes, raised my eyelids, but all remained dark and silent.

A familiar throat cleared itself.

"Um, again?" Roo's voice held a hint of laughter. "Frankie, we've been through this before."

"No, Roo, I know. I just tried opening my eyes but still can't see anything."

"Shit. Of course something would go wrong when Mama's not here."

I rubbed a hand across my eye, flinching when my finger collided with my eyeball. "Where's Mama?" I blinked away the pain. "Roo, my eyes are open, but I still can't see."

"Shit. I mean, don't worry. Mama's on her way. You showed up on the wrong side of the . . ." He coughed.

"The wrong side of what? Where are we?"

"The others will be here soon. Chickens don't see well in the dark, but we have other ways of navigating." His voice became a whisper. "Apparently some are even more effective than wolves' notorious night vision."

"Roo, where are we? It's someplace I know, isn't it?"

"You know," he said, his voice loud again, "I'm probably as surprised as you to hear this, but it's good to see you. I might even go so far as to say I was looking forward to this meeting."

I cocked my head. "You're just saying that to avoid answering my question."

"I beg your pardon." His voice was ice. "I may be avoiding your question, but that doesn't mean I'm lying. I'm not human, after all."

"Humans don't— We're not always— " I gave up. "Where's Cockroach?"

"So now you're eager to see him?" The rooster laughed in an at-me not with-me kind of way. "He's running late again, big surprise. He's always working on some top-secret project."

"And Nameless One?"

"Oh, he's here. But you can't count on him to help. I can't even remember the last time he said anything. Isn't that right?" he yelled to the sky. "Or is there something you want to tell us about what's wrong with Frankie's eyes?"

Silence.

"That's what I thought." There was a soft swishing noise I couldn't identify, then Roo's voice exploded in my ear. "They look fine, Frankie!" I jumped. The words vibrated in my eardrums. "Your pupils are even dilated," he said more softly. "Sorry, I didn't mean to scare you. I was just coming in for a closer look."

I rubbed my ear with the knuckle on my index finger. "Maybe so, but all I see is blackness." A frustrated *ugh* lodged in the back of my throat. "I feel like every time I figure one thing out, something else bewilders me."

A soft *hoo-hoo-ho-hooo* echoed above our heads.

"Frankie," said a familiar, throaty voice behind me. "Is everything okay?" Relief flooded me.

"She can't see again," crowed Roo. When I reached up

to knuckle my ear, he lowered his voice. "Her eyes are open, but she still can't see. I can't figure out what's wrong. They look fine to me."

Mama's feet crunched on dry leaves. Her warmth radiated against my leg as she drew close. I waited for her diagnosis.

"There's nothing wrong with your eyes, Frankie," the wolf said. "You just need to be willing to see."

"I'm trying. But it's not working." The wind tugged on my nightgown.

"I didn't say *try*. I said *be willing*."

"Of course I'm willing. You think I don't want to see you?"

Mama was silent for a moment. "Yes, I think I understand. That may be the problem. Frankie, stop trying to see us. The effort is getting in the way. Instead, be willing to see anything, whatever is here. Stay with the darkness and be willing to see if there's anything within it that wants to come into view. Anything, okay?"

"Okay." I wasn't sure what Mama meant but stopped trying to see the animals and focused instead on the darkness. Immediately it started to move and twist, shadows shifting all around me. Intrigued, I watched to see what the shadows would do. They roiled and rolled before beginning to transform into almost familiar shapes. Several to my right stretched into tall forms that resembled trees. On my left, small bits of light appeared, rippling amid the blackness in a pattern both regular and random. A stream.

More shapes emerged from the darkness until I found myself in the middle of a nighttime forest, moonlight reflecting off the leaves around me.

Finally, several shadows consolidated into a small ball of darkness close in front of me. The ball then expanded to form a sharp beak, arching tail, and two three-toed feet clutching a branch.

"Roo, I can see you!" His tail wagged back and forth once on each side.

I turned to where Mama's voice had come from and saw two yellow eyes in the darkness. Slowly the shape of the wolf materialized from the shadows. "Mama, I can see you too."

The wolf's eyes glowed. "That's great, Frankie. You did it."

"Where's Sweetpea?"

A rustling noise crescendoed and a small form came shooting out from behind Mama. "Frankie!" it yelled. "I missed you so much!"

"Sweetpea, I missed you too. You've grown. You must be twice as big as when I saw you last."

"My big teeth are coming in and look what I can do." The small squirrel ran past me to a large rock and climbed up, then hung upside-down along its face.

"That's amazing." I smiled. "I wish I could do that."

"I know, right?" She scrambled back to the top of the rock. "I walked the whole way to where we were supposed to meet without help. Mama only had to carry me a little after we found out you came here instead."

"That's great. Hey, Sweetpea, do *you* know where we are?"

"Of course," she said, oblivious to Roo's dagger stare. "We're in the woods. By the stream."

"Right." I laughed. "That's helpful. Thanks." I looked around. "So where's Cockroach? What's this top-secret project of his?"

"Oh, I'm here." The deep, rumbling voice came from everywhere at once.

"Where? I don't see you."

"Are you sure you want to know?"

I rolled my eyes. "Yeah, I'm pretty sure I do."

"Well in that case . . ." Something light tickled my shoulder. I screamed and flung it as far away as I could.

Distant thunder—or maybe a roach's laugh—rumbled through the trees.

"That's not funny!"

The thunder quieted. "No, I should say not. If that had really been me and not a twig, you would have broken an antenna." A shadow the size of a roach landed on the branch next to Roo. "We can grow them back, but it isn't easy. Though I do understand your disgust. Did you know that humans have over thirty million bacteria crawling on them at any given time?" He shuddered. "That's why we roaches always clean ourselves after touching one of you. Contamination goes both ways, you know."

A short speech I'd been practicing in the bath popped into my head. Reluctantly—extremely reluctantly after the insect's practical joke—I said the words out loud. "Cockroach, I've been thinking. I never thanked you for visiting the night Joe left. I know you were trying to help me, and I nearly killed you for it."

Cockroach spread his wings and tucked them away again. "You're welcome. I'm sure that wasn't easy to say, and I appreciate your appreciation. Though I do notice you stopped short of an actual apology."

I gave him a flat stare, then took a deep breath. "Okay. You're right. I'm sorry I tried to kill you."

"Thank you." His voice was softer than usual, but when he spoke again, it had regained its normal bravado. "See? We're living proof that no relationship is too far gone to be repaired. If you can try to murder me and I can forgive you, there's hope for this world yet."

I snorted. "Yeah, though I'm pretty sure we're even now that you tried to give me a heart attack."

"Frankie," Mama said. "Was there something you wanted to tell us?"

"Yeah, there is. I figured out what y'all were trying to

tell me, about Dr. Porter and Joe being scared. And it turns out that rats do communicate ultrasonically."

Roo's eyes narrowed. "I told you that already. How is that news?"

"Well, I didn't know for sure. Was I supposed to tell people I knew it was true because a rooster in my dream was quite convincing? Which reminds me—I must be losing my mind. I thought I saw you on the farm down the road from my foster mother's house—or hobbit-hole—or whatever, and I'm actually considering her claim that I could speak to animals when I was young."

"Frankie," Mama said gently. "It sounds like you think this is a problem."

"No. I mean, yes. I feel like I don't know what's up and what's down anymore. I know what everyone else thinks is possible, but not what I do."

"Then you are finally ready to discover the truth." Cockroach's deep, baritone voice radiated the authority of a documentary film narrator.

"What do you mean?"

"The only time we ever see the truth clearly is when we're confused. Otherwise we only see the things that support what we think we already know."

"But if I'm confused, how can I be sure? How do I know if I saw Roo or talked to animals, or if it was just my imagination—if y'all are just my imagination? How do I know what to believe?"

Cockroach cocked his head. "What do you think?"

"I don't know. I like the scientific method because you can design experiments to test your theories."

Feathers rustled. "Is that why scientists have never been wrong?" Roo's voice was steely. "Or why they understand everything about everything? Or why your science-based society has turned out so phenomenally?"

"Right. I suppose it has its limits."

The rooster grunted, his eyes narrow slits.

"Science is a good way to discover one kind of truth," Cockroach rumbled. "Though what you find always depends on who is asking and how you frame the question. Even the greatest human scientists admit that the observer affects the nature of what is being observed. And"—he tapped a foot against the branch—"Roo is right about one thing." The rooster grunted again. "Science certainly can't explain everything. Some things by their nature cannot be fully known."

I groaned. "Okay, so how do I know what to believe?"

"*Don't go by reports,*" the insect intoned, "*by legends, by traditions, by scripture, by logical conjecture, by inference, by analogies, by agreement through pondering views, by probability, or by the thought, 'This contemplative is our teacher.'*" He stared at me with small, dense eyes.

"So how *do* I—"

"*When you know for yourself that these qualities are skillful; these qualities are blameless; these qualities, when adopted and carried out, lead to welfare and to happiness— then you should enter and remain in them.*" He crossed his front two legs over his chest and looked at me as if that explained everything.

"Another Hafiz poem?" I asked.

"No," Cockroach said. "This one is by another very wise human teacher. Some might say a god. Though that is one of those unknowable truths, which depends entirely on who is asking."

"So what does it mean?"

"That's all I can say on the matter."

"Seriously?"

"Seriously. If I explained more, you might think you understood the truth about truth, and that would be a tragic disservice."

I glared at him but didn't push. He was terribly strong for such a small creature.

"Frankie." Mama pushed herself up to stand on all four feet. "Why are these questions so important to you?"

"I don't know. It just feels like I need to know the truth. So I know I'm not crazy. So I know what I should do." I thought of my father, then Dr. Porter. "So I don't humiliate myself or ruin my life."

Mama's eyes filled with tenderness. "Frankie, you could never humiliate yourself or ruin your life, any more than you could this stream. Say the water passing by us now were somehow dirtied. In a few moments the dirt would pass, and the stream would be clean again. You cannot ruin what is constantly changing."

"Or what is larger than you realize," piped in Roo. "I know your hopeless human eyeballs limit your ability to see, but even you must know that streams draw water from huge areas, and eventually join the ocean." The rooster's tone cut and comforted, like a warm knife. "You humans are unbelievably destructive, but some things are so big even you cannot ruin them."

The folds over Mama's eyes lifted. "That's right, Roo. I'm surprised to hear you say it, but you're absolutely right."

Roo hunched his head down onto his shoulders. "I do listen to what you say. Even if I don't always like to admit it."

"I believe you are forgetting who you truly are," said a voice so sonorous and loud I almost looked around for its source. I bent to get a better look at Cockroach. His chin was raised, and he stared at me with hard, dark eyes.

"That's my point," I said. "That's another reason I want to answer these questions. So I can find out who I am and why I'm here, since y'all won't tell me."

The roach's head shook. "You don't have to know who you are to know who you are not." I stared at him with eyes I hoped were as intense as his own. "You say you want to know whether or not you're crazy, and what you ought to do. These questions are coming from someone who sees herself with—to borrow our rooster friend's phrase—hopeless human eyeballs. You know how sideview mirrors have the warning: *Objects in mirror are closer than they appear?*" I nodded, wildly unsure how a roach could know this. "Well, your eyeballs should carry a similar warning: *Objects on retina are larger than they appear.*"

"Meaning what?"

"Meaning you see the small version of everything, including yourself."

"I have no idea what that means."

"You would if you let go of what you think you already know." The roach's antennae waved in a soft breeze. "You identify with the things that are easy to see. Your thoughts, your fears, your flaws. Your personality and performance. You think you are these things. No wonder you never feel good enough. No wonder you seek proof you're not crazy."

Roo had stopped preening and listened intently. Even Sweetpea was still as the roach went on. "You forget you are—to quote the rooster again—larger than you realize. Larger than you can possibly imagine." His bass voice vibrated over my skin, leaving goosebumps in its wake. "You forget you already have that which you seek."

"It doesn't feel that way." It was barely a whisper.

"To quote another wise human: *If the doors of perception were cleansed, everything would appear to man as it is, infinite.*"

How could you cleanse perception? What did it mean to be infinite?

"I appreciate your effort." My voice grew resigned. "It all sounds good, but I don't think it's enough. I still need to know if I'm imagining things. I still need to know what to do."

"Then you should find out," Roo said, his voice dry. "Gather more data. Isn't that what scientists do?"

"How? Are you saying—?"

Wheezing interrupted me. "Did . . . I . . . miss . . . anything?" The voice, like a boot scraping over rock, came from a small mound jerking through the darkness to my right.

"Shelly!" Sweetpea screamed. "You made it! But why are you so late? You missed, like, everything. Even Cockroach made it here before you."

The jerking stopped but the wheezing continued. "I practically ran . . . the whole way here." A long terrapin head protruded from the mound and stared at the squirrel with beady eyes. "Brash rodent . . . I take it . . . you've never heard . . . of the race between . . . the tortoise and the hare?"

Sweetpea shook her head.

"Long story short"—the turtle's mouth formed a grim smile—"the tortoise wins."

Sweetpea's eyes grew wide.

"Shelly, is that your name?" He didn't answer, so I turned to Roo. "Is he the turtle I found in Petaluma?"

"First of all," Roo said, "you need to give *her* a minute to answer. She's not the fastest chick in the brood." He nodded to the turtle whose head, sure enough, rose and fell with all the speed of an injured slug. "And second, have you ever heard of a male named Shelly?"

"I assumed it was because of his—"

"Her name is Michelle," said Roo in clipped tones. "We call her Shelly for short."

"Right. Makes total sense." I turned back to the turtle. "Nice to meet you, Shelly."

"The pleasure is . . . all mine."

I was about to ask her about crossing the highway when something pulled at me with the strength of a cyclone. I grabbed the branch Roo was sitting on so as not to be dragged away. "No! No, I'm not ready."

My alarm beeped and huge white spots opened in the scene in front of me. Panic rose.

"Bye, Frankie!" Sweetpea yelled. "Come back soon, okay?"

"I'll try." But she had already disappeared. "Roo, what did you mean about gathering more data?"

Roo opened his beak, but before anything came out, a vacuous blotch swallowed him whole.

"Frankie," Mama said, her soft fur brushing against my leg. "It's okay. You can come back whenever you want."

"How?"

"With time. You're designed to find your way back home. You always will. No matter how far you get, no matter how lost you feel. Denying its pull is actually much harder than following it."

I wanted to ask a thousand questions, but it was too late. The fur was gone and instead sheets lay tangled around my legs. White light poured through the window of my bedroom.

I lay there a long time, breathing hard, staring at the wall. The whiteness of the paint depressed me until I remembered that whiteness wasn't a lack of color, but all the colors combined.

And then I knew. What Roo had been trying to tell me. What I needed, without question, to do.

CHAPTER 10

The first step of my plan—the only part I was clear on—was to ask Lillian to meet me at the lab the next evening, when Dr. Porter would be gone for the day and Brian had soccer practice.

We sat at one of the lab tables, and I told her about my latest dream.

"I think what Roo was trying to tell me is that we're scientists, right? So if I want to find out if I really talked to animals, I should do an experiment."

"I knew it!" Lillian stood up in her excitement. "You do think it's possible you talked with animals when you were a kid."

"No." She sounded way too vindicated. "Maybe. I don't know. That's why I want to do the experiment. So I can know for sure."

"Great. I'm in." She sat back down. "So how are we going to test for animal-human communication?"

"I'm not sure. That's why I need your help."

A throat cleared behind me. "Did I hear someone say she needs help? Here I am, your knight in shining armor."

I glared even before turning around. Brian stood with a backpack and duffel bag and an overly-pleased-with-himself grin.

"I thought you had soccer practice," I said.

"Hello to you too." He walked over and put down his bags. "I'm beginning to understand that in your family, accusatory statements function as a formal greeting and welcome. Quite innovative, but so you know, in the rest of America we like to start with *Hello, how are you,* or, in informal cases, *What's up.*" He pulled over a chair and straddled it backward. "The head coach had an emergency, so practice ended early today. Lucky for you, I have some free time on my hands. So what is this little dilemma you're struggling with?"

Lillian opened her mouth, but I spoke before she could say anything. "It's not a dilemma, and we don't need your help."

Brian smiled, but his tone was sharp. "Hey, no problem. I was just offering." He stood up from the chair, still straddling it. "But I would have thought my usefulness was well-established in your last little adventure."

He almost sounded hurt. I'd tried several times to justify my irritation with Brian, but all I ever came up with was the vague sense that I didn't like him, and he didn't like me. It was circular logic, and I knew it. "Fine. I would welcome your assistance."

"Great. How can your knight in shining armor help?"

I immediately regretted my decision. "We're trying to come up with a test to find out how much, and in what ways, animals can communicate with humans."

"So your hypothesis is what, that rats are as eloquent as they are ticklish?"

I glared at him again. "My hypothesis is that some animals can communicate with humans using unknown, nonverbal methods."

"What, like, body language?"

"No, not body language."

"Telepathy then?"

"No!" My voice dropped. "I don't know. That's why I said 'unknown.'"

"So what's your plan?"

"I don't have one. That's what I was saying right before my knight in shining armor arrived."

He grinned. I had to admit his smile was beautiful, splitting open with light like the first edge of the rising sun when it warms you just by looking at it. It was almost too much. I forced my eyes to my hands.

"Well, if it were me," Brian said, "I'd start by testing dogs to see whether they really understand as much English as some of their owners think they do."

I groaned. "I said nonverbal. And besides, everyone knows dogs understand loads of words."

Brian raised his eyebrows and shook his head. "Au contraire. It's still unknown if they understand and process language like we do. They might just be reading tone, or body language."

"That's hard to believe."

"Most dog owners think they can talk to their dogs," Lillian said, "but science hasn't yet weighed in. I think it's a good idea."

I looked back and forth between them. "But I want to evaluate nonverbal communication. That's what I'm interested in."

Lillian put her hand on my knee. I hoped she wouldn't say anything to Brian about my dream. "I know, and we will. But this is a good place to start. Dogs are close enough to us that they're likely to have developed neurological processes for communicating with humans. Maybe if we can identify what some of those are, we can use them to investigate the existence of other forms of communication."

"Yep." The way Brian over-pronounced the p made it sound like a done deal. "And I know of an fMRI machine we can use. The only question is, will dog owners give us permission to restrain their beloved pets so they won't move and ruin the readings?"

I had an idea. "No. We won't be restraining anything."

"What do you propose, then?"

"We'll train the dogs to lie down without moving."

"You really think they'll be still long enough to run the machine?" Lillian's voice was curious, not doubtful, and I realized that was one of the reasons I liked her so much.

"Yeah, I do, as long as the owners are there. All the dogs I've ever known would be willing to do anything to make their people happy. The only question I have is whether the owners will be willing to take the time to participate as well."

Brian looked at me with an odd expression on his face. "They will. They'll want to know if their dogs really can understand what they say."

"I hope you're right," I said, though part of me didn't. It wasn't fair for one person to be right so much of the time.

"I know lots of people we could ask to participate." Lillian's head bobbed in excitement. "My parents have a shih tzu and know all the other dog owners in the neighborhood."

"Okay, I guess . . ."

"Frankie," Lillian said. "This is a good idea. It's going to work."

"Okay," I said again, trying to believe her.

CHAPTER 11

Patticakes, our first research subject, and Theresa, her owner, were perfect. A little too perfect.

They arrived at the lab twenty minutes early.

Brian, Lillian, and I were still getting everything ready. I was reviewing my notes when Brian said "Good morning" with so much enthusiasm I almost checked his butt to see if it was wagging.

A slender woman in yoga pants stood in the doorway holding a golden retriever on a leash. Her blond hair was as lustrous as her dog's.

"You must be Theresa," Brian said. "And this is . . .?"

"Patticakes." The woman glided into the room with a ballerina's posture, grace, and awareness that all eyes were on her.

"Nice to meet you." Brian stepped forward to shake her hand and held it for a long time, face flushed. Only after Patticakes barked sharply did he let go.

"Would you like a cinnamon roll?" Theresa asked.

Brian stared at her as if he hadn't understood the question.

"I made them this morning." She pulled a metal tray out of her bag and took off the clear plastic cover. Brian had one in his mouth and was mumbling about how good it was before Theresa could get the cover back on the tray.

Lillian coughed behind me.

"Oh, right." Brian wiped his mouth with his palm. "That's Lillian, and this is, uh, Frankie."

I doubly regretted letting Brian participate in the experiment.

Theresa walked toward me, so I held out my hand, but she either didn't see it or chose to ignore it and went straight to the fMRI machine behind me.

"This is the machine we'll be using?" She looked back at Brian.

"Yes, once we've trained Patticakes to lie still for long enough." His face was still flushed.

"Oh, that won't be a problem." Theresa tucked a lock of gleaming hair behind her ear. "When my husband told me what Patticakes would need to do to participate, I started working with her right away. She's ready to go now. We can start anytime."

Brian's face showed the same disbelief I felt on my own.

Theresa made an impatient sucking noise with her teeth and unhooked the leash from Patticakes' collar. She murmured something in the dog's ear, then patted the fMRI machine, which looked like a large bagel attached to a narrow cot.

The golden retriever jumped onto the raised platform.

"Lie down," Theresa said. Patticakes obeyed. "Now stay still." The blond woman held her delicate hand in front of her as she backed away. "Stay . . . stay . . . *staaay* . . . " Patticakes stared but didn't move. "See? Now watch this." She pulled a box of dog treats out of her bag and began to shake it while murmuring "*staaay . . . staaay . . .* " Patticakes' eyes widened, and I almost felt her stop breathing, but she didn't move.

"Wow!" Brian's expression tipped from captivation to worship. I almost wished I hadn't been right about dogs being willing to stay still. "How long will she stay like that?"

Theresa's smile was broader than a gold medalist's. "As long as I ask her to. She won't leave until I say 'okay.'"

Patticakes jumped up and barked, leaping off the plat-form to land by Theresa's feet. Theresa tossed her a treat. "See, she knows the drill even better than I do."

"Wow," Brian said again. "That's incredible. So phenomenal. Really..." He drifted off. I'd never seen Brian at a loss for words. "Just—wow. Thanks so much for training her like that."

"Oh, it was my pleasure." Theresa beamed.

I couldn't believe a married blond woman in yoga pants was really all it took for Brian to lose his sense. But then again, maybe I shouldn't have been surprised.

"We're all ready to get started then, right?" Lillian's busi-nesslike tone prompted me to add *no-nonsense professionalism* to the list of reasons why I liked her.

We got Patticakes back on the platform, only taking a minute longer to get her head positioned inside the bagel's hole. Lillian went into the room next door where the computer workstation for processing the imaging was located. She'd spent hours researching recent studies using fMRI machines, particularly ones that had to do with language and rewards, so we'd agreed she should be the one to see the images first.

Brian sat at a table with his computer in front of him, and I stood next to the machine with my notebook cradled in my arm.

"Ready, Lillian?" I called through the open door con-necting the two rooms. I could just see the top of her head over the monitors.

"Ready." She gave a high thumbs up.

"Okay," I whispered to Theresa, who had backed away from Patticakes and was standing next to me. "Go ahead and say to Patticakes in a neutral voice: 'Peter Piper picked a peck of pickled peppers.'"

Theresa gave me a funny look but repeated the phrase to Patticakes in a loud, flat tone.

"That's so interesting," said Lillian from the other room.

"What is?" Brian asked, leaning forward so he could see through the doorway.

"Nothing." Lillian waved her hand impatiently above the monitors. "I can't be sure yet. Keep going."

I turned back to Theresa. "Okay, now praise her, but do it in that same, neutral tone with no trace of approval in your voice."

"Patticakes," Theresa said in a monotone. "You're such a good girl. You really are. We love you very much." I had to admit she did a good job. She sounded like a robot.

"Fascinating," Lillian yelled.

"What do you see?" I asked.

"Nothing." Lillian waved her hand again. "Keep going."

"Now," I said to Theresa, "say it as if you're praising her, but use the words 'Peter Piper picked a peck of pickled peppers.'"

Theresa followed my instructions to the word. She sounded as if Patticakes had saved her entire family from a fire.

"No way!" Lillian yelled.

"What?" Brian and I both screamed this time.

"No, I shouldn't say anything until we're through," Lillian said. "We still have one more phrase, right?"

I groaned, turning back to Theresa. "The last one is to praise her like you normally would, in your usual tone."

"That's easy. Patticakes." Her voice was loud and warm. "You're such a good dog. So smart and sweet and well behaved. What a good girl you are. We love you very much."

Patticakes's ears moved forward, and I thought the excitement might be too much for her, but she stayed still, the only movement a slight wagging of her tail.

We waited a few more moments. "You good, Lillian?" I asked.

"Yeah," she called. "All good."

"You can let her know it's okay to move now," I said to Theresa.

"Okay, Patticakes," she said. The dog jumped up so enthusiastically she hit her head on the top of the machine. "Come here. You did such a good job!"

Footsteps sounded behind me. Lillian stood in the doorway with her hands on her hips. "It's so interesting. Though of course we can't be sure of anything until we've tested more dogs, studied the images, and run the statistical analysis."

We all waited, watching her, but she didn't continue.

"And what did you see that was so interesting?" The edges of exasperation crept into my voice.

"Oh," Lillian said, like she was surprised we didn't know. "Well, it looked pretty clear to me that Patticakes' brain was segregating and integrating both lexical and intonational information. She seemed to have a hemispheral bias for processing meaningful words, independently of intonation. And when intonational and lexical information were consistent, her septal area lit up."

Theresa stared at Lillian as if she had an alien crawling out of her nose. At least I wasn't the one on the receiving end of that look for once.

"What in the world are you talking about?" Theresa asked.

Brian laughed as if the question were a clever joke.

"She's saying that Patticakes understood your words in addition to your tone. The reward center in her brain was only activated when you said words of praise in a praising tone. Is that right, Lillian?"

Lillian nodded. "The words and the tone had to be consistent for it to register as a reward. Which means she understood what you were saying and wasn't just reacting to how you said it."

Theresa's fist pumped into the air repeatedly in a gesture at odds with her size and previous demeanor. "I knew it, Patticakes, you smart dog, you. Good job, girl."

"But that's not even the most interesting thing." Lillian spoke more quickly. "Her brain appeared to process what you were saying in different hemispheres. When you used meaningful words, her left hemisphere showed activity. When you used a praising tone, her right one did. It's remarkably similar to how humans process language, if I'm interpreting the images correctly."

I looked back and forth between Brian and Lillian. I didn't want to be the one to say it. Somehow that would make it less real.

Brian smiled at me. "It's true. If dogs have the same mechanisms for understanding language as we do, it means other animals might as well."

"It would also mean humans aren't as unique as we thought in terms of our ability to communicate." Lillian pushed a stray piece of wavy hair away from her eyes. "Assuming these results hold up with the other dogs, we've just taken a big step toward proving that animals may be capable of more than we thought."

"Frankie," Brian said, "this is really big. It was a great idea. Thanks for including me in it."

My irritation melted away. Let Lillian be cryptic. Let Brian be bewitched. Let Theresa be perfect. I just wanted to bask in the warmth of their words, in the pride on everyone's faces.

I was so light and expansive, like some giant, grinning parade balloon, I almost floated away.

CHAPTER 12

"Wait, you discovered that dogs understand simple commands?" my brother asked.

"No." The excitement leached out of my voice. "Simple phrases. We mostly used expressions of praise."

I could almost see James shaking his head on the other end of the line as he looked at his watch. "So you proved that dogs know when they're being praised? I'm sorry, Frankie, but didn't we already know that?"

"Yeah, but we didn't know if they understood the words or were just reading body language and tone. We found out they do comprehend the words, and their brains process them in a similar way to ours."

"And this was for which class? I thought you were studying the *human* brain."

I swallowed. "It wasn't for a class. A couple friends and I came up with the experiment and ran it ourselves."

"So this was your idea?"

"Kind of. I mean, not really. We designed it together."

The phone was silent. I leaned back against the trunk of a eucalyptus tree on the side of Stonewall Trail where I'd stopped to answer my phone. I smiled at a squirrel digging in the roots of another eucalyptus across from me. He looked at me with big, accusing eyes, as if asking what I found so amusing.

"Dad's worried about you, you know," James said. "He thinks you're getting off track, risking your reputation, not doing what you're there to do. He made me promise to try to talk some sense into you."

"I know. He told me the same thing. But I'm fine, James, really. I'm doing all my other coursework, and it's not getting in the way of anything else I'm supposed to be doing."

He grunted, then inhaled sharply, probably because he'd looked at his watch. "I've got to get to a meeting. But I've been wondering, have you been able to locate your birth mother's friend yet?"

"No, not yet. There's like a hundred Stella Richardsons out there. I've reached out to as many as I could, but the ones who have responded haven't been her."

"Sorry, Frankie. Stay positive. She'll turn up."

I wasn't so sure, but then, as if to prove me wrong, the understated tone of an incoming call filled my ear. I pulled the phone away and a long-distance number flashed on the screen. "James, I've got to go. I have a call on the other line, and I need to take it."

"Sure, Frankie. No worries. Talk to you soon."

"Good luck at your meeting." I didn't wait for his response before I swiped to the other call.

"Hello," I said. Silence answered. Was I too late?

There was a scuffling noise, then a somewhat husky female voice. "Ah, I'm trying to reach Frankie Connor," she said, making it sound like a question.

"This is she." I stood up, pulling my sweatshirt closer as the wind cut right through.

"This is Stella." Her voice was deep. "Stella Richardson. I got your message."

I started pacing. "Hi, Stella." Massive butterflies swarmed

my stomach even though I'd been through this before. "I'm looking for a woman named Stella Richardson who lived in California sometime around—"

"Yes, I know, Frankie." She cut me off without sounding impatient. "It's me. I believe I'm the woman you're looking for."

Questions about my biological mother—who she was, what she was like, where she was from—who my father was, all the relevant and irrelevant details of my birth, whether I had siblings, how many and where they were and what they were like—they all swarmed into my mind like flies to rotten meat. I couldn't see or feel or think through their thick buzzing.

Looking up at the sky, I tried to clear my head. The sun was a tiny golden ball about to be swallowed by an ocean of blue. *Wait*, it seemed to whisper. *First things first.*

I let out a long exhale. "That's great. Thank you so much for calling me back."

"How can I help?"

"I'm looking for information about my mother." It felt strange to refer to someone else that way. "I believe you knew her. She gave me up for adoption when I was born. I was then placed with a woman named Martha Forrester, whom I think you met."

Silence. "Yes," she finally said. "I remember her."

"It was Sundog—I mean Martha—who told me about you. She said you came by her apartment to check on me one time. She said you told her I was born . . . under duress, or something like that." I waited, but Stella didn't say anything. "Anyway, I was wondering if you could tell me more about that, and about my parents."

More silence, this time so long I checked my phone to make sure she hadn't hung up.

She hadn't. "Yes, well, I'm not sure how much help I can be. You were born under duress, but I don't know exactly what happened. Your mother was found unconscious just outside a hospital, already in labor. She wasn't in a car, and nobody knew how she got there. She did have her wallet on her, and they found my number in it, so they called me." She paused. "Unfortunately, I was traveling in India at the time. I didn't get the message until two weeks later when I got home."

"What about my father—my, uh, birth father? Were they able to contact him?"

"No." The word had sharp edges. "Your mother and father had only been on a few dates when she found out she was pregnant. He disappeared as soon as she told him."

My limbs must have weighed a thousand pounds each. I sat back down on the tree's roots and pressed my back into the rough bark of the trunk.

"So you don't know what happened before my mother got to the hospital? And you weren't there for the birth?"

"No. Like I said, I was traveling, and your mother never told me."

Strange, but I didn't want to pry. "Do you know where I was born?"

"Sure." Stella's voice grew stronger now. "Redwood Regional Hospital in Eureka. It's a beautiful facility. It backs right up against some of the most pristine forest you've ever seen in your life."

I realized I still hadn't asked the most important question. "What's her name? My mother, I mean. My birth mother."

Stella was silent again. "Isabella Days." The words were strained.

"Do you know where I could find her? I mean, do you think she would, I don't know, want to talk to me?"

When Stella spoke again, her voice was hoarse. "Frankie, there's something you need to know."

My breath stumbled on the way in. "What?"

"Your mother didn't want to put you up for adoption."

"She didn't?"

"No. She wanted to keep you, but she couldn't." She paused again, and when she continued, her voice was a whisper. "Your mother died during childbirth, Frankie. I'm so sorry. You have no idea how sorry I am."

Relief flooded me. I knew it made me an insensitive monster, but finding out that the first person who knew me hadn't wanted to get rid of me untangled all the knots in my belly. Thank goodness Stella couldn't see the expression on my face.

"That's okay." I managed a sober tone. "I mean, I'd rather know than not."

"I wish I could be more helpful; I really do. If you don't mind me asking, why are you reaching out now? Is everything okay?"

What could I say? That a bunch of animals in my dream had told me I wasn't who I thought I was, and I actually believed them? "Yeah, I'm fine. Everything's fine. I just got curious, that's all."

"Good." Her voice steadied. "It's been so long since I've seen you. I thought about trying to find you again after that night when you were a baby, but . . . I didn't want to intrude. You're happy though? Doing what you want to be doing?"

"I am. Happy enough." My words weren't convincing, even to me. "And I'm in grad school, which is definitely what I want."

"Good." She sounded relieved. "I'm so glad to hear that." Her words picked up momentum. "Feel free to reach out if you have any more questions."

"Thanks, I will. Thanks so much for calling me back."

She inhaled, like she might be about to say something else, but then exhaled before continuing. "Of course. Take good care, Frankie."

"Thanks, Stella. You too."

After hanging up, I sat with my back against the tree, the phone limp in my hand, the afternoon silent except for the small scraping sound the squirrel made in the dirt.

Relief faded into heaviness. The air was too quiet. The silence pressed in on me.

My birth mother was dead. I'd lost something the exact moment I found it. What did you do with something like that?

Shivering as the wind blew through my sweatshirt again, I stared out over the land that fell steeply to the crowded flatlands of Berkeley before ending abruptly in the distance in the smooth, dark waters of the Bay. I wished I could visit the animals. They were easy to talk to; people were more complicated. Plus, the people who might understand were too far away. My phone was lifeless in my hand, and I was too tired to search, scroll, and choose, let alone try to explain.

The squirrel stopped his digging and looked up, as if just now remembering I was here. He burst into movement, jumping onto the eucalyptus' smooth trunk, and running up into its branches. I lost him for a moment, then saw him leap from one branch to the next, still running at breakneck speed. Next thing I knew, he was on the trunk just above my head, staring at me with wide, dark eyes. He began to chitter, tail stuck straight up behind him, scolding me.

"Why are you complaining? I'm the one who just found out my birth mother is dead."

He grew quiet, cocked his head at me.

"I mean, it's not like I ever knew her, but just knowing she was out there somewhere, that I could talk to her someday . . ."

The squirrel chittered again, once.

"No, I don't want to call anyone."

He chittered again.

"Because I don't feel like it."

He launched into another round of energetic scolding.

"Fine, if it'll calm you down." I pulled up my phone and waved it at him, seeing the time as I did. "Shit!" I grabbed my bag and threw it on my shoulder. When I started down the trail, it was like something invisible tapped my shoulder. I turned back to the squirrel.

He was standing on the lowest branch, clutching his paws together and pressing them into his belly.

"I'm late to meet Lillian at the lab," I explained.

He pressed his paws further into the white fur.

"Goodbye?"

He didn't move.

"Fine. I'll talk to Lillian about it, I promise."

He skittered back toward the trunk, disappearing into the leaves.

I ran to campus as fast as I could, biting my lip the whole way there. My mind was filled with doubts and confusion and improbable questions, but not a single solitary answer.

CHAPTER 13

The first thing I did when Brian pulled his old, blue Cadillac in front of my apartment building was yawn so big I nearly unhinged my jaw. It was seven o'clock in the morning. On a Saturday. I covered my mouth and opened the passenger-side door.

"Morning, Sunshine." Brian's chipper tone irritated me. So did his face, which was fresher than an apple still on the limb. My face, a quick glance in the rearview mirror told me, looked like it had fallen off the tree weeks ago.

I mumbled something close to "Good Morning" and strapped on my seatbelt. It took a few tries to click it in. My brain was a bowl of warm mush.

"Ready to learn about your birth mother?"

"*Mm-hmmm.*"

We rode for a few minutes in silence as the Cadillac made its way to the interstate. After merging onto the 580, Brian turned to me. He stared for long enough I wasn't sure if the nervous jabs in my stomach were from his attention or the fact that he hadn't looked at the road in a really long time.

"I think I found a lab where we can do our next experiment." He finally turned back to watch the cars we whizzed by.

"I don't even know what our next experiment will be." The last word turned into another yawn.

"I know. But I wanted to be ready whenever you do come up with your next breakthrough idea, so I spoke with an old professor of mine in the psych department, and she's totally down. I could tell she had a beef with Dr. Porter, so I might have let it slip you've been a one-woman roadblock to his dreams of patriarchal hegemony."

Apparently everyone expected great things from me, except me. "Great," I said, or meant to say. It sounded more like a grunt.

"You're not a morning person, are you?"

"No. I'm really not."

"More of a night owl then?"

"More of a mid-morning to early-afternoon person."

His smile came easily, as always. "Sorry to make you get up so early."

"It's okay." I tried to make the mush form a coherent thought. "I'd like to get up earlier, but I've yet to find an alarm clock I can't outwit."

This time, his face stayed serious. "I think it was Robert Anthony who said 'when you blame others, you give up your power to change.'"

Anger shoved a spear into the base of my brain, waking me right up. I ground my teeth and turned to the window but didn't say anything.

The car's engine revved, and we picked up speed, passing a BMW. "What? I'm just trying to be helpful."

"Sometimes it's more helpful to not say anything."

The muscles of Brian's jaw hardened into high definition. "What is it with you, Frankie?"

"What is what with me? What does that even mean?" I spat the words like a hissing cat, all claws and bared teeth.

"Why are you so hot and cold with me? What have I done to you?"

I couldn't remember ever being hot with him, but his voice had that undertone of hurt again. I focused on a bunch of yellow wildflowers growing out of a crack in the median and took a breath. "You always have all these judgments and advice for me. But you don't even really know me."

"So that's why you don't like me? Because you think I'm judging you?"

"I don't *not* like you. It's just that I already have enough conversations with myself about what I'm doing wrong. I don't need somebody else joining in."

The smile returned, just barely. "I don't think you're doing anything wrong, Frankie. How do you think I know Robert Anthony's thoughts on blame? I only share what I've had to learn myself."

"Oh."

"Look, I know you didn't want to do this trip with me. The only reason you're here is because Lillian had her yoga teachers training this weekend."

I bit the inside of my cheek. "That's not totally true. I did want Lillian to come, but I didn't not want you to come. I mean, it was your idea to go to the hospital where I was born to see if anyone remembers anything."

I'd thought I was at a dead end after I called, and they said they didn't keep records from that far back.

Brian glanced at me. "Yeah, well, the reason I offered to drive is I hoped that if we got to know each other a little better, you might finally warm up to me."

Now I glanced at him. His jaw was more relaxed, but his eyes were tense, like he was bracing for something. "So let's get to know each other better," I said.

He exhaled, his shoulders sagging for a moment before he sat up straighter and repositioned himself in the seat. "There is something I'm curious to know more about."

"Okay."

"If you don't want to talk about it, I totally understand."

"What is it?" We passed a red sports car. How fast were we

going? I tried to gauge our speed by watching the stunted trees on the side of the freeway pass by and nearly got whiplash.

"You told us you're studying neuroscience because you're interested in depression, because you used to be depressed." He paused, his knuckles standing out white on the wheel. "What was your depression like? How did it start?"

Where to begin?

"We really don't have to talk about it if you don't want to."

"No, I don't mind." When most people found out I was depressed, they wanted to stay as far away from the subject as possible. Brian wanting to know more made me feel less like a leper. "I just don't know when it started. I mean, for as long as I can remember, I've had periods where I felt . . . down, I guess. But they'd come and go, and it didn't feel like a big deal. I always figured it was normal. But then when I started high school, things got worse."

"What happened in high school?" Brian's eyes remained glued to the road.

"I changed schools. All my friends went to one high school, and I went to another."

"Things didn't go as planned?"

"That's generous of you to assume I had a plan." The cars in front of us blurred as my vision went inward. "I was tired of feeling like I never fit in. I thought maybe if I started over, I would. But I never really made any friends."

Brian grunted. "So that's when you got depressed?"

"That's when things got worse. But I thought it was normal, you know, feeling alienated and insecure all the time. I mean, isn't that what being a teenager is all about?" I laughed, but it tasted bitter, even to me. "I don't know exactly when the depression started. For a long time I convinced myself I was fine."

"Did you ever consider going back to the high school where all your friends were?"

"I did. I transferred back my junior year. But by then, it was too late."

"Too late? You mean you spent too long at the other school?"

"Do these windows roll down?"

"Sure." He pointed to a giant button on the door.

I rolled the window down, closed my eyes, and let the wind blow against my face. "Too late because I'd already met Travis."

Brian shifted in his seat. "Travis?"

"A junior. Smart, handsome, punk. The coolest, calmest, most collected person I'd ever met. Nothing got to him, nothing mattered much. So, you know, the exact opposite of me. Obviously, I thought he was perfect."

"Obviously."

"We had gym class together my freshman year. Our teacher would sit all the *losers*—his word for those of us who didn't excel at badminton and dodgeball—on the bleachers. We'd talk while we waited for class to be over. Then, my sophomore year, he started inviting me to see his band play. We'd talk at his shows, and sometimes he'd invite me to go get vegetarian tacos with him and his friends afterward." I put my hand out the window and let it surf the wind in rolling waves.

"And then what happened?"

"Then we started hanging out just the two of us, and one day when we were at his house, he kissed me, and we started dating." My hand paused mid-roll. "And then he dumped me. Two weeks later. Said it wasn't working for him." I didn't recall his exact words. The thoughts in my head were too loud: *Of course. You knew this would happen the moment it started.*

"He broke your heart," Brian said.

"Pretty much."

"And then you got depressed?"

"And then I got depressed."

"What was it like?"

"It's hard to explain."

"If you don't want to—"

"No, it's not that." The blue hood of the Cadillac ate the road in front of us with an insatiable hunger. "It's just, when I'm depressed, it feels like I've been depressed my entire life. And when I'm not, it's hard to remember, like it never existed." I took a deep breath. "I guess at first it was a vague feeling that something was wrong, or more like everything was wrong, and there was nothing I could do about it."

"And later?"

"Later it felt like I was inside a thick, glass jar and everything else was outside of it. I couldn't touch anything or anyone no matter how hard I tried." I let the wind blow against my eyelids. "I remember this one beautiful, spring morning when my family was downstairs having breakfast, filling the house with good smells and happy noises. I knew I should be grateful—for the weather, the nice house, the loving family—but I couldn't feel anything except this sucking black hole that corrupted everything before I could touch it. It was the only thing that felt real."

I opened my eyes. Brian was looking at me, his lips drawn tight. I thought he would say something, but he didn't.

"Eventually the pain got so intense it was like wrestling a mountain. No matter what I did, it crushed me."

"That sounds awful." Brian's voice was hoarse.

"It was."

"So how did you beat it?"

"I wouldn't say I beat it. I still feel it lurking in there sometimes. But eventually, my family convinced me to see a shrink."

"You did therapy?"

"No, my dad wasn't into that kind of thing. He knew this psychiatrist from work, and my mom set up the appointment. I hoped he'd be able to tell me what was wrong with me, but instead he just asked me a bunch of questions about my symptoms—did I experience any changes in appetite, was

I having trouble sleeping, that kind of thing—then wrote something on a little pad of paper and handed it to me."

"Antidepressants?"

"Yep. But I didn't take them at first."

"Why not?"

"I've never liked the idea of being on meds."

"Doesn't your father work for a pharmaceutical company?"

"Good point. Maybe that's why."

"So when did you start taking the meds?"

"When I started thinking that death was the only thing that could possibly be stronger than the pain."

"Wow."

"Yep. It's a great motivator, misery."

"But at least you found a solution."

"I guess. It doesn't really feel like a solution to me . . . more like a temporary pardon."

"Why?"

"I still don't know why I get depressed. I mean, is it bad brain chemistry? A defective gene? Am I thinking wrong, feeling wrong, acting wrong? There are so many theories, but nobody can tell me for sure. If someone claimed to have solved your problem but couldn't tell you why it worked or what your problem was to begin with, would you believe them?"

Brian stared at the road ahead without saying anything. Had I shared too much? I looked back out the window, trying to distract myself with the bright blue sky, the golden hills, the big rigs we were passing at an alarming speed.

"How do you know it means there's something wrong?"

I jumped when Brian finally spoke. "Crying for hours on end without knowing why isn't exactly a benchmark of good health."

"Maybe it is. Maybe it's the rest of us who are messed up."

I shook my head. "And the pain? The self-loathing? The suicidal thoughts?"

"Look, I don't know much about depression, it's true. But my sister does, first-hand, and she swears it isn't a defect or flaw."

I sat up. "And what does she think it is?"

"I don't know. She's never been willing to explain it to me."

I slumped back down. "Right."

"But I do know this. For years in high school, my sister was a mess. She went from getting straight As in middle school to nearly flunking out her sophomore year. Eventually, she refused to leave her bed. No matter what I or my parents did, it didn't help. She tried to kill herself twice. The second time she had to go to the hospital and stayed in the psych ward for a month."

"Wow, that's awful. I'm so sorry. Is she okay now?"

"Yeah, that's my point. After they released her from the hospital, she started getting better. My parents assumed it was because of something she'd learned there, or in the therapy she started going to afterward. But they never asked." Brian looked over his shoulder as he prepared to pass another car. I forced myself not to check the speedometer. "So I did. I wanted to know what had worked after everything else we'd tried failed. She said it was simple. Someone she'd met at the hospital had explained to her there wasn't anything wrong with her. Something about a healthy response to an unhealthy world. Like I said, she wouldn't explain, but from then on, things were different. The depression still came, but it wasn't so intense. It'd crash over her, but it didn't drag her out to sea."

The words "healthy response" to describe depression stuck in my brain like food between my teeth. How could she be depressed and not believe there was something wrong with her? Especially when everyone else was saying there was.

Don't go by reports—a larger-than-life voice reverberated through my mind—*by traditions, by inference, by agreement through pondering views. When you know for yourself that these qualities, when adopted and carried out, lead to welfare and to happiness—then you should enter and remain in them.*

"Oh," I said.

"What?" Brian glanced at me.

"Nothing. It's just . . ." Was Cockroach saying it didn't matter what other people thought as long as what I believed led to welfare and happiness?

"It's just what?"

"It's just—" I searched for something I could say to him. "I just realized that you didn't go into neuroscience to make a lot of money. You wanted to find a way to help your sister."

His face darkened. "I'm not studying depression."

"No, I know. But you are asking questions that other people aren't. Like you did with your sister. You're finding out why some things help people while others don't. Neuroscience gives you a way to do that and get paid for it."

Brian's face flushed. Was he embarrassed, of all things? I would never understand men. "Maybe," he said.

His discomfort made me uncomfortable. I changed the subject. "Was it hard on you too? Your sister's depression?"

"Yeah, it was hard to see her suffer so much. But by high school I was more concerned about myself. She was my older sister, and I worried everyone at school would judge me because of her." Regret oozed from his sigh. "Real chicken shit, I know, but that's high school for you."

I imagined a nutrient-rich pile of steaming poop. "Where does that expression come from anyway?"

"Chickens aren't the world's most courageous creatures."

"I beg your pardon." Roo's bold stare and sharp words pressed against my mind. "They can't fly, live in metal cages, and are surrounded by animals bigger and stronger than they are who think they're delicious. I don't think it's lack of courage so much as proof of intelligence that they're not more daring. Give a chicken a fair, fighting chance, and I bet he's as gallant as a lion."

Brian looked at me, a small smile tugging at the corner of his mouth. "Maybe so. I've never thought about it that way I guess."

"Well, you should." I settled back into my seat and stretched my legs out in front of me. "We should all be proud to call ourselves chickens."

Brian snorted as he turned on his turn signal and began passing a giant RV. I turned to the window and smiled, for the first time not worrying about how fast we were going.

Brian pulled the Cadillac into a parking spot next to a giant, white Suburban. He turned off the car. "Are you ready?"

"Yep." But the only thing that moved were the butterflies in my stomach. I looked around the parking lot, then past it to where the forest crept up to the edge of the concrete, as if waiting for permission to cross. The stillness of the trees calmed the butterflies, and I reached for the door.

"Wait, Frankie?" Brian's voice held a note of uncertainty I hadn't heard before.

"Yeah?"

"Would you rather go in alone? I don't want to, ah, intrude or anything."

It was strange to see him so hesitant. "No, I'd like you to be there." Also odd was that I meant it. "Besides, this was your idea. If it doesn't work, I want you close for easy punching."

He grinned. "Then off we go."

The main part of the hospital was a rectangular building made of light gray concrete with a long band of tinted windows running the length of each floor. The maternity center, we learned at the information desk, was on the third floor.

When we got to the nurse's station, a blond woman with a round face and pink skin greeted us. I explained that I had been born here and was looking for information about my birth.

"How old are you?" the pink nurse asked, her expression filled with doubt.

"Twenty-five."

"I'm sorry. We don't keep records that long." Her voice was frustratingly pleasant.

"No, I know." I leaned forward. "I wondered if there might be anyone here who could give us more information. Maybe someone who worked here twenty-five years ago?"

The pink woman stared at me. I couldn't tell if she was doubtful or annoyed or both.

"You should have them talk to Jones," said a voice from behind me. I spun around. A compact woman in a white coat with dark brown hair arranged in intricate braids along her scalp stared at a chart in her hands. "He's been here forever." The woman didn't look up once while she spoke.

"Is Jones working now?" I asked. "Where might we find him?"

The doctor didn't say anything, just stared at her chart. After a moment, the nurse shifted her weight. "Um, I think so," she said. "A lot of the staff take their lunch around now. You might look for him in the cafeteria."

"Thank you. I appreciate your help."

When we were almost at the door, the doctor spoke again. "Big guy with short hair." I glanced at her, but she didn't look up. "Jones, that is."

"Um, thanks." I followed Brian out the door.

When we reached the cafeteria, my stomach rumbled, and saliva filled my mouth. I tried to focus more on the people and less on what was on their plates. People of every age gathered around small tables, from tiny babies to weathered men and women with white hair and transparent skin, many of them with heavy movements and sunken eyes.

Just as I was about to give up, we passed a water fountain and saw a large man wearing blue scrubs sitting at a table in the corner. His thick buzz cut was black in the middle and silver on the sides, and his light brown skin had the rich undertones of a harvest moon. He had a broad face and thick hands and was contemplating a large piece of broccoli pinned to his fork like a hunter's trophy.

"Um, Mr. Jones?" I asked as we approached.

The man looked at us. He had smooth skin despite the gray hair. "Jones," he said. "Just Jones. It's my given name, not my surname." He put his fork down and pushed his otherwise empty plate away. "I don't see how they expect you to fit this . . . tree of broccoli in your mouth or cut it with the plastic knives they give you either. This is a health facility, isn't it? Shouldn't they be encouraging us to eat our vegetables, not making it more difficult?"

"Um, yeah, I guess so." He didn't have an accent but spoke with a strong and soothing rhythm that had me paying more attention to how he talked than what he said.

Jones shrugged. "Well, could be worse. What can I help you with?"

"Uh, a doctor in the maternity ward suggested we talk to you." I regretted not asking her name. "I have some questions about my mother."

"Your mother?" Jones lifted an eyebrow in a way that reminded me of Brian.

"Yes." I tried to focus. "She was a patient here when I was born. Apparently, it was an unusual situation, and I thought, if you worked here then, maybe you could tell me more about what happened."

Jones smiled, and it reached past the corners of his eyes. "That's a relief. When a young woman comes along asking about her mother, a man with certain indiscretions in his youth can get nervous about what she's going to say."

I looked at Brian with wide eyes, then back at Jones. "No!" I yelled, then added in a softer voice, "Sorry, I mean, that's not what I meant at all."

Jones laughed. "It's quite all right. We're in a hospital, after all. If I'd had a heart attack, help would have been a table or two away." His eyes crinkled again. "So what can I do for you, kiddo?"

"Well, I'm adopted, and am trying to learn more about my past." I hadn't taken a proper breath since we'd arrived, so the words got more rushed the more I said. "I recently found out I was born here, in this hospital, and apparently my birth mother was found unconscious in the parking lot, already in labor. It was twenty-five years ago, in March, but she's not in the records. I just want to know if anybody ever figured out what happened to her, if you remember her, if you don't mind."

Jones took such a deep breath I saw his chest rise and fall. I followed along without meaning to. "I suppose there's a reason you can't ask your mother this."

"She's dead." My voice sounded too flat.

"And your father?"

"I don't know who he is. Not my birth father, anyway. Apparently, he ran off when he found out my birth mother was pregnant."

"I see. And who told you this about your mother arriving unconscious?"

"A friend of my mother's. I found her through my foster mother. Her name is Stella Richardson."

For the briefest moment I thought I saw a look of surprise cross Jones's face, but it passed so quickly I couldn't be sure. "And what was your mother—your birth mother's name?"

"Isabella Days."

"Twenty-five years ago you said?"

"Yes, as of last March."

Jones was quiet for a long time. He studied his wide hands in his lap, tapped his fingers on his thighs, looked up at the water stain on the ceiling. "Have a seat." He indicated two empty chairs at the table next to his. Brian grabbed them and set one next to me.

"I did work here then." Jones's voice was like a lullaby. "I had just started. You know, they say the only thing worse than being a janitor is being a young janitor." He shook his head. "It was true for me. I'd been to two years at the local community college and was preparing my application to transfer to UC Berkeley. It was a big deal for my family. Nobody else had ever gone to college, much less graduated. I was determined to be the first. But then my father got sick and had to stop working, and my mother's salary wouldn't cover food and utilities, let alone the medical bills. Plus, she needed to take care of my father."

Why was he telling us all this? My hands grew fidgety at my sides.

"You're probably wondering why I'm telling you this. Trust me, it's relevant. So after my father got sick, I had to—no, scratch that—I made the decision to quit college and go to work. I didn't have any experience or degrees, so my options were limited. Being a janitor was one of them. This job paid pretty well, and the hospital has a good name in the community, so . . . I started in late February exactly twenty-five years ago."

My heart stumbled. I leaned forward.

Jones leaned back and crossed his arms over his chest. I waited for him to continue, but he seemed to be finished.

"And when did you first learn about my mother?" I asked.

Jones uncrossed his arms, put them on the table, leaned forward. "Isabella Days?"

"Yes." I didn't quite keep the impatience out of my voice.

"I never knew anybody with that name."

I exhaled sharply. Luckily, Brian cut in. "Okay, so maybe you didn't know her by name, but surely you remember an unconscious woman in labor being admitted? Especially if it was your first few weeks on the job?"

Jones favored Brian with a lengthy are-you-kidding-me stare before smacking a hand on the table. "I know who you should talk to. Dr. Thomas Marrone. He was head of the maternity center at that time, has a memory like an elephant. He'll be able to help you out."

I stood up. "That's great! Is he up there now? Can you introduce us?"

"Oh, I would," Jones said, furrows of regret wrinkling his brow, "except he doesn't work here anymore. He retired ten or eleven years ago. He lives in Fairfax now. I don't have his contact info, but heck, I'm sure you could find it easily, technology being what it is these days and young people being so good with it." He leaned back in his chair and smiled.

I tried not to glare as we thanked him for his help and said our goodbyes. There was something he wasn't telling us—maybe a lot of things—but at least I had a lead.

Neither Brian nor I said anything until we got in the car. As I buckled my seatbelt, he turned to me. "Well, that was weird," he said. "Kind of like being on an episode of the Twilight Zone."

"I know. I'm sorry for dragging you into this."

"Dragging me into this? Really? I practically forced you to bring me along. Besides, I love a good mystery. This is the most fun I've had in months."

Was he being genuine or teasing me? It was hard to tell with him. I decided to give him the benefit of the doubt. "I'm glad you forced me to bring you along. It's been good to have you here."

"What do you say we go into town and get some lunch?"

"Sounds great."

By the time we got on the 101 to head back to Berkeley, I couldn't stop smiling. The road was wide open, inviting us to follow it all the way home.

CHAPTER 14

Nothing was working.

I'd tried for more than a week to reach the doctor Jones had told us about, the head of maternity with a memory like an elephant. When his wife finally called me back, she said he had Alzheimer's and could barely remember where he was most days. She'd asked him, but unsurprisingly he couldn't recall the details of some random birth — strange as it might have been — twenty-five years before.

Meanwhile, I'd hit a dead end in my other investigation as well. Lillian and Brian kept asking me what our next experiment would be, but I had nothing to give them. I'd spent more time than I wanted to admit failing to come up with an adequate idea, then going over and over the less-than-adequate ones like well-worn rosary beads, begging my brain to take mercy on me and offer a way out of my misery. But it never did. Instead, the more I thought about it, the more confused I got. And the more desperate.

I'd finally been broken down enough to ask Lillian and Brian to meet with me and talk it over. Brian had insisted we meet at the lab he got us access to in the psychology building on the north side of campus. The building, one of the newer ones at Cal, was a rectangular behemoth comprised of smaller rectangles of framed glass panes. The building stood out and was easy to locate, but the lab—room 25B—was nowhere to be found.

I'd searched the entire first floor, but the rooms all numbered in the thousands.

The second floor was the same, only in the two-thousands, and the pattern held on the third, fourth, fifth, sixth, seventh, and eighth floors as well. By the time I got to the top story, I was out of breath from all the stairs and stress and wished we had chosen a smaller building to meet in. I searched the stairwells for access to a hidden attic, but there was none. The eighth floor was as high as it went.

On my way back down, I checked to see if the stairwell went below ground. No such luck.

I walked over to a student waiting alone by a classroom door.

"Hello," I said.

"What's up."

"Do you know where room 25B is?"

"There is no room 25B here." He didn't hesitate to diagnose the situation. "You must be in the wrong building."

I wasn't. "Thank you," I said as genuinely as I could, which is to say, not very.

I asked five other people, none of whom had heard of room 25B. One pointed me to a building directory helpfully hidden behind a vending machine, but it also failed to mention any room numbers below 100 or indicate any kind of concealed passageway or secret annex.

Clenching my jaw, I called Brian. His phone went straight to voicemail. I dialed Lillian's number, and she picked up on the first ring.

"Hi, Frankie. Where are you?"

"I'm trying to freaking find room 25B!"

"Didn't Brian tell you? It's not in the main part of the building."

"Yes, I think I've thoroughly established that at this point." I spoke through my teeth.

Lillian laughed, but it didn't improve my mood. "It's underground. You have to take Stairwell C down as far as it goes. Don't try any of the other stairwells—they won't work. Once you get down here, you'll see a hallway—there's only one direction to go—and eventually you'll find us, on your right. We're—wait, what?" Lillian said something I couldn't make out.

"What's that?"

"Sorry, Brian says to tell you not to go in any other labs. Psychology faculty are secretive apparently. Make sure it's 25B before you open the door."

"He could have told me that himself if he would answer his phone."

"What? The connection down here isn't good. I couldn't hear you."

"Nothing. See you soon."

I found stairwells A, B, D, E, and F before entering Stairwell C like a desert pilgrim into an oasis. I walked down two flights and breathed deeply, repeating to myself *I am not inept because I failed to find a secret underground corridor.*

The stairway opened onto a long hallway so poorly lit I couldn't see the end of it. It disappeared into shadow like something out of a horror movie. Releasing a dramatic sigh, I started down the corridor. First on my right came Lab 1A, and just next to it, Lab 1B, twins conjoined at the head and mirror reflections of Labs 2A and 2B on my left. All the way down the corridor, pairs of large, metal doors gaped at each other across the hallway at regular intervals like giant, blank eye sockets.

The labs were large. I must have walked for miles before glancing up and seeing I was only at Lab 11A. There wasn't much to look at as I walked. Fluorescent bulbs flickered occasionally in the light fixtures, and now and then I passed a water fountain I assumed had been placed there so nobody would perish from dehydration on their long trek to the end of the hallway. The doors didn't have any windows, which made the labs even more mysterious.

I was beginning to wonder what so many large, hidden labs were used for when someone called my name. I turned around, but there was nobody in the hallway with me. The voice had been familiar, almost a growl, but was muffled and disappeared so quickly I couldn't place it. "Hello?" I called out, scanning the shadows at the end of the hall, half expecting someone to leap out as a bad joke.

Nobody did. But as I strained to see what was down there, something moved in the corner of my vision. Whatever it was froze when I looked straight at it, but two small orbs of light remained, just barely visible in the shadows. They almost looked like a pair of yellow eyes staring at me from the darkness.

I shivered. How much farther did I have to go? The rectangular plate next to me announced Lab 25A in neat, gray letters. Nearly crying with relief, I took another step to arrive at 25B, grabbed the handle, and pushed with what was perhaps a little more force than was strictly necessary.

The door lurched open and hit the wall with a loud bang. Bright light smothered me, making it hard to breathe. Two pairs of eyes stared at me under raised eyebrows.

"Everything okay, Frankie?" Brian's solitary dimple showed.

"*Mm-hmmm.*" I put my backpack down in a nearby chair and fussed with it carefully.

"You look like you saw a ghost." Lillian stood next to Brian in front of a metal table. "I knew one of us should have gone to look for you."

"I'm fine." I turned to Brian. "So why are we here, in such a top-secret location?"

"I already told you. This is the lab I found for our next experiment. It has all the equipment we might need plus comes with something even better."

"And what's that?" My words were limp. I wasn't in the mood for his shenanigans.

"Connections." Brian's smile was undiminished by my tone. "The professor who's letting us use it is on the selection committee for the Helen Wills Neuroscience Grant. It's not big but would give us a few thousand dollars and great credibility. Plus, I happen to know she's heard some really good things about you. So what's it going to be, fearless leader? What are we going to research next?"

Great. One more person with high expectations I got to disappoint. I slumped down into the chair next to my backpack. "I don't know. I don't have any good ideas. That's why I asked y'all to meet, so you could help me."

Brian perched on the edge of the table. "We could test cats in the fMRI."

I pulled my sleeves over my fingers, which were starting to go numb from the frigid underground air. "It's not a bad idea, but I want to do more than test for word recognition in another companion animal."

"I was kidding. Testing cats is a terrible idea. They'd never stay still once they realized that's what we wanted."

Lillian rolled her eyes. "I'd love to examine the brains of some wild animals to see if they share any similarities to what we found in the dogs. But I can't think of any . . . noninvasive ways to do it."

My frustration escaped in a hopeless, helpless moan.

"Frankie, you said you don't have any *good* ideas." Lillian spoke with the tone of a patient teacher. "What ideas have you considered?"

I fought to stay afloat amid the sinking feeling in my gut. "The only idea I've had is to test dogs to see if they can understand nonverbal cues."

"Like sign language?"

"No, I'm sure they can learn that."

"So what, like giving them commands without speaking out loud?"

"Yeah, exactly. But I don't know, I don't have a good feeling about it."

"Why not?"

I shook my head. I couldn't explain.

The last thing I wanted was to disappoint Lillian or Brian. They'd already done so much to help me, investing their time and risking their reputations. But this was the first time I'd had to come up with my own idea for an experiment, and the idea to test nonverbal commands somehow felt wrong. Not just wrong—it made me feel nauseated. I couldn't give up, but I also couldn't move forward with an idea that was doomed to fail. I was stuck.

"Can I ask you a question?"

I checked Brian's expression for any amusement, irony, or ill intent but for once his face was smooth and earnest. I nodded.

"Why are you doing all this? I mean, Lillian told me you want to know more about how animals communicate, but why?"

I bit my lip. I didn't want to tell him I was following the advice of a group of talking animals.

"Because of Charlotte. Right, Frankie?" Lillian spoke like she'd just pulled up a getaway car and offered me a ride. She didn't realize there was nowhere good this conversation could go.

"Who's Charlotte? One of the rats?"

"No, Charlotte was her cat when she lived with her foster mother. The cat disappeared and nobody could figure out where, except Frankie. She said Charlotte told her she was in a car, and sure enough they found her locked in a truck on the farm down the road, exactly as Frankie described."

Brian whistled. "Impressive."

I closed my arms over my chest. "She could have made the whole thing up."

"Could have," Brian said. "Doesn't mean she did. Do you know what I love about science?"

"No idea."

"It's the one field where it's okay to be wrong. It's part of the process. Only by being wrong can you figure out what's right."

Lillian leaned forward. "Do you know what *I* love about science?"

"What?"

"It doesn't give a fuck."

I blinked. "What do you mean?"

"Science doesn't care who believes something, how powerful they are, or how many other people they've convinced. It's the great equalizer, because truth is truth. And truth can surprise you. Or it may not, but at least then you know. Don't you want to know?"

I did. The animals couldn't be an ordinary dream—our first experiment had shown that—but what were they? How did they know things I didn't? Why were they appearing now, and what were they trying to tell me?

I was dying to know. But if telepathic communication was real, wouldn't somebody else have proved it by now?

Brian and Lillian's eyes were stuck on me, dissecting, digging, demanding. I had to do something, but I couldn't think of anything. My lungs froze and my heart boiled. The pressure built in my chest, stretching bigger and bigger like an inflating balloon. Eventually, it got so big that I realized either the balloon had to burst, or my mind might.

I chose. It wasn't so much a decision as a drowning person flailing about for anything solid within reach.

"All right." I sucked in as much of the subterranean air as I could. "Let's call some dog owners."

Getting the words out, deciding, seeing Lillian and Brian's excited reactions, I felt better. I felt relieved. I felt strong.

But beneath it all I also still felt like I might throw up.

———

After saying goodbye to Lillian and Brian, I headed to Tilden Park. It was a bit of a hike up some large hills, but I had energy I needed to burn off. As I walked, my mind spun, helplessly and rapidly, from one thing that could go wrong with the experiment to the next. I tried speeding my steps, but it didn't slow my mind.

When I reached the edge of the park, a call from my mother interrupted my thoughts. In an uncharacteristic twist, I rushed to answer.

"Hi, Mom." I stepped onto a trail and entered the welcome shade of some large, evergreen trees. "What's up?"

"I'm so glad I finally caught you." My mother panted as if she'd had to run to accomplish this feat. "Your father has some big news to tell you."

"Oh yeah? What is it?"

"I want him to tell you, but don't worry—it's good news."

"Okay." Awkward silence. "Can I talk to him?"

"Oh, he's not home from work yet." As if it were obvious.

"Okaaay . . ."

"How's school going?"

"School's fine." As soon as I said it, I realized my mistake.

"What's wrong, Frankie? You can tell me."

I didn't have the energy to resist one of her epic attempts at excavation, and she always unearthed what she wanted anyway. "I just agreed to do an experiment with Lillian and Brian that I don't feel good about."

"Why don't you feel good about it?"

"I don't know. I'm not sure I have a good reason. I just don't."

"I'm sure you'll figure it out."

"You and everyone else. But I don't think so. Not this time."

"Frances Connor." My mother's voice slipped into its full parental authority like a favorite jacket. "I can't believe you're saying this. I would think that Sweetpea proved you can do anything you set your mind to."

I gasped like I was in an old-fashioned movie and stumbled over a root on the trail. How did my mother know about Sweetpea? I'd never told her about my animal dreams. "Sweetpea?" I choked out.

"The baby squirrel you found when you were six."

"I found a baby squirrel?"

"Are you eating enough protein? Your memory is getting even worse." It was a familiar routine. My memory had never been good and provided a convenient and frequent opening for my mother to share her concerns about my dietary choices. "Are you sure you don't remember? When we walked to your bus stop one morning and startled a squirrel? And it leaped out into the road just as a car was speeding by?"

"No." I was more confused than ever. "So Sweetpea died?"

"No, dear. That wasn't Sweetpea. You were a wreck and threw a fit when I tried to get you on the bus, so you stayed home that day. You cried all morning. That's how I knew when you had disappeared, because the sniffling stopped. You were halfway up the oak out front before I could figure out where you were. When I made you come down, you were cradling her against your chest."

"Sweetpea? The baby squirrel?"

"Yes. You called her that right away and insisted we help her since her mother had died."

I reached a thicket of manzanita trees and stopped to touch the smooth bark on their crooked, maroon branches.

"I have no idea how you knew she was up there. We took the poor thing to a wildlife rehabilitator, but she took one look and said she was too young to save. She wanted to put her down, but you got hysterical. Wouldn't stop screaming and thrashing until I agreed we would take her home and do what we could. I thought she would die, but what choice did I have?"

I turned to continue up the hill. "Did she survive?" I couldn't believe I had no memory of any of this.

"Did she survive?" My mother's voice was almost comically incredulous. "*Did she survive?* That's the whole reason I'm telling you this. Of course she survived. She had you on her side. You made me hunt down every existing book and article on how to care for squirrels. You prepared her formula and gave it to her every two hours without a single reminder, even through the night. You slept with her, talked to her, sang to her nonstop, and saved that poor little squirrel's life."

"So what happened to her?"

"When she was old enough, we gave her to the rehabber so she could join a social group with other squirrels and be released. You didn't want to lose her, but you knew she belonged in the woods. You didn't stop crying for days." My mother's voice broke. "That's when I realized how special you are: determined to do whatever you set your mind to, and willing to break your own heart for the sake of those you love."

A lump rose in my throat. "Thanks, Mom." I swallowed and opened my mouth to wrap up the call, but my mother must have sensed it—her instincts were impeccable about that kind of thing—and she cut me off at the pass.

"Hold on a second, sweetie. I think I hear your father. *Mitch!*" My ears rang. "He's right here."

There was rustling, then my father's gruff voice. "Hello, Frankie."

"Hi, Dad. So what's the big news?"

"Oh." Like he hadn't expected me to know, or care. "The FDA approved the drug I'm overseeing."

"That's great, Dad. I thought James said you only submitted it a month or two ago."

"We did. It was an accelerated approval because of the nature of the drug, and because the in vivo results were so convincing."

"In vivo results?"

My father cleared his throat. "Animal tests and clinical trials."

"Oh." I thought of Wilbur, Calvin, and Hobbes. "Congratulations. That's fantastic." I knew how excited he must be. "Does that mean you can finally tell us what it is?"

"It's called Coramidol. It's a breakthrough treatment for heart disease. It's going to save a lot of lives."

"That's awesome. I'm really happy for you."

My mother's voice rose in the background. There was a muffled, intense exchange.

"Frankie." My father sounded defeated. "Your mother would like to know if she can buy you a ticket home for Christmas."

"That's . . . sweet. But tell her not to buy anything yet. I'd like to come home, but this is my first semester and I'm not sure how things work here yet. I need to find out if there's anything I have to do here first."

"Smart idea. I'll let her know."

"Thanks, Dad."

———

After hanging up, I stopped at an overlook to let the sun warm my face while I took in the view. Gentle, brown hills rolled to the horizon with shrubs collecting in their creases like rugged, green streams. All was still for a few peaceful moments, but as soon as I stepped back onto the path, my mind returned to its wanderings as well.

Here my father was advancing science, discovering cures, saving lives. Meanwhile I was—what? Trying to figure out if I'd had conversations with animals when I was a kid. Or worse, wanting to know if Roo was the rooster I'd seen on the farm down the street from Sundog's house, or Sweetpea the baby squirrel I'd rescued, somehow communicating with me from a distance.

Shame gnawed at the edges of my stomach. The worst part was, the more confused I felt, the more I wanted to speak with Mama and the rest, so they could make me feel better and tell me what was going on.

I really was losing my mind.

My eyes swung around, from branch to blue sky to brown root, seeking something real, something simple and solid to hold on to. They landed on two small, black spheres glistening from beneath a rock next to the trail. The spheres were eyes, but I couldn't tell what kind of animal they belonged to.

"Hi." I took a step toward the rock. The eyes grew wider. "What are you doing over there?"

The animal didn't respond, of course. She just stared at me.

I looked around. Nobody was coming up the trail. "What do you want? Come out from behind there so I can see you."

No dice.

I took another step, but as soon as I did the eyes disappeared. "Aw, come on. I just wanted to talk."

When I bent down to get a better view, my muscles froze. Fear spread from my core and into my limbs like water soaking through a blanket. I couldn't move. My hands trembled. My lungs sucked in shallow gasps of air.

And then, like the shadow of a flying bird, it passed.

I took a deep breath, and my brain unfroze enough to realize something. These weren't my feelings. They belonged to whatever was under that rock.

"You scared, little one?" I leaned in for a closer look but didn't see anything. "It's okay. I'm not going to hurt you. Here, I'll give you some space." I stepped back. "See? It's safe. You can come out now. You have somewhere you want to go? Go ahead. I won't let anyone hurt you."

For several long moments, nothing happened. Then, a black nose emerged from beneath the rock, followed by black fur, two dark eyes, and a white line running between them.

"A skunk!" My voice echoed off the tree trunks. The skunk's eyes grew wide, and she froze. "Sorry," I whispered. "Keep going. You're safe."

The white line ran all the way down the skunk's back, stopping just short of her wide, bushy tail. Walking on stiff legs, she took a couple steps, then stopped to look up at me.

"Go on. I've got your back."

She broke into a trot and crossed the trail. Soon, she disappeared into the shadows.

"Anytime," I yelled after her. "Really, it was my pleasure."

The whole way home I popped and surged like an electric current. The skunk was helping me understand something. I barely grasped the edges of the insight, and it was fuzzier than I would have liked, but I knew it had to do with my nausea about our next experiment, with how animals communicate, and with a bad assumption I'd made. I wasn't clear on the details, much less what to do about it, but I knew it was important.

It wasn't more than a small, flickering light in the darkness. I held onto it like a lightning bug between my hands, not wanting to crush it, but equally unwilling to let it go.

CHAPTER 15

I had officially given up by the time I heard footsteps on the ceiling.

After lying in bed for what must have been hours trying to find the animals, then trying to *not* try too hard to find them, then realizing that I was failing at both for what felt like the hundredth time in a row, I finally got up and went to the bathroom in the hopes of clearing my head. "*You can come back whenever you want*," I said in a nasal voice to my reflection in the mirror. I knew I was being juvenile but couldn't help it. Mama's assured words mocked me.

Lying back in bed, I took a few deep breaths. That's when I heard the footsteps.

It's odd I knew that's what they were. Barely audible clicks coming in rapid succession above me, they sounded more like dripping water or wind blowing a branch against the window. But I knew what they were. And to whom they belonged.

"Hello, cockroach," I said. I thought the footsteps belonged to an anonymous insect, a squatter in my apartment, not the intellectual one who liked to get into philosophical debates with me. I was wrong.

"Hello, Frankie." The familiar baritone shook the darkness above me.

I sat straight up in my bed. "Cockroach?"

"Yes, you established that already."

"What are you doing here?"

"You asked for help finding us tonight, did you not?" I tried to make out his form on the ceiling, but it was too dark, and he was too far away.

"I've asked for help every night for the last two weeks." I folded my arms over my chest.

"Ah, yes, well, I'm a cockroach, not a genie. I have other things to take care of, some of which might conceivably be more important than escorting you some place you already know how to find." It was the first time I'd ever heard a note of bitterness in his voice.

"I'm sorry." My repentance was sincere. "I appreciate your coming."

"I know you do," he rumbled, the bitterness gone. "It's not your fault. Come on, let's go. The night isn't getting any younger."

I got out of bed. The footsteps moved to the other side of the room. I followed, pausing when I got to the window. "Go on," the deep voice instructed.

"Wait, where are we going?"

"Are you still sleeping? Did you bump your head before going to bed last night? We're going to meet the others. I thought I made that clear."

"Yeah, I know, but how am I supposed to get there from here? You want me to jump out the window? We're three stories up!"

There was an impatient sigh, and I pictured Cockroach rolling his eyes. "Of course I don't want you to jump out the window." He paused. "Walking will do just fine."

I leaned over to open the window and stuck my head outside. Blackness greeted me in all directions—no buildings, no stars, no anything. Scooting closer, I stuck one leg through.

My foot landed on something solid. I put more weight on my foot and was relieved when it held. I brought my other leg over and stood there, in the middle of nothing, just outside my bedroom window.

"Good," said Cockroach, sounding like he was inside my ear. I jumped. He tapped my shoulder with an impatient foot. "But you're not going to find anything waiting around here."

"Which direction should I go?" The window had melted into blackness behind me.

"Any direction works." His back legs lowered his rear end to rest on my shoulder.

I started walking. After a few minutes of silence I said, "Cockroach?"

There was a brief pause, then he answered, "*Hmmm?*" as if he were lost in thought.

"Why can I sometimes find y'all but other times I can't?"

"Oh, you can always find us. You just don't believe it yet. It's like everything else you know. Your doubt gets in the way of seeing it."

I wanted to argue but decided against it. "I know who said that thing you told me about what to believe—to go not by logic or probability, but by what leads to welfare and happiness." Cockroach gave a noncommittal grunt. "It was the Buddha. I looked it up. He wasn't a god, or at least I don't think he was. I guess some people worship him."

"I know."

"Cockroach?"

"Yes, Frankie?"

"How do you know so much about humans?"

"I live in close quarters with them."

"Yes, but what I mean is, why do you know so much? Do all cockroaches quote religious texts and obscure poems?"

A small peal of thunder rang on my shoulder, and he bounced up and down. He was chuckling. "No, Frankie, they don't." His voice grew louder. "But to quote another smart human"—I stopped walking and looked at him in irritation, but before I could say anything he interrupted himself—"Oh, all right, it was Sun Tzu in *The Art of War*. 'Know your enemy,' he said." I began walking again. "'Know your enemy *and* know yourself,' is what he actually said, but nobody remembers that last part. Both are good advice if you ask me, but to answer your question, I gather as much information as I can about humans to better know my enemy."

I considered this. "I don't believe that."

Cockroach's legs stiffened on my shoulder. "You don't believe that someone who goes out of his way to create as many ways as possible to kill as many of you as possible is an enemy?" His voice boomed now.

"No, that I believe. But I don't think *you* see us as enemies."

There was a long silence, and for a moment I thought he was too angry to talk. But when he spoke again, his voice was quiet. "No, I suppose I don't."

I smiled, pleased with myself for having been right. It gave me the confidence to ask about the other thing on my mind since the last time I saw him. "What about reincarnation?"

"What about it?" His voice was only one note higher than usual but sounded squeaky in comparison.

"Well, when I was reading about the Buddha, I saw something about reincarnation. So then I started researching that, and I read that Hindus believe our souls reincarnate again and again until we attain perfection and reunite with our source. In the process, they think we enter many bodies—plants and animals at first—and then eventually, humans. Humans are the highest form that you get by creating good karma."

Cockroach's body went rigid. "So what's your question?"

"Well, is it true?"

Cockroach didn't move. "What do you think?"

"Part of me likes the idea. And it could explain some

things I learned today from my mother." Cockroach felt like a dam waiting to burst. "But I don't know. I think I want to believe it more than I do. And given the state of the world, the idea that humans are the highest form of evolution doesn't really make any sense to me."

The insect's body relaxed, his back legs lowering his bum to my shoulder again. "Yes, well, on that we can agree," was all he said.

We walked the rest of the way in silence.

———

Eventually the darkness resolved itself into shadows, some denser than others. Stray patches of light fell across the ground, which had become soft and forgiving. By the time the shadows had shifted into familiar, tree-like shapes, I could make out a slice of moon sitting low in the sky behind them. There were more stars in the sky than I remembered, and I realized the trees must have shed all but a few stubborn leaves still clinging to the branches above me.

Someone coughed. A pair of eyes glowed in the moonlight to my left. A higher-pitched cough brought my attention to several more pairs arranged at various heights in a semi-circle just in front of me. I stumbled trying to stop myself before I plowed right over them.

"Hi, Frankie," said a guttural voice I didn't recognize.

I turned to my left and inspected the eyes for clues. "Sweetpea?"

"Yes, it's me," she croaked.

"Is something wrong?" I stepped closer to get a better look. She was sprawled on her belly on a branch, looking down at me with bored eyes.

"No, everything's fine." She sounded irritated and bored. "Why do you ask?"

"You just sound a little different from usual."

"Well, I'm not a baby anymore." Her voice was even deeper than mine. "You shouldn't be surprised I don't sound like one."

A loud crow split the night in front of me. Roo stood on the ground with an open beak. "Our little girl is all grown up, Frankie." His voice was ironic, but his eyes were amused.

Right. It had been nearly three months since I'd first met them. Sweetpea did look almost full grown. I turned back to her, unable to suppress a smile. "Well, regardless, it's good to see you. I missed you."

The squirrel scrambled to her feet and opened her mouth. "I missed—" she began in what almost sounded like her normal voice. Then her eyes grew wide, and she looked back and forth between Roo, Cockroach, and me. "It's not terrible to see you either," she finished in a gruff voice and flopped back onto the branch.

My smile deepened and I turned to the other eyes I'd seen. "Hi, Roo. Hi, Shelly. Hi—" The third set of eyes were much too small to be Mama's. "Where's Mama? Who is this?" It was hard to see much beyond the glimmering eyes.

"You don't recognize Penelope?" Roo asked.

"Penelope?"

"You just met her today." Cockroach's low whisper tickled the inside of my ear.

I leaned toward the small animal. A stream of white trailed back into the darkness. "The skunk?" Nobody said anything. "Are you the skunk I met today?" More silence. "Does she not understand me?" I looked around at the others.

Roo cleared his throat. "She's a bit shy."

The skunk gave an almost imperceptible nod.

"That's okay. I understand," I said. "Did you make it to wherever you were trying to go?" Her nose lowered slightly, then lifted again. "I'm glad. It's nice to see you again." Her body trembled.

Cockroach still squatted like a statue on my shoulder. Sweetpea lay sprawled on her branch. Roo stood on one leg, appearing headless as he preened along his back, and Shelly rested with eyes closed and an upturned mouth, enjoying a nice nap.

"Where's Mama?" I asked.

Roo and Sweetpea both swiveled their heads to Cockroach. "She's on her way." The insect's deep voice was soft. "She'll be here soon."

"I'm here now," said a husky voice behind me. I turned. Two yellow eyes wound their way toward us.

"Mama! How are you?" I said it more as a greeting than a real question, but as the wolf came closer, her eyes were tight around the edges, and she lifted her paws as if they weighed a thousand pounds each. Roo and Sweetpea craned their necks forward, inspecting her as well. "Are you okay?"

She padded up to me and pushed her muzzle against my leg. I let my hand rest on the top of her head. "I'm great, Frankie," she said. "It was a long day. But everything is just fine. It's good to see you."

"It's good to see you too." Her fur was warm and soft. "Are you sure you're okay?"

Her mouth opened and her tongue fell out to one side in what looked like a lopsided grin. "Yes, Frankie, I'm sure. All is well. You don't need to worry about me, okay?"

"Okay." I was about to ask about her day when the strange, artificially low voice spoke again in a bored tone.

"Did you do another experiment?" Sweetpea stared at the ground beneath her as she spoke.

"No." I tried and failed to catch her eye. "But Penelope did help me realize a mistake I was making in my thinking."

Sweetpea started to sit up, a question in her eyes, then collapsed back down. "Whatever," she sighed.

A breeze tugged at my pajamas. The air was cold and dry and smelled like—what? I wasn't sure. Childhood? The gurgling stream and rocks and trees bathed in the moon's silver light all tickled a memory. "This forest seems familiar. Have I been here before?"

"Only…every…time…we…meet…." Shelly opened her eyes just long enough to roll them up to the night sky.

"No, I mean when I'm awake. Or in real life. Or whatever you want to call it."

Cockroach shifted his feet on my shoulder. "I believe you were going to tell us what Penelope helped you realize," he said into my ear. "I, for one, would like to hear what it was."

I clenched my fists, frustrated at never getting my questions answered but equally excited to share what I'd discovered. I decided to focus on the latter and, glancing at Sweetpea's stubbornly averted eyes, went out of my way to address my comments to the other animals. "This whole time I've been asking whether animals and humans can talk to each other." I paused, judging their reactions, but nobody moved. "Our dog experiment showed that some animals at least can understand the meaning of spoken words. Next, I was going to test whether or not they'd respond to unspoken words—like commands we didn't say out loud. But something didn't feel right about it to me."

Roo snorted. "Maybe the fact that dogs could have dozens of reasons for not doing what you wanted that have nothing to do with their ability to comprehend?"

Air hissed like a leaky tire as it escaped my mouth. "I hadn't thought of that. But yeah, it's true. What Penelope helped me realize, though, is that I was framing the question wrong. I was asking about an ability to understand language. But language isn't the only way to communicate, and it may not even be the best way. When I felt Penelope's fear, it conveyed more information than a thousand words could have, and in much less time.

It made me think: maybe there are other ways besides language to communicate. Like feelings, or images, or something else.

"It's like Mama said: *You have to be willing to see anything, whatever is there.* I only learned to see this forest taking shape from shadows when I stopped thinking I knew what would appear. Maybe our expectations blind us to what animals are truly capable of. I mean, how many things can animals do that we're missing because we don't look for them, expect them, even know how to see them?"

"Yesactly," said Roo, bobbing his head in satisfaction.

"Yesactly? What does that mean?"

"Yes . . . exactly." He looked at me like I was being obtuse on purpose. "Another example of how animals can make communication clearer and more concise."

"Yeah, um, okay. Great. So all I need now is to find a way to test that capacity for communication in a lab."

"Why would you want to do that?" Roo's voice was sharp. "You already experienced it for yourself with Penelope."

"Yeah." I shrugged. "But I want to know if it was real."

Roo made a disgusted noise, and Penelope flinched.

"The mind craves certainty in a world which has none." The words came in Cockroach's rich baritone, and I had to wait for the reverberations to end before I could respond.

"Who said that?" I rubbed my ear.

"I did." His dark eyes glinted in the moonlight.

"So what does it mean?"

"It means you can't ever know anything for sure."

"But if I could replicate it in a lab with witnesses and see what's going on in the brain, then I could find out—"

"You already know!" Sweetpea squeaked. She had jumped to her feet, her body rigid and her tail sticking straight up. "And Mama says you're almost ready to know that you know."

Was she talking about the question of who I was and where I was from or how much animals could communicate?

Either way, how could they keep insisting I knew what I so obviously didn't? "Cockroach just said it himself, Sweetpea. I don't know anything, not for sure."

"What makes you doubt that you know?" Mama's voice was so throaty and calm it sounded like it was coming from the earth itself.

"Well, for one thing, that kind of human-animal communication flies pretty aggressively in the face of conventional wisdom."

"Coming from a human, that's quite an oxymoron." Roo bobbed his head up and down, chuckling to himself.

"What is?"

"*Conventional wisdom.*"

"Oh. Maybe it is."

Mama cleared her throat. "And what else?"

"I don't know," I said. "It's not logical. It doesn't make sense. I guess I can't quite wrap my head around it."

Cockroach exhaled sharply, but it was Mama who spoke. "Yes, Frankie. That's just it."

"What's just it?"

"You're not using your full intelligence."

"What do you mean?"

"You're overthinking," Cockroach answered. "It's an easy mistake to make as a human, given your brains."

"Our brains?"

"Sometimes"—Roo's voice was muffled since he hadn't bothered to lift his head from where he was preening under his wing—"your highly-evolved, state-of-the-art, exalted human brains obscure more than they illuminate."

I scowled. "I don't understand."

Cockroach began to pace on my shoulder. "I think what Roo is trying to say is the mind is only a piece of the puzzle. Human brains are so impressive it's easy to believe they're all-knowing, unerring, infallible. That they're the only means for knowing things or making decisions. They're not."

I gave him a look I was sure he couldn't misinterpret.

"I see you doubt me," Cockroach continued, "but your own scientists have shown that some types of brainless, single-celled amoebas can solve mazes, and mimosa trees can learn and adjust their behavior as quickly as most animals."

"What does this have to do with my experiment?"

"Brains are fallible, just like anything else, which is why we're all given four ways to apprehend the truth." Cockroach held one foot—or hand?—in the air as he sauntered back and forth. "Don't get me wrong. Even if nobody else here is willing to admit it, I'll happily concede that I wish my brain could do the things yours can. Goodness knows the world would be a different place if it could."

I imagined a world constructed by cockroaches and shivered. "I'm still lost."

"What was the key to you communicating with Penelope?" Cockroach asked. "Or that squirrel right after Stella told you your birth mother was dead?"

"I communicated with that squirrel? I mean, I know I spoke to him, but he communicated with me?"

"Obviously."

"Then I'm really not sure."

"Of course you're not—we just established you can't be. Try to answer anyway. What did they have in common?"

I thought about it. "Well, I guess I was pretty upset when I interacted with that squirrel. And when I understood Penelope, she was pretty upset too."

"Yesactly." Roo's nod was solemn.

I stared at him, blank.

"Emotion!" he screeched. "One of your other sources of intelligence. Older than logic and language. You humans could learn a lot from paying more attention to it."

"But isn't that what gets us into trouble? When people act on their feelings without thinking?"

"Like what?" Roo asked.

"Well, like, some people feel they're better than other people who have a different skin color, and they do awful things to them that make no sense, like killing them, or enslaving them, or treating them like—well, like we treat animals."

Roo stared at me, motionless. "You mean to say you do the same things to each other that you do to us? Because you're different colors?" He cocked his head. "That's horrible. I mean, I've seen a lot of humans, and none of you are very impressive. No blues or greens or anything that catches the light. Just a lot of dull browns and beiges. I did see one who was bright red one time after working in the field all day. That was kind of pretty. Is that what you mean?"

I didn't know whether to laugh or cry. Explaining could take all night. "Yeah, something like that."

Cockroach shifted position on my shoulder. "You have to use all of your sources of intelligence together. That's the point."

"Okay." I held up four fingers and tapped the first two. "Thinking. Feeling. What are the other two?"

"Do you believe we're real?" Cockroach asked.

Why did he always answer my questions with another question? "Why does it matter what I believe? You're the one who pointed out I can't know anything for sure."

"What you choose to believe when the truth is still unclear matters more than you can imagine. Answer the question."

"Fine. Yes, I believe you're more than just my imagination."

"And why is that?"

"I don't know. Maybe because y'all know things I don't. Maybe it just feels true."

"Great. And where do you feel it?"

I hesitated. "You mean, where am I when I feel it?"

"No." Cockroach shook his small head. "I mean, where in your body do you feel the truth of it?"

"I don't know." I thought about it. "Maybe in my belly?

Like kind of a settling sensation? Or a weight or a solidness?" I framed everything as a question in a different way than Cockroach, but it wasn't any less annoying. I tried again. "I think it feels like a whirlpool has been swirling around inside my abdomen, and then all of a sudden the proper channels opened, and I can feel it draining and settling back to where it's supposed to be. Like a relaxing. Or an opening. Or an unfolding." It didn't even make sense to me, but Mama nodded her head against my leg.

"That's it," Cockroach said. "Instinct, intuition, intelligence, whatever you call it—your animal body is filled with the accumulated wisdom of millions of years and thousands of lifetimes. It's simultaneously aware of everything within you and everything around you, and it's constantly integrating information from both past and present. Needless to say, your body knows a lot. You just have to be willing to listen."

"Okay." I held up my fingers again. "So, thinking, feeling, and . . . sensing. What's the last one?"

Roo rolled his eyes. "You're smart, Frankie, but sometimes you're a little slow." I thought so hard I almost got a cramp in my forehead, but before I had any ideas, he prompted me. "Head, heart, body, and . . ."

"Spirit?" I yelled the answer in my excitement.

Roo hunched to the ground and spread his wings low in a defensive posture. After a long, frozen moment, he pulled himself up to his full height and ruffled all his feathers. "A correct if overly enthusiastic response." He glared at me.

"So how do you know what your spirit is saying?" I asked.

"That we can't tell you," Roo said, turning to preen his flank again.

I groaned.

"Spirit speaks differently to everyone," Mama said. "You have to learn how best to hear it for yourself. But you are learning. Every time you make it here, you're getting practice, and you get a little better at it."

You can come back whenever you want, Mama had said. Was that why I couldn't? Because I didn't yet know how to recognize my spirit when it spoke?

Mama turned her giant head to look up at me. Her eyes were golden in the moonlight. "The important thing, Frankie, once you've observed and listened to all four as best you can, is to trust what you know. There's no need to doubt."

"But how can I trust I know something when I can't be sure of anything?"

"Only a human would make certainty a prerequisite for knowledge." Roo sounded repulsed.

"So you're saying that I shouldn't try to find out if animal communication is real?"

One of Cockroach's feet tapped my shoulder. "That's another of the brain's inhibiting qualities. It tends to view everything in terms of should or shouldn't, good or bad. No, Frankie, there's no right or wrong here. We're not saying that you shouldn't do anything, just that you don't need to."

I thought about it. Then, remembering what I'd just learned, I felt about it. Every time I considered all the hidden capacities animals might have—including humans—I felt a surge of energy in my core. The desire to know more was a hunger in my belly. Even if I couldn't ever be sure—

I understood.

"Testing the capacity for language, especially through commands, is never going to show us what I really want to know." I met the eyes of each of the animals one by one. "I need to find people who have an emotional connection to animals and who can communicate in ways that go beyond words. I think my foster mother mentioned a school for animal communication—maybe I can start there. Then we can bring them in with the dogs again, or maybe the rats, and map which parts of their brains are active during the communication. Oh! And we can monitor what happens for them physiologically as well."

"You realize that won't prove anything." Roo had cocked his head and was studying me with his left eye.

"I know." I grinned. "But it might help me understand more, and that's what I really want."

Roo's chest puffed out. He looked like a proud daddy.

"Frankie," said a loud voice I didn't recognize. I looked around at Cockroach, Roo, Mama, Shelly, even Sweetpea, but they all just stared at me. I swiveled to Penelope. She'd taken a step forward into the light and was trembling violently.

"Yes?" I tried to be as gentle as I could. "Is there something you'd like to say?"

In a whisper so soft I had to lean forward to hear, she said, "Only your brain forgot."

"What?" I wasn't sure I'd heard right.

"The rest of you remembers who you are and where you came from. Just not your brain."

All that existed in that moment were Penelope's black eyes and the white stripe that faded into darkness behind them. Nothing moved except a fluttering in my belly. "So how do I hear the rest of me?" My own voice was a whisper now. "How do I remember?"

The skunk took a quick step back into the shadow and looked at the ground. "I don't know. You just do."

The air drained from my lungs, and my momentary excitement went with it. Penelope was trembling again. I felt sorry for her. "Why are you so frightened to speak? You have good things to say."

She looked up at me. The sadness in her eyes made my breath catch. "You would be too if everyone was scared to come near you."

I got down on my knees and kissed her nose. "Not everyone."

Something pulled at me, and the forest lurched away. Momentarily, it returned, and in that moment Sweetpea jumped to the closest tree trunk.

"Frankie!" she yelled. It was hard to hear her. Her voice wove in and out and sounded muffled.

"Yes?" I wasn't sure if any sound came out of my mouth.

"Frankie, please forgive me! I didn't mean it! I'm not too old to say I love you. I love you, and I can't wait to see you again. Come back soon!"

I wanted to tell her that I loved her too, that there was nothing to be forgiven, that I remembered my own teenage years too well to be upset by any of it. But the wind was strong and blew the words back into my mouth.

The next thing I knew, I was in my bed.

When I opened my eyes and saw the impossibly bright morning light spilling over arms and legs that extended away from me at odd and unlikely angles, the strangest thing happened. I was overcome by the feeling that I had just fallen asleep. It was as if the animals in the dark woods and the moonlight were my real life, and this room—my bed, my desk, the old fireplace, the 1970s carpet—were all part of some elaborate, improbable dream.

CHAPTER 16

"It changes your fucking brain." The dark waves of Lillian's hair vibrated with energy. She was more excited than I'd ever seen her before.

"Wait, what exactly changes your fucking brain?" We stood in line at the Mediterranean place. I stopped trying to figure out what to order from the menu board long enough to turn to Lillian.

"Meditation. Yoga isn't really about physical poses. They're just a means to an end. Did you know *yoga* means *union*?"

"Union with what?" I ignored my rumbling belly and waved someone else to go in front of us.

"Union with our true nature." Lillian's tone suggested she'd just clarified everything.

"Our true nature?" My eyes drifted back to the menu board. I should just get the mushroom wrap with extra greens like always.

"The part of us that's bigger than our personalities. We're not our thoughts and feelings, you know? We might *feel* sad, but that doesn't mean we *are* sad. The emotions are the clouds, but we're the sky. Same thing with thoughts. They come and go, but we don't have to believe them."

I grunted, remembering my last conversation with the animals three weeks before. "Yeah, I just heard something similar recently."

"Right, so meditation is a way to practice connecting with your true nature. We did a lot of it in our final training last weekend. At first it was hella boring, and I couldn't stop obsessing about the guy next to me who'd been correcting my postures all weekend even though I never asked him to."

"That's annoying."

"For sure. But after meditating for a while, the world just felt . . . I don't know, bigger. His correcting me didn't bother me so much. He was just nervous, you know? And it only pissed me off when I thought he thought he was better than me."

She looked at me, waiting until I nodded before going on. "So I got to thinking. So many of the world's problems come from people judging people who are different from them. If meditation made me more compassionate, maybe it could do the same for others. And maybe if we understood the neural mechanisms for how it works, we could find other ways to increase empathy."

"That sounds awesome. And like, kind of brilliant." I turned back to the cart and decided to add walnuts to my wrap. "Maybe you could show me how to meditate sometime?"

"Sure. I'd be happy to."

We took our wraps to a bench on the edge of the eucalyptus grove on campus. After a few bites, everything felt right in the world again and I became less like a toddler wanting to put everything in my mouth.

"When do you think they'll make their decision about the grant?" I asked. When I'd told Brian and Lillian about my idea to map the brain activity of people who said they could communicate with animals, they'd urged me to apply for the Helen Wills Neuroscience Grant.

"They should let you know soon. Definitely before winter break."

It was less than two weeks away, but from the impatience that flared in my chest, it might as well have been two years. I tried to distract myself by staring at the peeling bark on the tree trunks, which made streaky rainbows of brown, yellow, and red.

Lillian put her hand on my arm. "Brian's back from coaching the swim team at the invitational."

I tried to sound casual. "How do you know?"

"Because he's right over there." She pointed with her elbow.

I spun around. Brian grinned as he strode to us in a Cal sweatsuit, the thin fabric tracing the muscles of his legs with each step.

"Hi, ladies." Brian slowed to a graceful stop in front of our bench. "Beautiful day, isn't it?"

"Not really my favorite type of weather." Lillian scowled at the pale gray sky. "But I can see where if cold and damp are your thing, Bay Area winters might be quite lovely."

"Oh." Brian feigned surprise. "I guess I'm still feeling the warmth of our explosive victory over Stanford at the swim meet."

"Congratulations." I held up my hand for a high-five.

"Thanks." Brian winked and pushed his hand against mine.

"I'd congratulate you as well," Lillian said sweetly, "but I'm afraid if your head got any bigger, it might roll right off your shoulders." She put a hand on a hip. "Why do you hate Stanford so much anyway? I mean, I know they're our rival, but your passion is too zealous for school spirit alone."

Brian's face turned redder than Stanford's logo.

Lillian stared at him, her jaw muscles tensing and relaxing like she was literally chewing on the question. After a few seconds she clapped and pointed her index finger at his chest. "You applied to Stanford's neuroscience program but got rejected, didn't you?"

"I *never* would have applied to that piece of shit program. I have more pride than that." Brian's voice trembled. "I applied to them for undergrad"—his words pitched low—"and didn't get in."

"I knew it!" Lillian threw her hand up for a high-five but took it down when Brian's expression made it clear she was going to be left hanging. You could almost see her wrestling with her enthusiasm to rein it in. "I meant to say, their loss, man. Really. What losers."

Brian's eyes rolled upward. "That reminds me. Frankie, Dr. Porter wants to see you."

My good mood decamped faster than a dinner guest with diarrhea. "Why? Did he find out about our rat experiment? Does he want to kick me out of his lab?" Panic stirred in my belly. "Does he want to kick me out of the program?"

"Yeah, Lillian and I wanted to get in some big-time trouble, so we told him about the experiment." The sarcasm drained out of his tone. "He didn't tell me what he wanted. He just said to tell you to come by as soon as possible."

I was having a hard time breathing. "Did he sound angry when he said it?"

"Well, he never sounds particularly pleased when he says anything, but no, I wouldn't say he sounded angry."

I let out a long breath. "Okay." I crumpled the now-empty aluminum foil and grabbed the strap of my shoulder bag. "Thanks for letting me know."

"I'll go with you." Lillian began to wrap up her remaining salmon.

"No, that's really—"

"I'll go too," interrupted Brian. "Nobody should be alone when they find out they're expelled." Lillian and I stared at him, my eyes wide, hers narrow. "What?" He turned his palms up. "I'm being helpful."

"So helpful," Lillian murmured, picking up her purse.

I stopped when I reached the door of the lab and turned to Brian and Lillian. They didn't appear frightened, or concerned by the deafening noise of my pulse, so I took a deep breath and pushed open the heavy door.

Dr. Porter sat behind his big desk and stared at a piece of paper with a frown. He ran a hand through his salt-and-pepper hair.

"Um, Dr. Porter?" I winced when my voice squeaked.

He looked up. "Frances. And Brian and Lillian. I wasn't expecting you as well, but I suppose it's good you hear this too."

The knot in my stomach tightened. He wanted an audience to witness my humiliation.

"Frances, you remember our first experiment of the semester, correct?"

"The rat maze experiment on short wave ripples and replay?"

"That's right. I submitted it to the Annual Congress on Neurology and Neuroscience happening at the end of the month in Panama. It was accepted, and they've invited me to come lead a session on the results."

Why was he telling me this? Did he want me to congratulate him?

"The thing is, budgets aren't what they used to be, and the department's travel allotment has already been depleted. As a public sector servant, I'm certainly not in a position to fund a last-minute trip to Panama personally. Especially not with Christmas coming and my family—" His frown deepened, as did the lines on his forehead. "With certain unforeseeable changes being what they are. So when Brian told me you're going to the conference anyway, I thought we might give you a chance to redeem yourself."

What was he talking about? I turned back to Brian. He had a huge smile on his face but didn't say anything.

"Um, excuse me, sir, but why am I going to the conference anyway?"

Dr. Porter sighed and looked at his watch. "To present the results of an experiment from another lab. Or so Brian tells me. Why any professor would choose you is beyond me, but since you already have your ticket, I'm hoping you can represent our results without screwing up too badly."

"Um, sure? I'd be happy to try?" Dr. Porter looked like I did when I watched horror movies: repulsed, yet unable to look away. "But I don't actually have a ticket yet."

"I really don't care how you plan to get there. You do realize most first-year doctoral students would kill for the opportunity I'm handing you here?"

"Yes, sir. Thank you for the opportunity." Something stirred in my gut. Not something physical but a sense, a vague knowing. It reminded me of what the animals had told me about my body speaking to me. "Um, sir? About those results . . ."

He stared at me with eyes of ice.

"I'm sure you noticed." My voice sounded like a door hinge that needed oil. "The rats' sharp wave ripples, they replayed the routes through the maze forward and backward even though the rats only ran the route in one direction." I paused, but Dr. Porter didn't say anything. "I believe that suggests the *possibility*"—I was careful to emphasize the word—"that the rats were making mental models of their environment. It seems like we should mention the *possibility*—"

"There will be no talk of mental models in your presentation. That is unsubstantiated conjecture and has no place in our results. We'll discuss exactly what you *will* say later this week."

"Yes, Dr. Porter. I understand." My limbs felt like sandbags. I dragged them out of the room.

When the door shut behind Lillian and Brian in the hall, I let out a breath. "Okay does anyone want to explain to me what's going on?"

"I'm just as lost as you are," Lillian said. "You're going to have to ask Brian about this one."

Brian's face was smooth except for the crinkles at the edges of his hazel eyes. "Well, first of all, I should tell you that you do have a ticket to Panama. So you don't need to worry about that."

I stared at him. "But why am I going to Panama at all?"

"Oh, haven't you heard?" he said in the same fake-surprised tone he'd used earlier. "There's a big neuroscience and neurobiology conference happening there later this month."

"Very funny, mister. What I mean is, whose results am I supposed to be presenting besides Dr. Porter's?"

I could have sworn Brian's teeth glinted in the sunlight like we were in a cartoon. "You're like the opposite of an elephant. I can't believe you don't remember." He walked toward the building entrance. "Someone did this great experiment that showed that dogs understand human speech."

I grabbed his arm. "What are you talking about?"

His smile shrank from cartoonish to amused. "The conference organizers would be honored for you to present your recent discoveries on neural mechanisms for lexical processing in dogs."

"The results of our dog experiment?" I couldn't wrap my head around it.

"The very one."

"You sent them an abstract?" Lillian's tone was a relief; at least I wasn't the only one struggling to absorb this news.

"I did." Brian was nonplussed. "Right after I wrote up the results."

"Wow." I let go of Brian's arm. "Thank you, I guess."

"And I suppose you're welcome."

My brain began to warm up after the cold shock. "Why don't *you* go to Panama to present the results? You're the one who wrote the report."

"I'll be . . . otherwise occupied then." I opened my mouth to ask with what, but Brian shook his head.

"What about Lillian then? She's much better at talking about these things than I am."

"I'll also be otherwise occupied," Lillian said. "I thought about trying to go to that conference as an attendee, but my parents are making me take them on a Disney cruise that same week. Besides, it was your experiment. You should present it."

"I can't," I tried again. "I can't let you pay for my ticket, Brian."

"I didn't."

"Then who did? Dr. Porter said the department is out of funding."

He shrugged. "The athletic department has all kinds of frequent flier miles accumulated. I'm well-liked among the administrative staff, and they were happy to throw a few my way so the results of an experiment I'd worked on could be presented at a big-time academic conference."

My brain spun in hyperdrive trying to locate potential problems. "Dr. Porter didn't seem happy about me going at all. I don't want to antagonize him any more than I have."

"First of all, turning down the opportunity he's so magnanimously offered you is the absolute best way to antagonize him right now. But aside from that, don't worry so much about his reaction. He's just extra cranky because his divorce was finalized. From what I can tell, his kids don't seem so happy with him either."

"How sad," Lillian said. "Though not entirely surprising."

"Dr. Porter's not a bad guy." Brian held open the front door of the building for Lillian and me. "He's brilliant, and really does care about the people he works with. But for him, it's all about the results. If those are good, he thinks everyone will be happy in the end."

My brain wasted no time in spinning on to other obstacles. If I went to the conference, it informed me, I wouldn't be able to visit my parents over Christmas. Mom would be upset.

Dad might be too. James would continue to be the favorite. Still, I couldn't deny part of me was relieved not to have to go. My brain whirled to another realization.

"You lying liar!" I punched Brian in the shoulder. "You knew all along what Dr. Porter wanted, but you made me think I was getting expelled."

Brian grinned and rubbed his shoulder. "I think you accomplished that pretty well on your own. But I have to tell you, the expression on your face when you heard what he really wanted was priceless."

"Wonderful. And is there anything else you want to tell me before I have to humiliate myself in front of another professor or a few more classmates to find out?"

"Actually, yes." Brian's expression was serious now. "That Helen Wills grant you applied for? Word on the street is, you got it."

"Huh." My eloquence was astounding. "Wow. I mean . . . oh my God."

Brian squeezed my shoulder. Lillian had a huge smile on her face. I thanked them both and accepted congratulatory hugs. Brian's seemed to last a second or two longer than Lillian's, and I thought he pulled me tighter just before letting go.

At that point, my brain couldn't come up with any more excuses. I had no choice but to enjoy the happiness quietly washing over me.

CHAPTER 17

Physically, I made good time in my rental car on the drive up to Redwood Regional Hospital. Emotionally, I had one foot on the gas and one on the brake.

Part of me was desperate to see Jones again, to ask him more questions and dig out the truth. Part of me dreaded telling him I'd figured out he lied the last time we talked.

I pulled the nondescript beige car into what I hoped was the middle of a parking space. Everything looked the same as when I'd been here with Brian. Landscaped trees and shrubs in the parking lot were dwarfed by the dense forest nearly spilling over the curb behind them. I undid my seatbelt, gathered the remnants of my lunch, and walked on shaky knees to the main entrance.

I didn't know where to look for Jones, so I started with the cafeteria. Circling the giant eating area three times, I didn't see any trace of his thick, black-and-silver buzz cut, and it occurred to me that finding a janitor in a bustling hospital could take all day.

But then I got lucky. In a large waiting area next to the cafeteria, I walked past an empty janitorial cart. I had to break every unwritten rule in the code of ethics of waiting rooms and stare directly at one vulnerable person after the next, but

I finally saw Jones. He was bent over, whispering in the ear of a man with white hair and a tube winding out of his nose like a thin, transparent snake. When he finished, the man looked up at him with a grateful smile. He smiled back, warm as the sun, then stood up and noticed me staring at him.

The sun quickly set as he walked over.

"Hi, Jones." I tried to make my voice less shaky than my knees.

"Can I help you with that?" he asked in a cool, twilight tone.

"With what?"

He pointed to the remains of my lunch that I was still for some reason clutching in my right hand. "Oh." Why hadn't I found a trash can earlier? "It's okay. I'll get it in a minute."

He reached over, took the apple core and empty wrappers, and tossed them into the trash bag in his cart. My face flushed.

"What can I do for you today?" His voice was low. "I told you everything I could last time we met."

"Thank you. I just have a follow-up question, if you don't mind. Is there somewhere we can go to talk?"

He turned to walk down the hall, leaving his cart behind. I followed him past nurses' stations, closed doors, and a few empty examining rooms. He didn't look back once.

Just when I wondered if I'd misunderstood, if I was supposed to wait in the waiting room for him to finish his shift, Jones stopped and dug out a key from the ring at his waist. He unlocked a large, windowless door beside us and gestured for me to go in first.

The room was filled with metal shelves covered in blue-wrapped packages from floor to ceiling. "I'm sorry for bothering you again at work," I said.

"Don't worry about it. Now how can I be of service?"

I tried to calm the butterflies in my belly that felt more like baby dragons. "Well, last time I came here, you said you'd never met anyone named Isabella Days. You gave me the name of a doctor who treated my birth mother and said he might be able answer my questions."

"Dr. Marrone."

"Yeah. I left him a bunch of messages. Finally, his wife called back to say he's in the advanced stages of Alzheimer's and barely remembers where he is most days."

"That's too bad."

"Yeah, I know."

"So how can I help?" The musical cadence of his words soothed the dragons in my gut.

"I wondered if there was anyone else I could talk to." I still wasn't ready to call him a liar.

Jones stared at something far past the supply closet walls before shaking his head. "Sorry. I don't remember the names of any of the other doctors or nurses who might have helped your mother." He was more serious than the last time we'd spoken. There was no twinkle in his brown eyes. "What about your mother's friend? Stella Richardson, wasn't it? Can't you ask her for more details?"

How did he remember her name? "Stella doesn't know anything more than what she already told me."

"Yes, well"—his deep voice was low—"most people have a way of knowing more than they let on."

It was the best opening I could have hoped for. "Actually, I was thinking you might know more than you said you did last time." The dragons writhed.

But his skin remained smooth, and his eyes didn't narrow. There was even a hint of amusement when he asked, "And why is that?"

I licked my lips. "You said you'd never heard of Isabella Days. But you never said you didn't remember a woman arriving here unconscious and then giving birth."

"And why is it so important to know what happened to her? Isn't it enough that you lived? That you found a nice family?

That you have enough resources and free time to drive halfway across the state to ask questions in a hospital supply closet?"

The words suggested a rebuke, but his tone was gentle and curious. He might think I'd lost touch with reality, but if I wanted him to be honest with me, I needed to be honest with him.

"It's the animals." I pulled my shoulders back. "I keep having these . . . dreams . . . of animals, and they keep hinting that I'm from somewhere else. That I came here for a reason. I don't know. I've always felt like I never belonged anywhere, and then I found this out about my birth mother, and I thought maybe that's why. Maybe something happened when I was born that explains this constant feeling I have that I'm different, that I'm not . . . that I don't . . ." I trailed off, unsure how to finish, or maybe unwilling to.

Jones nodded as if what I was trying to say couldn't be clearer. "I get it. It's important to know who you are." He leaned in, even though we were the only two people in the closet. "I'd been working here about three weeks when they found a woman unconscious and going into labor not too far from the entrance to the hospital."

"Isabella?"

"No. I was telling the truth when I said I've never heard of anyone by that name." His voice was as smooth and unyielding as river rocks. "I am many things, but a liar isn't one of them."

"Sorry. I didn't mean to imply you were."

"I know." His voice was gentle again. "Anyway, nobody could figure out why the woman was unconscious, or how she'd arrived at the hospital. They didn't seem too keen to find out either. They were more concerned with making sure she and her baby survived. I, on the other hand, was young and still thought I deserved to know everything. I was determined to figure it out." He held up a hand with four thick fingers extended.

"I had four clues." He tapped his index finger. "First, where they found her. A nurse arriving for her shift saw her at the edge of the woods in the back of the parking lot. Far from the main road and nowhere near where a normal person would drop someone off in a hurry. Second"—he tapped his middle finger—"what they found on her. She was wearing long underwear, nothing else. Third"—he tapped his ring finger—"what they found beneath her. A blanket, dirty and badly torn. And underneath her, mind you, not covering her. Fourth"—he touched his pinkie—"what they found with her. When they cut away her clothing to do an inspection, there were no cuts or injuries; they found a few bruises, but nothing to explain her state. But one of the nurses working that night told me that when she went to dispose of the clothing, it was covered in dog fur."

I pulled the corner of my lip between my teeth. It didn't make any sense.

"You doubt my detective skills, I see," said Jones, but the twinkle was back in his eyes, had been since he started ticking off clues. "Heck, I would too, if I were you. And one thing I've learned in the last twenty-five years is that deserve it or not, there are many things we'll never understand. I never found out for sure what happened to your mother. But I did find one more clue before all was said and done, and it was a big one."

"What was it?" I grew dizzy as the closet, hospital, and entire world collapsed into the height and width of his dark brown eyes.

"We had four clues," Jones repeated, tapping each finger again in turn, "forest, long underwear, blanket, and dog hair. The hospital staff buzzed with theories about what had happened. Some thought she'd had a heart attack by the side of the road, where some kind person had picked her up and brought her here. Others thought she'd driven herself but collapsed when she got out of the car. I didn't know what had happened, but I knew everyone's theories were wrong. I went down to where your mother had been found and looked around." He peered around the supply closet as if looking for clues. "Sure enough, after just a few steps into the forest, I saw the footprints of the *ha-rak Li'riL*." He nodded, satisfied.

"What's a *ha rock lee real*?"

"*Ha-rak Li'riL*." The words tumbled then slowed like a river. "I'm Wiyot. *Ha-rak Li'riL* is our word for wolf."

Mama's golden eyes glowed in my mind. "There are wolves nearby?"

"No. Not usually. There used to be a lot, but they've been gone for many years. But sometimes, they cross the border to return to their homeland for a time. We all need to come home now and then."

I took this in. "So the dog hair they found on her wasn't dog hair after all?"

The ghost of a smile passed over Jones's face. "I suppose not."

Excitement thumped in my brain, making it hard to think. "What do you think happened?"

He shook his head, amused. "I don't know. Some things cannot be known for certain. If I told you my theory, you might mistake it for the truth and never come up with your own."

I wanted to argue; more honestly, I wanted to scream, but neither would do any good. "Why didn't you tell me any of this when I came here before?"

"It's not my story to tell."

"Whose is it?"

"Yours and your mother's. Go back and ask Stella what else she knows about your mom." Before I could respond, he opened the door to the hallway.

I followed him back through the corridor in silence. When we arrived at his cart in the waiting room, I put my hand on his arm. "Jones, I really appreciate your help."

His eyes were bright. "You're quite welcome. It's a relief to see how stubborn you turned out to be. You were so frail when you were born, I wondered if you were meant to be in this world. I'm glad to see you are."

The unexpected warmth gave me the strength to voice the other thing I wanted to say, the harder one. "I was thinking about what you said last time, about coming to work here when your father got sick and never finishing school." I searched his eyes for anger, but they remained calm. "I just wanted to say I think you're smarter than most of the people at my school, and I'd be happy to put in a good word for you in the admissions office."

Jones chuckled, the sound like a rock somersaulting down a slope. "I appreciate the offer, but I got my degree a long time ago."

Time stopped and my blood froze. My head sank into my shoulders like I was a turtle and could make myself disappear. How could I have made such an insulting assumption? Not to mention racist? What was wrong with me?

As the seconds ticked by, I realized I was making it worse with my silence. "I'm sorry." My voice was a horrifying croak. "I shouldn't have assumed—"

"Have you heard of the Indian Island Massacre?"

I shook my head.

"On February 26, 1860, after stealing much of our land, a group of local white men murdered hundreds of peaceful Wiyot people. We were holding our annual world renewal ceremony on the island. Mostly women and children were killed, hacked with hatchets, clubs, and knives. In 1850, there were two thousand of us. By the end of 1860, only two hundred remained. After the massacres, we were forced off our land, for our own protection they said, and confined to a reservation."

My lunch rose into my throat. "I'm so sorry."

Jones gazed at the creased and collapsed faces of the people in the waiting room. "I got lucky. My family stood behind me and one of the physicians here took a liking to me. He encouraged me to go back to school and become a doctor." His gaze fell onto the man with the white hair and the oxygen tank. He winked, and the man's face broke into a large grin. "I wasn't sure I wanted to at first, but wiping up blood and shit, you have a lot of time to think. My thoughts always came back to the fact that I'm here, alive—how that was never guaranteed. I wanted to do something to honor my ancestors. It occurred to me I could do that by stopping more blood from spilling."

My heart swelled. "You're a doctor?"

"Yes, an Emergency Room physician. I figured I understand trauma so well, I'm uniquely qualified to heal it."

I looked at the man with the white hair. A smile lingered on his lips. "They're lucky to have you," I said.

Jones's deep brown eyes probed mine for a long moment. "I could say the same for you."

I glanced back at the elderly man, his serpentine tube and tank, wondering who in the world was lucky to have me.

I must have wondered for longer than I realized, because when I looked back up, Jones had disappeared without a trace.

PART 2

CHAPTER 18

Somehow, it didn't occur to me that going to a conference alone meant I would be so . . . alone.

I'd obsessed about many things before arriving in Panama. I worried about what I would eat, what I would drink, how I would find my way around. Most urgently, I worried about whether or not to mention mental models in my presentation on the rat experiment. But I didn't once worry that being at a conference by myself would feel like being shipwrecked. Like saltwater when you're dying of thirst, there were people, people everywhere, but not a soul to greet.

I made a mental note—not my first—that my worries, though they always seemed infallible at the time, were spectacular failures when it came to predicting my actual struggles with any degree of accuracy at all.

There were too many people coming and going through the lobby. Most of them walked in groups of twos or threes—was I the only one who came without any colleagues or classmates? And those who did walk alone had intense expressions that didn't invite introductions.

I turned to head back up the stairs.

"There are a lot of people here, no?" A small woman with light brown hair and large, hazel eyes stood next to me.

"There are. I wish I knew some of them." I scanned face after unfamiliar face.

"You are here all alone?" She had a slight accent.

"I am." Saying it aloud made it feel like a confession.

Her smile made the room feel twenty degrees warmer. "Me too! My name is Tamara."

"I'm Frankie."

"A pleasure to meet you." She leaned in to touch her right cheek to mine and made a kissing sound. I pulled back, then instantly regretted it when I realized she was still leaning in, attempting a second kiss on my other cheek, which was no longer there. I forced myself forward, but she'd already straightened up, so I had to wait a second while she leaned back in.

I cringed at my awkwardness, but she only laughed. "Sorry, it's not usual here, but my mother accustomed me to kiss on both cheeks. It was her way of honoring our Spanish roots. I'm personally not as keen to remember, but it is a nice custom, I think." She nodded as if answering some unspoken question. "Frankie." She rolled the *r* like it was a piece of food in her mouth. "Where are you from, Frankie?"

"California." I remembered I was on a different continent and added, "The United States. What about you?"

"I am from here." She pointed a slender finger to the floor. "Well, the city, no? Not the hotel. Have you been here before?"

"No, this is my first time in Panama."

Her smile grew, warming another ten degrees. "Welcome! I hope you like it here. Where were you going when I interrupted you?"

"Oh. I was heading back to my room. I don't really have a plan yet."

"Perfect! Because I do. I'm going to buy you a *chicha de guanábana*, and then we will attend today's most exciting session."

"Sounds good to me." I took a deep breath, maybe the first since I'd left California. "I'll follow you."

———————

Tamara led us to a park just down the street from the hotel. We wound our way around playgrounds and beneath wide trees, watching bicyclists pass on a path that ran along the water. We stopped at the end of the park in front of a small shop. I still wasn't sure what a *chicha de guanábana* was and couldn't see inside well enough to make a guess. As we waited in the long line that snaked out the door, I mustered up the courage to ask Tamara the question I'd been trying to figure out since we left the hotel.

"So what's the most exciting session of the day?" Between finals and packing for the trip, I hadn't had time to look at the conference schedule before I left, and in my initial overwhelm at the hotel, I'd forgotten to pick up a program. The only sessions I knew anything about were my own, and they didn't start until the next day.

"Oh, it is not the what—it is the *who* I care about." She tapped her nose, where a few dark freckles contrasted endearingly with her autumn wheat complexion. "The session will be led by an up-and-going neuroscientist everyone is talking about." She brightened. "He is also American! He is from Boston."

"Why is everyone talking about him?"

"He's already been credited on more papers than most people two times his age. Most of the research ideas are his, too, even though he always works with senior faculty. And his research is very—cutting edge?" She looked at me to confirm the term. I nodded. "Please correct me if I make a mistake. It is the only way I will improve my English."

I wished, not for the first time, that I spoke Spanish. Any Spanish at all. "Okay, in that case, it's up-and-coming."

She laughed, a bright bubbly noise like water falling over rocks. "Up-and-*coming*. Thank you." She mouthed the words again silently, then nodded. "Anyway, today's session is on the role of orbitofrontal cortex gray matter volume in regard to trait optimism and anxiety."

"Interesting."

"Plus, he's really hot."

The lunch I'd eaten on the plane crawled back up my esophagus as I imagined a group of young grad students fawning over Dr. Porter and his rumpled sweaters. "Excuse me?" Maybe I hadn't heard her right. Maybe this was another hiccup in translation.

"Oh, yes. He is not my type, but it is fun to see the other ladies try to get his attention. My friend met him once and now carries a photo of him around with her. I have to admit, he is handsome. He looks like a movie star."

"Okay." I got curious to see this up-and-coming star. "Sounds good."

We stepped through the doorway of the shop—a smoothie shop, I guessed from the muted noise of blenders and the many fruits I'd never seen before—green, purple, yellow, red, and orange, some smooth, some prickly, some slimy—displayed on the counters.

"This is the best juice café in the city. How long are you here for? There is so much I would love to show you."

"Just until the conference ends. I leave on the last day."

"*Que lástima!* You have to see the Parque Natural Metropolitano and Casco Viejo. They're not far from here. Oh! And the San Blas Islands. Absolutely amazing."

"What's so amazing about them?"

"They are beautiful. Clear water, blue sky, palm trees, and lots of fish. But the best part is the people who live there. Some say they are the happiest people on the planet."

"Sounds great. Wish I had time to go."

"Maybe I have an idea." She winked, a sexy-and-I-know-it gesture. With her intelligence, friendliness, and eyes the color of a setting sun, I could imagine this neuroscientist was popular with the men. Or whomever she wanted.

"Changing the theme, do you have a boyfriend?" she asked.

"Wait, what?"

"Do you have a boyfriend or girlfriend in California?"

"Not really. No." Did all Panamanians get so personal so fast?

"Why not?"

Was it pity or confusion in her voice? Which would be worse? "I don't know."

She squinted through her dark eyelashes. "You said not really. That means there is somebody you like who likes you back."

I shrugged. "I don't know how much he likes me back. There is a research fellow I've been getting to know, but we're just friends."

"Ah . . . *amigos con derechos*." It sounded like a diagnosis.

"Friends with . . . what? What does that mean?"

"*De-re-chos*. It means rights. Like human rights, or . . . obligations."

Friends with rights. Oh. "Friends with benefits, we call it."

"*Perfecto*. You have a friend with benefits."

"Maybe. Not so many benefits yet. What about you? Are you dating anyone?"

Her expression decomposed like a rotting apple. "No, too much trouble." She looked like she was going to say something else but the person in front of us moved and the young man behind the counter waved us forward.

Outside, after we got our *chichas de guanábana*—smoothies made of one of the green, spiky fruits—Tamara turned to me. "By the way, I did not ask why you do not have a boyfriend because I think you should." She took a sip of her smoothie. "I asked because you are pretty and smart and kind, so I assumed you would."

Oddly, the voice in my head didn't argue. As I sipped the smoothie, which was creamy and sweet and complex, a cool breeze stroked my skin and the sun's warmth kissed my face. A relaxed, warm sensation began to fill me. By the time we returned to the hotel, I was no longer bothered by the frowning strangers surrounding me. I wasn't worried about arriving late to the session or not having read up on the topic. In fact, walking through the lobby, I felt snug as a snail in his shell, slack as a snake in the sun.

I did, that is, until we walked through the door of the conference room, and I saw who was speaking at the podium.

My whole body went rigid at once. Tamara must have noticed. "Are you okay?" she whispered as we scooted in to stand by the back wall. "What's wrong?"

"I'm fine." My eyes were glued to the podium. I couldn't believe what I was seeing. "It looks like your up-and-coming professor is my *amigo con derechos.*"

CHAPTER 19

"**A** professor from Boston?" I pushed myself against the back wall of the packed conference room, hoping Brian wouldn't see my face, which I could tell was bright red.

"I also do not understand." Tamara's eyebrows were creased with concern. "My friend who met him told me he taught at Berklee. We looked it up; the website said it was in Boston. He told my friend it was cold where he lived, so we assumed that was right."

Of course. The proper name of our school was the University of California at Berkeley, but nobody ever used its full name, so it would sound identical to the music school in Boston. And Bay Area residents, myself included, always complained about the cold, despite the temperate climate. "There are two '*Berk-lees*,'" I explained. "He's a research associate at the one in California."

Tamara's hands flew to her mouth. "I'm so sorry!" she whisper-yelled through her fingers.

"It's not your fault. I should have gotten a program." A wave of heat rose in my core. "Actually, he should have told me."

Brian looked like he was speaking to a group of close friends—he was relaxed, confident, and funny. He was explaining that his team had found that more gray matter in the brain correlated with more optimism and therefore less anxiety. It was the first time anyone had linked brain structure with personality traits, and it opened up new avenues for possible treatment of anxiety. He didn't use the word *breakthrough*, but it was clear that's what it was. I would have known it was a big deal even if every scientist in the audience hadn't been nodding their head up and down like they were at an Iron Maiden concert.

But Brian wasn't bragging. No, he was the poster child of humility and restraint, which garnered him even higher amounts of admiration from the people in the audience.

And that was the other thing freaking me out—just how many people that was. All the chairs in the room were full, and attendees lined the walls. Tamara and I had to peer over the shoulders of two rows of people standing in front of us, and every few minutes the door kept opening so somebody else could squeeze in.

Even still, I didn't fully understand how popular Brian was until after the Q&A when he stepped down from the stage and audience members swarmed him. He looked like a drop of honey overwhelmed by dozens of bespectacled ants.

I started to move to the door, but Tamara grabbed my arm. "You are not going to talk to him?" Her eyes were concerned again.

"Not now. I'll do it later when there aren't so many people trying to get his attention."

But Tamara didn't loosen her grip on my arm. Instead, she moved to the heart of the crowd, pulling me with her. People glared as we pressed by.

When we got within six feet or so of Brian, the crush of people became too thick to penetrate. We broke away to the side. Brian was deep in conversation with a short, balding attendee and didn't see us approach.

I shifted my weight from one foot to another, hunched over to make myself smaller, and tested Tamara's grip on my arm—maybe I could make a run for it. No such luck. Her hand was only slightly less firm than a steel vise.

By the time Brian had spoken to a few more people, I was ready to explode. Steel vise or no steel vise, I needed to get out of there. I turned to explain this to Tamara when I heard a familiar voice.

"Frankie!" Brian's gilded eyes pinned me in place.

I intended to walk over and give him a civil greeting like a friend. I'm sure that's what he expected, and Tamara too for that matter, because she finally loosened her grip on my arm. But when I used my newfound freedom to walk through the last ring of people, the greeting died in my throat. Instead, I punched Brian in the arm. "What the hell are you doing here?"

For a split second Brian's smile faltered, but he recovered quickly. "Don't worry, folks," he addressed the crowd, "that's how they greet each other where Frankie's from."

The crowd cackled and everything inside me shrank. I turned to go, but this time Brian grabbed my arm. "Wait, Frankie," he said, his smile gone. "I know I owe you an explanation. Will you give me a chance to explain? Can we have dinner together tonight?"

"Aren't you going to the conference dinner?" the woman in front of Brian asked. "You said you would give me advice on my next project."

Brian winced. "Right," he said to the woman. "Yes, I'll be there." He turned back to me. "After dinner then, Frankie? Will you meet me at the hotel bar?"

His eyes were earnest, his expression pained. Part of me wanted to say no, but the larger part wanted more than anything to say yes. Tamara's hand found mine from behind and squeezed it. "Yes." I exhaled. "I'll meet you there."

Brian's smile returned. "Eight o'clock?"

"Eight o'clock," I agreed, my own smile too far gone to find.

————

"He really likes you," Tamara said from the other side of the table. She sat in front of a mural of a stylized turtle made of repeating patterns and shapes in bright blues, yellows, reds, and oranges. The turtle was accompanied by similarly fanciful fish, lobsters, and crabs.

I wrinkled my nose. "Does he?"

She paused with her fork just in front of her mouth. "Of course. He invited you to meet up with him later, no?"

"He did." I pushed the few remaining grains of rice around on my plate with my fork. "I'm just not sure whether he did it because he felt bad, or because he actually wants to see me."

Tamara groaned. "We women doubt ourselves too much. We think it is humility, but really it is another form of pride."

"What do you mean?"

"*I* am terrible. *I* am a failure. *I* am not worthy. *I, I, I.* Pride, but in reverse. Thinking we are worse than everyone else is another way to say we are more special than they are. But nobody is special. Nobody is better or worse."

She had a point. "Okay, maybe he does really want to see me."

She gave a satisfied nod, golden highlights in her hair shimmering in the light. "Yes. It is clear that he does."

"What about you?" I didn't want to be the center of attention any longer. "You said relationships were too much trouble. Does that assessment come from personal experience?"

"Too much, if you ask me." She put her fork down and pushed her plate away.

"Can I ask what happened?"

"My father is a successful man. He owns a charter plane company. He always told me to have big dreams because I could be whatever I wanted to be. I believed him, until I fell in love." Her eyes were yellow embers—searing, shifting, starving. "Then I found out it is not true."

"I'm so sorry. Do you want to talk about it?"

She leaned back in her chair. "No. But love sometimes smells really bad."

I waged a valiant struggle against a laugh that rose in my throat. "Yeah, love stinks. My last boyfriend broke up with me in a note. It was so short it could have been a haiku."

Now Tamara fought a laugh. "Sorry, that is worse than awful. I hope you are not mad that it makes me feel better. Unhappiness loves visitors."

It took me a moment to understand. "Not mad at all," I said. "Misery does love company."

I worried that I'd ruined the meal for her, but by the time the waiter came to remove our plates, it was as if the topic had never come up. When he brought our dessert, she delighted in my mispronunciation of *cobanga*, then said she couldn't wait to hear what happened later with Brian.

When she said Brian's name, a tide of anxiety rose within me. I made a mental note to look up ways to increase gray matter volume in my brain.

CHAPTER 20

I arrived at the hotel bar first, of course.

When I had to squeeze between sweaty, drunk bodies just to get close enough for the bartender to hear me, I cursed Brian's current lifetime. When I had to order a drink with no milk or eggs or alcohol in broken, miserable Spanish I'd just looked up, I cursed his next one. And when I checked my phone for the tenth time and still didn't have any messages, I cursed any additional lifetimes he might be lucky enough to have.

Finally, at 8:09 p.m., a leonine man with a golden mane walked through the entrance. He wore the same clothes he'd had on during the presentation, only his fitted khakis were more rumpled, his dress shirt unbuttoned, and his eyes were heavy with bags as he scanned the bar.

When he saw me, a huge smile banished all the shadows from his face. "Frankie!" he called so loudly that several people near him turned to look.

I waved, and he made his way over.

"See, I do know how to give a proper greeting when I'm not in cardiogenic shock," I said.

"I know it was a bit of a surprise to see me here today, but really? A heart attack? Should I call a doctor?"

"Okay, maybe it wasn't physiological shock. But psychogenic, certainly. You gave me a psychological heart attack. Why didn't you tell me you were coming? It's not like you didn't have a thousand opportunities."

The woman next to us stared at Brian. She elbowed her friend and the next thing I knew, they were offering us their stools. Brian gestured for me to sit, so I did. I had to admit—knowing a celebrity did have its perks.

Brian turned to the bartender and pointed to my orange juice. "*Lo mismo, por favor.*" His accent was near perfect. Of course. Only after the bartender poured his juice and placed it in front of him did he turn back to face me. "I know, Frankie. I was afraid if I told you, you'd refuse to come."

"Yeah, I probably would have, because it doesn't make any sense for both of us to be here. Why couldn't you give Dr. Porter's presentation?"

Brian tilted his head. "You really don't want to be here? I would've jumped at the opportunity to present at a conference like this my first year in the program."

A piece of hair escaped from behind my ear. Even my hair refused to make things easy. "No, I'm grateful to present here. Terrified, but grateful. What I mean is, it was expensive to come to Panama. Why spend the money if you were coming anyway?"

"I told you, your ticket didn't cost anything, and the hotel room was paid out of a different department's budget. They had a surplus they needed to spend, or their budget would be reduced next year, so it was a win-win for everyone."

"That's not the point! You had to do a lot of work to get me here. Why, Brian? Why wouldn't you just present the paper yourself?"

His Adam's apple bobbed up and down. "I don't know. Maybe because I thought you'd do a better job. Or maybe because I was already presenting one paper, and that stressed me out enough. Or maybe because I didn't want to come by myself to another conference where everyone's more interested in my age and my stats and my hairstyle than in what I actually have to say."

I remembered what Tamara had said about Brian's notoriety and the way people had swarmed him in the conference hall. Sympathy stirred, but I shut it down. I wasn't ready to let him off the hook. "You certainly didn't look stressed out on the stage this afternoon. You looked more like a rock star performing for his fans."

Brian looked at his hands. "Looks can be deceiving. Tomorrow, you'll get to be the rock star, and the fans will all be yours."

My laugh came out more bitter than funny. "I don't think rock stars usually begin their set by throwing up."

Brian's smile softened his entire face. "You'd be surprised." He picked up his glass and took a long sip. "How do you think I slept last night?"

"Like a baby?"

"Actually, yes." He wiped his mouth with a napkin. "I don't have one myself, but I understand they take forever to fall asleep, wake up frequently, and cry for hours on end."

"So you didn't sleep well. Why not?"

"Good lord, Frankie, did you see how many people I presented to today? You're not the only one who worries about failing. I was nervous! I wanted to do a good job. I didn't want to get up there in front of all those scientists and fall on my face."

"Well, you definitely didn't fall on your face. Everyone loved you up there."

"Yeah, I know. I saw that once I got a few minutes into my presentation." He grimaced. "I won't lie. It felt good. Too good. When I sense the audience approves, it energizes me. I feel invincible, like I must be the best there ever was."

"What's wrong with that?"

"It's a double-edged sword. When I think the audience doesn't approve, things get ugly. I lose all my confidence, think I must be the worst there ever was. That's why I get so nervous. Because when I do well, it's great, but when I screw up, it's agony."

"I don't know. I've never seen you screw anything up. From what I can tell, you ace everything you try."

He laughed, and this time he sounded bitter. He took a deep breath. "The thing is, even when I do well, the satisfaction doesn't last. In the back of my mind, I have this voice that tells me I'm a fraud. Sure, I put on a good show, but what other people like is just a mirage, an illusion we invent together. If they knew the real me—well, let's just say they wouldn't be so impressed."

"Is the real you so different from what the rest of us see?"

"To be honest, I don't even know." He turned to the bar.

We sat in silence. Hunched over his glass, Brian looked less like a lion and more like a frightened rabbit. Something inside me softened. I wanted to lean over and give him a hug, but my muscles wouldn't move. Instead, I asked him a question I'd been wondering about for a while. "Are you going to leave Berkeley next year? I've heard rumors."

Brian turned back to me, eyebrows raised. "What, are you so eager to get rid of me?"

"No, but I hear you have your pick of offers."

His head dipped noncommittally. "There are several biotech companies recruiting me, but that doesn't mean I have my pick. The one I really want keeps stringing me along."

"Someone's stringing you along?" I slapped the bar. "Wow, the tables have turned."

He gave me a look of mock shock. Or maybe it was real. "I don't string people along."

"No, never."

"You're the one who keeps disappearing, going back to the hospital to investigate your birth without inviting me, complaining about being at a conference whose principal transgression appears to be that I'm one of the attendees."

"Okay, you may have a point. I'm sorry I didn't tell you I was going back to the hospital, but I thought you wouldn't want to come. And I'm not unhappy to be here. Just uncomfortable."

"What a relief."

"You know what I mean." I raised my glass of orange juice for a toast. "To good conversations at neuroscience conferences in beautiful places." Brian clinked his glass against mine. As we drank, the other thing he'd said bounced around in the back of my mind. I put my glass down. "So I'm curious, why biotech?"

Brian took his time finishing his juice before answering. "Good money mostly, but it's a growing field with opportunities for advancement."

"*Hmmm.*"

"What, you don't approve?"

"No not that. I guess I just didn't expect it, but it makes sense."

"What did you think I would do?"

I played with my glass on the table. "I don't know. Something different? Some kind of research nobody realized we needed until you pointed it out, and then it seemed obvious? I'm not sure. I hadn't really thought about it."

Brian's face tensed in thought, but he didn't say anything—just turned to the bartender and waved, pointed, and bowed over his steepled hands, ordering two more drinks without a word.

The silence gave me more time to think—too much, really. By the time I took my glass from the bartender, I could no longer keep my thoughts to myself. "I know I shouldn't ask this, but I can't help it. Why isn't Lillian here instead of me? I mean, I know she had a cruise, but she would have figured out a way to come if she were presenting. She's the one who should be here. She's so brilliant, and she works so hard—"

"I checked with Lillian after we spoke." Brian leaned back in his chair. "And she agreed that you were the one who should be here. The way you think about things . . ." His voice drifted off. "You're the one who initiated the dog experiment. And you recognized the possibility of mental models. You deserve to present the results."

My heart quickened. "So you think I should mention mental models in my presentation?"

Bits of amber I'd never noticed before flecked Brian's eyes. "I'm more interested in what you think."

"I don't think it matters what I think. Dr. Porter made it clear I was not to mention mental models under any circumstances. It's his experiment and his paper, so it's really up to him. He practically promised to hunt me down if I even thought those words during the presentation." I paused. "But then again . . ."

"Then again what?"

"Then again, I'd feel like a liar if I didn't say the results suggest the possibility that rats are capable of making mental models. It's so obvious, at least to me, and rats aren't exactly the world's most appreciated animals, so it seems like a real missed opportunity to right the scales, you know? What? Why are you smiling like that?"

"It's like I was just saying." He took a big gulp of his orange juice. "You think differently than most. It's a good thing."

"So what should I do? Break my promise to Dr. Porter or disappoint myself and regret it the rest of my life?"

"What exactly did you promise?" Brian's face was smooth. "Word for word?"

"He said, 'There will be no mention of mental models in your presentation,' and I said, 'Yes, Dr. Porter. I understand.'"

"So you can't bring up mental models *in the presentation*." Brian leaned toward me.

"No, I can't. Not without breaking my promise."

"But technically the presentation isn't the only thing you do when you're up there, is it?"

"No, you're right!"

"Only you can make it sound like you're arguing with me even when you're agreeing."

"Sorry, I mean, yes, you're right! So you think I should tell them everything?"

"I think what I admire about you is how true to yourself you are regardless of what others think." His eyes practically glowed with intensity.

"Oh my God, thank you." The swirling floodwaters within me drained. "You just saved my life." He kept staring at me. I had the idea he wanted to kiss me, but that was ridiculous. I straightened in my chair and looked away. "You have no idea how much that was stressing me out."

When Brian didn't say anything, I looked up. His smile was gone. "You really don't get it, do you?" he asked.

"Get what?"

"Nothing." He reached in his pocket and pulled out his wallet. "Hey, you wanna get out of here?"

I didn't. The idea of being alone in my room made me feel hollow, but I nodded anyway. I finished my juice, then followed Brian out of the bar, a dark cavern of disappointment expanding in my chest.

———

I had plenty of time to think on our way down to the lobby. People kept stopping us to talk to Brian, and even though he declined each request with a quick smile and a promise to make time later, it took us fifteen minutes to walk down two flights of stairs. By the time we reached the elevators and Brian told me he should let me get some rest for my big day tomorrow, I was ready.

"I'm not really tired yet. It's still early in California. Do you want to maybe go for a walk?" I held my breath.

He didn't answer right away, just stared at the elevator doors as they opened and closed. I began feeling dizzy. Finally one corner of his mouth lifted, and he offered me his arm. "Why, I thought you'd never ask," he said in a slurred drawl.

I sucked in air like a drowning bird. "Is that supposed to be a Southern accent?"

"Why, yes." He used the same tortured pronunciation. "Bless your heart for noticing. I'm not lucky enough to be Southern by the grace of God, but I do what I can."

"That's a relief." I put my arm through his. "For a minute there I thought you'd had a stroke."

He snorted.

As soon as we stepped out of the air-conditioned lobby, the warm night wrapped its arms around me, and the scents of earth and flowers filled my nose. I headed in the direction of the park Tamara had shown me earlier.

"What do you plan to do once you get your PhD?" Brian's voice was as warm as his arm where it touched mine.

"Study what exactly depression does to the brain so we can find better treatments."

"So you'll look for work in a pharmaceutical company?"

My shoulders bunched together. "Maybe. I'm not sure a new drug is what I'm after. There are already so many of them out there."

"So what, like a medical device or a biotech company?"

My foot hit the ground too soon. I stumbled. "I-I don't know."

Brian grabbed my arm with his free one to steady me. "Don't worry. You'll figure it out. I think it's great you want to help people with depression. Sometimes I think I should too, you know, because of my sister, but . . ."

"But what?"

"I don't really want to. Does that make me a terrible person?" His smooth skin creased as he looked to me for an answer.

"I don't think so. Depression is . . . complicated." Something about his expression reminded me of James. "Was your sister's depression hard on you?"

We turned into the park. Brian looked up at the trees, their forked branches reaching to the stars like so many extended prayers. "It was harder on my parents," he finally said, "but yeah, it was hard on me too. Though it probably would have been easier if I hadn't had my head up my ass."

I laughed at the image; I was being inappropriate given his sober tone, but I couldn't help it. "Why do you say that?"

"The fall of my sister's sophomore year, she got accepted into a statewide music competition. She was already starting to struggle, and music was the only thing she had any interest in doing anymore. My parents thought going would help her feel better and maybe inspire her to improve her grades, but they were worried about her being away from home on her own, so they made me go with her."

We walked around a small fountain, its shadowy water turning belly-up in constant acrobatic tumbles. "I was horrified. I worried my sister would do something embarrassing and everyone would know I was her brother and think I was crazy too." He stopped walking and turned to me. "I know now she isn't crazy, by the way, at least no crazier than anyone else. There are lots of ways to certify insanity, enough that anyone can qualify if you dig deep enough. But back then I thought she was just being dramatic to get attention. I thought she was choosing to be that way."

"Choosing to be so hopeless she wanted to kill herself?"

Brian conceded with a nod. "Yeah, I know. It's crazy. But I was just starting high school, and all I could think about was how everything would affect my place on the totem pole.

Anyway, I went to the competition with her. Sure enough, the first night, right after I'd finagled my way into the room of someone with a PlayStation, my worst fear came true. One of the teachers came running down the hall yelling my name. She told me my sister was having chest pains and couldn't breathe and was going to the hospital. My sister had given her my name. She wanted me to go in the ambulance with her."

"Wow. Was your sister okay?"

"Physically, yeah, but I knew she would be. We'd taken her to the hospital before for panic attacks, so I knew the symptoms. I knew they wouldn't find anything wrong with her."

"You must have been embarrassed when it happened again."

"No. I wasn't. Because I didn't go with her. I told the teacher I didn't have a sister, that she must be looking for some other Brian."

I grimaced. "Yikes."

"Yeah, *yikes* is right. My sister stopped trying after that. I didn't realize it until later, but that was when things began to get really bad. She failed her classes and stopped playing music altogether. That's why I thought she wanted to be miserable, because she wouldn't even try to do the things that made her feel better."

I flinched as if he'd hit me. My brother had said the same thing when I was depressed. I'd had no answer to his accusation but shame. "I don't know why it's so hard for some of us to be happy."

Brian looked down at me, his eyes soft. "You know, I've come to believe there's more to life than happiness."

"What do you mean?"

"I've never had a hard time feeling good, but I'm still not *happy*."

I furrowed my brows at him.

"I always have this feeling like there has to be more than

this, you know? I'm not *un*happy, but I'm also not—I don't know"—he looked out over the plaza—"satisfied. No matter how much I accomplish or how good I feel, I always want more. And if there's one thing I've learned from my sister, it's that there's more to life than feeling good."

"Like what?"

"Like caring about others. She hates to see anyone suffer. You know what she did when we got back from the music competition in high school? She told my parents I'd gone to the hospital with her. Later on, when we were alone, she told me she would have done the same thing I did if the tables were turned. She made me believe it too, even though it wasn't true. She knew I felt horrible for abandoning her, even when I didn't know it yet. I'd betrayed her, but she still didn't want me to suffer." His eyes were like polished quartz in the moonlight. "You remind me of her in that way. Your concern for the rats in the lab, and the risks you take to prove animals are smarter than we think . . . I wish I could be more selfless like the two of you."

My stomach twisted. I owed him an explanation I desperately didn't want to give. "It's not entirely selfless. I've been having these dreams."

"You mentioned before that a dream gave you the idea that rats might communicate ultrasonically."

"Yeah." My shoulders climbed to my ears. "I have these dreams where a group of animals talk to me and tell me things."

"What kinds of things?"

"That rats communicate ultrasonically. That I'm not who I think I am. That I'm not from where I think I'm from."

"Is that why you've been trying to find out more about your birth parents?"

I nodded, not easy to do with my neck muscles locked tight. "It's also why I've been trying to learn more about how much animals might be able to communicate."

Brian studied me as if I were an aberrant lab result. "So you think these dreams might be more than dreams?"

I nodded again, nearly pulling a muscle. "The animals tell me stuff, like the ultrasonic thing, that I have no way of knowing. They quote poetry I've never read by real writers I've never heard of. It's not that I think they're real necessarily," I hurried to add. "It's just I don't know what's going on, so I'm trying to find out more."

Brian inhaled audibly. "Why does it matter if they're real or not? Why is it so important to you to know for sure?"

I forced my shoulders down my back and stretched out my neck. "I don't need to know for sure if they're real. I just need to know they could be." The freedom of the realization was like a food I'd never tasted before. "I don't need to know they're real as long as I don't know they aren't."

"What do you mean?"

"I need to know the possibility exists."

"Why?"

"It's like you said: there has to be more than this. If there's a possibility the animals are more than a dream, maybe there's a possibility that despite all appearances and evidence to the contrary, I belong somewhere."

A strand of hair fell across my eyes. Brian reached out and tucked it behind my ear. "Frankie . . ."

I picked up speed like a lumbering locomotive cresting a hill. "That despite all the pain, something good might come from all of this." I waved in a circle, indicating myself, the plaza, the world.

"Frankie—"

"That despite my previous failures, I might actually succeed in doing one small thing to make this world better, something that actually matters."

"Frankie." Brian's voice was jagged, insistent. "Frankie, Travis was a fool."

The train screeched to a halt. "Wait, who?"

"The guy who dumped you in high school." His dimple peeked out from his cheek like a shy toddler.

"Why?"

"Because you're one of the most amazing people I've ever met." He drew me to him. His earthy scent enveloped me. "And I know you've already improved the world, because my life is so much better since you've been in it."

A charge of energy surged through me. He was going to kiss me. I now knew I'd wanted him to since the moment we'd met.

But the seconds rolled by, and he didn't move. The fountain's water chortled like a carefree baby in the darkness. The air grew cold. Maybe I misinterpreted the moment. Just because he liked me didn't mean he wanted me.

But then a deep, baritone voice rang out in my head. *The trick*, it rumbled, *is to see through our own fear to theirs.*

And I understood. With a trembling hand, I brushed Brian's cheek with the back of my fingers. It was warm and soft. My heart in my throat, I got on my toes and kissed him.

He kissed me back, softly but urgently, and when I began pulling away, he reached behind my head and brought me closer to him.

After a minute, he moved his head away from mine, his eyes liquid gold. "Thank you," he whispered.

"For what?" His body was warm against mine.

"For doing what I've wanted to for a really long time."

I smiled. "I should be thanking you."

"For what?" He took my hand in his and twined his fingers through my own. Electric sensations tingled where his skin touched mine.

"For proving anything *is* possible."

He didn't say anything, just pulled me closer, his body trembling where it touched my own.

I laughed at the irony. I felt at home for the first time I could remember, four thousand miles away from where I lived.

CHAPTER 21

When I fell asleep that night, I ran through the woods with something heavy in my mouth. It dragged on me, pulled me back, but I pushed forward, my commitment forcing me on. I couldn't drop what I carried. It was my responsibility. Too much depended on it.

The world around me shifted, rippling into a sunny yard with a tractor, truck, and barn in whose shadows I hid. The dry, soft dirt around me beckoned me to bathe myself in it. Green vegetables came up in the garden on the other side of the house, calling me as well—they would be moist and crisp and a little bit sweet—but I couldn't stop staring at a long, low building with no windows or doors across from the barn. Embers of anger and guilt erupted into flame within my breast. A nightmare unfolded inside those walls. I wasn't certain what it was, but I could sense the pain and suffering, and I had failed to stop it.

The scene churned again, and I watched, helpless, as several men demolished my home. The men sang and joked with one another as they ripped apart the sanctuary where my mother had fed and cuddled me. The memory of my mother filled me with sadness. Where the buzzing machines cut, they left gaping holes. What had been abundant and beautiful was in a flash nothing more than barren sky. Each violent crack, each branch that crashed to the ground like a fallen friend, ripped a matching hole in my heart.

The ground moved beneath me, and I was in a house looking down at two humans. They screamed at each other, taking turns, getting louder with each pass as if they were playing a game. Fear lay coiled at the heart of all human behavior, but I still had much to learn. How could they fail to see how much they hurt themselves when they attacked the other? I looked for clues, any hidden explanation. The male pointed his finger at the female, his face red. The female's face turned crimson too. Clearly, they both wanted the same thing, but each was refusing to give it first. Why? What was I missing? I froze almost too late. The female had turned to stare at me, was saying something soft to the male. He took off his shoe—in this they were united. I didn't wait to see what would happen. This part I knew and understood. I turned and ran back to the crack in the windowsill, back to the safety of the darkness from which I had come.

CHAPTER 22

hadows shifted. Light leaked through a thin curtain and revealed a bed, a small table and chair, and a suitcase on a stand next to a door. Nothing was familiar. Feet rose like a mountain range beneath a thin comforter. Human feet. Right. I rolled over onto my belly. Cool sheets pressed against my skin. I'd been dreaming, was now awake. In a strange place. A hotel. In Panama. With someone else. A man.

I pushed myself onto my elbows, looked around, but Brian was gone.

I swung my feet over the side of the bed and stood up—too quickly. A *whooshing* sensation emptied my head and darkness filled it. Dizzy, swaying, I lost again who and where I was, had no choice but to wait for it to return. Feeling crept back into my brain like blood into a thawing limb, and with it my memory.

A folded piece of paper I hadn't seen before rested on the table. Frowning, I remembered the last time a man had left me a note. I opened it anyway.

Sorry to leave without saying goodbye, but you looked like you needed your beauty rest. Thanks for last night. It was incredible. Hope you break a leg at your presentation.

I smiled. Brian had come back to my room with me after our walk. Being with him was a revolution, my cells flipping upside-down as we touched. Having his arms wrapped around me quenched a deep thirst I hadn't known I had. I had lain against his chest, my legs tangled with his, and let the well replenish.

The presentation. Shit. What time was it? I didn't remember setting an alarm. I searched around, fished out the small alarm clock from behind the table where it had fallen. 7:08 a.m. Falling back onto the bed, I released a sigh of relief.

It was going to be okay.

I had butterflies in my stomach, but they were the envoys of excitement, not the flag-bearers of fear. It was a minor miracle.

———

Standing on the stage later that morning, after breakfast and a shower, the insects in my abdomen remained enthusiastic. The faces that filled—or half-filled—the room seemed expectant but not critical, and they clapped politely when my name was announced.

I summarized current theories of sharp wave ripples, explaining that as mental replays of our experiences, they provided a possible mechanism for several tasks critical to learning: consolidating memories, incorporating information into cognitive maps, and planning future activities. I may have emphasized the cognitive maps part more than the others and paused a moment after I said it, but Dr. Porter couldn't fault me for citing previous research taken directly from our own report.

I went on to explain the setup of the experiment, how we observed mental replay in rats after they ran two different routes through a maze.

Then I got to the results. My hands shook, but it was still from excitement, not nerves. I explained how the rats' brains had replayed both routes through the maze in almost equal numbers, even though they ran one path more frequently than the other. There was no correlation, in fact, between the number of times they'd run a path and the number of times they mentally replayed it afterward.

This was the most important of our discoveries according to Dr. Porter. Our results suggested that hippocampal replay was not simply a reflection of an animal's most recent or frequent experience. Previous experiments hadn't shown this, and it suggested new possibilities for future research to better understand the exact mechanisms for learning within the brain.

I paused and examined the audience. A lot of people were looking down at the floor or at something in their laps. Good. They weren't enraptured by the official conclusion.

"There's one other result, however, I haven't yet mentioned." I took a deep breath and rolled my shoulders down my back. "Even though the rats only ran the maze in one direction, they replayed the routes both forward and backward, with nearly identical frequency." I paused, looking down at my notes for a long moment. "Thank you very much. I'm happy to take any questions you may have."

I scanned the audience again. Would it be enough?

The hand of a man sitting near the back wall shot into the air. Maybe so. "Yes, go ahead," I said.

"What do you think the significance is of the replay happening forward and backward?" He leaned forward in his chair.

I looked for Brian but didn't see him. "Well, I can't speak for the other researchers. I've already shared the official results contained in the report."

"Sure. But what do *you* think?"

I stood taller. My voice grew louder. "I believe the fact that the rats' brains went over routes they never experienced suggests they could have been making mental maps."

I searched faces for signs of skepticism and hostility. It was hard to tell for sure. A middle-aged woman in the front row wearing purple reading glasses and scribbling in a large notebook raised her hand.

"Why weren't mental maps mentioned in the report?" Only after she'd finished speaking did she look up to peer at me over the rim of her glasses.

I pulled up the phrase I'd rehearsed the night before. "Mental maps weren't part of the original research question." I was tempted to try to sway opinion against Dr. Porter but had decided being respectful would be best for all involved. "And there's no consensus on the research team about how to interpret those particular results."

The woman's eyes narrowed. I prepared to be skewered by further questions, but she just bobbed her head and went back to writing furiously in her notebook.

The next question was about the proportion of the replays in the different directions, and the one after that about whether there was any evidence the mapmaking influenced the rats' performance. My shoulders relaxed on their own. Not only was I not going to be attacked, but people were excited by the possibility of rats making mental models.

When the conference organizer announced we needed to vacate the room so the next presentation could begin, I was disappointed I wouldn't have time to call on anybody else.

As I walked off the stage, more than a few people came up to me, their voices animated as they shared related research or hypothesized about the implications of our findings. I was so caught up in our conversations, I didn't see Tamara until she stood right in front of me.

"Excellent presentation." She winked. "Though I thought the Q&A was even better."

The organizer waved her arms behind Tamara to get my attention. She tapped her watch and pointed to a few people already milling about on the stage, then inclined her head to the door to the hallway.

"Thanks," I said to Tamara. "Maybe we should take this out into the hall so the next session can get started."

"Yes, of course. I will not be long, but I have a surprise for you."

Curiosity stirred, but I didn't say anything. We made our way to the back of the room. Just as I followed Tamara into the hall, something warm grabbed my arm and pulled me aside.

"You did good, kid." Brian spoke into my ear without taking his hand off my arm.

"You were in there?" I turned to find Tamara and waved her over with my other hand. "I didn't see you."

"I got here late, and by then it was standing room only. I was in the back behind a couple tall Germans. Seems you're quite the rock star after all."

"Don't exaggerate. The room was only half full, at most."

"Maybe when you started, but by the end, it was packed."

Tamara came closer and nodded. "It is true. I walked in right after you started, and I almost did not get a seat. I think somebody may have been telling everyone it was going to be a fantastic presentation." She tilted her head to Brian.

"And I was right," he said.

I glowed so hard I could have lit the room. "Thanks, y'all." Tamara and Brian were staring at each other. "Oh, right. Y'all haven't met. Brian, this is Tamara. She's a grad student here at Panama Tech University. Tamara, this is Brian, a research associate at the *University of California* at Berkeley."

"Pleased to meet you." Brian stretched out his hand. The other one still held my arm.

"The pleasure is all mine. I am a big fan."

Brian's grip tightened on my arm. I spoke before things got awkward. "Tamara was just going to tell me about a surprise she has for me."

"Oh, yes." She turned to me. "I would be honored for you to accompany me to the San Blas Islands this afternoon.

We will return tomorrow morning, with lots of time for your other presentation." She turned back to Brian. "Would you like to come too? You would be most welcome."

My heart beat faster. "Really? There's enough time to get there and back before tomorrow afternoon?"

"Oh, yes. My father sometimes rents his planes to the people there to bring in supplies. There are some computers now they have been waiting to fly in. It is a very short flight."

"Then sure, that sounds amazing. Thank you so much."

"Oh good!" Tamara clapped her hands together and turned to Brian. "I hope you will join us as well?"

For once, Brian wasn't grinning. "I'd love to, but unfortunately, I can't." He let go of my arm, and I shivered. "I'm actually heading back to the States today. My flight leaves in a couple of hours."

I tried not to let my disappointment show. "You're not staying for the rest of the conference? Why not?"

He wrinkled his nose like he smelled something rotten. "Politics and the capricious nature of the free market. I couldn't spend more to come here than an associate professor was spending to go to his conference, and flight prices doubled if I stayed past today. Sorry, Frankie. I really would have loved to see you present about the dogs."

"It's okay." It was odd, trying to reassure him, like our roles had been reversed. "It's not like you don't know what happened."

He smiled, with both corners of his mouth. "Thanks for understanding. Seriously though, Frankie. You should be really proud of yourself. I know I am."

I went from sixty watts to a hundred. "Thanks. I am."

Brian pulled his phone out of his pocket and checked the time. "I need to head out. Nice to meet you, Tamara. I hope our paths cross again." He leaned over and kissed me on the cheek. The hundred watts turned into a thousand. "Break a leg," he whispered in my ear. "And thanks again."

"Thank *you*," was all I could think of saying.

He picked his way through the crowd like a cat, avoiding all the closely-packed people without leaving any trace or trail. I kept staring at the end of the hall where he'd disappeared until Tamara put her hand on my arm. "Do not worry. You will see your *amigo con derechos* again soon. And in the meantime, you are going to one of the most beautiful places on earth."

The sadness receded as I imagined blue sky, clear water, and sandy beaches as far as the eye could see.

CHAPTER 23

We sat on the smallest plane I'd ever been on. It had only four seats and a small cargo area in the back piled high with boxes. Tamara beamed at me. She'd been grinning like a slender version of a fat-Buddha statue since the moment I agreed to go.

"You are going to love the islands," she sang. "They are . . . they are . . ." She looked to the ceiling for words. "Magical. Totally magical."

"What's magical about them?"

"Oh. Oh. Oh. Well—" Her eyebrows drew together. "I cannot describe it. You have to see for yourself. But the people are amazing. The islands belong to an Indigenous group called the Guna. I told you some believe they are the happiest people in the world, no?"

"Yes. Maybe because they live in paradise?"

Tamara wagged her finger back and forth. "No. It is beautiful, but there are challenges too. The oceans are rising, causing more and more islands to disappear. And many villages are poor and have little access to drinking water, doctors, or sanitation. Plus, they are human, so of course nothing's perfect. But they have something else. Something bigger. They risked much fighting the government authorities and protecting their way of life. I think this is what makes the islands so special."

"What is it about their way—" I wanted to know their secret, what could be more valuable than clean water or healthcare, but the engine roared to life, swallowing the possibility of further conversation.

We flew over many shades of green, the patchwork alternating between light and dark, large and small. After less than an hour, one wing tilted higher than the other and a large expanse of aquamarine water swung into view, then gave way to a village—a collection of small, wooden buildings hugging the coast interspersed with palm trees and dirt streets.

It didn't look that magical.

We landed in a field just outside the village. Short, powerfully built people lined the runway, trying to catch glimpses inside the plane. A few ran alongside us but quickly disappeared from view.

As we deboarded, a man with small, round glasses approached Tamara and said something in Spanish. The only thing I understood was *Tamarita*.

"Maximiliano," Tamara said, turning to me as I stepped onto the dirt runway. "I would like you to meet my friend Frankie. Frankie, Maximiliano is the schoolteacher here."

"Nice to meet you." I extended my hand.

"The pleasure is mine." He took my hand between his deep ocher ones and held it for a moment. "We are honored by your presence."

A group of young men and women walked up to us, a few breathing heavily. Several clapped Tamara on the shoulder while others called out, "Tamarita."

Tamara greeted them with names I couldn't quite make out. When she got to the last woman, her grin faded. "Where's Colibrì?" Nobody answered her question. She *tsked*, then said something in a language I'd never heard before.

One of the women replied and Tamara closed her eyes, her face sagging. But a second later her lids flew back open, and soon she was back up on the plane, a computer box in her arms, dancing to the cheers of the young men and women below.

"These are the first computers to come to this village," Maximilano explained to me. "Now we will not have to travel to a city to do email or the internet."

"That's great," I said.

But his expression was darker than everyone else's. "I hope so," was all he said.

With the young men and women, we unloaded the boxes and walked them back to the village. As we passed the first buildings, dozens of children spilled into the streets. They raced to us in colorful clothing, shouting, and climbing over each other to put their hands on the boxes.

In between the children, I caught glimpses of bright-ly-colored tapestries hanging from strings between the buildings. Made of contrasting, interlocking lines and vibrant geometric shapes, they depicted birds, fish, butterflies, flowers, and unrecognizable beasts in colorful patterns. They were of the same style, I realized, as the mural I'd seen in the restaurant with Tamara. Was this the magic she'd mentioned earlier?

A cheer went up as the first computers reached a building of fresh wood with a bright metal roof. I squeezed through a tangle of people in the doorway to deliver my box inside. Just as I settled the computer on the ground, something tugged the bottom of my shirt. A small boy with black hair wearing nothing but red shorts waited for me to lean down, then yelled something in my ear. I couldn't understand a word of it, but he smiled at the end with such excitement it didn't seem to matter.

"He says your boat is ready," Maximiliano translated from behind me.

"What boat?" I looked around for Tamara but couldn't find her.

"The one that will take you to the lodge." Maximiliano put his box down as well. "You did not know? You are not sleeping in the village tonight. You are going to the resort."

"What resort?"

"On the island where the tourists stay. But do not worry." He put his hand on my shoulder. "It is not like other resorts. It is a lovely place."

———

The island wasn't big. It barely fit six wooden cabins that didn't even take up any space, built as they were on stilts over the water.

Blue sky and turquoise water stretched to the horizon in all directions, the sea so shallow you could see fish beneath the surface, as well as lines of shimmering sunlight that danced and shook on the sand with each passing wave. Inside the cabin, waves slurped the shore with peaceful regularity, like a hypnotist's clock, or a slow heartbeat.

I was just putting my bags down on my bed when Tamara stuck her head through the door. "Are you ready?" She was breathless from running.

"Ready for what?"

"A boat ride! Put on your swimming suit."

"Where are we going?"

"It is a surprise."

I didn't love surprises, but her last one had been pretty good, so I changed clothes and walked to meet her on the other side of the island at the dock.

The air stirred lazily, humid and cooling, causing the giant leaves of the palm trees to shudder with pleasure. I passed two women peeling potatoes outside the kitchen. They smiled and waved at me with the same enthusiasm they'd shown just a few minutes before when I passed by the first time on my way to the cabin. I waved back, grateful for their warmth, especially now that I was only wearing a bikini and a thin sundress.

When I got to the boat, Tamara was waiting with a man who appeared to be in his twenties, though it was hard to tell from his smooth, copper face.

"Frankie, this is Aresio, the lodge's naturalist."

I shook his hand, which was colder than I expected.

"Do you like your cabin?" he asked, helping me onto the boat.

"Yes, it's lovely. So relaxing."

A light went on in Aresio's dark eyes, making them shine. "Yes. Because of the wood."

"The wood?"

"We make our houses from wood because the spirits of the trees remain inside and protect us."

I imagined trees extending their limbs over the roof of the cabin and forming a shield to fend off storms, invaders, and loneliness. Something shifted within me, as if settling into place. "Very nice." I scooted next to Tamara on the bench.

Aresio pushed us away from the dock and into the shallow, blue water. While he busied himself with the engine, Tamara stared over the waves, beyond the horizon.

"Who's Colibrì?" I asked, my tongue causing the *r* to tumble rather than flutter.

Tamara looked at me, her eyes wide. "How do you know about Colibrì?"

"You said, 'where's Colibrì?' when we got to the village."

We passed an island that was nothing more than two palm trees and a circle of small rocks surrounding them.

"Oh, right. I forgot." Tamara looked back out over the waves. "Colibrì is my girlfriend."

"I thought you said you weren't dating anyone."

"Yes, I wanted to say she is my ex-girlfriend. She broke us last week."

I started to correct her, but her way of saying it seemed more accurate. "I'm so sorry. What happened? If you don't mind my asking."

"Of course not. She says she still loves me, but she was born on the islands and wants to stay here. She thinks it cannot work, that we are too far apart."

"Neither of you wants to move?"

Tamara's head shifted as she scanned the horizon. "It is not the kilometers that are the problem. It is the distance."

"I'm sorry, I don't understand."

"Colibrì studied marine biology at university. She likes Panama City. But she is also studying the traditional ways of her people. She believes they will be needed to heal the world's current sickness." Tamara turned back to me. Her amber eyes were fuzzy at the edges. "I love it here. I told her I would move here after I finish my program. But she thinks I cannot be happy here. It is too isolated, too quiet, she says, not enough to keep my big brain busy." She looked down at her feet. "I am a coward. I did not even argue. My father agreed with her, and I was scared they were right. I guess I can be whatever I want except the person who does what she wants."

"I'm so sorry," was all I could think to say.

Tamara tossed her head, the wind carrying her hair like brown waves behind her. "Do not be. What is meant to be will find a way. Colibrì has gone to some islands to the south to do research. We will not see her. And we are in San Blas! It is sunny, the sea is beautiful, and we are going to visit the wise ones. My sorrows are small next to this."

The motor quieted. We drifted onto the beach of an island that was just big enough to house a handful of palm trees, some piles of rocks, fallen coconuts, and a few small bushes.

"We're here!" Tamara said, hopping out of the boat to pull it farther up the sand.

"Are you ready?" Aresio slung a large bag onto his small frame and stepped off the boat.

"Ready for what?" I followed them onto the shore.

"To visit family."

My eyes scanned the island again, but nothing was large enough to hide any people. "So where exactly is this family we're going to visit?"

"Under the water."

"They're . . . scuba diving?" I tried to piece the puzzle together.

"Swimming." Aresio threw the bag onto the sand. He unzipped it, revealing snorkel masks and fins. "The fish, turtles, sharks, dolphins, whales—all animals are our family."

Something flapped within my chest, as if birds took wing with every word.

Tamara handed me a snorkel. "My grandmother used to say that humans are young souls in the world, born to learn and grow wise. If we are lucky, after many lifetimes, we gain enough wisdom and empathy to be reborn as animals—a great honor. Since some of the animals we see around us were humans in past lives who became wise enough to move on, she called them ancestor spirits. She would walk her father's farm every weekend to visit them and bring them gifts."

I stared at the sunlight dancing on the waves. What Tamara said was foreign, impossible, a frequency too high to exist, but it was also achingly familiar, as real as if she were telling the story of how my blood had gotten in my body, long forgotten but written in my cells.

"We visit our animal family to honor and learn from them." Aresio grinned. "And because they make us happy."

"See," Tamara said, picking up another snorkel. "I told you this place was magical."

I nodded, unable to speak, pulled on my fins, and waddled out into the turquoise water. Floating alongside Tamara and Aresio, I was careful not to stray too far until a bright yellow fish with black stripes swam up. He looked at me for a long moment, his dark eyes bursting with curiosity, then he turned to swim back the way he came, his tail end wiggling back and forth.

I no longer knew or cared where the others were. I swam after the yellow fish.

He led me to many more fantastic creatures. One fish's iridescent scales caught the light as she fed on the coral, her belly containing every color on the spectrum and then some. Another fish looked cartoonish with so much white surrounding her dark pupils that she made me think of the googly-eyes I used to love to use in art projects in grade school. Still another made me laugh as he swam by with large, sulky lips that looked puckered to kiss, all the while pinning me with a suspicious stare as if I might try to smooch him without his permission. Just afterward a large school of silvery fish who were headed in one direction turned about so abruptly and smoothly they looked like disparate elements of the same organism, taking my breath away with their synchronized grace.

Tamara and Aresio, the shore, and time evaporated from my consciousness like water from a heated pan. The sea's liquid arms held me afloat. Warm sun stretched across my back. Fish paraded their profound beauty before me, teasing me with it, drawing me deeper into the water, my tail wriggling to follow theirs.

The silvery school passed me again, ushering me into a new cosmos made not of earth nor sky nor water but of pure, brightly flashing life. Then something large on the sandy ocean bottom shifted and moved away.

At first, the ground itself seemed to stir, but as I got closer, a shallow mound distinguished itself, moving slowly along the ocean floor. Wide flippers extended off the mound, swooping into motion as it investigated various crannies in the coral. I paddled around to the side, careful not to move too much or too quickly. Large, heavily-lidded eyes regarded me from a pale-yellow head spotted with dark brown beauty marks. Oddly, the turtle's expression was warm and serene, as if I were a welcome part of her world and not some awkward, long-limbed intruder.

The memory overtook me like a tidal wave. Everything Sweetpea had begged me to remember hit so hard I couldn't breathe. And then, a few moments later, overcoming the shock, suddenly I could. My mouth opened reflexively to suck in a lungful of water. I spasmed, my body jerking. My flippers struck the sandy floor. I struggled to get my feet under me, but the flippers got in the way. I flailed my arms, but my body was too heavy. My lungs shrieked. A dark ring encircled my vision, drawing closer.

The turtle turned and swam calmly away.

I couldn't die yet. I needed to talk with the animals in the woods one more time.

CHAPTER 24

Darkness surrounded me.

I didn't bother putting my hand in front of my face to see if I could see it. I knew I wouldn't. I also didn't stare into the obscurity to see what shapes the shadows might form. I sensed that the only shadows I cared about weren't there—without looking, I felt their absence as sharply as an empty stomach or an icy breeze.

I got impatient. Just as I was about to call out, however useless I knew that would be, panting emerged from the darkness on my right. A moment later, the edges of a wolf's large body loped toward me. I looked around. The blackness eased and light had begun replacing it.

Mama stopped next to me, her chest heaving. "Is everything all right?" Her eyes glowed yellow.

"I'm fine," I answered before adding, "I think," vaguely recalling some sort of stress with a slight shortness of breath in my chest. "Why do you ask?"

"We didn't get the message you wanted to meet." Mama's breath was warm on my leg. "Then I woke to your alarm call."

I waved her concern away. "I'm fine. Where's everyone else?"

"They're on their way. Like I said, we didn't know you wanted to meet."

As we waited in silence, the light grew. Shadows resolved themselves into trees and familiar-looking rocks. Wind whispered through limbs above the uneven tinkling of the stream. I looked around for the moon and stars but didn't see anything. Instead, a dim glow emanated from the horizon.

Mama looked better than the last time I'd seen her. Her stance was more solid, her eyes more energized. As best I could tell, there was no longer an air of sadness surrounding her.

I was going to say something about it when loud, arrhythmic footsteps became audible on the other side of Mama. Roo ran to us, one eye wide and fixed on the wolf, his wings outstretched as his feet pounded the earth.

"Is she all right?" the rooster screeched even before he stopped running. "I was afraid this would happen. Humans are violent creatures. If anybody hurt her, I swear I'll—"

"She's fine," Mama said in her deep, reassuring voice. "She's right here." She tilted her head toward me.

Roo's eyes swung up to my height for the first time. "Oh." He sounded much more like his normal, acerbic self. "I see. Hello, Frankie. It's good to see you." His feathers all stood on end as he shook himself out. "For goodness' sake, if you're fine then why the dire alarm call?"

"I didn't know I made one." Something lumbered toward us in the corner of my vision—a four-eyed monster making grunting noises followed by soft, plaintive whispers. "What is that?" I asked.

But before anyone said anything, the beast stepped close enough to make out in the growing light. Shelly climbed off the back of what looked like the incarnation of darkness itself except for a strip of white peeking out here and there. As the turtle waddled her last leg onto the ground, she grunted. "Never realized . . . skunks were so . . . uncomfortable. . . . Did we make it . . . in time?"

"I'm fine."

Shelly looked up at me quickly—well, quickly for a turtle—with her mouth hanging open. Penelope trembled silently.

"No danger. All's well."

"Then why—" Shelly began.

"I don't know." My voice was impatient. "But now that you're here, there is something I'd like to tell you. Where's Sweetpea? Cockroach? Nameless One?"

"Nameless One is always here," Mama soothed. "I'm sure Cockroach and Sweetpea are on their way."

"I'm here," Cockroach rumbled from behind me. The light grew stronger, moving from twilight to daylight as I waited for the roach to approach. "You know, you can just let us know when you want us to come. You don't have to wake us up with some false alarm to call a meeting. Despite appearances, we insects need our beauty rest too." He made a deep, thunder-worthy chuckle as one of his front feet rubbed at an eye.

"Why is it daytime?" I asked as the sun peeked out from behind a tree. Colors sprouted around me like new buds in spring—green moss, brown leaves, gray rocks flecked with black—and the clear shape of bushes emerged where before there had been only vague shadows. "I always see y'all at night. What's going on?"

"You've never called us during the day before," Mama said.

My eyebrows bunched together as a loud scrabbling noise exploded in the treetop next to me. "I'm here!" Sweetpea cried, followed by more scrabbling. Her bushy tail streaked down the trunk. "Are you okay, Frankie? What's wrong?" When she pulled up short in front of me, her eyes were swollen with worry.

"Sweetpea..." Shelly drawled. "Why are you...so late. ...You missed . . . like everything. . . . Even Cockroach . . . made it here . . . before you."

It took me a minute to realize why the words sounded so strange in Shelly's mouth. Then I remembered—Sweetpea had said them the night I first met the turtle. The squirrel winced hearing them now.

"I'm sorry, Frankie." Her tiny hands writhed miserably. "I was napping. It took me a while to realize what was going on, but I got here as fast as I could."

I bent over and put the back of my hand flat on the ground. "It's okay, Sweetpea, There's nothing wrong. I'm fine. I just wanted to tell y'all something."

Sweetpea crawled onto my hand, her big eyes pleading. "Really?"

"Really." I repositioned her onto my arm in front of my stomach.

"So what do you want to tell us?" Roo's voice was sharp. "I'm dying to know why we were all assembled on such short notice."

I smiled at him before turning back to the squirrel who lay splayed on her belly across my arm. "Sweetpea." My throat constricted. "You're the baby squirrel I found whose mother had been hit by a car, right?"

Sweetpea sat bolt upright. "You remembered, Frankie? Frankie, how much did you remember?" Her voice was so high it sounded like it might break.

"But that was a long time ago," I continued, "so I don't understand how you're still alive."

The squirrel twisted on my arm, trying to get a better view of my face. "I'm her great, great, great, great, great, great-granddaughter. She was so grateful for what you did for her. And so am I." She attached her tiny gray arms to my belly in a hug.

"I'm so glad I was able to help her." I stroked her back, the fur dense and soft. "And that I now know you."

I turned to Shelly. "You're the turtle I moved to the side of the road." I waited for her to open her eyes and acknowledge me.

She hesitated a long moment before she did. "Yes . . ." She eyed me sharply. "Though I would have . . . made it . . . eventually . . . on my own . . ." Her eyes snapped shut again.

"Agreed. I apologize for any rough handling."

I turned to Penelope, who trembled as soon as my eyes met hers. "You're obviously the skunk I met in the park a few weeks back. We've already established that." I started to turn away before swiveling back. "You really don't need to fear me, you know. I'm not at all afraid of you."

Penelope's shaking decreased in intensity. "Thank you," she whispered. "That's good to know."

I looked into the treetops, but despite the lack of leaves, I still couldn't make out any owls. "Nameless One!" I called up to the high branches of the tree next to me.

"Um, he's over there." Cockroach indicated a double-trunked tulip poplar behind me with one of his feet. I searched its limbs but still didn't see anything.

"Thank you," I said to Cockroach. "Nameless One!" I called again, this time to the correct treetop. "You're related to the owl I saw in the park near my house after my parents told me I was adopted. The one who tried to tell me where I was from." I waited for an answer, even a simple *hoo*, but none came.

Sweetpea was squirming on my arm again. "Frankie," she squealed, oblivious to the intense stares of Roo, Cockroach, and Mama. "Did you remember? Do you know?" She caught the stares of the others and looked back and forth among them, half uncertain, half defiant.

I turned to Cockroach without acknowledging her questions. I wasn't ready to answer them yet. "You're the Cockroach who defeated me in the battle for my own apartment."

The roach drew himself up to his full height. "I was offering you companionship after a difficult breakup."

"I know." I grinned. "And I appreciate it."

"When did you put all this together?" the roach asked. "And when did you become so sure?"

I ignored his questions as well. "What I'm still unclear about"—I turned to meet the two dark eyes staring at me so hard they were about to bore holes in my skin—"is why Roo is here."

The rooster's head shot toward the sky and he flapped his wings. "Well." His voice was razor thin. "I know when I'm not wanted—"

"No, Roo, I'm glad you're here." I bent down to stroke him lightly between his wings with my free hand. He jumped at the first touch but after a moment he moved closer to me, and his body relaxed. "You've taught me so much. I count myself lucky to know such a wise and caring bird. What I mean is, I only saw you once at the farm near my foster mother's house, and that was after I'd already met you. I've seen lots of animals once, but they're not here. So why are you?"

Roo considered me carefully with his right eye. The green in his plumage was iridescent and beautiful in the light. "You don't remember another rooster on that farm a long time before?" His voice was quiet.

"No, I'm sorry. I don't."

His throat and chest expanded to twice their normal size as he breathed in, then returned back to normal as he released the air. "When you were still a chick living at your foster mother's house, she would sometimes take you to visit her friends at that farm down the road. One time you arrived just as they were trying to catch a rooster to"—he swallowed uncomfortably—"cook for dinner. When you realized what was going on, you wouldn't let them. You grabbed the rooster and refused to let go." Roo evaluated me with his left eye this time. "You were so stubborn and loud they eventually agreed. You helped take care of that rooster for as long as you lived with your foster mother. By the time you moved away, the young children who lived on the farm had all grown attached to him, and they kept him on. Since then, in honor of their kids, the family always keeps one rooster alive as a pet."

A heavy understanding dragged my insides to the ground. "Oh, Roo, I'm so sorry. No wonder you're angry with humans." My throat constricted. "You live, knowing that all your brothers are killed, and all your sisters are in cramped cages, never allowed to see sunlight or scratch in the dirt. You're all alone. The only one. You must be so—" I stopped, unable to continue.

Roo looked up at me, his dark eyes pleading. "I know it does no good to be angry. And I know not all humans are to blame. I try to remember that, I do. But no matter how hard I try, sometimes I forget." His eyes fell to the ground in front of him.

"Oh, Roo." His feathers were surprisingly soft. "You don't have to explain anything. I understand. If I were you, I'd feel the same way. Deserved or not, I think I'd hate them all."

The rooster's head lifted. "Really? You mean that?"

"I do. And the fact that you try so hard to help me proves how forgiving you are."

"That's true." Roo stamped his foot. "I am getting better."

"Roo," Mama growled. "We've talked about this. We all have our edge. You're working yours quite well."

"Right." Roo nodded vigorously. "Right, I'm working my edge. And doing well." He kept nodding as if to convince himself.

"So that brings me to you." I stood up and turned to Mama. "I don't remember meeting anyone like you in my waking life, and I'm pretty sure I would. So how am I connected to you? Why are *you* here?"

Mama's eyes seemed to dim for a moment, but they cleared so quickly I couldn't be sure. "You'll see soon enough, Frankie." Her voice was soft. "But it's not quite time yet for you to know."

"Okay, that's fine. I can wait." I luxuriated in their surprise at my lack of frustration like a cat in sunlight. "In that case, I suppose I should go ahead with the next thing I wanted to tell you." I paused, wanting to make them wait for the answer I had had to wait so long to find. "I remembered. Who I am. And where I'm from."

Six animal bodies froze, waiting for me to continue, the strain visible only in Sweetpea's pinched expression and her minutely vibrating body. How had I not realized it before? They felt so familiar to me, so comfortable. I could be my full wild self around them, all flashing teeth or trembling fear. It didn't matter. I could spread out all my smelly parts like last week's dirty laundry and it didn't erase their affection for me. Didn't impact it at all. Human love had never felt that way to me—it was much more fragile and easily withdrawn.

"I was one of y'all," I said. "We used to know each other. I'm not sure what type of animal I was, but I am one of you."

Several things happened at once.

First, the loudest noise I'd ever heard blew up beside me. After a moment, I realized it was the crow of a rooster. Before that realization sank in, a small object shot skyward directly above me. Somewhat belatedly, I realized the weight on my arm was gone, and again, somewhat belatedly, it dawned on me that the object was Sweetpea. She was stretched out to her full length in a triumphant arc across the sky, her heroic squirrel acrobatics in full force. When I looked past her, I realized there was no tree branch for her to grab onto. Her current arc was going to end in an unpleasant landing on the ground. She seemed to realize the same thing at the same moment, and she twisted around in the air, her eyes wide, her feet scrambling for something to grab onto.

Without thinking, I took a step forward—I'd make a higher and softer landing pad than the ground at least. As soon as I did, a loud moan pulled my attention downward. Penelope stared up at me with wide, hurt eyes—my foot was planted firmly on her bushy tail. I moved it quickly—well, quickly for a human. In that moment, claws raked into the soft skin between my neck and shoulder, and I let out a howl that sounded a lot like Roo's. Sweetpea clambered to get herself right-side up, then began yelling heartfelt apologies into my ear.

I stood still, trying to catch my breath until everything quieted down.

"Well, you certainly haven't lost your comedic sensibilities." Cockroach's rumble was dry.

"My comedic sensibilities?"

Before the roach could answer, Roo was yelling again. "That was hilarious." He hopped from one foot to the other, flapping his wings in delight. "I haven't laughed so hard since—ever, I think. Thank you, Frankie. I needed that."

I gave him a flat stare. "Happy I could help." I addressed Penelope with more emotion. "I'm so sorry."

Her eyes were still hurt. "It's okay. It was an accident."

"Yeah, but all the same, I'm really sorry."

Mama's muzzle nudged my thigh. "This is wonderful news, Frankie. I'm so glad you remembered."

"Yeah, but the thing I don't understand is why. Why did I return to being a human again? I mean, if Tamara's grandmother is right and with enough practice we move on from human forms to animal ones, then why did I come back?"

The wolf's eyes burned the same color as the sun that shone through the trees' naked limbs. "Human beings are a young species. In the beginning, when they first arrived, the rest of us provided food for them, looked after them, and taught them from the wisdom we had gathered over lifetimes. In return, they honored us and helped us when they could. They knew we share this world together for a reason, that we are related."

Mama paused, the only noise the sound of her panting. I wished the story would end there. "But as you well know, at some point humans grew up. They began to forget. A few worked hard and risked much to pass on the knowledge of our connection, but those with the most power started to believe humans are different, special, something more than the rest of us. Eventually, they began seeing us either as pests or a means to an end. They forgot who we are. They forgot who they are. They forgot how much we need each other. They no longer see that the damage they do to us they also inflict on themselves. And so the world has lost its balance."

She took a step forward, so close now her warmth radiated against my leg. "It is our sacred duty to care for and protect this world and all the inhabitants in it. So some time ago we asked for volunteers to take on human form again and help restore the balance."

My heart was so full it was about to burst, but my mind was an echo chamber. "So I am . . ."

"A brave, compassionate, and big-hearted soul who volunteered for a difficult task."

The other animals nodded in agreement, even Shelly, whose eyes were open.

I swallowed, waiting for a coherent thought to form. "And how do I do it? How do I help restore the balance?"

No one said a word. The forest floor rocked beneath me, and a searing white light flashed, replacing the scene around me.

When the animals reappeared, the forest behind them was gone. Only white space surrounded their forms. For a moment I saw them all in exquisite detail: Roo's iridescent green feathers, the proud curve of his tail. Sweetpea's large eyes and sweet, tiny paws. Penelope's dense fur and impossibly soft nose. Shelly's colorful carapace, the gentleness in her face. And Mama's quiet grace, the intensity of her eyes. I could even appreciate the beauty of Cockroach's efficient body and his delicate chin and antennae.

"So how am I to restore balance?" I poured the words out all at once as if upending a bag of groceries, knowing I didn't have much time.

They all opened their mouths, even Penelope, but before any sound reached my ears, the blanched light returned, and all was gone. A moment later, only Mama stood before me, surrounded by whiteness.

She moved forward until her head rested against my leg. "Frankie, you are one of the best of us. Never forget you have all the wisdom and strength you need within you. And we are all supporting you, no matter what. You will know when the time comes what you need to do."

I tried to believe her. "You promise?"

"I promise." She tilted her head, looked up at me. The skin above her eyes drew together. "I need you to promise me something as well."

"Sure, anything."

"Promise me that no matter what happens, you will love and have compassion for animals. All of them, Frankie. No matter what."

Her eyes were deeper than the space between the stars. A shiver washed over my body. "Is everything okay?"

"Everything is fine." Her tone conceded no ground. "Everything is exactly as it should be. Can you promise me this?"

"Yes, Mama, of course. I promise to love and have compassion for all animals, no matter what."

Air escaped from Mama's mouth and her body relaxed. "Good. I know you can do it."

I stroked Mama's soft back. Her spine lifted into my hand, and she stepped closer. Her warmth poured into me, accumulating, filling all the cracks and crevices, sealing all the leaks.

"Frankie," she finally said. When she looked at me, her eyes spoke of all times, of the beginning, and of the end.

"Yes?" I wanted to step into her eyes, live in the eternal spaciousness they protected.

"What you're doing isn't easy." Her large, grey head shook. "We always knew it wouldn't be. But you were willing to do it anyway, for all of us. We are grateful and owe you a great debt."

I couldn't take it anymore. I squatted on my heels and wrapped my arms around her large body. "I love you, Mama." The thick forest of her fur muted my voice.

"Oh, Frankie. I love you too." Her eyes welcomed me in. "More than you can imagine."

For a brief moment, I let it embrace me, this wolf's affection so alive and ancient that its heart beat against my own with the pulse of every being who ever lived. It wrapped itself around me, wings fluttering against my cheek, scales streaming alongside my skin, feet pounding against my bones, engulfing me, consuming me, burning through me until there was nothing left.

Mama's form and my own disappeared. In the remaining emptiness, the space where we had been, only affection remained, my love for her and hers for me, this immense and shining *we*.

CHAPTER 25

My body convulsed to force a flow of water up my trachea, a river trying to compel its current back upstream. I nearly choked again. Instinctively, I turned on my side. Coughed it out, little by little. My lungs screamed for oxygen. Eons later, the tiny river's flow shrank to nothing. I took a spasmodic breath in. The world settled.

Slowly, haltingly, uncertainly, I rolled onto my back. Sand and sky were replaced by two pale, drawn faces. I nearly choked again, this time on laughter that rose in my throat.

"What's wrong? Did someone die?" I pretended to look around for a dead body. The movement made me cough up more water but was worth it.

For a long moment nobody moved a muscle. Then Aresio's face relaxed into a grin, and Tamara threw her head back and roared.

For my part, I kept coughing and laughing until everything clamoring to emerge from within had spilled out into the sunlight.

CHAPTER 26

On the flight home, my bones were fortified by the rock-solid certainty that I was capable of anything.

When I got back to my apartment in the early morning hours, however, "anything" didn't appear to include keeping my eyes open. I lay on my bed and greedily collected the eight hours of sleep I'd lost on the plane. When I woke in the mid-afternoon, five texts from Lillian stacked up like cars at rush hour on the home screen of my phone, each one asking me to call her when I got home. Why would anyone ever send more than one message to say the same thing?

I called her back, and we decided to meet up for a late lunch.

———

"How was the cruise?" I slid into the booth across from Lillian at the vegetarian Chinese place not far from downtown.

"Oh, it was okay." She flicked her eyes to the ceiling to show her disdain. "You know how wretched cruises are, all waterslides and goofy dance classes."

Her expression was contemptuous, but the corners of her mouth had risen, almost imperceptibly. I took a guess as to why.

"Really, you think that's wretched? I personally wish I had more waterslides and goofy dancing in my life."

Lillian's whole body vibrated with excitement, and she leaned in close, lowering her voice. "Okay, I may have been playing it a little cool. The waterslides and dancing were awesome. It was hella fun." She gave a happy sigh and straightened back up in her booth. "But I'm much more interested in how your second presentation went at the conference. Brian already told me how amazing you were at the first one."

"Oh." I picked up the menu. "I don't know about amazing. It went well, though. The second one did too."

"That's not what I heard. I heard you knocked everyone's socks off. Brian says at least half the conference was at your presentation. That's so great, Frankie!" The people at the booth next to us glanced over to see what the noise was about.

"Thanks." I grinned despite myself, then let it fade. How could I explain to her what had happened with Brian? I searched for promising words as if pulling out the edge pieces in a scrambled puzzle. Lillian spoke before I had enough to string together into a sentence.

"Speaking of Brian"—she made a face like she'd just swallowed sour milk—"he told me to have you call him. He says he has something important to tell you."

"Why are you making that face?"

"The Golden Child has been too busy with important matters to say more than three words to me since he got back. The only reason I found out how the conference went was I was able to corner him when I ran into him in the lab. It's a minor miracle I got out of him what I did before he ran off like a frightened bunny rabbit."

"Weird. What does he have to tell me? Is it about the experiment?"

"He didn't say, but I don't think so. He did manage to get out that there may be an issue with using the lab he found. They moved some things around, and he's not sure if all the equipment we need is still in there."

"I'll check it out." The words were hollow. All my attention was devoted to guessing what Brian wanted to tell me.

"Also, I almost forgot. Dr. Porter wants to talk to you. Last time I went to the lab, he was there, and he bit my head off when I told him you weren't back from the conference yet." She winced. "I'm happy to go with you if you want. It can't be that bad, whatever it is."

"Thanks, Lillian, but I'll be fine. I'm starting to think maybe the more upset Dr. Porter is, the better I'm doing my job."

Lillian cocked her head and evaluated me with sharp, bird-like eyes. "What happened to you in Panama? You seem different somehow."

"Yeah, I guess I am." The truth of it was a new flavor in my mouth.

Telling Lillian everything—everything except the part about the animals, because no matter how well she understood me, it was a lot to ask of her to understand that—took a long time. She kept asking questions and wanting details, which I was happy to provide. By the time I finished, we'd paid our bill and were getting impatient looks from our waiter.

But Lillian wouldn't say goodbye until she'd told me about ten times how proud she was of me. When I leaned forward for a hug, she tensed with surprise at first, but then pulled me in close. Why had it never occurred to me to hug her before?

I walked back to campus and called Brian. It rang and rang, but he didn't pick up. I left a message saying Lillian had told me to call him.

The day was mild and clear, but it was winter break, and campus was quiet. Questions yanked the bright streamers of my thoughts this way and that like a gymnast in a particularly violent ribbon routine. Would I see the animals again now that I'd discovered what they were trying to tell me? Why did Brian give a message to Lillian instead of calling me himself? Were there others who had returned to human form like me, tasked with the same purpose? Should I call my parents to let them know how the conference went, or would they ruin my good mood? Could I really figure out how to restore balance? I might as well have been asked to save the world, and my mission felt too big, too ambiguous, too unwieldy to possibly fulfill.

The psych building was open, but when I got to the bottom of the stairway that led to the underground labs, the door was locked. I started to turn around when a man walked out of the nearest lab and through the door next to me. I slipped in behind him before the door slammed shut.

The noise from the slamming door echoed through the dark, empty corridor. My heart hammered in my throat. *There's nothing to be afraid of,* I reassured myself. *It's just a dark hallway. Nothing here can hurt you.*

I couldn't remember which side of the lab we'd been in before. Naked without a cell signal, I stood in front of the placards for 25A and 25B trying to figure out which was more familiar. Neither offered whispers of recognition, so I *eenie-meenie-miney-moed* it and went with A.

When my fingers touched the door handle, a shock of electricity shot up my arm and into my chest, causing my heart to hammer again. Wishing I weren't so high strung, I took a deep breath, turned the handle, and pushed open the heavy door.

The room was dark. Large shadows were indecipherable in the dim illumination entering from the hall. I pawed the walls with clumsy hands until I found a light panel and flicked up the first switch.

The row of lights closest to me came on, revealing a few empty, metal lab tables standing in the middle of the room. I still wasn't sure if this was the lab we'd been in before, so I flipped the next switch. A machine I didn't recognize appeared just past the tables, and some empty cages at the back of the room. This wasn't the right lab. I turned to shut off the lights and head into the room next door—quickly, remembering Brian's warning about professors not appreciating students poking around their labs—when my eyes landed on a third switch. Something told me to turn it on. My heart in my throat, I did.

Nothing new revealed itself. The back panel of lights threw a harsh illumination on the cages at the back of the room as if they were performers at the world's saddest improv show, but there was nothing there I hadn't seen before. Shaking my head, I was turning back to the light panel once again when I realized that that wasn't quite true.

Something new had appeared when the light came on, or rather, a lack of something. A mass of darkness had remained in one of the cages even after the fluorescent light spilled over it.

My limbs filled with lead, I inched to the cages. Most of them were empty, their metal bars gleaming in the harsh light. But the one in the back gleamed less, a shadow in its center. When I finally made out what the shadow was, my body collapsed in on itself like a sinkhole.

Mama.

In the middle of a coldly glistening cage, the giant wolf lay on her side with her feet tucked neatly under her. Her bushy tail wrapped tightly around her hind legs, as if trying to protect them from the frigidity of the metal. She panted, her eyes half-open, staring at something I couldn't see. And where her soft, furry belly should have been was another absence, one that caused my undigested lunch to rise up in my throat—a black fissure, a yawning chasm, an open, gaping cavity around which writhed intestines, fat, and blackened skin.

"Mama!" I fell to my knees. "*No . . . no . . . no. . . .*" My fingers trembled through the bars. Her body was too far away to touch. "No."

The abyss took form within me.

My hands fumbled for a door but couldn't find one. They stumbled over a latch in the back, but a fat padlock barred the way. I stretched my arms around the cage and tried to lift. My muscles strained and swelled and screamed, but the cage might as well have been glued to the linoleum. My eyes scanned the room, hunting bolt cutters, a hammer, any heavy object to smash the padlock. But the tables were empty.

I checked my phone again. No signal. Lillian had spoken to me from inside the lab next door, but maybe she had a different provider. Should I wait for a signal to try to call for help or go out for bolt cutters myself?

Just the idea of sitting and waiting made me feel like I was breaking out in hives.

"Mama." I knelt in front of the wolf. "Mama, look at me." The words caught in my throat. Her breathing was so labored, her eyes listless. "Mama!" A galaxy without light stretched between my extended fingers and her limp leg.

The abyss within me grew.

Finally, the wolf's big head lifted less than an inch off the floor of the cage. Her yellow eyes were sightless, but they rolled in my direction. "That's right, Mama! Look at me. It's Frankie. I'm going to get you out of here, you hear me? I just need you to hold on until I can get some help. Can you do that?"

Her husky voice echoed in my head. "Frankie . . ."

"Yes, Mama, it's me. You hang on, okay? I'll be back soon, so soon, and then we'll get you out of here."

"Frankie." It was the whisper of a ghost, so soft I couldn't be sure it was there. "Don't go . . ."

"I have to, Mama. I have to leave if I'm going to help you. You hang on."

Fighting every last cell in my body, I pried myself off the ground. Made myself look once more at the bloody ruin of her belly. Wiped my cheeks with the palms of my hands and forced myself to walk to the door.

"I'll be back soon, Mama. I promise."

I prayed it was soon enough.

CHAPTER 27

As soon as I was in the hallway, I pulled out my phone. Still no signal. I ran to the end of the corridor, out the door, up the stairs, across the hall, out the main door into the afternoon sun. With shaking hands I called up Brian's number. The phone rang and rang. Cursing him for never answering, I left a disjointed message. *Call me as soon as you can. It's important.*

I nearly dropped the phone trying to end the call. Taking a deep breath, I called Lillian next, because even if I broke the padlock, I still needed someone to help me carry the wolf to safety. Uncharacteristically, she didn't answer her phone either. I left another message, this one in a somewhat less shaky voice and with more useful information.

I debated going home for a hammer or taking a short bus ride to the nearest hardware store for bolt cutters. I wished I had more experience breaking padlocks. I'd learned everything they'd told me to in school, but all of it was as useless now as a dollar bill in a desert. Finally, I opted for bolt cutters since they seemed the more certain option. I was racing to the nearest bus stop when a familiar-looking head with salt-and-pepper hair bobbed purposefully toward me on the sidewalk. I looked around, but there was nowhere to run to, nowhere to hide.

"Frankie." Dr. Porter had a strange smile on his face I'd never seen before.

"Dr. Porter." My tones were clipped. "I'm actually in a hurry, so if we could talk later—"

"Oh, this won't take long." He waved my concerns away. "I heard the conference went well for you."

"Yes, very well." I edged toward the bus stop.

"I'm glad to hear it." He took three rapid steps, closing the distance between us. "Because it's likely to be your last."

Anticipation pricked my belly like a series of tiny daggers. "What do you mean?"

His breath smelled like yesterday's coffee. "I mean, you really shouldn't betray the trust of someone with friends on the Helen Wills grant selection committee."

No words came, so I didn't say anything.

"There will be no more experiments for you. Not in my department, anyway. It looks like they've reconsidered their selection and decided to go in a different direction. Such a shame." The creepy smile returned.

Something within me fell but then anger rose, pushing, filling, spilling. "Thanks for letting me know. And thanks for letting me use the rats in your lab to prove that they are ticklish and do communicate ultrasonically. Couldn't have done it without your help." I shouldered past him.

"Just wait until your exams!" he yelled after me. "By then there won't be a single professor in the department who will even consider passing you!"

When I reached the bus stop, the bus wasn't in sight. I pulled out my phone and called Brian again. It rang and rang before going to voicemail. I left another message asking him if he knew about the grant getting rescinded and what was going on with Dr. Porter. A few minutes later, the bus came. I boarded as quickly as I could.

The ride was torturous. Knowing what was at stake, every stop was not only frivolous but dangerous, stacking greater odds against me. It was my fault the traffic lights kept turning red. I was the one who decided to get on this crawling bus. When we waited at one stop for several minutes for the bus to kneel down and for the driver to strap a wheelchair into place, I pulled out a clump of hair. I hated myself for hating them, but I did.

Just as we finally, finally approached the shopping center with the hardware store, my phone rang. I dug it out of my bag while descending the stairs, answering without taking the time to look, assuming it was Brian or Lillian, someone to help. But my mother's voice greeted me. I bolted to the store.

"Hi, Mom. What's up?"

"Hi, Frankie." She sounded different from usual. "Have you seen the news?" Her voice was like a glass bottle left in the freezer too long.

"What news?" I walked into the hardware store. Where did they keep the bolt cutters? "Actually, can we talk about it later? I'm kind of in the middle of something."

"Jesus, Frankie, can you think about somebody besides yourself for five minutes?"

I froze. More icy daggers in my intestines. "What's wrong?"

"It's all over the news. I don't know how you could miss it. Your father's drug is under fire. People are saying they're having all kinds of nasty side effects, and your father is taking the heat personally. They're claiming he encouraged doctors not to report negative results during the trials. Reporters have been hounding him. They've even shown up at the house and tried to get me to talk. I've never seen your father this upset, Frankie. You need to come home. He needs your support."

"Okay, Mom." I tried to keep the relief that none of my family was in immediate danger out of my voice. I walked to the sign I'd seen for tools. "I'll do what I can."

"I don't believe you!" My mother's voice was so loud I had to pull the phone away from my ear. "Whenever you require anything, your father bends over backward to help you, but when he has the audacity to need something. . . . I don't know why you refuse to spend time with us after all we've done for you, but you owe it to your father to come home now."

Anonymous tools lined the shelves. None were bolt cutters. "I'm sorry, Mom. I'll try, okay? And I'll call Dad soon. Now's a really bad time, but I promise I'll help Dad as soon as I can."

"I hope so, Frankie." Her voice calmed. "For his sake and yours, I really do."

I hung up just as I reached the bolt cutters. Grabbing the biggest pair, I ran back through the maze of displays to the registers.

Lines snaked everywhere. I chose the shortest one, tapped my fingers on the counter, peered over shoulders with narrow eyes. Obnoxious, I knew, but I couldn't help it. The cashier made a mistake and had to start over. The manager came over to reset something with her key. The man in front of me pulled out his wallet more slowly than I'd known a human could move and counted his change out in five cent increments.

Finally, it was my turn. It took all my remaining patience and self-control to stand there long enough for my total to appear in green, blocky letters on the register. I handed over the money with shaking hands, grabbed the receipt, snatched the bolt cutters, dismissed the proffered bag with a rude wave of my hand, and ran out the doors.

The bus was nowhere in sight. I claimed the spot closest to where I imagined it would stop. My phone began to vibrate violently in my bag. When I saw who was calling, my heart thumped the same way.

"Brian."

"Hey, Frankie." His voice was calm, detached, assured. "Welcome back."

"Thanks. Did you get my messages?" My voice was continents away from his—tight, impatient, squeaky.

"I saw you called, but I haven't listened to my voicemail yet. I do have something to tell you, though, and it's kind of important."

I scanned the oncoming traffic—no sign of a bus. "Okay. You go first then."

"To be honest, I'm not sure how to say this." The arctic pinpricks returned to my belly. "I, uh . . . well, after we went to the hospital, I had this nagging doubt. I didn't want to upset you, so I didn't say anything, but then you went back on your own and found out more, and I thought it was okay to do a little digging around. I didn't hear back from city hall until after I got back from Panama, though, and then you were still gone, so I couldn't—"

"Brian, for God's sake just tell me." A bus was coming into view, but it was the wrong number.

"Your mother's name wasn't Isabella Days, and she didn't die. Stella Richardson is your mother."

I couldn't feel my body or the ground beneath it. I was a disembodied gasp falling through space. "How could you possibly know that?"

Brian exhaled. "It didn't make sense that Jones remembered the incident but didn't know the name Isabella Days. I wondered if it was possible—if maybe . . . for some reason Stella didn't want to tell you she was your mother, so she pretended to be your mother's friend."

"She's not my mother," I whispered into my phone's plasticky mouth.

"Frankie, I'm pretty sure she is. I mean, your birth mother at least. I got to thinking: even if the hospital didn't keep birth records from that far back, the city should. I checked with city hall in Eureka, and they confirmed that the name Isabella Days appears nowhere in their records the month you were born. But their files do show that a Stella Richardson gave birth at Redwood Regional Hospital on March eighteenth to a healthy baby girl."

I closed my eyes and doubled over, unable to breathe. "Why?"

"Look, I don't know. I'm sorry to be the one to tell you, but I thought you should know."

A picture of Mama's ruined body and her missing abdomen intruded into my thoughts. I stood bolt upright, my eyes wide open and scouring oncoming traffic once again.

"Brian, there's another problem. I need your help—"

"What is it? Did something go wrong with the experiment? Dr. Porter was hinting at some type of trouble, but he wouldn't tell me what it was."

"No, I mean, yes, there's a problem with that too. Dr. Porter told me I'm not getting the grant. But that's not what I—"

"Frankie, be careful with him, okay? That man knows how to hold a grudge, and he's vindictive enough to go out of his way to make things hard for you."

Wasn't he the one who encouraged me to go against Dr. Porter's wishes at the conference? "Yeah, he made that pretty clear, but what I really need your help with is something much more—"

"Maybe there's still a way. I could talk to someone on the selection committee, find out what went on. Maybe it's not too late."

"Brian!" I was a raging river ready to jump its banks. "I don't care about the grant, okay? I don't care about Dr. Porter! Can you just listen for a minute?"

"Okay." His voice was stone. "I'm listening. What is it?"

"There's a wolf, in the lab next to the one you found for us to use. She's in a cage. With a lock. It's too big and heavy for me to lift by myself, but—"

"Wait, hold up. A wolf? In the lab? What are you talking about?"

"Yeah, I saw her when I went to make sure we had the equipment we needed in the lab. But I went in the wrong one. She's in a cage. She's not doing well. I have to get her out, but—"

"Frankie, calm down. There must be some mistake. It wasn't a wolf. There are no wolves in the labs. Dogs, maybe. I think there may be a few studies using dogs, but no wolves. And you can't mess with someone else's experiment. I'm sure they're taking good care of the dog, so you don't need to—"

"Wolf, Brian! She's a wolf! And she's going to die if I can't get her out of there. She's missing half her body; I can't even imagine how much pain she's in. I have to get her out. I have the bolt cutters, and I'm heading back to campus now. I just need someone to help me carry her once I get the padlock off, and—"

"Slow down." Brian's voice went from stone to knife. "You can't just barge in and mess with someone else's experiment. It's not right. And there are rules about the treatment of animals in the labs. Sometimes things look bad, but they use anesthesia. You need to trust that they're doing what they should and focus on your own experiment."

"No." I had a knife of my own. "No, they are most definitely not doing what they should, and I will not let her suffer any more than she already has. I'm going back there and getting her out whether you help me or not."

"I stuck my neck out to get a lab for you!" Other people at the bus stop looked at me, at my phone. "Don't do this. Some of us need to get jobs and can't afford to antagonize all the professors. This isn't just going to affect you. Don't drag me into your pointless little war!"

"It's not war, Brian." Hot, angry tears streamed down my cheeks. "It's just something I have to do."

"Well, leave me out of it then. And don't ask me to help you in the future, okay? I'm done. Maybe it's a good thing Dr. Porter killed your grant. Good scientists don't let themselves get so emotional."

The river jumped its banks but had nowhere to go. I wanted to scream. I wanted to smash something. I wanted to slam down my phone.

I swiped the red button and threw it in my bag.

I was barely aware of the steps of the bus as I boarded them, the passengers who shifted out of my way as I stalked to the back. I'd known from the beginning I couldn't count on Brian. I couldn't believe I had trusted him, let him in, actually believed he cared about me.

I tightened my grip on the stainless-steel bar running from floor to ceiling as if it were the only thing keeping me out of a pit of self-loathing despair.

———

By the time I got back to campus, it was a zombie wasteland. A dim twilight stretched over everything, and an eerie silence swallowed all sound. Lillian still wasn't answering her phone. I ran into the psych building and down the stairway to the double doors guarding the entrance to the labs like a blank-faced Cerberus missing one of his heads.

It was then, staring at my mangled reflection in the glass, my fingers stretched toward the handle, that I knew I had failed, and why.

The door wasn't going to open. It was locked. I'd learned as much less than two hours before but had forgotten in my panic. Cursing, I yanked at the door anyway, but it refused to budge. I banged on the glass as hard as I could, hoping it would shatter, but it didn't. It was thick. Solid. Unbreakable.

I banged and shook and kicked, but I might as well have been a hummingbird trying to move a boulder. Turning my back against the door, I slid to the floor. What was wrong with me? Why didn't I prop the door open when I left? I'd known the door was locked, could have planned for it, but now there was nothing I could do. Mama—who had asked me not to go, who I'd promised not to leave for long, who was trapped in there, suffering and alone—was going to die, all because of me.

Thought after bloody thought pummeled me, each one a blow to the gut. Eventually my brain must have grown tired after so much time in the ring. It retired back to its corner, sat down, prepared for the next round.

A small silence descended.

In the stillness, a different type of thought arose, a voice not from my brain but from somewhere deeper, a remote region long overgrown with brambles of neglect.

You helped all the other animals, it whispered. *That's why they were in the woods with you. Why would Mama have been there too, if not because you're going to help her?*

I took a deep breath. Strength flooded back into my body. I remembered that I'd heard Mama's voice in the hallway the first time I met Brian and Lillian at this lab. If she'd been there for that long, one more night shouldn't hurt.

You can still be with her, the voice whispered, so soft it would be drowned out by the breeze of a butterfly's wings.

How? I asked it in my head, then out loud, unsure how this part of myself communicated.

An image of Mama in the cage filled my mind—her thick fur, her chest rising and falling with each shallow breath, her head pushed up against the cold metal bars. Moved by instinct, my body knowing what to do, I wrapped my arms around her in my imagination, cradled her against my chest.

"You came back." Mama's murmur was frail, almost inaudible, but there was a strength, a steadiness to it as well.

"Yes, Mama. Of course I did."

Something moved in the shadows next to the wolf's head. Multiple feet tapped metal and the darkness rearranged itself into an insect shape that stared up at me with familiar eyes.

A smile formed like a grub in my chest, though I was too heavy for it to take wing. So this had been Cockroach's top-secret mission, the important work Mama said he was doing that made him late to our meetings.

"Cockroach is here too, Mama. We're both here for you. It's going to be okay."

Her body relaxed against mine. Her breath deepened. "Of course it is." She almost sounded like her normal self.

I leaned against the cold metal door that exiled me from her body, but in my mind I could feel her soft fur, her warm skin, the power rolling off her in waves despite her condition.

I let the truth of her words wrap its arms around me, holding me as close as I held her.

———

The next morning I woke up before my alarm and walked to campus in darkness, repeating a silent prayer that the blanket I'd brought would be enough to drag Mama to safety.

I took my first real breath of the day when the door at the base of the stairway conceded access to the underworld with a firm tug. My second came in the hallway outside lab 25A, the oxygen gifting me the strength I needed to swing open the heavy door and reveal its hidden contents.

Mama lay in the cage just as she had the day before. Her belly was a bloody, black crevasse. Her tail was tucked tightly around her legs. Her head was on the ground, her eyes closed. With shaking hands, I pulled the bolt cutters out of my bag and removed the padlock.

An otherworldly wail filled the room. I was aware of that before I registered the cold, stiffening body beneath my fingers. More than logic, it was the lack of warmth, the chasm where something tender and full had been just hours before, that brought home to me what was going on—Mama had lied to me. Nothing was going to be okay ever again.

Giant eagles of sorrow beat their wings within my chest. *Not again* repeated over and over in my mind.

I had just enough time to lean over Mama's beautiful body, kiss her on her forehead above the wise, golden eyes that would never open again, whisper into her ear that I loved her one last time, before the abyss swallowed me whole.

PART 3

CHAPTER 28

A harsh noise stole me from the darkness.

My implacable phone. I rolled over in bed, did my best to ignore it.

The cacophony subsided, but only for a moment before it began shrieking again. Grunting my frustration, I turned back over, grabbed the punishing device, pressed the button to silence it.

Or thought I did. A disembodied voice rose out of the discarded hunk of plastic, glass, and metal. "Hello?" it asked. "Hello?"

Moaning more frustration, I picked up the phone. "Hi, Lillian." My voice was flat.

"Frankie!" The word exploded out of the phone. "You picked up!"

"Yep, I guess I did."

"How are you? Are you okay? I've been worried about you. Why didn't you answer any of my messages?"

My brain couldn't even register all the questions, let alone begin to come up with answers. I settled on the last one. "I haven't had a chance." Only a half-lie, depending on how you interpreted it.

"Well, I'm glad you picked up now. Do you wanna meet for lunch?"

"I'm still in bed."

Disappointment filled the silence on the other end of the phone. Or maybe it was disapproval. "I can wait . . ."

"I'm not hungry." I wasn't being fair and knew it. "Sorry," I added.

"It's okay, Frankie." *Just barely,* her tone implied. "But I'm worried about you. Are you okay?"

"Yeah, I'm fine." Another lie. This one less than half true.

"Listen, I'm sorry about the grant. And the wolf. And . . . everything. I know it must be hard."

"I don't care about the grant." That part at least was true.

"Well, then I'm sorry about the wolf."

"It's not your fault." More truth.

"But I wasn't there for you when you needed me. I don't know if you listened to my messages, but I dropped my phone in the toilet as soon as I got home from the restaurant. It was completely destroyed. It took me five days to get another one, and in the meantime I didn't have anyone's phone number. I went by your apartment, but I guess you weren't home." Guilt, or maybe regret, laced her voice.

"It's not your fault," I repeated. The best I could offer.

"So do you want to talk about what happened?"

The barren, white ceiling of my bedroom swallowed the world. "Not really." I could hear her frown through the phone. "Maybe we could go for a walk later today." She was hopeful, resolute.

"Maybe." I was neither.

A heavy silence descended between us. Too heavy to lift. Then Lillian sucked in air. "Hey, what classes are you taking this semester? I thought you might be in a couple of mine, but I didn't see your name on the list."

I felt bad for her, doomed as her efforts were. "I haven't registered for anything yet."

"Frankie!" The cry was immediate and jarring. "It's been

a week since registration opened. All the good classes are full. Maybe all of them are full."

I closed my eyes, replacing vacant white with infinite black. "I don't think I'm going back."

The silence was even worse than the cry. I squeezed my eyes more tightly shut.

"You have to go back. They'll kick you out of the program if you quit like this. If you need time off, talk to your adviser. If you apply now, maybe you can take a leave of absence next semester. Maybe—"

"I don't want to go back. I don't think I'll ever want to go back."

I could hear the frown deepening; could see the two, telltale vertical lines appearing on her forehead.

"I know you're having a hard time. But come to a class with me on Thursday. It's on the neurobiology of consciousness, and I think it would be really interesting to you to see how it applies to animals, and—"

"Can't." I opened my eyes. "I have plans on Thursday."

"Oh, yeah?" Her voice rose, hopeful again.

"Yeah. I'm going to jail."

"Wait. What? Why?"

"Because I'm going to break the law." I sighed. "At a protest. Against fur."

"Why would you do that? Couldn't you just protest without breaking the law?"

"Sure. But I want to go to jail."

More silence. "Frankie, I don't think—"

"It's a good idea. Yeah, I know. But it is. It's the first good idea I've had in a long time."

More silence. "What law are you going to break?"

"Probably several. We're going to chain ourselves to barrels so we can block the entrances to a major department store. So nobody can get in and shop for the day."

"Because . . ."

"Because humans are cruel, violent creatures who massacre innocent animals—including other human beings—so that rich people can get richer and then show everybody else just how rich they are."

A shorter pause this time. "I see. You don't think it might be more effective to simply educate people with flyers or something?"

"I don't." I pushed myself up against the headboard. "Other people will be doing that, but I personally don't want to waste my time. People don't buy fur because they don't understand how cruel it is. They're just too selfish to care."

"And you think you're going to change that by breaking a law, getting a criminal record, and getting kicked out of the program? If you get convicted—"

"I don't care if I'm convicted! I don't care if I get a record. And I definitely don't care about getting kicked out of that fucking program." I gulped down air. "All that matters is protecting more animals from the cruelty of humans. But I don't expect you to understand that. You only care about your grades and proving to everyone you deserve to be here. Well, I'm over it. I don't care about those things anymore. I'm going to do something that really matters."

Silence. Then Lillian spoke in a voice so tight I thought it might shatter. "At least I'm not so dense I think that throwing a tantrum will do any good. Or too selfish to care." And then her voice did break, into thousands of piercing pieces. "Fuck, Frankie! After all the shit I've done for you!"

The anger stung, but it was a welcome surge of life in a sea of death. "Thanks for the noble sacrifice, Lillian. I'm sorry to have ruined your perfect, perfect life."

The phone turned to ice against my cheek. "How did you say it just now? You're over it? Yeah, well, I think I'm over it too. So. See you around, I guess."

I started to say something, but the line went dead.

A missed call from my mother stared up at me from my home screen. Hoping she didn't hate me as much as I deserved, I threw the phone on the table, turned over, and tried to go back to sleep.

CHAPTER 29

The morning of the protest, I got up well before dawn, left my apartment in the dark, and caught the first train to San Francisco. When I walked out of the subway station and past a few run-down hotels, the cold effortlessly penetrated all four layers of my clothing.

It wasn't long before combed-over poverty transformed into conspicuous wealth. I passed endless displays of over-priced clothing, jewelry, and handbags, all perfectly lit despite the hour, all screaming silently of life's meaninglessness.

When I arrived at the protest, I found the red-haired woman I'd spoken with before.

"You won't be getting arrested," was the first thing she said. "Not today, at least. What you choose to do on your own time is entirely up to you." From her wide, toothy smile, it was clear she thought she was doing me a favor.

She wasn't.

It hadn't been easy to drag myself out of bed that morning—it had been excruciating. I'd used up the last dregs of my energy and willpower, all so I could do one, small thing that mattered, finally, after so many days of feeling powerless.

And now this woman was telling me even that was beyond me.

"Why not?" My voice sounded whiny even to me.

"One of the trucks we were gonna use to transport the barrels wouldn't start this morning. They couldn't get it to work, and we couldn't find a replacement with zero notice. Without all the barrels, we can't create an effective blockade. The cops would just remove us in like ten minutes, and we'd go to jail before anyone could even see we were here. There's no point."

The cold void stirred in my belly. Still, I tried. "But even if it doesn't shut them down, going to jail would still make a strong statement, right? Like in the news?"

The fiery waves of her hair shook. "No, in this town, activists get arrested so much, nobody cares anymore. You've got to do something different to catch people's attention."

My life was as pointless as a thousand-dollar handbag.

"We're still going to protest," the woman said. "We'll hand out flyers and let them know we're serious about this. And you can get arrested next time, when we come back."

It didn't matter. That would be too late. But she obviously believed we could do some good today, and I didn't want to burst her bubble. "Okay. So where are the flyers?"

She pointed. I walked over and grabbed a stack, then found a street corner as far away from the other protestors as possible.

For a while, no pedestrians came by. When a few began to file past, they looked vigorously in the other direction, slowing their hurried strides just long enough to walk in wide circles around me. It seemed a lot of work to escape talking to me or taking a flyer.

But as the morning wore on, the sidewalk got too crowded for them to give me such a wide berth. Sometimes they saw me when it was too late to pretend they hadn't. "Would you like a flyer?" I asked. Nobody volunteered to take one, so I tried a different tactic. "This store sells fur."

I offered the information in the spirit of an insider's stock tip, but they acted like I was trying to hand them dirty toilet paper.

I overheard another protestor asking people if they wanted to help animals. People—at least some of them—seemed willing to take flyers from him, so I tried saying that, as nicely as I could, as I held out my offering. Still, nobody willingly acknowledged I existed.

Finally, a man about my age in a blue suit with a red tie and a fake-vintage suitcase paused to look me in the eyes. I held out a flyer, grateful for the kindness.

"Get a job," he said, turning away before I had a chance to respond.

I ran after his pointy leather shoes. "What makes you so sure I don't have one?" He didn't slow or make any indication he'd heard me.

"Hey!" I grabbed his shoulder. "Hey, don't ignore me."

He spun around, studied me with sapphire eyes. "Tell me then, why are you out here?"

"To stop people from selling fur. It's wrong."

"No, I know what your message is. I saw your signs on the way over." He waved a dismissive hand at my flyer. "I'm asking why you think blocking a public intersection and inconveniencing innocent people is going to help you accomplish anything."

"If people knew that this store sold fur"—I tried hard to believe it—"they wouldn't shop there anymore."

He snorted and rolled his bright blue eyes. "Your naïveté is adorable. Leaving that aside for a moment though, why shouldn't stores sell fur?"

A few people had stopped to watch our exchange. I swallowed. "Foxes and minks are wild animals. But they're kept in cages so small they literally lose their minds and mutilate themselves before they're anally electrocuted, gassed, or poisoned. A hundred million are killed every year. And that doesn't include the millions of wild animals who are caught in cruel leg-hold traps before they're drowned, clubbed, or suffocated."

"And?" He prompted me with raised eyebrows.

Flames licked the inside of my chest. "And isn't that enough suffering for you? Or what, you think animals don't feel pain?"

"No, I'm sure they do. But that's the way of things, right? We're carnivores. Top of the food chain. We kill other animals to survive. No use getting bent out of shape about it, is there?"

"We're omnivores, actually. And it's one thing to kill something to survive—quite another to kill it for convenience or greed. And even if you put aside the fact that most people eat way more meat than they need, there's no way to justify how we torture the animals before we kill them. But that's all beside the point anyway, because nobody around here needs fur to survive. We're torturing animals so that what—we can look good? Or prove to everyone else that we have more money than they do?"

He shrugged. "Survival of the fittest, right? We're smarter and stronger, so we use them however we want. It's just the way things are. You can't change it."

I was an over-inflated balloon. "But we can change it! If people like you would just be willing to try."

His grin was so patronizing I wanted to punch him in his pretty little face. "A lot of people resisted Darwin's ideas, but in the end they had to accept them. Survival of the fittest is a fact of life, like it or not. Nothing's going to change that. All you're accomplishing here is pissing off a lot of people and making them late for work."

Pressure pounded through every inch of my body. A cage holding the broken body of a wolf floated in front of me, making it hard to see the man in the blue suit or the people gathered around us. My mouth tried to form words, but my throat was squeezing itself shut. The pressure was going to rip me to pieces. I had to do something. Anything.

I realized I was staring at his briefcase only a split second before I found myself reaching for it, ripping it out of his hands. I only half-registered the wide-eyed look of shock on his face before I saw myself—as if watching a character in a movie with no control over her actions—run to the curb and hurl his bag in front of the wheels of an oncoming bus.

My abdomen settled. When the huge wheels crushed the bag and something crunched inside, I had a moment of utter satisfaction. All was finally right in the world.

I turned back to the sidewalk. Two ice-blue eyes screamed at me. "You're insane!" His movements were jerky—other people were holding him back. "You crazy bitch! What the fuck is wrong with you? My laptop and phone were in that bag! What the fuck!" He kept going, but I didn't hear what he said.

My own blood was too loud in my ears to hear anything else. I turned, wove through the crowd, sat down on the curb.

None of the onlookers came to talk to me. Neither did the protestors. Nobody said anything to me as I stared at my feet, a rushing in my ears, an erratic hammering in my chest. Was it possible something had exploded inside me—a blood vessel, an organ, maybe a demon?

Something tapped my shoulder. I turned around. A man stared at me with furrowed brows. It took me a moment to realize he was a cop. He said something to me in a quiet voice. I said something back. His brows were still furrowed as he stood up and indicated his car, which he'd pulled onto the broad sidewalk and was waiting with the door open. I didn't need him to tell me to go get in the back. I knew it was where I belonged.

It looked like I would be going to jail today after all.

CHAPTER 30

The worst punishment jail offered me was giving me so much time to think.

There was no shortage of other discomforts for those of us waiting to be processed, like having to use a toilet in plain sight of anybody walking down the hall or treating us like we were already guilty—which I was, I had to remind myself when the guards seemed overly gruff.

They shuffled me around like a hot potato from one holding cell to another, finally leaving me with twelve other women in a small room with a television blaring. The only places to sit were two benches along the walls, both of which were full when I arrived, as was most of the floor, so I made my way to the toilet, the only available real estate. I was so tired that I laid down on the painted concrete and slept in twenty-minute intervals. I couldn't sleep longer because either my hip would start aching or the aggressively cold air would make me start shivering, so I had to stand up and jump around for a few minutes before lying back down and trying again.

Guards at the door interrupted my routine now and then, calling my name like it was an accusation. The first time it happened, despite my despair, my heart surged with the hope that I was being released. But they just handcuffed me and dragged me to someone's desk to record my name, then injected me back into the cell. The same thing happened a few more times as they gathered my fingerprints, photo, and other information. Each time the guard came, I would ask questions about where I was headed and what was going to happen, but none of them bothered to answer.

But by far the worst part was having so much time to wrestle with my thoughts. At first, my mind sought all the flaws in my character, things I'd done wrong, and poor choices I'd made with the pre-programmed determination of a heat-seeking missile. Eventually, as time wore on, the missile's energy faded and became more scattered, like a flock of easily-startled crows that would take flight at the slightest noise or provocation. Their accusatory wings whispered that I'd failed once again and wondered if I would ever find anything to do that I was actually good at. They reminded me that the woman who gave birth to me didn't want me, that I'd somehow managed to alienate the parents who did, that Brian and Lillian hated me, and that I'd basically either disappointed or failed everyone in my life who ever tried to be there for me, even—and especially—the one creature who had loved me most of all.

I was alone. My current situation just made that fact more obvious. Nobody knew where I was, and they wouldn't have wanted to help me even if they did. I settled onto the floor and tried to get comfortable so I could do the only thing that made any sense—give up.

Which is why I was so surprised when the guard who called my name took me not to another desk or cell but a room I hadn't seen before with a long metal bench running down the middle. Behind a glass window was a petite woman in the same gray-blue uniform as the other guards. She had large curls piled on top of her head and rows of shelves behind her. When I stood in the doorway, confused, the woman waved me over, then handed me a bag with my last name, first initial, and a series of numbers written in permanent marker over it. Still not understanding, I stared at her. She waved the bag at me. "Here are your things."

I put on my hoodie and relaced my shoes, then walked through a door opposite the one I came in. Only then did I allow myself to believe that they might be releasing me. There was something different about this room. It was bigger, less harshly lit. There were chairs in it instead of benches, and they weren't bolted to the ground. The people in the chairs wore normal clothes and looked worried, but not desperate.

Several moments passed before I realized someone was trying to get my attention. She was sitting in a chair to my right, just inside my peripheral vision. She had a book in her hand that she was waving at me, and I recognized the book before I recognized her. It was a textbook we'd used in one of my classes last semester.

"Hi, Lillian." I slid into the seat next to her, staring at her feet on the brown, tile floor.

"Hi, Frankie. How was jail? Everything you'd hoped?"

"Maybe more." My voice was soft. "What are you doing here?"

"Really? I borrowed my parents' car and waited in one of the most depressing rooms I've ever been in for the last three hours—I had to move my car twice, by the way—so that you could imply I shouldn't be here?"

I swallowed, the dry squeak echoing in my ears. "Sorry, Lillian. I didn't mean it like that. I meant, how did you know I was here?"

"Oh. That red-haired woman from the protest called me. When you got in the cop car, you left your bag behind, so she grabbed it and used your phone to find my number. I guess I'm your most frequent contact, so she let me know what happened and dropped off your bag." She leaned over and pulled my backpack out from under her chair. "Don't say I never gave you anything."

"Thank you."

"Well, I wasn't going to throw it away."

"No, I mean, for that, but also for picking me up. And for not hating me. And for everything you've done. I really do appreciate how much you've done for me."

"Just promise me you won't go back to jail."

My gaze dropped to my feet. "I don't think I can." Before she could say anything, I added, "But I won't do it again over something as stupid as this."

"It wasn't stupid." I looked up in surprise. She was shaking her head. "Thoughtless. Short-sighted. Ridiculous, maybe. Foolish, definitely."

My face flushed.

"Which isn't at all like you." Her brown eyes softened. "And of course I don't hate you, Frankie. It takes more than a few harsh words to get on my bad side."

Warm waves of gratitude flooded me. "I'm so sorry, Lillian. I know you care about way more than your grades. I was being unfair and unkind."

"I wasn't exactly the queen of compassion either if I remember correctly." She stood up. "What do you say we get out of here?"

"Yeah, I can't wait to get home." I squatted down to pick up my bag.

"Oh, no. We're not going home."

I froze mid-squat. She must have been kidding, but when I looked over, her eyes were dead serious. "What do you mean? Where are we going?"

"You'll see," was all she said. Now she did smile, but it was the leer of a hungry feline, and it didn't make me feel even the slightest bit better.

CHAPTER 31

After we left the jail, Lillian drove us across the Bay Bridge. She exited the 80 at the first opportunity, and I soon lost track of where we were. We were headed north, I thought, and we stayed close to the water, but winding our way through access roads and side streets, my inner GPS got tangled.

Where was she taking me? Had my parents found out what had happened and flown out to yell at me? Were we headed to her parents' house? Some sort of scared straight program? A hospital?

My mouth went dry. Was Lillian going to check me into a mental health treatment center? I was pretty sure she could, whether I wanted her to or not. It seemed the most likely option—the most logical—and would explain the long drive, her secrecy about our destination, the oppressive silence that sat like a third passenger between us.

But when Lillian pulled the car to the curb, we were in front of a small stucco house. The front yard was paved except for two beds of flowers growing on either side of the walkway. I searched my memory but was sure I'd never been here before.

I followed Lillian through the gate in the metal fence surrounding the yard. Instead of going up the main stairs to the front door, she walked around the side of the house and into the backyard. The concrete extended all the way to a two-car garage that sat at the back of the property like forgotten stucco offspring. Lillian rapped on the rollup door.

A loud guitar squealed for a moment before diving into silence. Then the door squeaked as it rolled into itself, revealing a space far bigger than seemed possible from outside. Dozens of green plants covered the floors and tabletops, and through the jungle, red, yellow, and orange flowers big and small peeked out.

In the corner, an electric guitar rested on a stand next to a microphone, speaker, and amp. Framed, professional-looking concert posters, many of which were for a band called Underwater Tea Party, made a colorful backdrop to the equipment. Farther down the wall were a few thick, wooden shelves that held small, potted plants, bowls of fruits and vegetables, and glass mason jars filled with things I couldn't identify. In the far corner was a bed, neatly made, and the most beautiful mural I'd ever seen of a tree that extended up the wall and onto the ceiling, stretching its brown branches and wide leaves over the mattress like a benediction.

I was so fascinated by the room that at first I didn't see the woman standing to my left with an apron on her waist and a smile on her face. When I registered her presence, all I could think was how beautiful she was—tall and thin with tanned skin, freckles, and golden hair that cascaded over her shoulders like a semiprecious waterfall.

"So, Lillian tells me you're having a breakdown," the golden woman said.

"I did something foolish." My voice wavered. I hoped she wouldn't ask what I'd done. "But I wouldn't call it a breakdown."

Her blue eyes were fixed on mine. "Oh, it's not a bad thing. Some people call them breakthroughs to make it more palatable, but why put lipstick on a pig? You might as well be honest with yourself."

I wasn't sure if I was the pig in her metaphor, or if my meltdown was. I stared at her.

"Right." She wiped her hand on her pants. "Sorry, I'm not always so good with the niceties." She extended her hand. "I'm Gracie. I think you know my brother, Brian. Lillian thought it might be helpful for us to talk."

Was this my punishment for acting out?

I glanced at Lillian, who gave me a flat look, then turned back to Gracie, shook her hand, and introduced myself.

"Would you like a smoothie?" Brian's sister indicated a blender on a table next to the wall with the shelves. "I'm guessing you might be pretty hungry after spending the night in jail."

I looked at Lillian again, this time more angry than apprehensive. She gave me the same flat stare. "Sure, thanks," I said. "I am pretty hungry."

"I find that eating well helps with the depression." Gracie began pulling things out of bowls and mason jars. "That and exercise. And music, of course. I don't know what I would do if I couldn't play. What helps you when you feel depressed?"

"Um, I'm not really depressed. Not anymore, anyway."

"Really?" Her voice was bright and casual. She tossed a few peeled bananas into the blender. "Because from what Lillian told me . . ." Freezing, she looked up at me. "Right." Her tone softened, grew sympathetic. "You know, it's not a bad thing, Frankie. You've got to stop seeing it as some sort of disease or deficiency. There's nothing wrong with you for feeling depressed sometimes."

"I don't really feel depressed anymore. I'm on meds." At least I could say that much truthfully.

"Medicine can be a good thing." She peeled kale off its stems. "But the problem is, it makes us think it's fixing something that's broken. It's not. There's nothing broken about us."

I remembered the dozens of articles I'd read about the defects and dysfunctions of depression and swallowed down the sticky shame that rose in the back of my throat. "Isn't that kind of the definition of depression? Or any mental illness?"

Gracie threw the kale onto the table and groaned in disgust. "No. That's just what they say because experts hate to admit when they don't know something." She pushed her hair away from her face with her forearm. "Look, if depression were really caused by a deficiency, don't you think they would have figured out exactly what it is by now?"

I rubbed the back of my neck. "Maybe."

"Lord knows they've tried hard enough. But every time scientists think they've figured it out, they find new evidence that undermines their theories." She tossed the kale into the blender, then added soymilk, berries, and some powders from a few mason jars. "I used to think the same way you did. I figured something *must* be wrong with me—I mean, good lord, I certainly felt broken—and I thought someday someone would figure out what it was so I could fix it for good. But they never did, and then I realized why they never would."

Gracie turned on the blender, and I tapped my fingers on the table while I waited for it to quiet down so she could continue. But when it did, she just poured the smoothie into three glasses without saying anything else.

"And why is that?" I didn't manage to keep the irritation out of my voice.

"Because I don't think depression is a defect. I personally find it a healthy response to an unhealthy world." Gracie seemed angry, but not necessarily with me. "Shutting down when the world is falling apart isn't a sign of dysfunction. Plunging forward like nothing is wrong is what doesn't make any sense.

Have you seen the current state of the world? Depression won't let you keep living in denial. It's a forced stop. Like any pain—it gets our attention and directs it to where it's most needed."

"You really don't think there's any physiological basis for depression?" Lillian's tone was somehow both challenged and challenging.

"I can't say for sure. There may be physiological differences, but I'll never believe they're defects, and they certainly don't make what we're feeling wrong." Gracie handed us our glasses, then raised hers. "To mandatory time outs."

Lillian and I echoed her as we clinked the toast.

"So if the problem is the world," I asked, "does that mean we'll never get better?"

Gracie's eyes were serious. "Not at all. We can heal the world. We just have to start by healing ourselves."

"And how do we do that?"

"By doing the opposite of what our culture tells us to."

"What do you mean?"

"I should start by saying everyone's depression is different. That's why they get such different results when they try to study it. It's a complex beast." Gracie wiped her lip with the back of her hand. "But I'm certain when *I* feel depressed, it's because I'm neglecting my soul. We're always in our heads in this culture. Thinking about this, worrying about that, planning for the future. We think we always need to be logical, rational, prepared. We think we can solve everything by thinking."

Brains are fallible, just like anything else, Cockroach's voice rumbled through my head. *Which is why we're all given four ways to apprehend the truth.*

"But we need more than logic," Gracie continued. "More than money or status or survival. We need love, compassion, and kindness. Humor, beauty, and awe. We need the incomprehensible vastness of the ocean, the stillness of an ancient mountain, the power of a raging storm. Most of all, we need belonging and meaning. Without it, a part of us starves. It happens so slowly that most of us don't even notice. But our souls do. They speak to us when our guards come down. Or they make us so miserable we have no choice but to listen."

Spirit speaks differently to everyone. You have to learn how best to hear it for yourself. The words echoed in my head in the husky voice of the wolf, untethering a deep sadness in my breast.

"So you think your depression is your soul speaking to you?" Lillian asked.

"Absolutely." Gracie punctuated the word with the clink of her glass on the table.

"How do you know what it's saying?" I put my own empty glass down.

"Oh, that's easy. The things that bring up the opposite of depression—that make me feel energy, or love, or that there's good in the world after all—those are the things my soul is pointing me to."

My fingers tapped the table again. "But depression sucks. Why would your soul cause you so much pain?"

"Oh, I'm sure it doesn't want to, but I have a high pain tolerance. Do y'all want another smoothie?"

I waited for Lillian to say yes, then I did too.

Gracie's attention got lost in fruit bowls and mason jars. My impatience passed the high-water mark again. "What does having a high pain tolerance have to do with it?"

"Oh." Gracie paused, holding a mango mid-peel. "My soul had been trying to talk to me for a long time before I finally heard it. It started with a whisper, but I ignored it. It spoke up a little louder, but I didn't want to hear it. It tapped me on the shoulder, then eventually punched me in the gut when I refused to listen. But I'm stubborn, and like I said— high pain tolerance. So I still ignored it. That's when it got desperate and did whatever it took to get my attention—which it turns out is full-on, hard-core, knock-you-on-your-ass depression."

"So when you listen to your soul, you don't get depressed?" I asked.

Gracie emptied the mango peel into the blender. "Not exactly. Depression isn't something to be eradicated. Thinking it can or should be—that's the kind of thinking that brings it on in the first place. I still get depressed sometimes and don't know why. But it happens a whole lot less than it used to, and it doesn't kick my ass in the same way. And yes, when I listen to my soul, depression recedes, sometimes even disappears."

As the blender buzzed, an urgent question bubbled within me, but it was too primordial to put into words.

The blender stopped. "I'm making it sound easy," Gracie said. "It isn't. And I didn't learn this all on my own." I pictured her with her own team of animal advisers. I imagined hers would be led by a golden mountain lion. "I saw a great therapist for a long time. And I was in some support groups too."

All at once the primordial ooze in my brain solidified. "What if your soul is telling you to give up?" The words burst from my mouth as if propelled by a foreign power.

Gracie studied me over the pitcher, her eyebrows drawn together. "Well, often what the soul needs *is* to let go—of relationships or efforts that aren't supportive of who you are. Or of whatever it is you think should or shouldn't be happening."

"No." I stomped my foot like a five-year-old. "I mean, what if your soul is telling you that you're too inept to ever find what you're looking for?"

Gracie poured more green smoothie into my cup. "That's not your soul talking, Frankie. It's your brain."

Sometimes—it was Roo's acerbic voice this time—*your highly-evolved, state-of-the-art, exalted human brains obscure more than they illuminate.*

"I've done some really absurd things."

"Who hasn't?" Gracie leaned over her elbows on the counter. "Listening to your soul isn't exactly something they teach us in school. We may know how to do it when we're kids, but we've all forgotten. You have to learn how to do it again, and that takes time and help. A lot more of it than you'd think. Believe me, if I can do it, you definitely can."

Her perfect hair, unblemished teeth, and Martha Stewart living space belied her words. "I don't think so."

"Right." I realized that Gracie had the same dimple Brian did. "Tell me the most absurd thing you've ever done."

I shifted my weight to the other foot. "I said some really mean things to Lillian the other day."

One of Gracie's perfect eyebrows arched. "I didn't return any of my friends' messages for over two years. Pretended I didn't know them when I ran into them."

"Okay." Her words cried a challenge. I shifted my weight the other way. "My mother's been begging me to come home for over a year now, but I refuse, even though I know how much it hurts her. And my father's going through a hard time, but I can't get over my anger at him long enough to even hear his side of the story."

Gracie nodded, serious. "Yep. Okay. I used to tell my mother—the woman who gave birth to me—that I wished I had been adopted by a crocodile, because it would have made a more loving and caring parent. It was the first thing I said to her every day, my special way of saying *Good Morning*."

"I threw a man's briefcase beneath the wheels of a bus because he told me to get a job!"

A slow smile crept over Gracie's face. "Yep, I win." She sipped her smoothie, taking her time. "I've been arrested for three outbursts, the least offensive of which involved me, my neighbor's Mazda, a *Choose Happiness* bumper sticker, and a baseball bat."

I hated those bumper stickers, almost as much as I despised the ones that said: *If we're not supposed to eat animals, why did God make them out of meat?*

"So your neighbor didn't choose to be very happy about the damage to his car?" Lillian asked.

I laughed, tension bleeding out of me.

"No, he was quite hypocritical about the whole thing, actually." Gracie winked. "Listen, depression sucks, no doubt about it. But it's also taught me a lot. I'm no longer willing to live a life without purpose. And I think it's part and parcel of my gifts. Not that the tendency to get depressed makes me creative, but it's the flip side, you know? Part of being sensitive in a culture that isn't. Maybe if our world were different, it would be easier. I don't know. But I do know if I hadn't gone through hell, I wouldn't have nearly so much to give the world. I wouldn't be able to properly appreciate amazing people like you. And I definitely wouldn't be able to help the kids."

"What kids?" Lillian leaned forward, her glass already empty.

"I teach a music class for kids who are struggling with depression. Which reminds me." Gracie put down her glass and picked up a stack of papers from the corner of the table. "Some of my students are opening for my band next month at the Fillmore. I'd love for y'all to come if you can make it." She handed Lillian and me a flyer.

"You're in Underwater Tea Party?" I'd never seen Lillian's eyes so wide.

Gracie looked at the flyer as if confirming for herself. "Yep. Singer and lead guitarist."

"You guys are huge!" Lillian gasped. "Didn't I just read in the Weekly that you're about to sign a deal?"

"Yep. Which is why I'm finally in a position to move out of my parents' garage."

Gracie invited us to sit down, and Lillian proceeded to ask a million questions about what it was like to be in a band

and what her bandmates were like and where she got her inspiration. By the time we stood up to leave, the sun stretched long rays through the doorway from low in the sky, and I'd worked up the nerve to ask Gracie one last question.

I waited until we'd said our goodbyes and Lillian had started back down the driveway. Touching Gracie's arm before she could step away, I leaned in close and whispered my question in her ear. She showed her dimple one more time and said, "Of course." She pulled a pen out of her pocket and wrote a number on the back of the flyer she'd given me.

I thanked her, promised to come to her show, and walked back to the car, hope stirring to life within me like a new leaf unfurling in the first days of spring.

CHAPTER 32

My phone stared up at me, a challenge in its darkened face.

I reminded myself of what Dr. Barnes had said, and the definition of vulnerability she'd had me look up: *Susceptible to physical or emotional attack or harm.* If this didn't qualify, nothing did.

I picked up the phone and scrolled until I found the right number, pressed the button before I could talk myself out of it again. My stomach tightened with each successive ring. I held my breath and waited for someone to pick up.

For what felt like forever, nobody did. I was planning what to say in my voicemail when the ring was interrupted by a slight pause and then a strange voice that said, "Hello?"

It took me a minute to realize who it was. "Why are you answering the phone at Mom and Dad's house, James?"

"I'm housesitting for them while they're in the mountains. Why? What's wrong? Mom and Dad have been worried sick about you. What's going on?"

"Nothing. I've been busy."

"Really? How busy? Mom says she's left you like two hundred messages, but you haven't responded to any of them. They would've flown out there already just to make sure you're still alive if your friend Lillian hadn't called to let them know that you are."

I froze. "What exactly did she tell them?"

James made an impatient noise. "Just what I said, Frankie. That you're under some stress but not to worry because you're still alive and kicking."

"Okay, thanks for letting me know."

"Look, Frankie, is everything all right?" His voice softened. "Are you sure you're okay?"

"Everything's fine." Dr. Barnes's voice explained in my head that depression is an absence of connection, and connection requires vulnerability. I took a deep breath. "Well, maybe not fine, exactly."

"What's going on?"

I told him. It was easier than I expected. In fact, once the words started pouring out, I didn't think I would be able to stop if I wanted to.

When I finished, a heavy silence descended on the line. I figured James was trying to find a clever way to either point out my lunacy or say *I told you so.*

"That must have been hard," he said instead. His voice was strangely quiet. "Why didn't you tell me sooner?"

"I was embarrassed. I mean, I destroyed the possessions of a total stranger."

"No, I mean about the rest of it. About your birth mother, and the grant, and the wolf. That's a lot to deal with, Frankie. Maybe I could have helped."

My lungs expelled more air. "I don't know. Maybe I was embarrassed about that too. I mean, y'all told me not to alienate my professor, but I did it anyway. And the woman who gave birth to me lied to keep me out of her life. And sometimes . . ." I trailed off, not sure I wanted to say the words that were leaping into my head.

"Sometimes what?"

I took another deep breath. "Sometimes when I'm feeling bad, you make it sound like I'm doing something wrong. Like if I could just handle things as well as you, I'd be happy. Like it's yet one more way in which I fail to live up to my brother's shining example."

The phone was quiet for a long time. James cleared his throat. "Frankie." His voice was hoarse. "I don't think my example is quite as shiny as you think."

"What do you mean?"

"Most people don't think having five jobs in seven years is a sign of success. My former bosses sure didn't when I told them I was moving on. And I know Mom and Dad worry about my inability to settle down."

"But you get every job you apply for, and every girl you ask out says yes. You're always traveling to amazing places and taking Mom and Dad out to dinner, and you have tons of friends you're always doing cool stuff with."

"Frankie, I never feel good about what I'm doing. I mean, it's never enough. I'm always wondering if there isn't something better out there. I'm like a cat chasing a laser that disappears the moment I pounce on it."

"You really feel that way?"

"I do. And you know, I probably should have told you this before, but I've always been jealous of your ability to commit."

"Seriously?"

"Of course. Ever since you were little, you've been dedicated to what you care about. Like, stubbornly dedicated. You don't care what other people think, and you don't let anything or anybody stop you until you've helped those you set out to help or finished what you wanted to do." His voice got quiet. "You have no idea how many times I've thought about asking you how you do it, but I always chicken out."

"You know," I said, miles beside the point, "chickens are more courageous than most people give them credit for."

His laugh soothed my remaining rough edges. "Well, you would know. Listen, Frankie, I'm sorry I haven't been better at helping you when you're depressed. Sometimes I just don't know what to say when I see how much pain you're in. But that's another thing I admire about you. You're so strong. I don't think I could have gone through what you have and handled it so well."

"Handled it well? Are you kidding me? Did you hear the part about me going to jail?"

He chuckled. "You managed it better than I would have, that's for sure. I probably would have ended up in the hospital, and then jail."

An imbalance tugged at the back of my mind. "I'm sorry too, James," I said, attempting to true the wheel. "For being too caught up in my own worries to see you might need my help too."

"Don't worry about it, kid." For once I didn't mind him calling me that. It felt affectionate, not belittling. "Hey, sis, you sound really different today. What's going on?"

Being vulnerable might have been helpful, but that didn't mean I wanted to have so many opportunities to practice it. "I've started therapy," I whispered.

"What?"

"I've started therapy."

James's voice rose about three octaves. "What? Really? Are you going to tell Mom and Dad?"

"Probably not. I don't want to worry them."

"Yeah, good call. Just keep ignoring them. Nothing puts people at ease like refusing to talk to them."

"I know. I'm going to come home soon. It's just . . . what if they don't want to see me?"

"Frankie, Mom's been begging you to visit for over a year."

"I know, but I mean . . . what if I end up disappointing them even more?"

"I think they'd rather be disappointed than abandoned."

"But what if—"

"I don't know much about love, sis, but I do know families show up for each other, no matter how hard it is. And family welcomes you back home, no matter how long you've been gone. That's what it means to be family, whether it's the one you grew up with or the one that you choose."

Something within me settled at the truth in his words. "Thanks, James."

"Anytime, sis." After a moment he added, "You're both, by the way."

"Both what?"

"The family I grew up with, and the family I choose."

My throat constricted, and it was hard to get any words out. "I love you, James."

"I love you too, Frankie."

By the time we hung up, I didn't even have to talk myself into it. I just went online and booked my ticket home for the soonest date I could find. Or rather, the soonest date I could make.

Because my brother had helped me realize there was still one crucial, overdue, and virtually impossible thing I needed to do before I left.

CHAPTER 33

Crucial or not, I almost didn't do it.

When I gave my name to the lady behind the counter at Enterprise, she said there had been a mistake and they didn't have the type of car I'd reserved after all.

"That's okay." *I can go another time,* I was about to say. I hadn't slept well the night before. I was tired. Maybe what I was about to do was too drastic, too soon, or too much to handle in my current state.

But the woman behind the counter wasn't done. "We're going to upgrade you to the next class of car for free. Would a convertible Mustang work for you?" She said it with a bright smile I frankly didn't share.

But deep in my bones I knew my resistance was cowardice, nothing more. And I knew the guilt and disappointment I would feel if I bailed now would be far greater than whatever discomfort I might experience if I went through with my plans. So I took the Mustang, drove without stopping, and stepped out onto the landfill before I could change my mind.

A huge mound of garbage spread out before me like the rendering of a mountain made by a madman. Bits of bright blue, red, and yellow plastic poked out from a more understated background of dirty brown mixed with gray. A breeze blew and carried with it the smell of rotten eggs and something else that burned the inside of my nose. A flock of seagulls flew over the far end. On the edge to my right, a pack of large, yellow bulldozers slept nose-to-nose, as if trying to minimize their intake of the hostile smell.

I turned in a half circle. I'd hoped to have a sense of which way to go, like a dog who knew how to return home from hundreds of miles away, but all I felt was revulsion.

I'd had to make multiple phone calls and beg more than once to find out where to come. Apparently, the University didn't like anonymous callers asking how they disposed of the dead animals in their labs. In the end, I'd had to ask Lillian to ask one of her other professors. It turned out that the school had a vendor that picked up its biohazardous waste, but Lillian's contact wasn't sure of the name. I called three different providers of waste management services before I found the right one. When I asked what they did with the "waste" after incineration—I felt nauseated calling it that, but the man on the phone didn't understand what I meant when I used the word "animals"—he explained to me twenty times that nothing dangerous or contagious could survive the level of heat in their ovens. Only then did he admit they hauled their ashes to the local landfill. It took me two more calls to find out which landfill that was.

I should have taken Mama with me, I thought for the hundredth time. *I never should have let them dispose of her like some worn-out shoe they no longer had any use for.* But she was so heavy, and I was so upset, that I hadn't thought I could carry her body far enough, even if I could get it out of the building without anybody noticing. And Brian's warning that my actions weren't just affecting me had been ringing in my ears.

At least I was here now. Whatever remained of Mama's beautiful lupine body was somewhere in this giant pile of briefly used and long forgotten trash.

"I'm sorry, Mama," I whispered. "I am so, so sorry."

I pulled the flowers I'd picked on campus from my backpack. Closing my eyes, I imagined the great wolf in front of me, her dark fur thick, her gold-flecked eyes soft, her power barely concealed.

The chasm in my chest expanded.

How did you say goodbye forever? What words would be enough?

"I love you, Mama." My shoulders collapsed at the memory of her ruined body. "I'm sorry you suffered so much before you died." My upper body heaved, as if trying to expel the sadness. "I'm sorry I couldn't help you more."

Rivulets of warm water trickled down my cheeks. Words began flowing alongside them.

"You saw me for who I really am. You held up the brilliant truth of who I could be like a mirror, made it feel not just possible but inevitable. You loved me so much"—I choked on the words—"you loved me so much, there was no room to wonder if I deserved it. You taught me how big love is—how there's nothing it can't hold."

I took a shuddering breath. "I'll always be grateful, Mama. And I promise I'll do my best to accomplish what you sent me here to do."

I placed the pink and yellow flowers on the gray ground, wishing I knew where the wolf's ashes lay. I realized that her remains weren't the only ones in this artificial mountain. The ashes of millions of rats like Calvin, Hobbes, and Wilbur; mice, hamsters, and rabbits; cats, dogs, pigs, monkeys, and who knew how many other types of lab animals must all be clinging to the bits of the plastic out there too. Their bright, curious eyes stared at me through the bars of cages, unable to comprehend their incarceration. The enormity of it hit me like a hurricane, stirring up a tidal wave of anguish too big for me to hold. It broke over me, water running down my face now in torrents, rivers, floods far too wide for me to stem.

Other discarded bodies accumulated in my imagination as well—the billions we ate or imprisoned for food, the millions we skinned for fur, the untold numbers we murdered in our houses and yards for convenience without a second thought or robbed from the wilderness and sold or mounted on a wall. I suddenly realized the problem wasn't that they gave their lives for us, but that we weren't grateful—we didn't even recognize their tremendous sacrifice on our behalf. They gave us everything they could, and we threw them away.

The animals' unacknowledged gifts and broken bodies piled high before me until the mass was larger than Everest, my despair a bottomless ocean. I sank into it, falling to my knees, its salty water engulfing me, drowning me, overflowing out of me.

I felt I could cry the rest of my life without draining that sea of sadness, but after a long time, the sobs diminished until small gaps of stillness broke in between them. The gaps stretched longer and longer until the convulsions finally dissipated, leaving my body in peace like a spirit escaping its host.

"To all the animals we've ever used without permission or abused without remorse," I shouted so they could hear me from the highest mountaintop, "I apologize on behalf of all humans. To the billions we've killed without gratitude, I hope you're now at peace. To all our animal family, know you are loved and appreciated. We owe you a debt of gratitude. We're still here because of you, and some of us know this."

My body floated, strangely light, as I made my way to my feet. Dirty plastic stretched to the horizon, but inside I was clean and clear, like a stone scoured by heavy rain, or a clogged channel opened by a raging flood.

"Goodbye, Mama," I whispered.

A warm, glowing peacefulness answered, expanding within my breast—one last, precious gift from the wolf.

CHAPTER 34

I tried to remember all the details, significant or not.

Behind me on the left, where the land flattened out to the creek, there was a large, double-trunked tulip poplar. In front of that, several large boulders jumbled on top of one another like a flock of heavy birds. On my other side sloped a hill, smaller trees and bushes marching down its side but stopping short of the bottom to create a small clearing. Directly in front was the stout stump of what must have once been a massive oak.

It was dark in the shadows, but silvery light fell here and there in patches between the trees and covered the front half of the stump. Wind tugged at my nightgown for a moment before releasing it and moving on. The air was crisp and clean, and water tinkled softly over rocks beyond the boulders to my left. Other than that, and the occasional rustling of leaves by the wind, the night was quiet.

Or it was, at least, until a small, sweet voice emerged from the shadows. "Is she here yet, Mama?" it asked.

And then, causing my heart to skip a beat, the throaty response: "Yes, I believe she is."

"Then why can't I see her?" The small voice again, impatient.

Answered quickly, with a gentleness that pulled the scabs off my newly healing wounds: "Because she can't see you yet. Give her a minute, Sweetpea. This is all new to her."

It was too much. I was about to stop—to open my eyes and remind myself I wasn't actually standing in a dark forest with ghosts but rather sitting on a plane, flooded by artificial light, relegated to the center seat and much too crowded by the very real people sitting next to me—when a familiar, sharp voice spoke from behind me.

"That's when I asked if you realized we were all waiting for you."

I spun around. A tall rooster stood in front of me, his tail feathers arching proudly behind him, his eyes black diamonds.

"Roo!"

"Hi, Frankie." The rooster's voice was hoarse. "I'm afraid I still can't match Sweetpea's enthusiasm. But it's very good to see you."

"It's good to see you too." I blinked my eyes hard. Still, the forest remained.

"What are you doing here?" Roo asked. "We thought you'd given up."

"Given up? No, I— I was trying to remember the first time I came here so I could write about it, but then—then I heard your voice behind me. This isn't part of my memory, is it?"

"No. I got the call like always, so I came. The others are on their way."

Before I could stop it, the name flew out as if propelled from a cannon. "Mama?"

Roo flinched. "No, Frankie. When a form leaves that world, it's gone from this one too."

All the air escaped from my lungs. I nodded, the sadness too high in my throat to speak.

Roo cocked his head and considered me for a long time with his right eye. "What exactly happened to her? She just . . . disappeared one night. I know that means she died, but I don't know how."

"You didn't know where she was?"

His feathers swayed as his head shook back and forth. "No. Cockroach told us some people were doing terrible things to her, but he never said what, or why."

"How do you know that I know?"

He cocked his head the other way and I stared into his left eye. "Well, you were gone a long time, and you didn't really believe she was going to be here. Mama always said you would find her when you were ready."

"I found her, but I failed, Roo. I'm so sorry. I let her die."

Roo's voice was sharp again when he answered. "You weren't supposed to save her, Frankie. That wasn't the point. But tell me what happened. How much did she suffer?"

I winced, remembering the gaping hole in her side. "A lot, I'm afraid. They were doing experiments on her. I don't know what kind, or what they were trying to learn. But she was by herself in a cage in a lab, and they had removed most of her abdomen."

Roo's eyes were huge, and he stared at me, his body perfectly still. "I see." His comb trembled.

A small sob erupted from above me. The silhouette of a petite adult squirrel quivered on a branch. "Oh, Sweetpea," I said.

"How could you, Frankie?" she asked. Each word caused the pit in my stomach to grow.

"I tried to help her, Sweetpea. I wanted to get her out of there. But the cage was locked, and I had to get a tool to break it, and by the time I returned, the building was closed, and I couldn't get back in until morning." The breeze blew across my skin, raising goosebumps. "By then it was too late. She had already died."

Sweetpea made a rapid clicking noise at the back of her throat. "I'm not mad about that. Mama told us you wouldn't be able to keep her alive. I'm mad because you abandoned us. I didn't think you were ever coming back."

"I didn't mean to abandon you. I didn't think I was capable of coming back."

"We told you, you can come whenever you want!"

"I know. But after Mama died, it just felt . . . different somehow. Like the doorway to see y'all had slammed shut."

Her small head veered back and forth. "It didn't. It was open the whole time. You just never walked through."

I looked at the ground, then back up at the squirrel. "I'm sorry. I wanted to see you. I guess I just forgot how for a while."

She peered down at me with eyes as hard as rocks. "You promise?"

"I promise. I missed y'all more than you can imagine."

Before I knew what was happening, she'd leaped off the branch, landed on my shoulder, and was nuzzling her nose against my neck. "I missed you too," she said in the same sweet voice I remembered.

"Where are the others?" I asked Roo, but it was Sweetpea who answered.

"Right there." She pointed behind me, where a quiet skunk and surly turtle sat next to each other on the tree stump. Cockroach rounded the edge to join them.

"Hi, Penelope. Hi, Shelly. Hi, Cockroach."

"Hi, Frankie," they each replied. We settled into a heavy silence.

"I can't believe I'm never going to see her again," I finally said.

"But, Frankie—" Sweetpea started to say.

"We're all sad," Roo cut her off. "But Mama knew it was going to happen. She prepared us. She made sure you were ready before she went."

His words made me remember something I'd thought about a lot the first few days after Mama died. "Why didn't she tell me where she was sooner? I could have helped her if I'd had more time."

Roo exhaled sharply. "We already told you. Saving her wasn't the point. That's not what she wanted."

"Why not? Why would she possibly want to suffer like that?"

The rooster looked at me, and it struck me that something was different about his eyes. They were soft, I realized, like liquid shadow. "She didn't want to suffer. That's just the situation she found herself in. What she wanted was to help you see things through her eyes."

"What do you mean?"

"*If the doors of perception were cleansed,*" Cockroach rumbled, "*everything would appear to man as it is, infinite.*"

I stared at him and chewed my lip.

"She wanted you to see that we're always with you," Roo said, the dark liquid of his eyes threatening to spill over.

My hands clenched. "By leaving me? You're not always with me. Mama's gone. And even if I could've come see y'all, I didn't know how. I feel like it's been forever since I talked with you."

Sweetpea stood up on my shoulder. "Frankie." She had the tone of a teacher disappointed by her student's obstinance. "I talk to you all the time. I ask you how your night was when I get up in the morning. I tell you what I eat for breakfast, breakfast snack, lunch, lunch snack, dinner, and dinner snack. I ask you what you're doing, and if you've found any good new trees recently. I tell you when I dig up something interesting and ask what you dug up that day. I always say goodnight before I fall asleep. You just aren't listening."

I tilted my head. Did she really believe I should be able to hear her?

Roo cleared his throat. "We all do, Frankie. We're always reaching out to you. Whether you're paying attention or not."

Understanding clicked into place. "Okay, I get it now. You mean, like you're thinking of me. As in 'sending me your best.'" I made quotation marks with my fingers. "Or like, you're 'with me in spirit.'" Sarcasm dripped off the words. "That's great, but it's not the same as really being together, like physically, in the same room."

The rooster's sigh weighed a thousand pounds. "No, Frankie. I don't think you do get it. We're always with you. As in, we exist within you."

Sadness floated into my throat again like a log rising to the surface of a river. I swallowed it. "You mean I made you up? You're a figment of my imagination?" It was hard to get the last word out.

Roo just looked at me with his dark, molten eyes.

"Only to the extent that the rest of the world you see and walk around in is a figment as well," a baritone voice boomed from my side. "For that exists within you too."

I turned around to face Cockroach. "Are you saying the world is all a dream?"

The roach snorted. "No, Frankie, I'm not Descartes. The world is real, but not in all the ways you think. You think because you're in a distinct body, you're all alone. Humans speak of themselves as if they're independent from everything else. Separate. Exceptional. As if they no longer belong to the kingdom of Animalia or the larger world."

"They talk of nature as if they're not a part of it," Roo added, walking over to the base of the stump. "As if what happens to others has no effect on them."

"You feel separate," Cockroach rumbled on, "when in fact everything you see around you"—his front foot made a wide arc that included the hillside, the boulders, the creek, and everything in between—"is a part of you. And you're a part of it."

"How do you mean? Like, spiritually?"

I heard a groan and looked up. Shelly's eyes were open, and she was rolling them to the sky. "Aren't you . . . a scientist? Don't you study . . . what things . . . are made of?"

"I suppose so." I was thoroughly confused.

But the turtle's eyes closed again. It was Penelope's timid voice that offered an explanation, so soft I had to lean down to hear. "We're all made of the same . . . things. I forget what they're called."

I scratched my head. "Atoms?"

"That's it. They combine and recombine, but it's still all the same ones. Maybe some of yours were in a skunk in a previous life." Her lips drew back into a toothy grin.

"Maybe that's where my courage comes from," I whispered to her. Her smile grew.

"Energy too . . . is neither created . . . nor destroyed," Shelly droned, not bothering to open her eyes. "Just recycled . . . in different forms."

"Like it or not, humans are part of the same ecosystem as the rest of us," Roo said. "And the ecosystem becomes a part of them as well, when they breathe the air, drink the water, and eat the"—he coughed a few times and ruffled his feathers—"plants. When they eat the plants."

"Mirror neurons," I said. The animals looked at me. "Our brains are wired to mirror the experiences we see others having. Like if we see someone who's feeling sad, we get sad too. Some people think it's the basis of empathy and being able to feel what others are going through."

Cockroach took a step forward. "If you pay attention, you'll see evidence everywhere that despite appearances, we are all intimately connected—physically, emotionally, and spiritually. In the most important ways, we are one and the same."

"Okay." I rubbed my forehead. "I can believe that. But what does that have to do with Mama? She's dead. One and the same or not, she's gone."

Sweetpea shifted position on my shoulder, but before she could say anything, the baritone voice went on. "Yes, she is." Cockroach's legs sagged for a moment before firming again. "But as our carapacial friend pointed out, energy is neither created nor destroyed. What you cherished in her is also within you. Her wisdom, strength, and compassion—they're all yours. The love she gave so generously—it still exists. Only now it's a part of us."

"She's in my heart," I murmured.

Cockroach's head bobbed up and down. "She's been in your heart since the day you were born."

My heart thudded. My head grew light. The strength of gravity tripled, dragging every last cell toward the earth.

"If everyone's always with me," I asked, my voice lead, "if you're all a part of me, if Mama isn't truly gone, then why am I so sad?"

"It's okay to be sad, Frankie." Cockroach's voice shivered through me. "It's how you let go. How you reorganize your-self around the space she left behind."

"And what about anger?" I asked. "Is that okay too?"

Cockroach opened his mouth, then closed it. "Yes," he finally said. "Of course it is."

"Good." I pulled myself up to my full height. "Because I can't stop thinking about the horrible people who tortured Mama. Roo was right. Humans are cruel, selfish, violent crea-tures who will do anything to anybody if they think they'll benefit. They have no concern for anybody except themselves. They have to be stopped."

Roo stared at a point in the distance. Penelope was grimacing. Sweetpea was flinching as if I might strike her. "Okay," I said, "not all humans. But a lot of them, right?"

For a long moment nobody answered. Then a subterranean voice rang out. It was more deep than loud—I wasn't sure if I heard the words so much as felt them vibrate in my bones—but my entire body froze with their forcefulness.

"Do you see the irony yet?" it asked.

I looked around at Sweetpea, Roo, Penelope, Shelly, and Cockroach. They were all staring up at the branches far above us.

"Nameless One?" My voice sounded higher than a baby squirrel's.

Again the vibration. "Not yet, I see." There was no sound after that, but the branch above me lurched and a giant shadow in the shape of an owl appeared above it. "You say these people have no concern for anybody else. And yet when you condemn them, you are not truly concerned for them, are you? You only seek to end your pain—which is, as it happens, their motivation as well. Do you not commit the same crime you accuse them of? Caring only for yourself?" The owl's huge head swiveled—I thought he was an owl, though he was the size of a small bear—and two large eyes reflected the moonlight at me. "Don't forget that you're hoo-hooo-hoo-hooo"—there was a noise like a giant throat clearing—"hoo-hooo-hoo-hooo"—the throat cleared itself more violently this time—"hoo-hooo-hoo—hooman too. Human. Oh, that is a tricky one to say."

"I suppose that's true," I said.

"Good," the bottomless voice vibrated. "I hope I don't have to come down here again. It makes the little ones nervous."

Sweetpea trembled on my shoulder, and Penelope was trying to squeeze herself under Shelly. Even Roo looked a little edgy despite his defiant stare.

A breeze pushed against my face. When I looked up, the owl-bear shadow had melted away.

"Great," I said into the ensuing lull. "I'm no better than the people who tortured Mama. So why send me here to help the animals?"

Silence answered. Everyone was perfectly still.

Roo was the first to speak. "Frankie, you're not here to help us."

"But that's what Mama told me. Humans have forgotten their connection to the natural world. I was sent back to help them remember, to restore the balance and protect the animals."

I expected an acerbic response, sarcasm at least, but the rooster's tone was patient. "Once again you've forgotten that you're not separate. Frankie, you are here to protect animals. Only we're not the animals you're here to save."

"You mean, I'm supposed to help . . ." I took a step backward.

Roo nodded. "Yes, you're here to save humans."

I had no words.

"Do you really think . . . *we're* the ones . . . who need help?" Shelly somehow stared down her nose at me despite being so close to the ground.

"I guess—I guess I don't know."

"Frankie," Cockroach growled. "Do you remember how sad you were when you thought the white wolf had abandoned you?"

The implacable sadness throbbed in my chest as if I were five again. I nodded.

"Can you imagine how much more painful it would be if you'd never seen the white wolf to begin with? Never run beside her? If you didn't even know that kind of love existed?"

My heart froze. I nodded again.

"Good. Then you can see why humans need your help far more than we do. And why they deserve it."

"I don't know that I'd say that they—that *we*—deserve it." My voice was sullen.

"You yourself pointed out that you have mirror neurons," Roo said. "On some level, humans must feel the suffering they cause others." His eyes were augers. "How much pain must somebody be in to inflict *that much suffering* on someone else and not even notice the effect on themselves?" The image of Mama in her cage was reflected in his eyes.

"A lot." A reluctant admission.

"Has she forgotten . . . the promise she made Mama . . . already?" Shelly's eyes didn't blink open once.

"You know about that?" I asked.

"Of course . . . I know." Her mouth snapped shut.

"I promised to love and have compassion for all animals, no matter what." I'd wondered why the wolf thought she needed to make me promise something so obvious.

"And by animals, she primarily meant . . ."

I glared at Roo. "Humans."

"Hey," said the roach. "If they were easy to love, they wouldn't need your love so badly."

"Fine," I said. "I get it. Humans are the ones I'm here to help. I'll try. But nothing you say is going to make me like it."

"You will in time." Cockroach's tone was gentle. "As you learn how to come home more and more."

"But what if I don't learn? What if I can't?"

"Don't worry." Sweetpea soothed me with soft strokes on my shoulder. "The more you walk down a path, the easier it is to travel."

Five pairs of literal and figurative eyebrows rose, and we all turned to look at the squirrel. Even Shelly deigned to crack an eye to stare at her.

"What?" Sweetpea scrambled in a half circle to look at all our faces. "It does, I swear! I should know. When I first came here, I used to get so turned around that Mama had to come get me. But the more I did it, the easier it got. Now I don't have to even think about it when I come." She stopped and her eyes opened wide. "Wait, y'all aren't staring at me because I said something wrong . . . you're looking at me because I said something right!" She clasped her tiny paws together under her chin. "Oh my gosh, I just taught Frankie my first thing!" Her teeth were large and white in the night.

"Sweetpea," I said. "It was hardly the first thing you've taught me, but it was amazing. Thank you."

A bright light flashed, and the forest disappeared from behind the animals for a moment before returning. "Bye, Sweetpea," I said. "See you soon." She answered by wrapping her arms around my neck. "Bye, Roo." He grunted a response. "Bye, Penelope. Bye, Shelly. Bye, Cockroach." They each waved a foot at me, except Shelly, who may or may not have inclined her head. "Bye, Nameless One. And thank y'all. I couldn't do this without—" But before I could finish, all went white.

And then it stayed white. Just as I started wondering if something had gone terribly wrong, a soft, rhythmic clicking moved toward me. I looked down. A large, brown insect walked steadily across the achromatic ground.

"Cockroach?"

"Yes, Frankie?" He tilted his head up to look at me.

"Are you sure I can do this? That I'm capable of restoring balance?"

"Of course you are. And you won't do it alone. We're all with you, and the others who went back, too."

"Other animals have gone back to human form?"

A chuckle thundered. "What, you thought you were the only soul wise and courageous enough to go back to help?"

Questions jumped in my mind like grasshoppers fleeing a brushfire. Who were the other volunteers? Did I know them? How many of us were there? Did they all have meetings with animals too? How could I find them? Was everyone's mission the same? But none were imperative at the moment, and I didn't have much time. "How do I do it, Cockroach? How do I restore balance?"

"You can't *do* anything to create wholeness—it's the natural state of everything. You simply must find where it resides within you, and act from that place."

Wondering where wholeness lived made me remember where it didn't. "And what if I get depressed again? I get lost when I'm depressed and can't find anything good—let alone wholeness."

"You don't lose your way because you're depressed. You get depressed because you've lost your way." He must have felt the shame welling up in me because he added, "Everyone gets lost, Frankie. It's just that your animal body won't let you stay lost for long."

"What do you mean?"

I couldn't tell if Cockroach was rolling his eyes or just straining to look up at me from so far below. *"You must have seen yourself by now."* His voice thundered and filled every empty particle of the void around us.

"I mean
the real Self. It must have at least passed close
by one day, maybe even stepped on your toes.
Or dragged you somewhere.

That Self, upon your seeing it, gave you the idea
of how eternity could be endured, because of a

tremendous enchantment you felt for a grace
emanating from all things, and your soul now
the epicenter. Your own presence, upon every throne.

Such an incandescence you emanated, and so
magnificently sovereign you felt, that rightfully,

*rightfully, all your ideas of God would look very
pale if they had the audacity to stand next to
you, when your sight was clear . . .* and all your
power revealed."

Silence settled again. Was he making fun of me? I bent
down to get a better look at his eyes. Something stirred
there that I'd never seen before: tenderness. And admiration.
Affection radiated off him in waves like heat from an
industrial-sized oven. Cockroach wasn't just trying to teach
me, I realized. He really cared for me as well.

"I love you too, Cockroach," I said.

"Glad you finally understood." His mouth opened—into
a smile.

The ground shook beneath me and all went dark.

———

When I opened my eyes, I was back on a plane rocking with
turbulence. In the middle seat, I couldn't feel my feet, and
the people next to me had each taken the entire armrest to
themselves. The plane rocked back and forth like a bucking
bronco, the lighting was unnatural and harsh, and cold air
assaulted me from above.

But I couldn't stop feeling how lucky I was.

CHAPTER 35

When I stepped off the escalator into the arrivals lobby, I was greeted by the same frozen, lopsided smile my father always adopted as soon as anyone pointed a camera in his direction.

I understood. I had mixed feelings too. My own smile was half-plastered on, covering new cracks in my faith in my father. What scared me was I wasn't sure how deep they ran.

I gave my dad the customary hug. "Where's Mom?"

"She, uh, had to run an errand." He reached over me to take my suitcase.

We fell into an awkward silence. I didn't manage to break it until we'd passed through baggage claim and were headed out to the car.

"I'm sorry about your drug baby, Dad." I knew this was my first real chance to make good on my promise to Mama, and I'd practiced what I wanted to say on the plane, but it came out stiff and flat, and I wasn't sure how much I meant it.

"Not your fault," my father mumbled as we stepped into the street.

The noise and colors and chaos of people rushing in and out gave me cover to ask the question I didn't want to ask but needed to know. "Was it yours?"

"Are you asking if I instructed the doctors not to report negative findings during the trials?"

I swallowed and nodded.

My father took a few more steps in silence. "Not directly," he said, turning into the parking deck. "But I was so determined to get approval . . . I heard what some of the doctors said during their media interviews about being scared of me, thinking they'd get blacklisted if they didn't show positive results. I never said that." His dark blond hair shuddered. "But thinking back on our conversations, I can see where they got that impression."

Judgment and embarrassment sped through my veins like I'd just mainlined some kind of toxic drug cocktail. How could my own flesh and blood, the man who raised me, the hero I looked up to—how could his values be so backward?

"How could you?" The words tumbled out sharp, meant to draw blood.

My father didn't say anything. Just stared at me with large eyes that were soft and unprotected at the edges before crumbling in on themselves like ancient columns that could no longer bear their own weight. The slump traveled down his body—his head nodding, his shoulders sagging, his feet shuffling between steps.

I'd never seen my father like this.

How much pain must somebody be in to inflict that much suffering on someone else and not even notice the effect on themselves?

Roo's voice transformed the toxic cocktail into something sweeter.

Compassion.

My father felt bad about what he did. Even if he didn't say it, I knew it was true. He needed my help, not my judgment. "I know you didn't mean to hurt anyone, Dad."

I wasn't sure if he heard. "You know, Frankie," he said, stepping onto a staircase, "no matter how hard you try, you never end up where you think you will."

"Believe me, I know." I followed him up the steps. "I've failed enough times to at least learn that."

"That's not what I mean." My father stopped walking and turned to look at me. His eyes flared like blue suns. "As a kid, I never thought, *I want to make drugs when I grow up. I want to be cooped up in a lab all day. I want to yell at my colleagues and make pills that create side effects that require other pills to treat them.*"

"That's not fair, Dad. You've made medicines that helped a lot of people."

"No, I know, Frankie. Of course it's complicated. It's not that my job doesn't do any good, or that nobody should want to do it—it's just *I* never wanted to do it."

"Really?"

He nodded, his shoulders straightening. "When I was a kid, my mother couldn't keep me in the house. I'd disappear outside for hours at a time, only coming back in when it was too dark to tell Adam from Eve. If you would've told me then I'd end up working inside a windowless laboratory ten hours a day, I never would've believed you."

"So how did you get into R&D?"

"Did your mother ever tell you I served in the Peace Corps?" My father's voice was far too calm for having just blown my mind. He started up the steps again.

"What? No! You were in the Peace Corps?"

"Yep. I served in Ghana, just after college. It was all I could think to do with a degree in botany."

"Wait, you majored in *botany*?" I checked the nearby cars and columns for hidden cameras or famous television personalities.

Dad grinned ruefully. "Believe it or not, your father was an idealist. I loved exploring the forests when I was a kid, and I was still young enough in college to believe I could find work doing the same thing as an adult."

"But you told me—" Something told me now wasn't the time to bring up his efforts to discourage my own less conventional dreams. "Never mind. So what was the Peace Corps like?"

"Life-changing." We passed row after row of cars without slowing down. "I met the most amazing people. The ones I was serving with, and the people we were serving. And I learned about neglected diseases."

"Neglected diseases?"

"Diseases that impact almost a billion people, causing serious pain, disability, and death. But they primarily affect people in poorer countries, so they don't receive the same amount of attention as the diseases most common here."

I studied my father as he strode to his car, racking my brain to dredge up memories. Had I ever seen this side of him before? The smallest, quietest hint of it? I came up empty-handed. Had he given me no clues, or had I failed to see them?

"When I got back to the US, I decided I wanted to find cures for neglected diseases." My father stopped next to his BMW. "I figured that with my botany degree, I could use plants to find new treatments and really help the people I'd grown to care about in Ghana." He grunted as he lifted my bag into the trunk. "Why are you bringing rocks home with you, Frankie? Aren't our stones as good as the ones in California?"

"They're not quite as heavy." I moved to the front of the car and settled into the passenger seat.

My father got in the other side and started the car. "I decided to go back to school so I could get a job in Research and Development at a pharmaceutical company." He turned around to back out of the parking spot. "Only—" He stopped the car and looked at me.

"Only what?"

"Only it wasn't what I thought it would be. I first realized it while I was in school, but I told myself it would be different once I got a job. Then when I got a job . . . things were already complicated."

"What do you mean, complicated?"

"Well, for starters, we'd already had your brother and were talking about getting you. I don't know how much you know about adoptions, but they aren't cheap." He backed out of the parking spot and guided the car to the exit. "But if I'm honest with myself, it wasn't about the money. It was that I liked some parts of my new job. The respect people had for me. The way they listened to me. The power I had to persuade. And more than anything, I didn't want to admit I'd made a mistake or wasted so much time and money."

"If you had power to persuade, why couldn't you do the things you wanted to?"

"I tried, Frankie. I really did. But persuasion is one thing, and the power to make decisions is another. When I floated ideas to my supervisor, he'd always say the same thing: 'Show me the numbers, Mitch. Labs, FDA approval, and smart people like you cost money.' I went home every night for months and tried to make the numbers work, but I never could.

"I tried to get others to join my cause, but they all dismissed me as impulsive and reckless. Pretty soon nobody wanted to be on my team. After about six months, I realized it was never going to happen and I was just creating more problems for myself." He handed a bill to the man in the booth. "It took me a long time to win back my reputation and respect. Years and years, and it left a bitter taste in my mouth that never went away."

"And you didn't want me to make the same mistake."

"Yes, only I think I may have been wrong about what mistake that was."

My father never admitted he was wrong. He never apologized. It was my mother's biggest complaint about him. The scandal had rattled him more than I'd realized.

"I've always admired your idealism, Frankie," he said. "The way you care so much about things and try to make them better regardless of what others think. But I've also always feared it too. It leaves you so open and exposed, so vulnerable. And that's dangerous. There's far more selfishness and cruelty in the world than anyone likes to think. So yes, I've always worried where your heart is going to lead you."

I bit my lip. "I understand. I can be pretty — "

"No." The word was fast, a forced stop. "That's where I was wrong. I used to think that strength was not putting yourself in a position where you might feel pain. But you've taught me what strength really is — having the courage to face and feel anything. Your heart is beautiful, Frankie. I shouldn't have discouraged you from following it. I'm sorry. That was my mistake. It doesn't have to be yours."

His words slipped into a crack in my heart, smoothed and soothed it.

A green blur of trees slid by the window. The world had flipped into its own negative in the blink of an eye — light shone where there had been shadow, and shadow gathered where there had been light. My father, an idealist. Admitting he was wrong. Telling me to follow my heart. I remembered what the animals had said in our last conversation about who needed help and stumbled over a final inversion — the one who needed help wasn't me.

"Thank you, Dad." I wondered if the words would work.

"For what?"

"For this conversation. For the apology. For always loving and caring so much about me."

I would have sworn there was nothing else my father could have done that would have surprised me more than he just had, but when he turned to me, he did.

His bright, blue eyes were moist.

"Are you crying, Dad?" I couldn't keep the disbelief out of my voice.

"Of course not." He turned back to the windshield. "There's a bug in my eye."

Our laughter cascaded out the windows, streaming behind us like a tail, a trail, a path back home.

CHAPTER 36

After my father left to go back to work, I spent forty-five minutes pacing, waiting, and moping alone in my parents' house. Somewhere in my ramblings, I misplaced all the nice things I'd planned on saying to my mother.

I tried to avoid the conclusion that she was punishing me—even though she was clearly avoiding me after begging me to come home for over a year—but the idea lodged in the back of my mind like a boulder, and as my thoughts ranged far and wide, they kept stubbing their tender toes on it.

It wasn't like I was trying to be hurtful. She always made everything about *her*. It wasn't my fault I'd gotten depressed, or that I hadn't had the energy to talk to anyone. And I really couldn't go flying home every weekend like she expected, not while having my own life, anyway. She wanted too much from me—demanded too much—and when I couldn't give it to her, she punished me like a sullen child, "running errands" and keeping me waiting for almost an hour when I was finally able to make it home.

I was sitting in the back yard watching a bright red cardinal fail to hide himself in an azalea bush when her car's tires crunched on the small rocks in the driveway. I resolved not to give in to her latest guilt trip. She wanted me to apologize for doing something wrong when I hadn't. I wouldn't give her the satisfaction. I didn't go inside when her car door slammed and the front door creaked open, and I barely turned around when she said my name behind me.

She stepped through the French door. "How was your trip?"

I shifted back around to face the yard. "It was fine."

"Good." She pulled a chair next to mine and folded herself into it. "Your father said you two had a good conversation."

"I guess so." I fiddled with a broken piece of wicker on my chair. "So apparently you were too busy with your errands to come pick me up at the airport, but you had enough time to gossip about me with Dad."

Her sigh was almost louder than her words. "I didn't come pick you up because I didn't want to crowd you." She glanced at the broken wicker and a small frown pulled down the corners of her mouth. "I know I can be a little overwhelming at times, and I thought I'd give you some space. Plus, I figured you had things to talk over with your father. Alone."

"Really? And is that why you waited"—I pulled out my phone and checked the time—"*over an hour* to come home? You talked to Dad. You knew I was here by myself."

The frown disappeared, replaced by an amused smile. "If I'd have known that leaving you by yourself for an hour would make you so excited to see me, I would've done it a long time ago."

"I knew it!"

"Knew what?" The smile departed as quickly as it had come.

"That you're trying to manipulate me, like you always do. You'll do anything to make me do what you want."

The corners of her mouth tightened. "That's not fair, Frankie, and you know it."

"What's not fair is you expecting me to come home whenever you want without caring what I have going on or how I feel about it. And then, when I finally do come home, you ignore me and act like you don't even want to see me. Like I'm some kind of terrible daughter who doesn't deserve the time of day."

My mother didn't say anything, but her face grew darker, her lips more compressed, her eyes more dangerous. My muscles tensed, bracing for the imminent explosion. But just when I couldn't wait any longer, her eyebrows lifted, and she guffawed as if I'd just made the funniest joke she'd ever heard.

"What?" I demanded. "What's so funny?"

She released a few more howls, then took her time to wipe tears away from the corners of her eyes with the edge of her sweater. "It's not easy when someone you love leaves you and you don't know why or when they'll be back, is it?"

"No." I sounded like sullen toddler.

"Well, if you ever want to be a mother, then you'd better get used to it." She dabbed her eyes again with her sweater.

"That's funny, because in my experience, it's the mothers who do the leaving."

She dropped her sweater and looked at me with a large crease between her eyes. "You're referring to Stella?" Her voice was soft.

"James told you about Stella?" She nodded. "Well, the bright side is I now know why I never feel like I belong anywhere. The first woman who knew me couldn't wait to get rid of me."

"Oh, Frankie." My mother reached over to put her hand on my leg. "You don't know that. You don't know her circumstances, or what she might have really wanted." She smoothed my leggings over my knee. "And what about me? I chose you, sought you out, and brought you home because I wanted you so much. Doesn't that count for anything?"

My throat tightened. "It might if everything I did didn't disappoint you."

My mother opened her mouth, then shut it again. "This being human thing isn't easy, is it?"

Sometimes my mother could read minds.

"Frankie, you don't disappoint me. I'm proud of you and the life you've built for yourself. I just miss you. You used to need me more, you know, and I guess . . . I guess I miss those days. It's hard when someone you care for so much, someone you'd do anything for—it's hard when they suddenly don't want you around anymore. It can break your heart, if you let it."

I knew she was talking about herself, but her words reminded me of a different conversation I'd had not long before. I was trying to place it when my mother spoke again, her voice soft now, and tentative. "It's funny, you worrying about disappointing me, when I'm the one who should be apologizing to you."

I pulled my head back to get a clearer look at my mother's face, but nothing in her pained expression answered my question. "Apologizing? For what?"

"For not talking more openly about your adoption." I started to interrupt her, but she held out her hand and shook her head. "No, it's true. Ever since the night you ran away, I knew how hurt you were, but I thought it was my fault. I couldn't face the guilt, so I tried not to talk about it. I know you sensed that, because until this year, you never brought it up. You must have felt so much loss and anxiety about your adoption, but I left you all alone in your pain. It was cowardly and selfish."

Something in my chest clicked into place like a puzzle piece filling a decades-old gap. A half-second later, my own words echoed in my ears. *I promise to love and have compassion for all animals, no matter what,* I'd said to Mama the last time I saw her. I loved my mother, but had I ever really had compassion for her? Could you have compassion for someone if you never stopped to consider how they might be feeling?

"Mom, I appreciate you saying that, but it's okay. It was a difficult situation, and honestly, I've always felt how much you love me. I really never meant to avoid you. I just felt so terrible, the thought of talking to anyone seemed too overwhelming. But I do still need you. Obviously. When I wasn't talking with you regularly, I landed myself in jail."

She laughed. "Did I ever tell you about the time when I moved to New York?"

"Um, no." I wasn't sure I could handle both my parents blowing my mind in the same afternoon.

"The summer after my senior year in high school, I had a whirlwind romance with a man on break from college in New York. When he left to go back to school at the end of the summer, I was heartbroken. I decided that instead of going to college in Massachusetts, I was going to move to New York to be with him. But I didn't tell my family because I knew they'd talk me out of it."

"You didn't."

"I did. I was so excited to surprise my boyfriend and be reunited with him, I wasn't going to let anything stop me." She grimaced.

"What happened?"

My mother gave a throaty laugh. "My boyfriend was surprised. So was his girlfriend when she answered the door."

"Oh, no. That's terrible."

"Terrible," she agreed, "and ultimately fortuitous."

"Why? What do you mean?"

"I moved back home and started mid-year at the University of Georgia. It meant I had to live with my mother for an extra two years, but it also meant that I was there in time to meet your father."

I stretched out my limbs as if absorbing the story like sunlight. "So you're saying if you can recover from something like that, then there's still hope for a screw-up like me?"

She wrinkled her nose. "I'm saying we all screw up now and then, and it doesn't have to be a bad thing."

I leaned my head on her shoulder. "Thanks, Mom. You're the best."

"Only after my daughter." She rested her head on mine.

We sat like that, watching the yard in silence for a long time.

And one by one the words of another mother grieving the loss of her children came to mind.

Human beings are a young species, Mama had told me. *In the beginning, we provided food for them, looked after them, and taught them from the wisdom we had gathered over lifetimes. But at some point they forgot. Eventually, they began seeing us either as pests or as a means to an end. They forgot who we are. They forgot who they are. They forgot how much we need each other.*

The reassuring weight of my mother's head on my own and the warmth of her hand on my leg satisfied a hunger deep in my chest. How could I not have seen that I missed these moments too? I'd been carrying around an emptiness I didn't even know was there until it was filled.

Not unlike the rest of humanity, estranged sons and daughters of the earth. Only our need still aches.

It really could break your heart, if you let it.

CHAPTER 37

I decided to make the hardest call last.

First I called Brian. The phone only rang once before he answered, a little breathless.

"Frankie?"

I spoke before thinking. "No, it's the ghost of Christmas past."

His laugh was generous. "I didn't think I'd ever hear from you again. Why didn't you return any of my messages?"

"I, uh . . . was feeling a little under the weather for a while. Sorry about that."

"Yeah, Lillian told me." He inhaled, then exhaled, only to inhale sharply again. "Look, I'm the one who should be sorry. I should have been more supportive. I should have helped you when you needed it. And I shouldn't have said those things about you being a bad scientist. It's not true."

The irony was too much. I couldn't keep the laughter out of my voice. "I appreciate that, but I've been wondering if maybe you weren't right after all. I'm not sure I'm cut out to be a scientist."

"No way! You ask good questions and have great instincts. And you're fearless. Science could use more of that."

"Thanks." I twisted the end of my shirt around a finger. "But I don't mean it like that. I mean, I'm not sure I want to be a scientist. I'm thinking about leaving the program for good."

"No, Frankie, don't give up. I know you've had some setbacks, but the first year is hard for everyone. It'll get easier, I promise."

"It's not about being easy or hard. It's about being happy."

"Are you sure you won't be happy in time?"

I searched inside for some small piece of certainty but found none. "No. There are things I like about science, and I worked hard to get here, and I have no idea what else to do. But. . . ." I let my voice drift off.

"But what?"

"It doesn't feel right." I didn't know how else to explain it, and I couldn't defend what I didn't understand, so I changed the subject to another thing that pressed uncomfortably against my chest. "Hey, Brian." My voice fractured. "What would have happened if I hadn't called about the wolf?"

"What do you mean?"

"Would we have dated?"

Silence. Then: "I'd like to think so."

"You'd like to think so."

More silence. "I really like you, Frankie."

"But—"

"*And* I'm not always so good at choosing what I like. I worry too much what other people think."

I appreciated his honesty, but it stung. "You worry what other people would think of you if you dated me?"

"I worry what other people will think of me no matter what I do. It has nothing to do with you." He exhaled. "Most of all, I guess I worry what *you* would think if you really got to know me. As you've seen, I can be a real chicken shit—er, human shit—sometimes."

"That's good. I wouldn't want to go out with anyone who isn't as frightened as I am."

"So does that mean we can go on a date when you get back?"

"If you promise not to yell or run next time you get scared, then sure."

"I promise," he said without a pause.

A memory of his lopsided grin kicked my heart into high gear. "Good. Then I look forward to it."

"Me too," he said. "More than you know."

After hanging up with Brian, I dialed another number from which I'd missed multiple calls, though it had been longer since I'd missed them.

Again a voice answered after only one ring.

"Hello?"

"Hi, Sundog. It's Frankie."

"Frankie." She made my name sound like a song. "It's so good to hear from you. How are you?"

"Better now. I'm back home visiting my family. How are you?"

"I'm doing great now that I've heard your voice. Is there anything I can help you with?"

I looked at my hands. "Actually, yes. I was wondering if I could come stay with you for a little while when I get back to California. I have a tent I could pitch in your yard, and—"

"*Yes!*" I had to knuckle my ear to get it to stop tickling. "Of course. I would love that. But you don't need a tent. You can sleep on my couch. I got an extra-large one for just this reason."

"Are you sure? I know I wasn't very . . . friendly the last time I saw you."

"Oh, Frankie, I'm sure it isn't easy to meet a foster mother you haven't seen in over twenty years. And I laid a lot on you with my talk of chakras, and the whole communicating with animals thing. I really did intend to be more subdued, but then when I saw you, your energy was so—" She paused. "I got excited. It felt like old times, and I slipped into old habits. Part of the reason I kept calling was I wanted to apologize."

"You don't owe me an apology. I'm the one who should be sorry for how rude I was."

"No apology necessary. I'm just glad you're coming back. I can't wait for you to meet Patrick, Big Red, and Skinnyjon Jones."

"Who are they?"

"A rabbit, house finch, and baby squirrel I've been rehabilitating. I guess I didn't get around to telling you when you were here, but when you were a kid, your love of animals inspired me so much I became a wildlife rehabilitator after you left."

"That's awesome. I can't wait to meet them either." An idea broke free from the morass in my mind. "Hey, have you ever thought about adopting any chickens? Or, more specifically, an exceedingly-opinionated rooster? I know one who could use a new home."

Sundog's laugh welcomed the world into its warmth. "Well, there's certainly plenty of room here, and I do miss the fiery debates about current affairs I used to have with friends when I lived in the city."

Excitement surged in my chest. Maybe I wasn't as crazy as I thought. Or maybe I was, but I was in good company.

By the time I hung up with Sundog, twilight had begun dulling the peach-colored walls of the room. It was getting late. My parents were probably hungry. I stood up to go downstairs so we could eat. But a quiet voice in the back of my head whispered that there was plenty of time. *Call her*, it said.

I dialed the number scrawled on a card I'd been carrying in my wallet for months.

This time the phone rang longer than I'd thought was possible. The rhythmic tones went on so long that I jumped when a woman's deep voice interrupted the sound.

"Hello," it said in a flat tone.

"Hi, Stella. It's Frankie."

There was a pause. "I know." More silence.

"I, uh, was wondering if I could ask you a few more questions."

"Of course, Frankie." Her tone was less than convincing. "Go ahead."

"Well, ah . . ." My stomach twisted. "After we spoke last, I drove up to Eureka and visited Redwood Regional Hospital."

"You did?" It was the first time her voice contained any emotion.

"Yeah, and um . . . they didn't have any record of Isabella Days giving birth there." I spun the card with the phone number around on my leg.

"That's odd." Her voice was colorless again.

"Yeah, I thought so too. And so did my friend who came with me to the hospital. So he did a little research in the county birth records"—there was a sharp intake of breath—"and he found there's no record of Isabella Days there either. But a Stella Richardson did give birth at Redwood Regional Hospital on March eighteenth."

Nothing for a long moment, then finally a long, slow exhale. "I'm so sorry, Frankie. I should have told you when we spoke before."

"Then why didn't you?"

"I was trying to protect you."

"By lying to me? Really?"

"Okay, maybe I was trying to protect myself."

"From what? From me? Am I that horrible?"

"Of course not." Her breath blew across the phone's speakers again. "I wasn't lying when I told you your birth mother didn't want to give you up."

"So why did you?"

Silence again. "I was terrified out of my mind. I didn't think I could handle being a mother. I was struggling with depression at the time, and—is that an issue for you too?"

I wondered how she'd known until I realized that I'd grunted at the word *depression* like someone had struck me in the belly. "Yeah, it is."

"Yes, well, it runs in the family. So you know how everything feels overwhelming when you're depressed? Like you can't do anything right, and it feels impossible to take care of yourself, let alone anyone else?"

"Yeah. I know."

"I convinced myself you would be better off without me. I didn't want to give you up, but I thought I was doing the best thing I could for you."

My hand found the center of my chest, stayed there as if trying to keep something inside.

"I imagined you with a loving mother and father in a stable home with siblings." Her voice was weak, as if she wasn't sure the words could stand on their own. "When I called and found out you'd been placed with a foster mother, it occurred to me that maybe I'd been wrong. I went to see you at Martha's with the intention of picking you up. I was going to take you back with me."

"Really?"

Her husky voice strengthened. "I won't lie to you anymore, Frankie. I promise you that." She took a breath. "That's why I was skulking about the window." She gave a dry chuckle. "I'm not a natural burglar, that's for sure. When Martha found me and I told her I was friends with your mother, she was so sweet and sympathetic that I realized you *were* better off with her, even if it was only temporary. Did you know she went to Harvard?"

I threw the card on the floor. "I heard something like that."

"She was a successful management consultant in New York before moving to California. She was only thirty when she realized it wasn't for her. Within one month she'd quit her job, packed up her belongings, and was on her way to

Humbolt. She was planning to foster lots of kids like you, but you were her first and last. It was too hard for her when you left. She told me that once when I called to check on you. Broke her heart to see you go."

Sundog's endless tears during my visit with Lillian took on new meaning. "Wow. I had no idea."

"When you called me, I almost didn't call you back. I was a wreck for so long after you were born, some part of me worried I'd never recover if I reopened that wound."

"So why did you?"

"In the end, I couldn't help myself. I couldn't stop thinking about you, and the desire to hear your voice was . . . overwhelming. It just seemed like a safer option to continue the lie rather than risk telling you the truth."

I exhaled then, my cheeks puffing out in a long, deep breath. "Thanks for telling me all this."

"Of course. So how are you? Are you depressed now?"

"I was recently, but I'm not at the moment."

"Good." She hesitated. "You asked about the circumstances of your birth the last time we talked. Do you still want to know?"

I leaned forward. "Yes, of course. But I thought you didn't know what happened, or why you were unconscious."

She was quiet for a moment. "That was another partial truth. I don't *know* what happened, but I do have some clues."

I stood up and paced around my childhood bedroom as she told me the story.

"I was living in Oakland at the time. A friend invited me to go camping. Her uncle had some land in Eureka that was beautiful, she said. I was seven months pregnant, but my friend pointed out that if anything happened, the hospital was just a mile away from her uncle's house. At the time I was starting to have panic attacks, and being in nature always helped me relax, so I agreed to go."

Outside my bedroom window, the bare branches of trees reached to the sky, making invisible offerings to the heavens.

"I was all packed and ready to go when my friend called me," Stella said. "She had the stomach flu and couldn't travel." The glass was cold beneath my fingers. "She told me I should go anyway, that her uncle would be fine with it. Normally I wouldn't have considered camping alone while seven months pregnant, but . . ."

"But what?"

"But I felt this . . . this pull to go. I'm not sure I can describe it. It was like a magnet pulling every particle of my being to that land in Eureka. In the face of that force, staying home didn't feel like an option." The wind howled outside my window.

"So I went by myself." Her voice was matter-of-fact. "It was quiet and uneventful at first. I arrived and met my friend's uncle, walked the trails on his property, managed to cook myself dinner on the stove my friend had lent me. I watched the sun set—it was a fiery red, I remember—and went to sleep soon after. The last thing I remember for sure is lying on my blanket listening to the splashing of the creek nearby."

She inhaled deeply and released it slowly. "Everything that happened after that is a blur. I remember feeling very hot. In my dreams, I was trudging through a desert. Then I was in the middle of a volcano. I was getting covered with magma like the bodies at Pompeii. Just when I was about to be buried completely, I woke up. There was a loud crackling noise, and a flickering light. When I turned away from it, I found myself staring into two large, golden eyes that seemed to glow in the darkness."

A crow took off from one of the trees beyond my window in an explosion of raucous caws. I jumped.

My soul settled slowly back into place. "What was it?" I asked.

"I can't be sure." Her voice was soft. "The rest of my dreams were even less lucid. I was mostly running from shadows. But at one point one of the shadows stopped chasing me long enough to transform into the body of the largest animal I've ever seen. It was dark gray, unbelievably graceful, with huge paws and ears, and when it turned its giant head to me, I saw the same golden eyes." She paused. "I started to run, but when I looked into those eyes again—this is going to sound so strange—but when I looked into her eyes again, they filled me with love."

The image caused a tremor in my chest, a tremor that broke loose and rattled through my legs, my arms, my hands.

"A wolf." My voice whispered like the wind outside my window.

"Yes. But just after I had that vision of her, when I was still filled with that warm, expansive affection from her eyes, I woke up in a hospital bed, nine inches dilated and about to give birth."

A warm tear rolled down my cheek. "She was helping you." I wasn't sure if I meant it as a question or a statement of fact.

"Maybe." Stella's words slowed to a crawl. "I never saw her again, but I can still call up that feeling of being filled with love just by remembering the look in her eyes."

The crow swooped down with a few others to harass a large hawk sitting in a tree across the street. "It was a wildfire?" I asked.

"Yes. It started well east of where I was camping. Arson, they thought, though they never found out who did it. It burned twenty-nine hundred acres."

"And you don't remember seeing it come, or getting out of your tent, or running away from it?"

"No."

"The wolf, she found you unconscious from the smoke and dragged you to safety?"

Stella hesitated. "I can't say anything for sure, Frankie."

"But you think she did? That's what you're saying?"

"I want to believe she did. But like I said, I don't remember anything clearly from that night. It's much more likely I made it to the nearest road without remembering, or that somebody found me unconscious and drove me to Redwood Regional. It wasn't my friend's uncle—he'd gone to spend the night at his girlfriend's house—but maybe someone saw a strange car in his driveway. A wolf dragging me on a blanket not just to safety, but to the nearest hospital, sure makes a nice story, but it doesn't seem very likely."

That last phrase was too familiar. I'd said the same thing to myself so many times I'd made canyons of doubt in my brain.

But then I remembered Jones. "Stella." The hawk beat his powerful wings to rise above the angry crows. "When I went to the hospital, I spoke with a doctor who was working there the day you appeared. He said a nurse found what looked like canine hair all over the clothes you were wearing."

"Frankie, my roommate at the time had a dog." Her voice had deflated. "All my clothes were covered in dog hair in those days."

I tapped my fingers against my thigh. "But that's not all. The doctor was curious about what had happened to you, so he went back to the spot where they found you unconscious." My fingers drummed faster. "He saw wolf tracks in the woods nearby. Wolf tracks, Stella. I know that doesn't prove anything for sure, but it's got to be enough to believe."

"Maybe." Her tone was noncommittal. "It still doesn't make any sense."

Since when did the truth make sense?

And with that thought, in that moment, with that wolf haunting my mind, I understood. It didn't matter if Roo, Sweetpea, Cockroach and the rest were living animals or not. It didn't matter how our conversations happened or if they could be scientifically proven. All that mattered was that I believed in them. That's what made me happy, made me wise, made me whole. That's what made them important and real—as real as I am—even though I may never know in what way.

And in the same moment, in the same way, my decision about school became obvious. In fact, it wasn't a decision at all—it was just the truth, sitting there inside me where it'd been all along. The truth was, neuroscience wasn't for me and I wasn't for it. I'd known it, deep down, probably before I'd even started. No matter how I'd fought it, denied it, or tried to change it, it hadn't budged. It had only weighed me down. And if I was ever going to be free of that burden, I was going to have to welcome its heavy weight.

I felt lighter already, having acknowledged my truth and given it wings.

"A friend once told me not to believe things based on legends, logic, or probability," I told Stella. "He told me to believe only what I find through experience leads to well-being and happiness." The last crow flew off, having accomplished her mission. "I don't know, but I found that helpful. I mean, maybe truth doesn't always care about what's reasonable."

"I suppose believing that the wolf helped us wouldn't do any harm."

"Seems to me it's already done some good. It brought us together, right?"

My birth mother was quiet. When she spoke, she had to try three times before she could get a word out fully formed. "I—thank you, Frankie." She paused again. "This means more to me than you could know."

It occurred to me after I hung up with Stella that my whole life I'd walked around with the invisible conviction that because I was adopted, I wasn't loved like everybody else. I always felt I didn't belong anywhere, and without realizing it, I'd assumed I never had a mother who really wanted me.

I laughed out loud then, that my highly-evolved, state-of-the-art, exalted human brain could make such a huge mistake. The truth was, all this time I'd had not just one mother who loved me, but three.

And that was just counting the human ones.

EPILOGUE

Fourteen months later

A symphony, that's what it is.

I exhale with relief at discovering the right word to describe what I'm experiencing. This early in the spring, everything feels alive—the tiny, green leaves on the trees that look like babies compared to their fallen forebears. The young plants pushing themselves up through the detritus of last year's growth with unsullied optimism. Even the moist, fragrant earth and the brilliant blue sky seem to whisper and sway as if animated with a life force of their own.

There's a depth of richness in the cumulative effect that's difficult to describe. All around me, the forest is sounding perfect notes of beauty. One elegant branch crosses another at just the right angle. An inexplicable white circle on a tree contrasts perfectly with its dark gray bark. The iridescent trails of slugs climb a trunk just above my head and catch the light, creating an intricate pattern of interconnected lines. Everywhere I look, individual wonders painstakingly layer with an infinity of others.

The forest is a symphony of impossibly orchestrated beauty.

I stand still for a long time and let its music wash over me. Eventually the joy subsides, and I continue my walk through this slice of old-growth forest, the traditional land of the Muscogee People.

It's only been four months since I was last in Atlanta, but it's been seven years since I've visited this park, this trail, the leaves on this path that muffle the sound of my footsteps. How strange that in all my visits home during that time I've driven across the city with my parents on many occasions but never ventured the one block from their house to the park at the end of the street. I suppose it seemed too ordinary, too pedestrian, hardly worth revisiting, especially since my childhood dog died and nobody's needed a walk.

Except today, apparently, I did.

I made it clear to my parents when I decided to come for a month that I would need plenty of time alone to write. I'd been living with Sundog for a little over a year and figured that an extended trip home could both give her a well-deserved break from me and allow me to spend more time with my parents and brother. Plus, even though the book has been coming along well overall, I've been struggling to write the prologue, and I thought a change of scenery might help. I knew it would be a challenge to write with my parents around, so I'd warned them—and when I say *them*, I mean my mother—that even though I'd be staying in their house, the situation would be more like it was with James, who's taken a permanent job with the company he was serving as a consultant. I'd work during the day, they would go about their business, and we'd see each other in the evenings.

They were all nodding heads and eager acquiescence before I bought my ticket, but ever since I arrived, my mother's found a hundred and one reasons to be near me. Most of them involve food or favors of some kind, and I really get now she's just expressing her love for me, but while understanding and forgiveness are great, they don't help me get any writing done.

This morning I was packing up my computer and trying to figure out how to get to the nearest café when my father knocked on my door and informed me he was taking my mother on a shopping trip that would likely last all day. I might have thought it was a lucky coincidence if my father hadn't proceeded to tell me I could use his home office to write in, instructed me to put on music if the silence was too much for me, and then cackled like a maniac the entire way to the front door.

It was a sweet gesture. The only problem was, as soon as I sat down in my father's comfy office chair and spun it around a few times, the words dried up. Just like that, my mind was as blank as a cloudless sky. It's the same thing that always happens when I try to write the prologue—arguably the most important part of the book—but for some reason today it was even worse. I wondered if my father had created a self-fulfilling prophecy with his joke and tried tapping my foot on the floor, humming to myself, and putting on music, but nothing worked.

That's when an image of the park down the street popped into my head and sat there, unobtrusive, as if pretending it had been there all along. Why hadn't I thought of it sooner? I'd jumped out of the chair and found my shoes.

Now one of those shoes slips off a rock I'm balancing on to cross the small stream and splashes into the water. I rescue it with a curse, cold water soaking the tip of my sock. When I regain my balance, something darts away across the surface of the creek.

I bend down. An insect with a long body and even longer legs rests on top of the stream. His legs reach out in six directions like the extended oars of a tiny boat. Where the creature's feet touch the surface, minuscule indentations push against but don't break the water. The insect's ability to walk on water is impressive, but only when my glance falls below his body to the shadow beneath do I see something truly incredible.

On the sandy bottom of the stream swim six circles of shadow, each varying in size but all far larger than the insect's tiny feet. The amazing thing is, unlike any other shadow I've ever seen, each darkened circle is surrounded by a fiery ring of light. Six full solar eclipses occur simultaneously, unannounced and uncelebrated on the discarded leaves and mud of the forgotten streambed.

I straighten up, taking a deep breath as I do. Clearly there's more to this world than I can ever know. So many of the things I thought I understood have turned out to be wrong. Meanwhile, what I dismissed as wishful thinking has turned out to be real, if not in the ways I imagined.

It's almost enough to make you doubt your sanity. Only, I've never felt more lucid in my life.

Leaving the neuroscience program wasn't easy. Lillian, my father, and even Brian tried to convince me to reenroll. Worse, a deep sadness lodged in my chest when I made my withdrawal official. I wondered then if I'd made a mistake, if I'd lacked faith in myself or given up too soon.

Tamara was the one who helped me see that giving up can be a good thing when life is calling you somewhere else.

Three months after the conference, she quit her program and moved to the San Blas Islands to be with Colibrì. She realized she felt more herself when she was on the islands, like she was only a shadow imitating the real thing when she was in the city. All her worries about being bored and restless turned out to be unfounded. "I've learned my brain doesn't need to be busy," she told me. "It only needs to be challenged." And she has plenty to challenge her in learning from the islanders, the land, the water, the animal ancestors, and the natural struggles of being in a committed relationship.

Tamara's courage inspired me to admit once and for all that the road I had been on—while a good one—belonged to somebody else. But she wasn't the only one who helped me find my way. There were the animals, of course—Roo and the rest—who taught me to be willing to see anything, whatever was there. That was huge, but if I'm honest, some of the greatest help I received was from Dr. Porter.

He destroyed my defenses, laid me bare, cut me to the bone until there was nothing left between me and the truth. Without him, I might still be a scientist, not dedicated to writing a book about the extraordinary experiences I've had—who knows, without him, maybe I wouldn't have had those extraordinary experiences—and it turns out writing is more fun and satisfying than anything else I've ever done. Besides, if any human is suffering and scared and in need of the compassion the animals have helped me to find, it's him. So I wrote him a letter, explained how he helped me, thanked him, and wished him the best.

Making science wrong is tempting, given how many animals suffer in its name and its presumptuous belief that what it can't observe or explain doesn't exist. Part of me wants to condemn Brian, Lillian, and my father for their unquestioning faith in the scientific method. But I've learned enough by now to know that as I just saw with the insect's shadow, lightness and darkness don't usually show up quite as you expect.

Lillian has decided to focus her studies on the neuropsychology of connection. She's researching what happens in the brain and nervous system when people become disconnected and view themselves as superior to some other group—whether people or animals, she told me, it's really the same thing. She's also studying what happens when people feel their kinship with all other people and forms of life, no matter how different, in the hopes that the patterns will suggest ways to help people become kinder, more connected and compassionate. She glows when she talks about her research, and I have to admit it could help make the world a better place. Way better.

Brian, meanwhile, can't stop talking about using science to uncover our ignorance. I didn't understand what he meant at first, but after a long conversation, I realized that he wants to use the scientific method to discover the limits of what we know. *Of what we can know*, he corrected me. He's so excited about the idea that he turned down the offer he worked so hard to get and landed a job with a think tank. His current track is less lucrative and prestigious than the biotech role would have been, but it allows him to determine what type of research he'll do. It also means he didn't have to move to the South Bay, where the drive would have been even longer to Eureka. He comes up to visit once or twice a month. So far, he's been true to his promise—he's gotten scared plenty of times but hasn't yet yelled or run. We recently started making plans for moving in together.

Even my father has found a way to make science his own again. He's now the director of a brand new, fully-funded non-profit dedicated to conducting research on neglected diseases. Most of his former colleagues think he's lost his mind, but he's been surprised to realize how much he no longer cares.

Sometimes so much clarity in everyone else's path underscores the uncertainty in mine.

I follow the trail beneath a beech tree that's leaning over it as a protective mother might her child. I'm aware I could easily slip into a panic that I have no idea what I want to do after I finish writing my book. Truth be told, I'm nearly done, and not even the whisper of a plan has come to me. But I've gotten better at recognizing what my heart and body are trying to tell me, and am hearing the quiet, guiding voice of spirit more and more. It's harder than I imagined—what the animals didn't tell me is that in order to hear the wisdom, I have to feel the pain—but I do have the sense that when the time is right, I'll know what to do.

As if thinking about the quiet voice woke it up, it stirs in my belly. Today it isn't speaking so much in words as tugging me away from the turn the path is taking and toward the babbling creek instead. I follow the pull.

Within a few steps, I'm face-to-face with a tree whose girth reminds me of the great sequoias I saw when my family drove me out to college. Reaching both hands out around its trunk, I can barely encompass half its width. Thick roots the size of my thighs radiate out from its base, following the curve of the earth before disappearing beneath it. Above, giant, gnarled limbs extend in all directions, splitting into smaller boughs which then divide themselves into branches, which split yet again into thousands of tiny twigs like crooked neurons reaching to the sky.

How brave, given the state of the world, that this tree is willing to stretch so many tiny feelers out to see what it can find. Or maybe *brave* isn't quite the right word. Maybe *heroic* is the better choice. Neurons are designed to create connections, after all, and I've been thinking a lot about how so much of my suffering—so much of our suffering—comes from a lack of connection—to ourselves, to others, to the life all around us. And here this tree is, not only offering food, shelter, and shade to any who come near, but thousands of opportunities for connection as well.

I read once about Buddhist monks who spend their lives praying in caves for the enlightenment of all living beings. When I first read it, I thought, *What a colossal waste of time.* But now I see things differently. Who's to say the world wouldn't suffer more without the good wishes of all those monks? And who's to say trees aren't doing the same thing, silently pouring their energy into the world in dedication to the well-being of the rest of us?

I reach my hand up and place it on the tree's craggy surface, roughly across from my heart. I close my eyes. The bark is hard and jagged against my skin. A deep and vibrant spaciousness, as strong as stone and just as still, expands outward from the heart of the tree until it stretches from limb to root, enveloping me completely.

I'm filled with that calm strength. And then, as quietly as it came, it washes over me and recedes.

I stare past the trunk and try to catch my breath. Something is familiar about the clearing beyond the tree. As if commandeered by a power larger than me, my feet carry me around the left side of the giant trunk, my right hand still tracing its rugged bark. I float into the magnetic glade.

A thick, double-trunked tree comes into view. A stream gurgles contentedly behind it. In front of the tree, a large, moss-covered rock blocks my path. More than one rock, really—several boulders are tumbled together one on top of the other. They tickle a recent memory my childhood adventures here can't explain. I'm trying so hard to place it that I almost miss the biggest clue—a waist-high stump with a flat, broad top. If I squint, I can almost make out a large rooster perched on it, his iridescent feathers intermittently catching the moonlight.

I'm holding my breath but can't seem to force any air into my lungs. Roo, the real-life rooster, now lives with me in California. We adopted him some months back after persistent conversations with his previous owners. He's now part of Sundog's quickly growing family, along with twelve hens who came with him, most of them geriatric aunts and grandmothers, and a few chicks we ordered online.

Speaking of geriatric, Cockroach nears the end of his life. I'm sad that he'll soon be gone, but he's assured me that he's had a full life, is ready to go, and has generated plenty of offspring who are smart enough to pick up where he left off in guiding me. He even suggested I keep an eye on *their* offspring for one with a particular proclivity for philosophy. Even after all this time, the idea of cockroach reincarnation doesn't disturb me nearly as much as the thought of getting close enough to interrogate hundreds of baby cockroaches about their thoughts on the meaning of life.

Could Sweetpea be nearby? I shake my head. It doesn't matter. Any effort to locate her would be both futile and unnecessary. She's the easiest for me to find, and when I asked her once exactly where she lives, she looked at me with a mixture of pity and concern and said "in a tree" before scampering off.

I haven't run into Shelly or Penelope since I first met them, and they're far off in California anyway. Nameless One might be in these woods, but it's the middle of the day, he's probably hidden and sleeping, and I'm not sure I want to hear any hard truths right now anyway.

Which brings me to the final animal I met in this glade, the one I can neither easily remember nor possibly forget.

A poem drifts into my mind like a leaf on the wind. I first found it when I was researching the lines of the poem Cockroach recited in our initial meeting, but I didn't really take note until I came across it again while getting ready to write that scene in my book. It's another poem by Hafiz, the fourteenth-century Sufi mystic who wrote the poem Cockroach quoted, and since I read it again, I haven't been able to get it out of my mind:

The earth is a host that murders its guests.
But what can die?

All dying just removes more of the husk
over the soul's vision.

All dying thins the veil over a wondrous
world within.

I'm still not sure what it means, but something about it haunts me like a soul seeking resolution in the afterlife.

A young tree on the far side of the stump catches my attention. It's strange to call it a tree—it barely reaches my thigh—but I recognize its gingerbread-men-shaped leaves as those of an oak. I don't remember seeing it before, though it's usually nighttime when I'm with the animals, and I'm not sure I've ever looked past the stump.

I walk over and stroke the soft surface of the leaves. Do all trees exude the same spaciousness as the one I just experienced? I place the palm of my hand against the tiny trunk and wait, sensing. Nothing at first, but then a murmur passes over me, like an echo of what I felt before.

Only it isn't an echo. It's smaller, but it has the same potential for power within it. It's more like a—what? Bud? Foreshadow?

"Ghost," offers the quiet voice in my mind.

I shake my head. The voice sounds different today. Normally, it's like hearing myself, only more softly, but just now it seemed deeper and hoarser and kind of . . . amused. It almost sounded like—

"No," I say aloud. "No, *no, no, no, no.*" I don't need to be any crazier than I already am.

But even as I'm saying it, my heart races with an impossible hope.

"And why not?" asks the voice. "Is it so unbelievable?"

"Yes," I answer, nodding vigorously. "Very much, actually." But that doesn't stop me from kneeling and nestling my face against the bright, green leaves. As I close my eyes and take a deep breath, her expansive love envelops me.

"Mama." My voice breaks alongside my heart.

"Frankie." Her growl rumbles inside my head. "Beautiful Frankie."

"Oh my God, I've missed you so much." I wipe my cheeks with the heel of my hand. "Is it really you in there?"

"Of course," Mama says in her husky voice. "I am in everything."

"Including this tree?" I hold my breath, waiting for the voice in my head to confirm my sanity.

"Especially this tree."

I wish there was something besides a spindly sapling to hug. "There's so much I want to ask you." I rest my hand against the base of the tree. "About the lab, and how you died, and what happened after—"

"Frankie." I wait for more, but there's only silence.

"Yes, Mama?"

"Did you really think I would leave you?"

My mind flies to the prologue I'm having such a hard time writing. I whisper, "Doesn't everything we love eventually leave us?"

"The white wolf." It's a statement, not a question, but I nod anyway.

"She left me, Mama. I wanted her to come back more than anything, but she never did. Not once."

"You still don't understand." Her voice is sad, not accusatory.

I shrug my shoulders.

"The white wolf is not a sorrow, Frankie. She is a promise and a gift."

"What do you mean?"

"She never left you. There has never been a moment in your life when she hasn't been running beside you."

I sigh. It doesn't feel like enough. "And the promise?"

For a moment, only silence. "She is your true nature, and you will find her again and again and again. In many things, and eventually, in everything."

"How?"

No voice answers me, but the image of the simultaneous solar eclipses on the bottom of the streambed flashes through my mind. "Mama?" Only silence answers. "Mama!" Suddenly the silence feels thick, as if it's not just the absence of sound but also the emptiness of space. I stand up. "Mama, am I losing you again?"

A warm, throaty laugh fills my ears. "Of course not, Frankie. You are discovering what cannot be lost."

I sink to the ground. What could that possibly be in a world that murders its guests? Even this tree, small as it is, won't last forever. I've seen too many stumps in forests and empty lots waiting to be developed to pretend otherwise.

"Are you coming?"

I jump at the sudden words. "Coming . . . where?"

Again, only silence answers. I close my eyes and take a deep breath, trying to be patient as I wait for a response.

And then it comes. Not in the form of a voice, but as a spark of excitement somewhere deep inside me.

The spark lights up the gloom behind my lidded eyes, a flickering, fiery thing that surges into flames, a bonfire, an all-encompassing blaze. The blaze spreads into every corner of my being, scours it clean, then pushes beyond to fill the space around me with shifting, licking light.

Everything extraneous burns away. What's left is tiny, minute, no bigger than an acorn, but so dark and dense it's as if the entire universe has compressed itself inside me.

Something pushes out beneath me. What looks like a thick, white snake grows from my base, stretching, strengthening, seeking.

Energy explodes in my core. I'm pulled in opposite directions. After what feels like forever and the blink of an eye, a massive pressure releases. The light around me shifts, taking on a more solid, concentrated quality and expanding into recognizable shapes—trees, dirt, leaves. Despite the increased solidity, I sense spaciousness around me, as if all constrictions are gone, and I stretch upward to fill the void.

Soft umber turns to hardened silver and sorrel, which eventually turn emerald and azure. A larger picture takes shape, though I don't see so much as sense its presence. Vibrant green extends on all sides of me, interrupted frequently, and for long stretches, like holes in a well-worn quilt, but nevertheless continuous as it climbs and falls, climbs and falls, riding the curves of the land.

Beneath the green, a different type of quilt unfurls, this one almost invisible. Fine filaments nestle in the fertile darkness beneath me waiting to be fed. Extending outward in all directions, they join with other filaments, which join still others, forming a tangled, twisted web that has no end.

I feel every part of every living thing that it touches as if it were my own.

Sun warms my innumerable, fluttering leaves. Raindrops wet my countless shivering crowns. Wind caresses my infinite swaying limbs. And the billions upon billions of beings whom I shelter kiss me, tickle me, thrill me with their touch.

I welcome all of it inside me, gathering everything I can. At first so much wild energy threatens to topple me, but as I grow bigger and bigger, all the tremulations, the storm and the murmurs, the sensations exquisite and crude, then even the inevitable loss become like the whisper of an owl's wings inside the enormous cavern of my being.

I expand. Before long, I'm so large the entire sky, all the stars and planets, and even other galaxies pulse within me. They continue spinning and revolving, but soon they too grow small, becoming no larger than a reflection in the eye of a gnat flying in a great abyss.

I am the abyss—empty, endlessly expanding, limitless. I'm so large I no longer feel where I end and anything else begins. Nothing else exists. Nothing that is not me.

And then I realize my mistake. My fundamental misunderstanding. The abyss—the emptiness that I've feared, that I've been ashamed of, that I've carried inside me as long as I can remember—it's not empty after all. *I* am not empty after all. Rather, I'm filled with a power, a wild and fierce and tender power.

I immediately recognize it as the love of one supremely compassionate wolf. But who knows? Maybe it would appear entirely different to somebody else.

There are many things in this world I cannot be sure of. The one thing I do know is this: Freedom and love are all that there is, all that have ever been.

BOOK CLUB QUESTIONS
FOR *THIS ANIMAL BODY*

1. What does having an animal body mean to you? How does thinking of your body as "animal" change how you relate to it and to the world around you?

2. In the beginning of the story, Frankie feels like she doesn't belong anywhere. When in your life have you felt like an outsider? What helps you feel a sense of connection to the beings and places around you?

3. The animals in this book speak of four sources of intelligence: head, heart, body, and spirit. Which is easiest for you to tap into? Which of the others would you like to tap into more, and why?

4. Do you think our relationship as human beings with the natural world is troubled? If so, what can we do to repair it, individually and collectively?

5. Over time, Frankie comes to see animals as her family. How do you define family? How do you feel familial relationships are different from other types of relationships?

6. At one point, Cockroach says, "You don't lose your way because you're depressed. You get depressed because

you've lost your way." What do you think he means by this? Does it feel true to you? Why or why not?

7. Which of the animals' messages resonated most for you? How might they help you in your own life?

8. Mama makes Frankie promise to have compassion for all animals, no matter what. For which types of animals, including humans, is it easy for you to have compassion? For which types is it hard? What situations or circumstances make it more difficult?

9. When in your life have you lost your way? What helped you find it again? Did any good come from getting lost?

10. Why do you think Frankie relates so much better to animals than to human beings?

11. At one point, Frankie says, "I suddenly realized the problem wasn't that [animals] gave their lives for us, but that we weren't grateful—we didn't even recognize their tremendous sacrifice on our behalf." Do you agree? Why or why not?

12. If you had your own personal circle of advisors, what animals would be on it? What plants? What other elements of nature?

CREDITS

Poems and Excerpts:
"How Eternity Could Be Endured" and "But What Can Die" from the Penguin publication *A Year With Hafiz: Daily Contemplations* by Daniel Ladinsky, copyright 2011, and used with permission.

"So Many Gifts" and "Now is the Time" from the Penguin publication *The Gift: Poems by Hafiz* by Daniel Ladinsky, copyright 1999, and used with permission.

Scientific Studies and Articles:
The experiments performed in the story are based on the following scientific studies:

Replay of recent experiences in the hippocampus of rats suggests they're making mental maps:
Gupta, A. S., van der Meer, M. A., Touretzky, D. S., Redish, A. D. Hippocampal Replay Is Not a Simple Function of Experience. Neuron, 65 (5), 695-705. https://doi.org/10.1016/j.neuron.2010.01.034

Rats leap and make ultrasonic vocalizations when tickled:
Ishiyama, S., Brecht, M. (2016). Neural correlates of ticklishness in the rat somatosensory cortex. Science, 354 (6313), 757-760. https://www.science.org/doi/10.1126/science.aah5114

Dogs can understand word meaning and tone:
Andics, A., Gábor, A., Gácsi, M., Faragó, T., Szabó, D., & Miklósi, Á. (2016). Neural mechanisms for lexical processing in dogs. Science, 353(6303), 1030–1032. https://doi.org/10.1126/science.aaf3777

ACKNOWLEDGMENTS

Many humans have contributed amazing gifts to me and this story.

Thanks go first to my father, Mike Walters, who loved and supported me in every way he could during our time together. I still feel his love from beyond.

I'm deeply grateful to my husband, Helton, for his large and loving heart. Always generous with his encouragement and support, he never hesitates to remind me how much he believes in my capability and vision. I'm beyond lucky to have such a strong and worthy partner.

I am indebted to my mother, whose exquisite poems and generous sharing of them inspire all my creative endeavors. She's always believed in me, from the time before I could read when she typed my dictated stories, to more recent days when she read my earliest drafts, giving me helpful feedback and—more importantly—the confidence to keep going. My whole life she's encouraged me to discover and express my truth, and she's been by my side through the ups and downs while I've attempted to do just that.

Barbara Shirkey has also offered unwavering support through all the ups and downs. She, along with Jen Canon, Elizabeth Chur, and Kay Hunt, read the first draft at a time when Frankie and the animals were not yet sure exactly how they wanted to be in the world. These generous (and, given the length of the first draft, incredibly patient) people gave insightful feedback at a critical time in the story's growth.

Others contributed invaluable feedback in later stages—Margo Geller, Shirin Ardakani, my sister Carolyn McCarthy, and my father. Special thanks go to Margo for getting me to admit what I always knew, and to my sister for always looking out for me in all ways.

I am grateful as well to my critique group—Anthony Miller, Neville Carson, Denis Hearn, Kenn Allen, and most of all, Susan Crawford—for their input and ideas. Susan always gave thoughtful and powerful feedback that helped me see things from a new perspective. Her encouragement, humor, and willingness to mark up the entire manuscript were priceless.

Finally, I'd like to thank the people who have dedicated their lives to increasing connection in the world, particularly nature connection. The ideas of many, including Robin Wall Kimmerer, Jon Young, and Richard Louv, among others, have inspired, informed, and encouraged my own.

Then there are the non-human animals.

I owe a debt of gratitude to the robin whose piercing, knowing, and patient eyes not only gave me the idea for this story, but also wordlessly counseled me to write it.

Similarly, I'm indebted to my animal family—from the cats, dogs, and horses we had growing up, to my wonderful, demanding chickens, to the many beautiful and wise wild animals I meet daily in my yard and on my walks. Each one reminds me that there's an abundance of magic and mystery out there, that we all have gifts to give just by being who we are, and that despite the state of the world, our true nature is connection.

Finally, I'm grateful for everything anxiety and depression have taught me about pain and suffering and love and compassion and wholeness.

———

I would be grateful if you considered leaving a review of this book on your preferred site. New authors, indie authors, and books like *This Animal Body* can only thrive with the support of wonderful people like you who take the time and energy to let others know about them. If you enjoyed this book, please spread the word in whatever way feels good to you.

ABOUT THE AUTHOR

Growing up in Atlanta, Meredith often wandered nearby forests looking for animals and magic and writing stories about what she found. After getting a BA in literature from UC Berkeley, she spent ten years trying to figure out what she wanted to do with her life. Her adventures included volunteering for a nonprofit in Mexico, getting an MBA, and working for a social enterprise startup. Her short story collection, *The Adventures of Little One*, was published in 2018. Eventually, she moved back east to be close to her human and non-human family. She now lives in Atlanta with her husband, working as a life and career coach helping others rediscover their lost magic, and writing stories about what she finds on her wanders through the woods.

Author photo © Bonnie Heath

SELECTED TITLES FROM SPARKPRESS

SparkPress is an independent boutique publisher delivering high-quality, entertaining, and engaging content that enhances readers' lives, with a special focus on female-driven work. www.gosparkpress.com

Squirrels in the Wall: A Novel, Henry Hitz. $16.95, 978-1-684630-22-6. In Squirrels in the Wall, humans and animals share heartbreak and ignorance about the nature of death. Together, they fashion a collage of a human family and its broader habitat, filled with dogs, cats, bees, turtles, squirrels, and mice, illuminating the tragicomic divide between humans and the natural world.

Pursuits Unknown: An Amy and Lars Novel, Ellen Clary. $16.95, 978-1-943006-86-1. Search-and-rescue agent Amy and her telepathic dog, Lars, locate a missing scientist who is reported to have an Alzheimer's-like disease—only to discover that someone wants to steal his research for potentially ominous purposes.

Child Bride: A Novel, Jennifer Smith Turner, $16.95, 978-1-68463-038-7. The coming-of-age journey of a young girl from the South who joins the African American great migration to the North—and finds her way through challenges and unforeseen obstacles to womanhood.

On Grace: A Novel, Susie Orman Schnall. $15, 978-1-940716-13-8. Grace is actually excited to turn forty in a few months—that is until her job, marriage, and personal life take a dizzying downhill spiral. Can she recover from the most devastating time in her life, right before it's supposed to be one of the best?

Found: A Novel, Emily Brett. $16.95, 978-1-40716-80-0. Immerse yourself in life-changing adventures from a nurse's perspective while experiencing the local color of countries around the world. *Found* will appeal to not only medical professionals but those who are drawn to suspense, romance, adventure, and self-discovery.

So Close: A Novel, Emma McLaughlin and Nicola Kraus. $17, 978-1-940716-76-3. A story about a girl from the trailer parks of Florida and the two powerful men who shape her life—one of whom will raise her up to places she never imagined, the other who will threaten to destroy her. Can a girl like her make it to the White House? When her loyalty is tested will she save the only family member she's ever known—even if it means keeping a terrible secret from the American people?